# The Crosses Of Aiolos

## (A Tale of Wind & Wallets)

To Sue, with best wishes,
from Keith. 20.9.10

*Keith Milligan*

4-Winds House Publishing

First published by 4-Winds House Publishing in UK, 2010

4-Winds House Publishing
four-windshouse@hotmail.com



Cover Design & Photography by Keith Milligan



ISBN 978-0-9566383-0-4

*For Annie, for believing and believing.*
*For Mike, for good advice on a warm summer evening.*
*For Chris, for enabling.*
*And for RP & MT for fighting the good fight.*

'While the mice in the field are listening to the Universe...
the Developer is peering at the field...
behind him stands the whole army of madmen's ideas,
and shareholders, impatient to cash in the world.'

*Ted Hughes*

# Part I

# REVELATIONS

# PROLOGUE

Wipers clunking, Willie Dee negotiated the last bend into town and night turned into nightmare. Clouds of impenetrable brown murk swirled up in front of him, masking the streetlights. At gutter level the Range Rover's full beam showed torrents of whitey-foam/brown-malt-vinegary water surging towards him.

100 yards away a police officer emerged from the gritty brown clouds. The copper waved him down, indicating the side of the road. For months and months, no, maybe getting on for two years, they had warned them and warned them about this.

But the developers and their backers hadn't listened. Willie and his friends had been brushed aside in the stampede for Big Wind. The dash for cash was on.

They had fought Big Money, Big Government, and the biggest PR campaign for decades. But the unholy trinity had steamrollered them. And the all-important hydrology survey had been overlooked.

Now what they feared had happened. And it was worse than anything he could have imagined. The powerful halogen lights above the loading bay of the Storm-n-Shine factory burned through the swirling grit like gleaming stars in a faraway galaxy. But nothing else was visible. It was like something from Dante's seventh circle of hell. Except for the noise of the sirens.

Willie drove into the side of the road and cut the engine, watching as the young policeman trudged up to him through the dense brown fog and muddy water. His face was streaked with filth and there appeared to be smudges around his eyes from tear stains. He held a grubby white handkerchief over his nose and mouth. He looked more like a stressed-out squaddie emerging from combat than a copper, Willie thought.

He lowered his window and an alien atmosphere surged in. Huge, clogging particles of grit, moisture, and a funny smell like island malt whisky. Peat, that was it. The young copper leaned in close, showing the red-raw whites of his eyes. Close up, China-blue eyes, pocked red acne scars, he looked about 20.

'You'll have to turn round and go back, sir. The road is closed for emergency rescue work.' The young man blinked hard, bit his lip. 'Could be days...weeks even...it's a disaster...'

'What happened?' Willie heard himself say, knowing full well.

'Hard to say yet, sir...'

'Christ, what a mess,' Willie said. He could have told the copper exactly what had happened. They'd warned of it often enough. Peatslide.

'Just get out of the way, sir, please. Quick as you can,' the police officer said, 'Let the emergency vehicles through. Ambos, fire guys...' his voice trailed off, not wanting to mention the unmarked undertakers' vans he'd also been briefed to wave through.

Willie looked at the young policeman and felt the instinctive pity of an older man for a younger one pushed way beyond his comfort zone, dealing with horrors beyond his years. Struggling, but coping.

'Will do, officer,' he said and nodded. The boy copper touched two fingers to the brim of his flat cap in salute and spun on his heel.

Willie turned the key in the ignition, did a u-turn and headed the 4WD back the way he'd come towards the alternative way home near Woolton. As he changed gear something rattled, it had been doing it spasmodically for about a month. Something else to sort out.

Suddenly his face was flooded with light. A fleet of chequer-banded cream ambulances, sirens screaming, hammered past him heading for the old mill.

He felt stiff from his 200-mile drive. He resented being forced into this unlit, hairpin-bending, 700' climb up to the moors in the dark. Then something clicked. His tiredness was numbing his humanity he realized and suddenly felt guilty. What was he thinking about with those poor bastards down there trapped in the Storm-n-Shine factory?

What he, Verity, Carter and Phyllis had foreseen was unfolding like some apocalyptic Greek tragedy. Poor old Jumper Lonk was dead, Verity was banged up and townspeople had been left without their spring water or in respite care. Now this.

Down there in the old mill innocent people lay dead or dying. Waiting to be dug out of the hillside that had slid down out of the dark and engulfed them.

As a professional photographer, visualization was a big part of his job. Only amateurs just snapped what they saw in front of them. Pros imagined what could be achieved and constructed their pictures to suit.

In his mind's eye he saw thousands of tons of wet peat and rotted pit props travelling around 100 mph downhill. He saw the black mass smashing through the back wall and doors and windows of the mill. Then roaring through the work spaces choking men where they stood. Screams for a moment, then silence. Please God they were all killed quickly, not left to choke or suffocate.

The horror of it made him gag. He stopped the car, got out into the thin drizzle and vomited. He wiped his mouth with the back of his hand and rested his arms on the roof of the Range Rover, facing away from the mill.

He filled his lungs with the chill night air and took deep breaths. The east wind ruffled his blond hair. This is what the high Pennines is all about, he thought. Rain, wind, cold. Millstone grit and heather. Dirty sheep. Space. A beautiful wilderness place still. Except for the bloody wind farms.

On clear nights you looked up and the sky was like navy velvet with twinkling gems some drunken Greek god had spilled. Not tonight though. He felt he could almost reach up and touch the low cloud.

With an effort of will he forced himself to turn around. He didn't like looking at ugly things, but he'd been forced to do that this last 2 years. He felt a savage joy as he looked back on the crimson and yellow flames dancing around the downed turbine on the far side of the valley. It seemed as big as a bloody thumbnail in the black void. Then the vengeful feelings drained. And he felt heartsick as he thought of the men trapped inside the mill. From what you could see it looked like half the hill had slipped away. He held out little hope, except for a quick death.

Slowly he hoisted himself back behind the wheel and resumed the blacked-out upward climb. Tiredness strained his eyes, making them water. He rubbed them but it didn't help.

After negotiating the 9th hairpin bend on the upward single track road he emerged on to "the tops", high above the valleys. The road up had narrow passing places but no lighting and he blessed his luck he hadn't encountered a drunk going the other way. There was a long drop over the edge if you miscalculated.

Now he was on the tops the road widened into a long level road through small, sleeping hamlets. For hundreds of years they'd called it The Long Causeway. It was the old straight track the Bronze Age people had walked, high above the wolves, bears and bandits in the woody valleys.

Even without streetlights it was a much easier drive. But he knew he was too tired to be driving really, even without the emotional upset.

Since he'd turned the car in front of the mill he'd come around almost 270 degrees. The burning oil from the flaming turbine was clearly visible now he was up high.

After about 5 minutes he turned left onto the rough track that led to his old laithe house.

There were no lights on in the neighbours' cottages or Jumper's old farmhouse as he drove down the lane. At the end Greenwood Royd lay outlined blacker than the darkness like some ancient, supine beast.

It exuded the security of having outlasted many crises these past 400 years.

He eased the 4WD into the courtyard between Greenwood Royd and the outbuildings and turned off the engine. Then forced a thin smile as the stillness woke Nelson in the boot. The black lab shook himself and did his customary four-foot fandango, stamping his paws as he revolved and stretched, impatient to be out now they were home.

Willie opened the front door and the dog shot along the hall and into the kitchen. He could hear him slurping from his water bowl. Stale water or fresh seemed to make no difference.

He turned on the lights and headed for the stairs. Then the lights failed. It had happened before when there had been problems with the wind turbines. No electricity, so no 24-hour news on the radio or telly.

No matter, he'd find out soon enough the full horror story, he thought. The latest sacrifice they'd all been forced to make for Big Wind.

Two years earlier...

# 1

Thursday November 1st

The man and his dog were invisible. A thick fog had settled on the tops of the Pennine valleys around first light. Its cotton wool density created a new and frightening world where sound was muffled and you could only see your feet. Within moments of stepping out into this grey murk the man's eyebrows and hair were sodden. The black stone farmhouses, ranged along the contours, were as isolated and cut off as they had been in the 1500s. Each in its own veiled universe.

Invisible sheep that stood stoic through the wind-driven hail and sub-zero temperatures of the night now bleated. Cut off from their sisters in the fog, they cried out eerily like lost souls.

The man could barely see his boots as he kept to the smooth, uneven stone flags of the 16th century packhorse trail. Suddenly something ran hard across his knees and the dog's backside. He yelled. The dog barked. The ewe screamed. Then it disappeared as fast as it had come.

It was hard to say who had the biggest fright, him the sheep or the dog. He laughed with relief as his heartbeat slowed back to normal. But still...

'The heck with this, Nelson,' Willie Dee said. 'I'm afraid that's it for today.' It was a day when even the most hardened dog walker would quit early, he told himself. It was one thing blundering into a sheep. Quite another blundering into a bewildered bull or stallion, or a cow with calves. It was no fun when you couldn't see. In fact it was positively dangerous. Ironically, just as dangerous as the city when you couldn't see. The animals could still kill you.

The day had begun like any another with Willie Dee crossing his fingers and counting his blessings. As he had everyday since he'd sold his photographer's business and moved from the concrete canyons of London to this Pennine fastness. When things were going too well it was like a challenge to the gods, he thought. But now wasn't the time to think thoughts like that, he chided himself.

They trudged back to Greenwood Royd, his old laithe house, and went in through the back door. He took off his lovat cap and Barbour, took the dog's old brown towel from behind the door and began to dry his paws.

As soon as he was dry Nelson padded over the stone flags of the big kitchen to a cardboard box in the corner. Delicately he removed a worn yellow tennis ball and brought it over to Willie. He dropped it at his feet and watched as it rolled gently to bump his boots. He looked up at his master expectantly. Then dropped his eyes back to the tennis ball. *Come on, dozy.*

'Okay, you haven't had your full walk,' Willie said. 'So now you want to play cricket?'

"Cricket" was part of the dog's vocabulary. He wagged and trotted off to the other end of the long kitchen, mounted the two wooden steps and stood in the doorway to the dining room.

The rules to their indoor cricket were simple. Nelson being a dog, and therefore challenged in the batting department, was always 25 all out. Nonetheless, he defended the wicket formed at the top of the step by the narrow doorway into the dining room. If Willie got the ball past him, Willie scored a run. Similarly, if Nelson either blocked the ball with his body or took it in his teeth, it was a wicket down. The dog, a natural retriever who loved ball games, would play all day.

But the 40-ball game was just long enough to keep the dog seriously focused and not too long to be a bore for the man.

Soon enough the indoor cricket match was nearing its conclusion. Nelson was 25 all out as usual, and Willie was 21 for 9.

Willie fixed the well-sucked yellow tennis ball in his off-spin position, then changed his mind at the last minute and lobbed it. The ball went through the air like a dud grenade, plummeting after 15 yards towards the batsman who rose skilfully to take it in his teeth.

21 all out.

'Okay, Nelson, you win.'

The one-eyed black Labrador thumped his tail on the floor. He knew the words "you win". He came bounding down the kitchen steps to his tall, middle-aged owner and followed him over to where the Marrobones lived.

'There you go, you win The Bones. Again,' Willie said. As he spoke, he took a Marrobone from the cardboard box next to the bread bin and half-chucked it into the excited dog's mouth, being careful to keep his fingers out of the way.

It was the one problem they hadn't cured since they'd got Nelson from the rescue centre. He'd had one eye kicked in and been badly starved by his previous owner who'd fed him the same rations as his other dog, a tiny Yorkshire terrier. Some people. When Willie first went to pat him Nelson ducked and ran.

They'd soon overcome that. But after a year of starvation Nelson could never believe he'd get enough food every day.

His fierce clumsiness to eat reflected his memory of all the days he'd gone stomach-grindingly hungry.

Knowing this upset Willie every time he gave the dog a treat. It reminded him of the abuse. Once he had been a swinging Seventies photographer, but he had always considered himself a serious, civilized man. He hated denial and restriction and the spoilers of this world: the wowsers, the proscribers, the joyless ones.

The front door banged and after a moment his wife's voice called out along the hallway. 'Are you playing with that poor dog again? You'll wear him out.' The woman entering the kitchen was tall and slender-limbed, green-eyed, red-haired and tanned with galaxies of faint freckles, like some exotic big cat. Even at 40 she was a looker.

'Hi, Bolly,' he said, as she came around the kitchen door. 'The fog stopped the usual 2-hour trek. We were bumping into livestock all over the place. Got a bit dangerous. So we had to curtail the walk and Nelson felt cheated.'

Something else had happened which had spooked him even more. But he didn't mention that. Close to home the winter sun suddenly burned a hole in the fog and the world lit up. And from over a dry stone wall had come this enormous feathery sussuration. Up from the field behind the wall rose a black cloud of squealing starlings. As it climbed over them it twisted and turned like a giant black ever-changing teardrop. Momentarily the swarm blocked the sun out. It felt like a dark shadow passing over them and he shuddered. Then he shook himself and watched.

Each of the starlings was fast changing position and yet they still maintained this twisting, turning teardrop shape as they whirled over the countryside.

Everyday up here something like that happened. The seasons changed, the weather changed, the light constantly changed. To an artist or photographer it was balm for the soul. When he came back into the present, Bolly was laughing.

'Excuses, excuses,' she was saying. 'You can't leave that dog alone. I think you love him more than you do me.'

'Never, Bolly Dolly,' he said, going over to her and slipping an arm around her to draw her up and kiss her. They'd been married 6 years and it felt like 6 days. Her real name was Verity. But everyone from her London advertising days called her Bolly Dolly in memory of a certain champagne she'd favoured.

'Post for you,' he said, lifting a white envelope and a small brown paper package from the oak farmhouse table. 'A letter from the Open University and a parcel - could be that new hat you were after.'

She took the letter and the obviously book-shaped parcel from him. 'Funny man,' she said, shaking her head and opening the letter.

'So?'

'The letter is about doing an Eng Lit course with the OU. You know I always regretted not doing it after the sixth form. Thought I'd look into it. The book's a critical review of Ted Hughes. Nothing you'd like.'

Too right, Willie thought. His taste ran to Ian Rankin, Michael Connelly, Peter Temple, and that French woman, Fred Vargas: crime novels. Although of late he had to admit he'd been brainwashed into a sneaking regard for the former poet laureate, Ted Hughes. You couldn't live up here in these wild Pennine hills without feeling his spirit all around you. Ted Hughes knew all about wind and rain and shifting light, black rocks, frost, snow and ice, suffering sheep and of course the moors themselves. What was it he said? "Moors are a stage for the performance of heaven".

He looked thoughtfully at the post where it lay.

'Will you do the course then, do you think?'

'Don't know. Maybe I'm best off as I am, just mugging up on Ted and all his works. Might even write a book about him myself one day,' she said, looking thoughtful. 'Wonderful as Harvey Nicks is, I need to stop myself turning into a lady who just shops and does the garden. Maybe I will try and write a book about him. I've been making notes.'

Have you indeed? he thought. That was news to him.

'Here,' she said, rummaging in her Tesco bag, before producing a folded-up newspaper. 'I'll swap you. Something to take the pressure off that poor dog. See if anything's happening in sleepy little Cloughgreen.'

She passed him this week's edition of the Cloughgreen Recorder. Grinning roguishly, he took it from her. 'You know we buy it for you really, all the small-town gossip and pictures of the mayoress opening things...' he said.

It was a family joke. They both knew he thought it was a small town rag. Even so he always flicked through just to check nothing earth-happening was going to change their rural idyll. But Bolly devoured it, knew exactly who was who, what was opening, what was closing, who was new golf club captain, which cricket professional was coming from where, which pubs or restaurants were changing hands, who was selling their house, who had got married or died or both.

Page 1 was unpromising, he thought. A granny's triumph at Fat Club, four stone lost. Sundry traffic accidents and burst water mains. The announcement of a new optician's opening. What the mayor had done next. Same old stuff, just the names changed from the previous week to protect the guilty, so far as he could see. He turned the page and read on, still standing, while Bolly went out to hang her coat up. It was a small paragraph on page 3 that had him spluttering.

'My God,' he bellowed. 'How could they?'

Bolly Dolly came running, her high heels clattering on the grey stone-flagged floors. 'What's wrong? What's happened?' Willie Dee was normally a pretty laid back bloke. He never yelled.

Without a word he passed her the Cloughgreen Recorder, his thumb underlining the offending piece. 'It would appear the barbarians are within the gates,' he said. She looked down at the paper, trying to see what had upset him.

'Do you mean this bit about the proposed new wind farms?'

'Too right.'

'Well, what's the problem? We agree the climate is changing. We recycle. We insulate. We use low-energy light bulbs and stuff...'

'Have you seen how many turbines they want to put up?'

'Four new wind farms, it says,' she said, checking.

'That's seventy odd more turbines, if you look closely.'

'Well, they're good aren't they? I mean, they're green. They'll help save the planet. Why all the fuss?' She stood, hands on hips, legs akimbo, smiling in disbelief and incomprehension. The green dress clung flatteringly to every curve.

'Have you any idea what another 78 turbines up here will look like. It'll be like an industrial estate, steel and concrete everywhere. It'll completely destroy the scale of the countryside. It's just too many to absorb.'

'You're a Nimby,' Verity said, laughing. 'Not in my beautiful back yard, eh, Willie?'

'It'll be in a lot of other peoples' beautiful back yards, as well as ours. You'll see 'em for about 30 miles on the tops of these hills.'

'It doesn't say exactly where they want to put them.'

'No, but you can bet they'll be where they're the biggest eyesores. There are just too many of them already, that's all. Another 78 and we'll look like an industrial zone, not a rural community. If I'd wanted to live somewhere like Scunthorpe or Port Talbot I'd have moved there. *Pace* Scunthorpe and Port Talbot.' He held his hands up.

'Well you can see the 24 at The Delf already if you look left from our back garden. That doesn't seem to bother you.'

'My point exactly, I'm already an Imby - In My Back Yard. You can see plenty of them at the Delf from my back garden already. I thought that was my sacrifice. My tolerant contribution. I didn't expect to be knee-deep in these things when we moved here.'

'Calm down, Willie. I'll make a cup of tea.' She went and filled the chrome kettle and took out the Yorkshire Tea he liked from the orange-banded pack. 'Dear me, I can't remember ever seeing you like this,' she said. 'This is not like you at all. What on earth is the problem?'

'I can just see it in my mind's eye, that's all.'

Bolly sighed. 'You and your imagination. It could be nothing like you imagine. You should just wait and see.'

'It might be too late by then.' He looked her straight in the eye. 'Look, some folks can't see things till they bump them on the nose. I visualise things very clearly. It's the way I am, you know that. I can't help it.'

He could feel the back of his neck going warm and red as his blood pressure rose, so he sat down on one of the old curved back wooden chairs at the kitchen table. He never wanted to argue with Bolly. Rarely did.

'It's just I have such a bad feeling about this,' he said. 'And I don't quite know why. It's not the turbines themselves, it's the numbers and it's the whole world they're gonna destroy up here. And I bet those bastards in Downing Street who want this, never mind the developers, don't even have a clue what they'll be ruining, never mind caring.'

'Just think though, it's for the good of the planet. I'm sure it won't be as bad as you think. They could all be miles away, anyway.'

'No. There are just so many of them they're gonna ruin this whole countryside that your sainted Ted Hughes wrote about. He'd be rolling in his grave if he could see this happening in his back yard ...' Willie sighed and rubbed his eyes with the back of his hands. 'I don't know, it's a beautiful world and there's always some buggers want to ruin it...'

There was a silence until the kettle clicked itself off. Bolly Dolly poured the water onto the teabags in the big brown earthenware pot and put the lid on. Trying to lighten the mood, she started to dance around him skittishly, pointing at him and darting away.

'You're a Nimby, you're a Nimby, you're a Nimby,' she chanted. Her husky voice singing this childish chant sounded ridiculous. Even so, normally he'd have laughed along with her and pretended to chase and catch her. Instead he saw red.

'I'm not a fuckin' Nimby,' he said, and was immediately horrified at what he'd said. Bolly stopped dead in her tracks and went white.

'You swore at me,' she said, her husky voice gone shrill. 'You swore at me. For the first time ever.'

'I didn't,' he said, confused and embarrassed. 'Not at you, at the situation... At the situation,' he repeated, 'not at you.'

He could have saved his breath. She turned on her heel and left the room. Which shocked him. She wasn't a shrinking violet to be upset by a bit of bad language. That he knew. She had been PA to two directors of a successful London ad agency and slept with them both. During the stresses of deadlines, last-minute client changes and general cockups she'd heard more blue language than a police sergeant on a Saturday night down the Elephant and Castle.

But she was right, he thought. He had never sworn in front of her before. For 6 years they'd had an old-fashioned marriage which suited them both fine. No matter what had gone before they loved and respected each other. When she'd asked him to marry her he'd been stunned and amazed and, being 15 years older, flattered. He would never have dared to ask her. He knew he made her laugh. He knew he excited her in bed. And he'd made a few bob. But he also knew that none of these things made him in any way unique.

So why she loved him was a mystery. 'I love you because you're such a great appreciater of life,' she'd told him on their wedding night. 'You just drink life in with your eyes and transform it. You're an artist.' And that was as close as he was going to get, he reckoned.

He looked down at Nelson. But the dog was embarrassed by the raised voices and looked pointedly at the floor. *Don't make me take sides.*

He thought of going upstairs after her. But it would be no use. She'd likely throw something at him. Bolly had her father's Irish temper. You just had to sit tight and let it blow over. At least she never normally held grudges or sulked.

Willie dragged himself off to what they jokingly called The Music Room, angry with himself and confused. He walked around the redundant white grand piano which he'd attempted to teach himself to play and failed. A rare failure in his golden life. Started much too late. Now there were cases of Bollinger sitting on top, *en route* to the fridge. They'd once been placed there temporarily and for some reason it was now where they kept them. One of those accidents of an easy-going, haphazard marriage. Looked oddly classy though, somehow, he thought absently. Nice props.

He picked a Vaughan Williams CD from the rack and selected 'The Lark Ascending' track.

He closed the door, put the CD on, jacked up the volume and settled back in his green leather armchair. Nelson flopped on his crossed feet and looked away. Wanted to be near master, but not sure. Didn't like raised voices and didn't want a kicking like he'd had in the old raised-voice days before Willie rescued him. Low profile.

The clear notes of the strings started quietly, mimicking the low level flutterings of the sky lark. Willie waited with yearning anticipation as the music triumphantly built, matching the songbird's progress as it sang its way in soaring spirals up into the clear blue sky, high above the moor.

Six years ago, locked amongst London's concrete canyons, making his way between ad agencies for meetings, he wouldn't have understood this music. Now he could open his back door, put on a pair of green wellies, summon an unthinkingly faithful black dog and go and hear real larks ascending over the moorland.

Genius as Vaughan Williams was, not even he could better the real thing. Every time he heard a lark ascending on the moors, Willie stopped and marvelled. Nelson too looked upward as the tiny chorister soared.

Now those metropolitan bastards wanted to invade the moorlands for millions in subsidies and a thoughtless promise given by a discredited British politician half a world away in Kyoto. A man who, to give him his credit, Willie thought a decent man. But who on this occasion had courted popularity and a future legacy without really thinking through the feasibility of what he was signing up to.

Why was it the bastards always wanted to spoil the best things in life, he wondered? Sex. Love. The human body. Freedom. Wilderness. The bastards always wanted to control people. Or say no. Or destroy things for a fast buck. Sometime he felt his understanding of life hadn't moved on much since he was a six-year-old kid in the playground watching two bigger kids pushing a speccy kid's arm up his back and giving him Chinese burns. Why do these awful things? he'd wanted to ask. Then slowly the realization had dawned on him. Because they could. That was all the reason they needed. Because they could.

Later he'd refined this early epiphany into a realization that a lot of evil stuff didn't necessarily come with horns and a tail but grew out of an uncaring disrespect for men or beauty or anything not personally understood. The bastards were everywhere.

As an anthropology graduate he knew all about taboos. Way back in the day he'd photographed some slightly *risque* nude shots for some export mags. He'd liked the idea of showing teenage boys and old guys in priest-ridden places what naked women really looked like.

He chuckled to himself. Pretty innocent stuff. That really was back in the day. In the early Seventies. Now you could go on the Net and check out what your neighbour's wife looked like in the buff. The vicar's wife even, he chuckled. All the young women seemed to be exhibitionists now. And maybe that wasn't such a bad thing. Better than repression anyway. Live and let live. Letting people enjoy life was what it was all about.

He sighed and let himself slip back into the lyricism of the music, his spirits following the rising and falling of Vaughan Williams's lark.

When the music finally died away with one lingering call it felt to him as though the real skylarks outside had already become extinct. And maybe they would be, hacked open by steel turbine blades. The ones that hadn't been crushed by bulldozers.

He had always been an equable man. These strong feelings were alien to him. Why on earth had he so jeopardised his relationship with Verity, the amazingly loving Bolly Dolly?

He was also a thoughtful man. If just the idea of these coming wind farms upset him this much... then he would have to look into it.

Troubled, he dragged himself over to his CD rack and fished out a Vaughan Williams choral piece, 'An Oxford Elegy,' about a scholar gypsy long dead in the 1600s. From a poem by Matthew Arnold.

He turned the CD to play and took the bottle of Glenfiddich from the oak drinks cabinet, together with a crystal glass tumbler. It was a bit early, but what the hell.

He poured himself two fingers of the whisky, sat down in his green leather armchair and allowed himself to wallow in the rich timbre of the narrator's voice. His eyes hit the expensive original photography on the Music Room walls unseeing. Black and white prints from some of the great early pioneers. Anselm Adams, Edward Weston, Bill Brandt, even a Cartier Bresson. Beautiful images.

The elegiac feeling of the music suited his mood perfectly. Already he felt something precious was mortally threatened. The speaker finally came to the last stanza:

'Why faintest thou? I wander'd till I died.

Roam on! The light we sought is shining still.

Our tree yet crowns the hill,

Our Scholar travels yet the loved hillside...'

The music was a much-loved piece that usually gave him consolation. He even knew a blasted tree on the moors that clung to life so tenaciously he thought of it as his own Scholar's tree - 'that single elm-tree bright against the west...while the tree lived, he in these fields lived on'.

But now Willie felt uncharacteristically pessimistic and he didn't like himself for that at all. He was an intuitive man and he felt the shadow of some blight falling over their lives.

He wasn't the sort of guy who ran around flailing his arms and shouting the odds; it wasn't his style. He just dug in and sorted things. He'd been a very successful businessman as much as a top photographer, but how could any one individual fight a big corporation hungry for easy pickings, a fanatical wind farm lobby and a prime minister looking to leave a green legacy?

The hell with it, he thought, he may well have to try. He took his glass and walked over to the row of mullioned windows the weavers had installed to provide light in the 1600s. The laithe house had been the first primitive textile factory, where people worked in their own homes. All those windows might have seemed a luxury; but it was chiefly a way to see to work the fleeces. Looking out he saw nothing to lift his spirits. The fog was low about the house still, thick and grey as a dirty dishcloth with no light or colour. It could lay low and damp like this for days up here.

When it came down to it, Willie thought, his knowledge of wind farms was as blank as the view from this window. Like Bolly, he'd always assumed they were a good thing. But so many of them... And if there were going to be so many here, how many more would there have to be throughout the country in all the other high, wild places? And if this technology was so great why did there need to be so many? The unanswered questions disturbed him.

Friday November 2nd

Nelson licked him awake at 5.57, 3 minutes before the alarm went off. The dog was accurate to plus or minus 5 minutes. He opened his eyes slowly, clicked the alarm off.

The window was on the latch to let air in. Outside he heard the crows squabbling. The wind was ululating in the power lines. Eerie. Savage. Strident as eastern women at a funeral. And a length of wooden guttering banged rhythmically in its loose metal holders against the roof.

From a chink in the curtains he could see the gale had blown off the previous day's fog. It made him feel better, more positive. If you could see, you could walk. And if you could walk, it made your head feel better, you could make proper decisions.

He looked sideways at Verity. She ceased being Bolly Dolly when she was angry and reverted in his mind to being Verity. He smiled to himself at this distinction. The way his mother had called him William (Bad) or Willie (Good) when he was a boy.

'You awake, Verity?'

'"This house has been far out at sea all night,' she quoted,

The woods crashing through darkness, the booming hills,

Winds stampeding the fields under the window..."'

Willie recognised the poem as the start of 'Wind', one of the blessed Ted's. Bolly had spoken it without opening her eyes and looking at him, so he knew he was not yet forgiven. She had too passionate a nature to sulk, but she was quite capable of letting him know she was still upset if a spat remained unresolved. So resolve it, you idiot, he thought.

Looking at her, the blizzard of pale brown freckles on her face and chest, her long red hair splayed out on the cream pillow, he knew he would always be helpless before her beauty. So resolve things, you idiot, make your peace.

He got out of bed and walked to the window. Surprise, surprise, it was wild and wet outside. Although the fog had lifted, the far ridge was obscured by low cloud. The sky was one big grey wet blanket. Beneath it the landscape looked like a hairy old tweed sports jacket left out in the rain, drab greens, dead browns, black rocks. The wind was coming in sudden house-shaking gusts. Something, somewhere, was still loose and banging. The wooden gutter, he hoped.

Sighing, he reached up behind the bedroom door for his dressing gown to cover his goosebumps and padded off over the carpet, out the door and down the steep and narrow 16th century stairway. He'd heard the central heating come on half an hour earlier and the millstone grit walls were 18" thick but it still felt chilly.

He knew his journey was necessary, as it was every morning. Night owls like Bolly needed gentle awakening or they showed their claws. He took the new jar of Colombian coffee down from the cupboard in the kitchen, pierced the foil and inhaled deep of the strong roasted aroma. It was only instant freeze dried stuff, but the smell from a new bottle was always a sensual treat.

His attention was caught by the racket of the crows whirling outside the window. Pennine crows he considered the sleekest, most murderous-looking birds he had ever seen.

Bigger than small hawks, they were normally super-confident. Quite ready to hold down and murder an ailing sparrow or two. But this morning they were in turmoil. They screeched loudly in complaint as they were backhanded around the sky by invisible hands. Just oily black rags tossed hither and thither.

Suddenly Willie realized they were having trouble flying, controlling their direction. The racket they were making was their life force screaming in protest: "We want to live. We want to live. Don't whack us up against stone barns. Don't rip our heads off on taut power lines. Don't drive us into windscreens. We want to live".

He stood watching for a while, fascinated by the noise and the wild gyrations of the birds in the gale. Then he remembered he was there to make Bolly's coffee.

Just after he turned away there was a loud bang on the window directly behind him. Startled, he spun round and looked out. An enormous crow, maybe a raven, lay stunned on the path between the window and the lawn, its head lolling, shaking its crusty beak as though disbelieving what had just happened. Willie caught more black violent movement out of the corner of his eye and raised his head. A murder of crows still hung in the air, being batted to and fro by invisible hands.

The crow that had bashed its head on the windowpane abruptly keeled over on the path, and lay feet in the air, motionless. Reminiscent of the Pythons' dead parrot joke, but not funny at all. Sudden death when least expected. Whack. Dead. Just like that. He instinctively thought of going out. To do what? It was beyond help. Doubtless its chums would be back to devour it in calmer conditions.

Death before breakfast. The countryside was like that, he had found. But it still shocked him. He dragged his eyes away from the dead crow/raven and made the coffee. Sometimes, even after 6 years up here on the moorland tops, the sheer brute force of the wind awed him. People who lived in towns and cities had no idea of the destructive power it wielded over these exposed moorland farms. Capricious, unpredictable and violent, the wind held dominion over this place, he thought. It killed even the predators. Shaking his head, he took Bolly her coffee in bed, and quickly got dressed.

But the dead crow bothered him. Or at least the thought its erstwhile companions would come back to devour it on the patio. He went outside, past the firethorn to the garden shed and took out his red work gloves. Close up the bird seemed even larger. When he picked it up it felt monstrous heavy. The eye, frozen open by sudden death, was mid-blue around the black pupil. The thick plumage ran through shades of blue and emerald to purple and black.

But what most caught his eye was the beak. It had sandy encrustations on the top mandible. Some sort of growth? Or just wear? Where the lower mandible exited the head there were black striations, clipped and layered as a coal seam. Or a notched sabre, he thought grimly, thinking of the use the crow had made of its beak.

Still marvelling at the iridescent plumage he carried the crow down to the blackthorn hedge at the foot of the garden where the old fox had gone to die. No point in being squeamish. If he left the corpse here some other scavenger would benefit. But he and Bolly wouldn't have the mess left on their doorstep.

A walk on the moors with Nelson usually put Willie in a good humour. But this morning his mood was black, pervaded by a sense of foreboding and imminent loss.

Bolly Dolly had obviously not forgiven him for being an alleged Nimby or swearing. And he was irritated she hadn't grasped the magnitude of what was about to befall them. This whole beautiful landscape they lived in was going to be destroyed. And not just the immediate landscape but the whole damned region if these grasping developers got their way. They were like some terrible virus probing the body for a soft spot, ready to rush in and colonise it.

Well, we would see about that. Took him a while to lose his cool. But he could be damned tenacious once he sank his teeth into something. Nelson was nudging his leg.

'A biscuit? But you haven't done anything yet.' Nonetheless, he took a brown gravybone treat from his left hand pocket and tossed it to the dog. Nelson wagged happily and loped away in search of new sniffs.

The shifting beauty of the moors and the seasons usually exhilarated his senses but this morning he realised he hadn't seen a thing. He'd battled his way though clinging mud and a headwind to the 60-minute turnaround point without noticing anything.

He had been looking inwards, seeing Verity, the blizzard of pale brown freckles on her face, the direct green eyes, her long red hair splayed out on the cream pillow. He knew he would always be helpless before her beauty and now she was giving him the cold shoulder. He had slept with many beautiful women, famous models, household names from glossy magazines and Page 3. It was a perk of the job. But he had seen the same women without makeup in the morning. And he saw Verity through the lens of love. She had qualities he had neither sought nor found in those casual relationships. So far as he was concerned his marriage was for ever.

The only way to sort this out was to poke about and find out why the bastards wanted to put so many more wind turbines on the moors up here. Maybe his gut feeling was right. But then again maybe Verity was right and he was just being a Nimby. He needed to find out.

# 2

Friday November 2nd

Dr Edwin Newall was in a bad mood when he picked up the Cloughgreen Recorder from the coconut mat behind the front door. The day had started badly when, hungover, he had descended to the kitchen to find some none-too-clean white knickers discarded on the tile floor. Lifting them between finger and thumb he dumped them in the pedal bin on top of the remains of last night's chicken vindaloo takeaway.

His drunken debauch of the night before slowly began to filter back to him when he heard the rumbling of the plumbing. Penny Wragg must still be in the upstairs bathroom.

Gaia! she was still here. He had given up on God, aged 13, when he had realized God was just a manifestation of human need. It amused him, as a Green, to invoke instead the name of the Earth goddess, Gaia.

Anyway why hadn't bloody Penny Wragg taken her soiled underwear and just buggered off home like she was supposed to? She knew he didn't encourage her staying over. Once they'd had it off, they had nothing to say. It was just an arrangement they had. After all this time, she surely knew that as well as he did. He must have passed out and she'd taken advantage and stayed anyway.

He'd come back and caught her with a pot of paint the week before, touching up some skirting boards. As though she owned the place. Or at least as though she lived there. The spare key had been a mistake. Gaia, he'd really have to watch that. The last thing he wanted was her moving in.

Anyway, too late now, he'd have to try and put a good face on it. He poured himself some fair trade Columbian coffee and generously sweetened it.

Then he glared out of the rain-spotted French windows at the glimpses of hills and moors above the town which he could see above the houses from his dining room table. Hateful, bloody useless things, those moors, sullen, green deserts. He almost dared them to speak back in their own defence. What bloody use were they to Cloughgreen? Ugly dead land. He hated the sight of them, reminding him as they did solely of missed opportunities for the town.

But after 10 years of being glared at the offending landscape had no defence. They were just drab and dreary empty moors which he imagined no-one ever visited. Green nothingness where nothing much lived and nothing deserved to live. They were holding up the whole sustainable regeneration of the town below them where he lived, Cloughgreen.

Grumpily, he looked at the front page of the local rag, the Cloughgreen Recorder. It featured a large picture of some obese granny who'd been going to Fat Club and lost 4 stones. A geriatric peasant. Irritatedly, he ripped the paper open and ... suddenly the sun came out.

What with Penny Wragg and her discarded soiled knickers still in attendance he'd forgotten what the date was. But there it was, the initial, rather coy announcement. Tucked away on page 3, quite small, just one thin column, the declaration he'd been awaiting for months. Ursa Power had officially stated their intention to seek planning approval for 4 new wind farms. Only 4, mind, not the full 8 he'd hoped for. Still, 4 would serve the purpose for now. Could still be 78 giant new turbines. That was what they were putting in for.

He was still smiling idiotically when Penny Wragg, stooping self-consciously because of her 6' height, sidled around the dining room door. Her shoulder-length, mousy hair drooped in wet rats tails from where she'd washed it. But she compensated by wearing her trademark purple tights, a yellow miniskirt, black top and blackish-purple lipstick. It was funny how she always looked so different after a couple of bottles of claret and a few glasses of Southern Comfort.

'Great news,' he boomed. 'We're finally going to stick it to those apathetic bastards in the valley that being green means being proactive.'

'Wonderful,' she said, helping herself to a piece of buttered toast from his plate. Gaia, how he hated her doing that. Still, he ignored it. This was the Big Day. The start of great things for Dr Edwin Wellington Newall, and for this valley whether they liked it or not.

He, Doctor Newall, planner extraordinaire, urbanist supreme, a man who had trained other town planners, had a vision that would change not just this valley, but the face of an entire region. Wooltonside, with Cloughgreen in the lead, would be an exemplar of green politics for the whole of Britain, maybe even the world. It would make him famous. And there was no reason why it should not make him rich as well.

Men of vision, like himself, should not be impeded by the apathetic masses. Particularly when the whole future of the planet was at stake. Green fascism, schmashism, what did he care what they said? He had the old traditional view of himself, Planner as Hero.

If the bastards wouldn't listen to reason, as they hadn't, then they must be led by the nose to do the decent things. One day they'd wake up amazed at how transformed and how Green was their valley. And then they'd thank him. Though they wouldn't know what had hit them until it was too late. Because that was the only way you could deal with these knuckle-dragging backward types.

He closed his eyes and tried to imagine it - 4 new wind farms. Right here on the green deserts. The biggest of them, if they got it through, would have 25 turbines. 25 turbines! Each of them the revolutionary new 410' height. Roughly 2 ½ times the height of the existing ones at The Delf wind farm.

That would show 'em. Really show 'em! The totemic power itself would be immense, standing proud on the high ridges sending out invasive Green signals throughout the whole of Northwest England, reminding people of the Green Imperative, making it impossible for the plebs to ignore them. To make the political point you wouldn't even have to turn them on. They would be so monumentally *there*! Gaia, how it made his heart sing. On sunny days they would look like an enormous sculpture park, that kinetic stuff that moved in the wind and light.

They would command the heights all around Cloughgreen. If they got 'em all through the planning processes they would completely surround the town down here in the valley. Smiling benignly down from the heights as they supplied the people with Green renewable energy for decades. Sending a signal to the whole country that Cloughgreen was taking a proud and responsible stand...no matter what those apathetic bastards who lived there wanted. He was in a high state of excitement and wanted to be rid of Penny Wragg as quickly as he could, the better to focus on the next steps. So he deliberately didn't offer to drive her home. She hadn't said a word over breakfast, just sat there chewing his stolen toast, bovine, looking down at her plate. Gaia, she did irritate him sometimes. Mostly when he was sober.

He was about to show her the door when he had a better idea.

'Penny,' he said, 'I'm late. You know how tetchy people get if I'm late for a meeting. You wouldn't be a pet and do last night's washing up before you go, would you?' He knew she had a job to go to, working for that prat Gerry Stansfield, but that wasn't important; it was only provincial advertising. Or design. Or whatever it was she did. Advertising tents and camping stuff.

Instantly she looked up, one hand sweeping lank hair off her face, two bleary un-contact-lensed eyes looking blurrily at him, but smiling, grateful to be of use. Like a beaten dog thrown a bone. Beaten was how she mostly looked, he thought, with that ridiculous tall girl's stoop. Though she bloody well asked for trouble, with her victim's attitude.

'Okay. I don't mind,' she said. 'I'll do it when I've got my "eyes" in.'

'Good girl.' He started heading for the hall.

'Edwin...'

'Yes.'

'You'll think I'm being silly...'

'What?'

‘Well, just thanks. For last night.’ She smiled insipidly and he winced. For what, drunkenly ripping her pants off?

‘It’s okay. I have to go. Be in touch.’

‘Yes,’ she said passively, looking back at her plate.

Newall picked up his beautiful Gucci briefcase - 2 years on, it still gave him pleasure - put the Cloughgreen Recorder in it and headed for the station and the trip to his office in Manchester.

He had tried cycling in for a year, to set a good Green example. But the ice and the frost and the wind and the rain and the traffic and the Pennine hills had all proved too much. What did it matter? That had been only a small personal gesture, this would be so much more. And only he had the specialist skills and vision to pull this off.

Now he was almost delirious with happiness. Not just 78 turbines, but the new giant Mark Tens, too. That would show the bastards. From a height of 5’5” he had no illusions that size did not matter. 5’5” tall, with black hair, his father’s broad shoulders, a small paunch and a strut like a fighting cock he knew the figure he cut. He disliked tall men on principle.

His second most humiliating experience ever had been instigated at his public school by the Wellesley College’s first Rugby XV. For no reason that he could ever fathom, except “we like to hear you squeal”. The bastards had ambushed him, aged 13, on his way from the art room and spirited him into the gym where they had stripped him down to his underpants and vest and strapped an old motorcyle helmet on his head. Then they had organized an impromptu dwarf-throwing contest, seeing who could hurl him furthest on to the piled up foam mats.

Chalky White MA, (Oxon) and rugger Blue, the Head, had felt compelled to phone his father, Colonel Ned "Nasty" Newall and tell him of his son's bruises.

Colonel "Nasty" Newall was well-known to the Head from parents' evenings. Wellesley College was run like a military academy. Its whole intake was made up of the sons of officers and NCOs. But "Nasty" Newall was a case apart. 6', gaunt-skulled, yellow-skinned from many years in the sun, he had long, hairy arms and was frankly simian. He was one of those men best described as a 'fighting soldier'. Psychologically resembling a case of stale nitroglycerine, Colonel Newall had been lethally deployed by his masters in most recent hell holes the British Army had fought in: Aden, Malaya, Cyprus, Oman and many more covert sinks. Perhaps because of his limited imagination he always returned unscathed.

Listening to the man ranting down the phone and demanding to take on these bullyboy 18-year-olds man to man in the gym, one hand behind his back, and teach them a lesson, Chalky White had a thought. On the one hand, some action had to be taken. He couldn't allow an epidemic of dwarf-throwing to break out in the school. On the other hand, did this obnoxious, ageing infantry colonel really think he could tackle 15 fit young men? One way or another it seemed like a win-win situation.

Chalky White accepted the invitation and commanded the First XV to entertain Colonel Newall behind closed doors in the gym.

One after another the colonel placed his fist or boot between ribs or teeth or square into genitals or eyes until he succeeded in making young Edwin Newall the most hated boy in the College. Hardly broke sweat.

Dr Newall tried never to think of his father if at all possible. Colonel Newall was everything he loathed. Tall. Physical. Thug. Macho. Team player. Thicko.

His father had made him the non-team-playing, dirty tricks activist he was. So although he'd taught planning for 10 years at Manchester Uni, he'd always known he could never be part of a department there or in any municipal planning office. No, he wasn't a team player; he was a brilliant virtuoso performer. He had used the time to acquire acolytes among those he trained and to cultivate contacts in planning departments, local councillors and companies until the day he'd put his own shingle up: Dr Edwin Newall, Urbanist & Planning Consultant. He had thought romantically of these contacts he'd cultivated as 'sleepers', embedded in organizations where he could awake them when the Green Time came. And now it was starting to happen. The Green Time was coming. The Cloughgreen wind farms, wonderfully exciting in themselves, would be the covert key to his Purity Valley regeneration scheme.

His mind whirred with pleasure at the thought. This was the start of the whole Green revolution he had been planning for over a decade. He liked demonstrating his intellectual superiority. What was the point of being brilliant if other people didn't recognize it? The only point of knowing all the Planning Regs was so you could bend 'em like Beckham for the cause.

They'd called him Big-Ead when he was a kid at that dreadful school. An unfunny schoolboy joke about his name, his height and his precocious knowledge. But now Dr Edwin Newall would show 'em all, oh, yes. He might be small, but he was a Goliath of planning.

After all these years of frustration things were beginning to move at last. He clicked his knuckles and smiled. Good.

He strode out and down Radical Road, a street of large Victorian red brick villas on three levels. His address had given him sly pleasure since the day he moved in. He ran his hand cheerfully along the tops of the low privet hedges. He'd often wondered why they'd given the road its name. It must have been the shiny red brick, he decided. In a town built almost entirely of the local millstone grit, shiny red brick was definitely making a statement. That definitely would have been radical.

He almost floated the 100 yards to the corner and turned into Park Lane and then into Manchester Road. Although it was winter it felt like spring, the wind actually felt bracing. He was soon level with the little arcade of shops facing the park, the Happy Dragon takeaway, Jimmy's barbershop, the newsagents and Tout Vitesse bike shop (aka Emil's). Emil, born in Bradford to French parents, kept a replica Tour de France leader's Yellow jersey and a string of plastic onions in his window and wore a black beret. That Emil. He waved cheerily to him sporting his beret in his doorway. Must try and sell him the bike back.

In no time at all he'd passed the cop shop, the main shopping strip on Manchester Road, The Prince of Denmark pub and the Town Hall and was into the station.

The purple 3-car unit hissed its doors open and he could hardly get on past people standing in the doorway. He started to exclaim Gai...but stopped and smiled. What did it matter today if he had to stand all the way to Manchester?

He rode the rails into Manchester happily watching his inner movie, giant steel blades glittering in the sun sending out a huge spiritual Green message to the whole planet. Other passengers wondered at the silly grin on his face. But he never even noticed they were there. His 10-year old plan for Purity Valley and a new responsible way of life was starting to move.

When she heard the front door close Penny went upstairs in Dr Newall's house and popped her contact lenses in. Then she applied her waterproof mascara and eyeliner. You could never have too much of that. She believed the slight magnification of the contact lenses made her eyes look massive. After her long, purple-clad legs they were her best point.

Satisfied she looked her best, she went downstairs and did the washing-up. Then she went and got the hoover out of the old pantry that served as a cleaning cupboard. As she hoovered the living room where they'd eaten the takeaway on their laps she discovered her foil tray of leftover red masala sauce next to the settee.

She tsked under her breath and took it out to the kitchen pedal bin. She scooped it in before she realized she'd plopped it on top of yesterday's knickers and Dr Newall's vindaloo tray.

Whilst it was a surprise - she certainly couldn't remember putting them there - she just shrugged. If she couldn't remember, it must have been fun. Marks and Sparks would provide.

After thinking for a minute she went back upstairs, through all the tastefully muted hessian walls and carpets to Edwin's bedroom.

She took a pair of plum-coloured jockeys from the top drawer of his dresser and rubbed her nose in them, but they only smelled of conditioner. Disappointed, she shucked off her shoes and tights and wriggled the jockeys on under her tight yellow mini. They rucked up a bit under her bum but that couldn't be helped. VPL was the least of her problems.

Then she went across the landing and couldn't resist a last look into Edwin's study. There were a lot of books on the wall surrounding the door frame. Then there was a desk facing out into the garden with an expensive black laptop on it. Through the window you could see a small lawn and then the tall reeds and large white pebbles surrounding a deep frog pool with a water feature; the Buddhist meditation garden Edwin had built himself in the Japanese style.

Apart from the tidy desk with the computer and peripherals, there was a small nest of 3 plain oak tables. Each contained a chess set on top with a game obviously in progress. One table carried a card reading Moscow, the next said New York and the smallest one read London. On the right hand wall was a large international clock with 3 dials showing the present times in each of the three cities.

Before they'd had a drink the night before Edwin had had to email his latest chess move through to New York. He was cross because he said the guy must have got some grand master in to help. His opponent had suddenly started winning and that just never happened, Edwin said. The guy must be cheating. She believed him. He was clever, he never lost. She'd heard him speak. God, how he could speak.

Beneath the international clock on the wall was a line typed on thick gloss photo paper, blown up and framed: 'THE LONG VIEW IS EVERYTHING'. On the left hand wall was a medium size green mask of the Green Man, his grotesque face surrounded by twigs, branches and leaves. There were others distributed around the house. It was all linked up with respect for nature and the planet. One night she'd asked him why he exclaimed Gaia and he'd talked for nearly 3 hours about it.

'Gaia is the name of the Greek Earth goddess, the daughter of Chaos,' he said, smiling. 'But I say it really in recognition of the Gaia Theory which was started by a brilliant, brilliant guy, a NASA scientist called Dr James Lovelock.

'Roughly speaking, he had this breakthrough idea which suggested that the Earth, the planet, was a living entity, which was self-regulating to keep itself hospitable as a host for all the other living species.'

Penny remembered his eyes gleaming as he talked. She loved people who were enthusiastic, who believed in things.

'Properly speaking, it's more often referred to as earth system science. He defined Gaia as "a complex entity involving the Earth's biosphere - those bits of the Earth occupied by living organisms - atmosphere, oceans and soil; the totality constituting a feedback or cybernetic system which seeks an optimal physical and chemical environment for life on this planet.' She knew he could tell she couldn't follow it all. Her eyes were probably glazing over like when she'd listened to her science teacher. But still, he had touched he hand gently.

'All it really means is that for millions of years the Earth has been quietly regulating itself to make it pleasant as a host for all the other living things,' he said. He stopped and put a Polo in his mouth and offered her the tube, which she accepted. He sucked a minute then started speaking again.

'Lovelock pointed out that despite the Sun's energy having increased by 25-30% the surface temperature of the Earth had remained constant. And the atmospheric composition had remained constant despite the presence of methane - I won't bother you about why that matters. And finally, the salinity of the oceans had remained constant. All of which is very good news for living things here on Earth.' Then his face clouded over.

'The bad news is that we are overwhelming Gaia with man-made waste products, suffocating her with excess carbon. It's why we've got to take Green issues seriously. Why we really have got to cut the carbon now.'

God, when he talked like that she could listen for ever. She knew some people said he liked the sound of his own voice too much. But if you knew as much as he did, why not? You had the right to tell other people. Probably had a duty even, if you were serious-minded like he was.

She went to his main desk and riffled through the mail, looking for anything from Irene Vine. Councillor Irene Vine, if you please. Widowed and on the lookout. Penny knew they'd slept together, had even plucked up courage and asked him about it once.

'Just a mercy fuck one Christmas. It meant nothing. It's just she's useful to me. She's on a lot of planning committees and quangos, puts in a good word for me locally when contracts come up. Business really.'

She wondered if Irene Vine saw it like that. Probably not, knowing Edwin. Still, no trace of her here. No giveaway purple envelopes with green ink, smelling of perfume. Just loads of boring stuff about renewable reed houses, industrial wind turbines, revolutionary new concrete, bore holes, geosomethingorother, tidal power, solar panels, submerged turf houses and god knows what. Plus the latest edition of the wind farm journal from the UK Wind Commission. So, no immediate threat then from other rivals.

Penny clasped her hands in silent ecstasy. What infinite joy it would be to live in this wonderful, roomy, tasteful house with this genius of a man, the good Dr Newall. All the plain muted colours indicated conservative bachelor tastes, but she had some wonderful vibrant travel posters she could put up to liven the place up with splashes of colour. And some reproduction Kandinskys. She was sure he'd appreciate that.

Outside the parish church bell chimed, breaking her reverie. She checked her original Mickey Mouse watch, one of her most treasured possessions, a design classic. Ten o'clock. More than enough time to face up to scruffy Gerry Stansfield and his knife-and-fork-cut brown beard and his cynicism and start knocking out all those boring catalogue layouts for Storm-n-Shine (Attire & Camping Gear).

Hundreds of layouts showing happy campers in sunny settings wearing Storm-n-Shine clothes, using Storm-n-Shine utensils and living in Storm-n-Shine tents. Ditto the winter catalogue. Smug-looking outdoor types looking warm and happy in brass monkey conditions on the moors. Crap. She'd once thought of doing the alternative, realistic winter catalogue with people looking like frost-bitten Magwitch or Captain Scott, purple with frustration at tent pegs frozen immovably into cast-iron ground. It was alright for Gerry. He worked on all the outside photo shoots and commercials, the exciting stuff. She laid out thousands and thousands of little insets and cutouts in the voluminous catalogue, almost going cross-eyed. Then again he was the boss.

What the hell? If you couldn't be late now and again what was the point? Sighing, she took a key off a hook in the kitchen, went to the shed and extracted Edwin's little-used, red and silver mountain bike. May as well save some time getting into work. She was sure Edwin wouldn't mind. The frame was a bit small for her long legs, but who cared? She returned the key, locked up and went back to the bike. Pausing before she got her leg over the crossbar she opened her handbag, and took a quick look around. There was nobody about so she had a heart-starter from her vodka flask. She'd noticed recently that the booze was giving her greasy skin and dry hair. So what? Edwin never complained.

# 3

In a small country town dominated by pubs with names like The Shepherd's Rest, The Fox & Chickens, The Pack Horse and The Farmer's Arms, The Prince of Denmark had cultural pretensions.

Willie looked up at the Prince's inn sign, racketing on its iron mount in the wind. A limelight-faced, camp-looking Hamlet in baggy black tights posed with Yorick's skull which bizarrely had a lit candle inside it.

For entirely different reasons the sign offended him, Gerry and Jumper. They had remarked on this to Wesley, the Ronny Corbett lookalike, who was the landlord. Hilda likes it, he said, referring to his giantess wife. She says he looks like the sort of lad who wouldn't make trouble on a Saturday night. The four of them had sniggered. There was definitely that, Willie thought. Anyway one day Willie had started calling The Prince of Denmark the Hamlet and it had stuck. Shorter.

Standing on the corner he looked at his watch. 12-58. May as well give them 2 more minutes. Gerry was often late because of last minute advertising panics. But Jumper was old school. Punctuality was the courtesy of kings etc.

As Willie watched the side street next to the Hamlet, a venerable, muddy brown minibus stopped and disgorged 12 elderlies. Apart from telltale bulges, they appeared unisex, all anoraked, trousered, booted and woolly-topped. To his amaze the faded lettering on the side read Sheffield South Side Ramblers. Ramblers? They looked more like outpatients for Woolton General.

Nonetheless, they soon pulled their packs on and staggered off in the direction of the Tourist Information Centre. They trooped past him holding their map cases out in front. Big city folk. You could tell city folk on the moor by the way they pretended you were invisible, avoided eye contact and walked or jogged straight past as though on dangerous city streets. The locals recognized other human beings and stopped to chat. Cultural differences, town and country; it didn't matter. Even if they didn't stop and chat, it made Willie feel good. They were refreshing their souls away from all the steel and concrete.

He could identify with that.

The ramblers' crocodile was slow but purposeful as a column of soldier ants. They drifted relentlessly on, hoisting a metaphoric two fingers to age, wind and impending rain. Cloughgreen's rugged landscape attracted walkers and runners the year round. The pubs, tea shops and market stalls did good trade.

Good luck to them, Willie thought. He turned his head and looked the other way, down Manchester Road. He spotted Jumper and Gerry coming around the far corner. A couple of minutes later the three of them entered the Hamlet. Mob-handed.

Wes, the Ronnie Corbett lookalike landlord, was wearing his Saturday show-off yellow waistcoat. He beamed at them. 'How's the Gang of Three?' he asked, smiling.

'Bolshy,' Gerry Stansfield said, sharp as a tack.

'*Plus ca change then*, eh? The usual? Pinta lager, pinta Gweens, pinta Black Sheep?'

'That'll do,' Jumper said.

The three went through to their usual table in the small snug and huddled around the smokey fire. Through the open door of the big new Sports Bar with the giant Sky TV there were the sounds of raucous football appreciation from the young bloods. The three friends normally met Monday and Friday lunchtimes. Quieter. But this was an emergency and Jumper had forgone his usual Saturday afternoon sport at the rugby club.

We probably look an odd trio to the lads from the Sports Bar, Willie thought. If they notice us at all.

They were all around 6' tall, but Willie and Jumper were lean and wiry. Gerry was soft from a sedentary life huddled over a layout pad and a Mac.

At 73, Sam "Jumper" Lonk was the oldest. Jumper was a tough-looking, bachelor farmer who would have passed for 20 years younger. He got his name from having been an international showjumper and from all the farmers' wives he had ridden.

Jumper was not a cuddly man. He was hard and bony with a purple hatchet nose and a mass of white hair. He had an animal directness that women found appealing. What he lacked in looks he made up for in athleticism. And a good few women had passed him on to girl friends in need of comfort. Jumper was Cloughgreen born and bred, like Gerry.

Gerry Stansfield was 45, an art director and graphic designer who ran his own small ad business in town and lived above the shop. They'd met briefly when Gerry had done a stint in London advertising. The creative community of London advertising was like a small village, everyone knew everyone. Willie sometimes thought of Gerry as Friar Stansfield, the cynical Cistercian who'd seen too much disappointment. He had a tonsure-like bald spot surrounded by shoulder-length thick brown hair and a jagged brown beard that looked as though it had been cut with a knife and fork. But the pale blue eyes were worldly enough.

'Well,' Jumper said, 'Meetin' on a Saturday like this and missin' the rugby... it had better be important.' Jumper was a product of his age: "sportin'" on Saturdays, "churchin'" on Sundays, social engagements that defined his week. It being a Saturday he was wearing his "sportin" rig: scarlet cravat circa 1955, spotted red and white breast pocket hankie, hounds-tooth sports jacket, beige cords, tan brogues on his big feet.

Willie couldn't help himself, he was like a man obsessed and blurted it right out. 'What does anyone know about the wind farms?'

'Only that The Delf's been there about four and a half years now,' Gerry said, yawning and scratching his ample gut. 'But you were in Greenwood Royd when they were putting them up.'

'No, I meant the other 78 they're thinking of putting up on the moors round Cloughgreen.'

They both looked blank.

'Eh?' Jumper managed.

'Jesus,' Gerry spluttered.

'78?' they said together, appalled at the figure. 78 of anything was a lot to get your head around.

'And they'll all be 410' high. It was in this week's Recorder,' Willie said. There was a stunned silence, so total you could only hear the soft thud of metal driven into cork from two old guys playing darts in the far corner. It was halftime in the Sports Bar and the noise had dropped to a steady drone.

'Jesus wept,' Jumper eventually spluttered.

'Dr Newall is the bloke to ask about wind farms,' Gerry said.

'Who's he?'

'He's the local wind farm fanatic. He goes out with Penny Wragg. You know, Penny as works for me? Wears purple tights all the time.' He reflected briefly and shook his head. 'Don't know why Penny sticks with him, mind. Seems to treat her like shit.'

'What's he like, then, this Newall?' Willie asked. Gerry took a swig at his lager, wiped his mouth with the back of his hand and pulled a face.

'Dr Newall, if you please,' Gerry said through clenched teeth. 'Thinks he knows everything and knows nowt. Arrogant little fucker. Spoken to him a few times. Looks down on you as though you're a piece of shit. Insists you call him *Doctor* Newall, at all times. And he's not even a proper doctor either, not a medical one.'

'Little bloke, wavy black hair. Struts round like a bantam with his chest out and his head back. Wears 'orrible bow ties. Proper little dapper dan. It's a small town, you must have seen him around,' Jumper added helpfully.

'Can't say I have,' Willie admitted. 'We must move in different circles.'

There was a  raucous cheer from the Sports Bar. They'd kicked off again. Jumper and Gerry looked at Willie. What next?

'Doesn't sound like Mr Popular,' Willie said.

'Oh, he ain't got no friends. Town this size, everyone's got his own Dr Newall story. Loves 'imself too much. Like I said, dunno why Penny sticks with him. The times I've seen her come in with red eyes. He treats her like shit, but she can't see it. I bumped into him once in the gents at The Bird i' The Hand. Told him if he didn't want Penny he should do the decent thing and tell her so. "What business of is it of yours?" he said. "Fuck off, peasant."'

Gerry indicated the top of his chest. 'Only comes up to here, the little bastard. I was about to teach him some grown-up manners when someone else came in for a leak. Amazes me he doesn't get thumped daily, his attitude. Still, he's the sort of guy who'd call the police rather than fight back like a man.'

Jumper, who'd been considering the foam on his Guinness, suddenly looked up. 'He's always writing about Green rubbish in the Recorder letters page. Strikes me as one of those blokes who's lost all his common sense fast as he's passed his exams. Like one head couldn't contain both, the learning and the common sense. Lot of college lads like that. All theory, no common sense.' Willie looked at him, knowing full well Jumper had been to agricultural college and was brighter than he let on.

'So he's highly qualified?'

'Oh, yeah,' Jumper snorted. 'Dr Newall would be first to tell you that. But like Gerry says, he's not half as clever as he thinks he is. Have to be Einstein and Henry Kissinger rolled into one to be that. He's always banging on about these windmills. Fact is, they were obsolete 400 years ago. That's why they went over to water power. Worse, he's one of these Green nutters who wants to get rid of all the modern inventions like cars and planes and fridges and go back to the Dark Ages. Sailing ships, horses and carts.'

'That's right,' Gerry agreed. 'Ideally he'd like to go back to the water-driven mills they used to have. And for Cloughgreen to be industrial again. Everyone just a cobbled street away from their work. No nasty cars, see. Just the sound of clogs in the dawn trudge to the mill.'

'Bloody hell...' Willie said.

'Like I said, no common sense, but he knows he knows best,' Jumper said. 'Anyone who lived through the mill times in Cloughgreen, like I did, wouldn't want to see all that back again. Pea souper fog every winter from the chimneys. People herded into dark satanic mills for long hours and paid peanuts. Dying before their time. When I was young you couldn't grow roses for the smoke even up where we are, Willie. Or lots of other stuff, for that matter. Cabbage white butterflies actually evolved into cabbage blacks. Can you believe that? Thirty-odd years without mills and they're white again.'

'He surely wouldn't want polluting industry if he's green,' Willie said.

'He wants all the moors and green valleys round here turning back into industry. Low carbon, but industry. And he won't worry how menial it is. He'd love to have us all out on the moors in all weathers quarrying stone, mining fireclay or digging lime out for fertilizer - the good old days. That's what the moors were used for and that's what they should go back to so far as he's concerned. He's been banging on about it for years. Back to the future.' Jumper let loose a low growl under his breath and swigged his pint. Gerry shook his head and passed his hand over his face.

'Like Jumper says, he wants all these local industries on our doorsteps so everyone walks to work. No cars, see. He hates cars. No quality of life either living on top of the works. Even when they let you out you lived in the shadow of the mill to remind you. That's why so many rambling clubs were started up here. Just to get away from the mill and up into the clean air on the moors for a few hours.'

Hearing about Dr Newall Willie felt the same chill of intuition pass through him as when he first read about the planning proposal. 'The good doctor must be very pleased at the prospect of getting all these new turbines. What does he actually do?'

'He's a planner,' Gerry said. 'As in town planner. He calls himself an urbanist, if you please.'

'Jesus...the last thing this little town needs is a clever Green bastard who wants to "urbanize",' - Willie made pointers in the air with his fingers - 'our beautiful landscape and knows how to do it.'

'Well he won't care what anyone else thinks; that's for sure,' Gerry said. 'He knows he knows better. He's a smart arse.'

Willie spoke very quietly. 'And this bloke, this "urbanist",' he said the word as though it stung his mouth, 'is mad keen on wind farms?'

'Lives for it, to judge from his letters.'

'Well, if we're going to stop these 78 new wind turbines springing up all round Cloughgreen we're going to have a fight on our hands. I take it you gentlemen feel the same as I do.'

Gerry and Jumper looked at him, then Jumper spat ostentatiously into the fire. Willie looked away, shocked at his vehemence.

'Apart from saving the landscape, I'd like to remind that bastard his shit smells the same as everyone else's,' Gerry said, smoothing a hand through his jagged brown beard. 'Arrogant git.'

The conversation seemed to have reached a natural conclusion and Willie suddenly felt like a leak. He excused himself and got up to go. Gerry asked if he'd like the same again. He nodded.

Walking back from the gents he couldn't help noticing how Gerry and Jumper looked pretty much the same age, even though Jumper was nearly 30 years older. His tall, bony figure looked trim and fit, face relatively unlined. A tribute to riding out every day and a diet of red meat and Guinness plus carrots and onions in winter, lettuce, tomatoes and chicken in summer. And a lifetime heaving sheep around. Not to mention other men's wives. Jumper was a sort of life force.

Now he sat erect, deep in thought, behind his great purple hatchet of a nose, while Gerry was slumped back against the wall, eyes half-closed, beaming seraphically as he took in Fleetwood Mac's Albatross from the 60s jukebox.

As Willie sat down, Jumper spoke. 'Wouldn't mind a spin in your missus's new Mini Cooper...'

'You'll have to ask her yourself, Jumper. She won't even let me drive it.'

'Get away!'

'It's true, she's very possessive about it.' Willie considered for a moment then smiled a bitter little smile. 'Maybe if you said you supported these new wind farms...'

'How do you mean?'

'We've fallen out over the new wind farms. That's partly what this conversation has been all about. She thinks they're all pink and fluffy and God's gift to humanity and they are going to save the planet. I'm a bit worried we're going to be overwhelmed by all this concrete and steel in our faces.

Seems to me like we could suddenly be living on an industrial site. And I'd like to know if being swamped by the things is worth it.' Willie closed his eyes and rubbed his hands through his curly blond locks. 'Anyway, she's not really talking to me.'

Gerry opened his eyes. 'Oh dear, Willie,' he said. 'Oh dear.'

The atmosphere in the small front room of the Hamlet was conspiratorial and thoughtful. They had fallen silent when Wesley Douglas, landlord and Ronnie Corbett lookalike, came to collect the empties from the table.

'These all dead?' They nodded.

'What are you lot plotting?' he asked in his usual jokey way. 'Blowing up Parliament? Taking over Man United?'

'Making Big Hilda laugh,' Gerry Stansfield said, referring to Wesley's large and largely humourless wife.

'Oh, you do that already, Gerry,' Wesley said, making Willie and Jumper titter. 'Be careful, mind, she'll be up from the cellar soon and I can't always control her.'

'We know that,' Jumper chipped in, his purple hatchet nose gleaming. Jumper had a sneaking fancy for Big Hilda and her enormous, shelf-like bosom, but she was a powerful woman. 'You might care to use the whip a mite more often,' he added helpfully.

'Take a bigger man than me,' Wesley grinned, turning on his heel.

'We know that, too.'

'Calm down, Jumper,' Gerry said, patting Jumper's arm, 'he doesn't mean you'. Jumper gave him a dirty look.

'Enough of this frivolity, gents,' Willie said, suddenly serious. 'Let's get back to the wind farm issue. You know me. I've got no idea about this sort of thing, finding stuff out and protesting.' He took a pull of his Black Sheep bitter. 'People dream up crazy ideas and bring them to me on the backs of envelopes and I make their idea happen. But I'm no good at finding stuff out.

'We need a writer. Someone who knows how to poke around and ask a few questions, find out what's really going on with this new wind farm caper.'

'Makes good sense to me,' Jumper said.

'Yeah, but who?' Gerry said. 'My mate Keene down in London is smart, but he's an ad writer. You really need a journo who knows how to ferret around, get the facts.'

'Now you say that, I think I know who, too,' Willie said. 'I used to do a lot of pack shots for 'The Grocer'; it's the trade rag for the grocery business telling retailers about new lines. Anyway this guy used to write for The Grocer. His name's Charley Fort. He's no Pulitzer Prize winner, but he's an old pro. He knows the ropes, knows how to find stuff out.'

'Do it now,' Gerry said, handing his flash new mobile over.

'I would, but I'll have to check out my old Filofax first for his number. Gerry snorted into his lager, soaking his raggedy brown beard, his blue eyes flashing.

'Filofax! Where've you been the last 20 years?'

'I don't even have a mobile,' Jumper said.

'Yeah, but you're...oh, forget it, Jumper.'

# 4

Monday November 5

Dr Edwin Newall parked his rusty, red 2CV a block away from Ursa Power's address. He hated the 2CV, as he hated all cars. But the fact was, unless you lived somewhere like London, where there was fantastic public transport, you just needed one. He also felt guilty that he was wasting fuel by not keeping the tyres regularly inflated and getting the plugs changed; but he just couldn't be arsed. He could hardly bear to look at the smelly old thing, much less fuss over it.

Ursa Power's *pied a terre* in Rochdale looked distinctly unpromising. An anonymous office above a small greasy spoon in a 3-storey redbrick Thirties shopping arcade. This wasn't what he'd had in mind at all.

A top of the range silver Merc and a black Porsche Carrera sat at the kerb. Incongruous visitors from another planet.

The smell of over-used fat rankled in his nostrils beneath the smell of frying sausages and bacon as he approached the open door to the side of the cafe. Dr Newall felt a pang of unease; he was potentially risking a lot, who was he signing himself up with?

A small silver plaque inside announced that Ursa Power were situated on the first floor. The bare wooden steps sighed and groaned alarmingly as he went up.

A similar silver plaque adorned a seriously heavy oak door on the landing. He knocked twice, pushed and walked into another world.

A large spacious room with doors off it contained a grey, deep pile carpet, heavy red drapes and expensive chocolate-coloured leather settees grouped around a low steel and glass occasional table.

Two expensive-looking black laptops sat side by side on the table.

'Dr Edwin Newall,' he said and the two elegant men in their early forties rose to meet him. Their suits probably cost more than his annual income, he thought. He had dressed in a 100% wool suit with a 100% Egyptian cotton shirt and black Oxfords from Church's. The keynote was supplied by a green silk bow tie, deliberately meant to be the colour of folding money. He believed in symbols.

The blond man strode quickly across to grasp his hand, the dark-haired man held his ground. They both looked like they worked out in the gym, making him aware of his incipient paunch.

'Dr Newall, how do you do? I am Ilya Bakunin, MD of Ursa Power. And this is Arkady Shevalenko, our Finance Director.'

'Pleased to meet you,' Newall said.

The dark-haired man strode forward and offered a bone-crunching, dry handshake. 'How do you do. You come very well recommended. A degree in architecture as well as town planning. Excellent.' There was a pause as the blond-haired man hesitated, wondering how much to say. Then he seemed to decide and he spread his arms wide.

'We are both ex-Red Army men. I was a colonel in the KGB. Arkady was a major in *spetsnaz*, special forces. Then later I was his commanding officer.'

'As he is once more,' Arkady said, grinning.

'Since then,' Ilya continued, 'I have an MBA from Harvard as well as my degree from St. Petersburg. As does, Arkady.'

The blond man smiled and made a mock bow. Newall smiled, this was more like it. 'Impressive,' he said.

'Sit down please, Dr Newall. It is good that we meet at last.' Newall did so, sinking into the low settee. The other two men sat also. 'Coffee please, Victoria,' the MD said over his shoulder.

'Coming up,' a plummy English voice replied.

The blond Russian leaned forward. 'Anyway, we meet at last. The consultancy contract we have offered you is generous enough?'

'Extremely generous,' Newall said.

'You are sure it is enough? And you are here to sign it?'

'It is very generous, as I said. And yes, I am here to put pen to paper.'

'Good, because we believe we are paying for the best local planner available. We have a talented planner on board already, but nothing must be left to chance. Local knowledge may be vital. Do you know, we found this wonderful site overlooking the Solway Firth and the locals wouldn't let us develop it. And do you know why? It is unbelievable'

'They have about 10,000 barnacle geese migrate there every winter?' Dr Newall suggested.

'Exactly. You must have heard about it. We couldn't believe it. A few damned birds can prevent a major investment project here in the UK. Astonishing, no?' Doctor Newall gave a sort of philosophical shrug. More than a few damned birds, surely? Even he could see that.

'Anyway, it is of paramount importance we win this contract whatever opposition there may be...many, many millions are at stake over the next twenty-five years.'

Newall smiled and nodded his agreement. Understood. Wondered whether maybe he should have asked for more?

'And the bank arrangements are set up? You have supplied us your details?' Bakunin continued.

'Yes, they should work like clockwork.' He was looking forward to receiving his first-ever statements from an offshore bank in the Caribbean. He was definitely moving up in the world.

Ilya Bakunin sat back, placing clasped hands behind his blond head. 'Yet you look surprised, Dr Newall? You were expecting Russian mafia perhaps, with Molotov cocktails and AK47s?'

'No,no, not at all. It's just that outside and in here...'

Ilya Bakunin smiled again, displaying some very white and expensive American dentistry. 'This is just a temporary base up here for our fleeting visits,' Bakunin said. 'We thought it politic not to be too close to the natives in Cloughgreen while we blow the wind of change through their town.' He tightened his lips reflectively. 'Few people like change. But change there must be.'

'Wise move, Mr Bakunin, the peasants may well revolt.' The Russians were displaying a surprising grasp of the ignorance and resistance to change they were up against, Dr Newall thought. That was encouraging.

'Call me Ilya, please,' Bakunin said.

'And Arkady,' the dark-haired assassin said. 'We are going to be comrades, we must not stand on ceremony.'

'Then you may call me Edwin,' Newall said.

'Not Dr Edwin?' Arkady said, teasing.

'Edwin will suffice,' Newall said, who normally insisted on being called Dr Newall. Who in truth thought of himself as Dr Newall even on the lavatory. Discarding his doctorate would be like racing bollock naked through the streets. Still. Think of Purity Valley. He could be plain Edwin for a price.

'Anyway, Edwin, what a splendid enterprise this is, eh? We Russians provide the seed corn and your Government will carry on paying us for another 25 years. What a good wheeze, eh? We save the planet. We help Britain's renewables. We make buckets of money. And everybody is happy.'

Arkady Kovalenko, the Finance Director, grinned wolfishly. 'We see our investment as foreign aid. Truly.' He laughed and then leaned forward. 'The generous British government guarantees make it the chance of a lifetime for entrepreneurs all over the world. You know there are other wind companies being formed by French gentlemen, Yanks, Scandinavians, even Burmese chaps. It's like an English Klondike. They call it the dash for cash.' He laughed again loudly. 'None of us has ever done this sort of thing before. But as you know your Government has guaranteed us subsidies for 25 years.' He smiled happily.

'We have merchant banks and lawyers in place. And wind turbines are not rocket science; it is such a simple technology. A one-off negotiation and then we're sitting pretty for 25 years. What's to go wrong?'

It's all such a simple game for you fat cats, isn't it, Newall thought. *Advance to GO! Collect £20,000,000.* He waited a moment, letting the silence build before dropping his pebble into the still waters.

'Only planning permission,' he said, crisply. 'That's what can go wrong. The peasants aren't just going to roll over, you know. Even if they are thick and can't see beyond the ends of their noses.'

'But now we have you Edwin, hey?' Kovalenko said, rubbing his arm warmly as though he were a West African juju. Dr Newall pulled his arm away briskly. Aaghh, Kovalenko was a toucher and space invader. *Noli-me-tangere.*

Hiding his distaste, he quickly recovered his composure and waved his hands airily. 'If the investment expertise to get this Green venture going comes from overseas, then so be it. The planet is down on its knees suffocating from excess carbon dioxide. The change to sustainable, renewable resources must be as swift as possible.'

'Well said,' Ilya, the blond MD said, clapping his hands together gently. 'The patient is already critical, eh?' He pursed his lips and put his head on one side quizzically.

'And time is money,' Arkady added.

'You realize, if we are clever, this may be only the start?' Dr Newall said. Both the Russians jerked to attention and looked hard at him.

'Really, how so?' Ilya Bakunin creased his eyes up and fiddled with his four-button cuff.

'Well,' Newall lowered his voice and leaned forward confidentially. 'I cannot go into details yet, but there is a planning loophole you might exploit to get in at least another 78 turbines if we are successful with this application. If we get these through we are away and running. These are only the thin end of the wedge.'

Ilya Bakunin showed his white teeth in a smile of genuine pleasure. This little English popinjay may be worth more than they thought. 'Better and better,' he said.

Dr Newall made a little moue and opened his palms wide. 'Some of the extra turbines may have to be a little smaller. But I envisage hundreds more in this very same area. I see how we could make this area between the Lake District and the Peak District wind farm capital of the UK. There are no areas of natural beauty here. Apart from the Bronte village of Haworth, there aren't even cultural sites to be wary of. It's just green desert. Worthless as it stands.'

'Bravo, well spoken, Edwin,' Arkady said, 'I like your passion. I see you are a true believer in wind farms.'

'As are we all,' Ilya said smoothly.

A slim young woman with cropped corn-blonde hair and big blue eyes brought the coffee out on a tray.

She wore a sunflower design tee shirt and a short black micro-mini. Newall almost gasped out loud. Perched on strappy heeled sandals, she had long coltish legs, splayed above the knee with a gap you could drive a bus through. You could almost smell her sex, he thought.

'There you are gentlemen,' she said, beaming faux-innocently as she put the tray down, pretending to be unaware of the oceans of lust she was stirring.

'Victoria, could you bring your latest PR release through for Doctor Newall to take a look at please? And could you bring out the Stolichnaya and three glasses?'

The young woman smiled warmly. 'Of course, Ilya.'

When she had gone, Arkady leaned closer to Newall. 'Victoria Flowers is our pubic relations girl, Edwin.'

'Public Relations, you mean.'

'On the contrary, we do mean pubic relations, Edwin,' Arkady said, roaring with laughter. 'Victoria went to Benenden, you know. Daddy's a lord. She goes like a rat up a drainpipe. You should try her some time.' They both laughed fit to bust again and Dr Newall felt like he was getting out of his depth. MBAs maybe, but what vulgarians. But then he could hardly keep his eyes off Victoria's thighs himself as she passed him the PR Release.

'We'll talk about it later,' Ilya Bakunin said, dismissing her.

Newall found it difficult to concentrate. His eyes were hitting the page, not taking anything in. In fact he was worried he was actually getting red under the collar. With men like this you had at least to pretend you were one of the lads, a vulgarian. But he didn't want to embarrass himself.

Then his eyes alighted on one sentence in the PR release. "One proposed site at Cloughgreen will provide 85% of Woolton's Govt sustainable energy quota...' My, how the peasants of Cloughgreen will like that, he thought. They hated the town of Woolton and all of its metropolitan works with a passion. The hatred went back years to all the occasions when Woolton prepared borough maps and forgot to even put little Cloughgreen on them. And to the disastrous social engineering experiment when Woolton had "decanted" hundreds of their problem families onto the Mancan Green estate in Cloughgreen. How Cloughgreen's citizens would love to be playing host to wind farms on Woolton's behalf. They would see it as them shovelling more of Woolton's shit for Woolton MBC.

'Has this gone out yet?' he asked mildly.

'It's on the website,' Bakunin said proudly. 'First thing we did. Victoria's idea, to be fair.'

'Right,' Newall said. So too late. They had already lit the blue touchpaper. This was going to be tricky. How to explain to two Russians and their eager-to-please high class southern counties 'tail' the micro-politics of the northern tribes?

Dr Newall appraised them as they drank their coffee. The overtly macho aura they gave off as men's men was disconcerting. There was a physical menace about them. They had MBAs so they must be clever, but not so clever or subtle as him. They seemed to lack guile, be bull at a gate. Perhaps it was a gate he could lean on?

'May I speak openly?'

'Of course.'

'Even if it is criticism?'

'Naturally. That is why we are paying you. To find faults and smooth our path.'

'Alright, then you should understand the local politics between Cloughgreen where you want to put the turbines and Woolton, which is the authority which will impose them.' He explained quickly how the PR release would be viewed in Cloughgreen. The response was instant and impressive.

'Arkady, tell the girl to remove it from the site. Immediately.' The scary ex-spetsnaz guy nodded and rose to his feet. After he'd left the room Ilya Bakunin turned to Newall.

'Good thinking, Edwin. Is there anything else?'

'Okay. I think you should have concealed the fact that you plan 78 turbines.'

'We have. We plan many more in Scotland and Wales and Devon.'

'No, here I mean.' Arkady inclined his head, baffled.

'Why?'

'Well, some of the peasants might be alarmed by the number. It might have been better to introduce the 4 different wind farms at intervals, piecemeal. Disguise the number of turbines there will be in this area. Use subterfuge. Try and sneak them in under the radar. Always play the long game, revealing your hand at the last moment...sometimes only after years...' He became aware that Bakunin was staring at him.

For dramatic effect he locked his hands together and placed them over his eyes. 'Frankly the best way to treat the peasants is by using the Mushroom Principle.'

'The Mushroom Principle?' Bakunin looked blank.

'Feed them shit and keep them in the dark.'

Ilya Bakunin laughed a great Russian belly laugh. 'Good, very good. I have not heard that one before. We are going to like you, I think, Edwin.'

He waited until the laughter had drained away and made a point of looking serious. 'But our lawyers say there is one big advantage to linking them all together when they are close like this.'

'What is that?'

'The lawyers say that when the grouped total energy output of the turbines reaches a big enough size it may then be considered a site of national importance. Then it can be referred to the minister of state over the heads of the planning inspectorate. If the minister of state wants it, he can have it. He can invoke national importance and it doesn't matter what the planning authorities think.'

Doctor Newall whistled. 'Very clever. You have some smart lawyers. I didn't know that,' he admitted. 'The more things like that we have up our sleeve, the better.'

Arkady Kovalenko rejoined them with a bottle of Stolichnaya and three small glasses. 'The PR thing is sorted,' he said.

'Good, then let's drink gentlemen. Do the honours please, Arkady.' Arkady poured and then Ilya rose to his feet with the other two joining him. He winked broadly: 'Cheers. Here's to Sites of National Importance and to The Mushroom Principle.' Then he and his Finance Director drained their glasses. Under pressure Doctor Newall drained the remaining two thirds of his. It took his breath away.

Ilya beamed. 'Good. we will make a Russian of you yet.' Gaia! Doctor Newall thought through his fume-filled brain.

'To prevent any further mishaps, may I suggest I write some local PR for the local rag, try and organize some other Green local support, influence the peasants?'

'Good thinking,' Ilya said.

'Now before we get down to reviewing our application, are there any more local bribes you foresee we will need to pay?' Arkady was saying.

'More what?' Doctor Newall heard himself asking.

'Apart from yours.'

'Mine is a professional contract.'

'Sorry, yes, Arkady was clumsy, Doctor Newall, ' Bakunin said quickly, looking hard at his colleague. 'That's what he meant. Of course, it's quite different. Here, let's have another vodka.'

Arkady stood up, drew his heels together. 'Stupid. My English. I apologize,' he said.

'No problem,' Newall said, thinking, your English is as good as mine, chum. Even if it is a bit American at times.

'The word I was looking for was "sweeteners". For those lowly paid in the local government... the planners, perhaps?'

'No,' Newall almost screamed. 'That will not be necessary. They are professionals. And idealists. They would be insulted. And there is the law...'

'So, we will not insult anyone. And we have no need to break the law. Cultural differences, that is all.' Bakunin rubbed his right forefinger across the end of his nose, then made a calm down soothing gesture with his hands and poured them all another thimbleful each of vodka.

Arkady Kovalenko looked out of the window, yawning, and Dr Newall felt a frisson of fear run through him. These men would do whatever it took. It should have pleased him mightily. But although he shared their enthusiasm for the desired end result, they worried him in other ways.

'Good,' he heard himself say. 'So let's get down to the real nitty-gritty, let's look at the contract.'

Bakunin got up to fetch his briefcase from the other side of the room, next to his desk. Before he reached the desk he stopped and half-turned, the semblance of a smile on his smoothly shaven, cologned face.

'One last thing, Dr Newall, before we formally engage you. You did imply you had special connections with Woolton

MBC. That's partly why you've got the job. That and your local knowledge, of course.' He raised a quizzical eyebrow. 'These special connections are still in place, we take it?' He paused and smoothed his trouser crease before looking up. 'Just in case there are special circumstances and we need to call on them.'

Edwin Newall smiled. 'Of course.' No need to tell them he'd trained two of Woolton's planners, Angie Snow and young Steve Rathbone. They owed him. But the fewer people who knew of the connection, the better.

As Bakunin double-checked the contract and presented it to him Newall felt Kovalenko's cool blue eyes on him. Both these men had expensive educations and good manners, yet they exuded a raw primal magnetism like an aura. Naked power came off them in waves. And he was scenting it the way animals ran before a coming storm.

Despite their expensive suits and haircuts, manicured nails and silk socks they emanated a faintly suppressed air of physical violence which frightened him.

These men were undoubtedly highly intelligent, but they were not remotely like the planners and academics he was used to dealing with. It was disturbing to realise his main allies actually frightened him. Arkady Kovalenko in particular. He was the sort of man who looked at every woman in the room to check her bedworthiness and every man to see whether he could physically take him out.

Newall knew it would be no contest. He might be able to influence these men, but he would never be able to lead them. When he signed their contract he would have crossed some ill-defined Rubicon. Perhaps it was inevitable that a Green idealist and two capitalist bloodsuckers would be uneasy bedfellows?

With a mixture of fear and excitement, he took Ilya Bakunin's fountain pen and signed his usual large, languid signature.

'Good,' Bakunin said, beaming and extending his hand. His grip was firm but not macho.

Arkady Kovalenko took the contract and scanned it briefly. 'That's a very big signature, Edwin,' he said.

*What was that supposed to mean?* It was only his usual half-page scrawl. Big intellect, big signature. He was about to say something when he caught Bakunin shoot Kovalenko a look. Okay, leave it. Then the two Russians signed. Small, beetling signatures both of them, as if trying to conceal themselves. Or as though they were ashamed of them. Small minds, small signatures.

Kovalenko extended his hand, took his and duly cracked his fingers till they hurt, as he knew he would, smiling as he did it.

Dr Newall resisted the temptation to massage his bruised fingers. 'There is one last thing,' he said. Then he used his good left hand to extract a small note from his inside pocket.

It was written on the lined yellow legal pads he favoured. A conceit.

'What's this?' Bakunin took the scrap of yellow paper and unfolded it. 'The Bus Boys,' he read aloud, 'and a phone number.'

'What does that mean?' Kovalenko asked. Dr Newall smiled.

'The Bus Boys can be very useful to you. They don't call themselves that of course. But for a few bob, plus beer and sandwiches you can bus loads of them in to support a demo on a site, attend planning meetings, write letters to the planners, distribute pro-wind leaflets in town...whatever you like. The phone number is a bloke called Kevin Duff, their leader. Die-hard pro-wind man in his thirties. Lives for it. Bit of a tough nut. Milkman in real life.' He paused, thinking of Duff. 'No, I think the wind movement *is* his real life.'

'But, a sort of local militia,' Kovalenko said, thoughtful. 'I like it.'

'And all for beer and sandwiches, you say?' Bakunin asked.

'Well, they do like a little backhander, but they're very reasonable. They'll do it for peanuts,' Dr Newall said. 'The oposition call them "Rent-a-Mob".

'Ugly,' Kovalenko said. 'I prefer local militia.'

'Yeah,' Dr Newall said. 'They're a funny lot. A few are die-hard wind supporters. But a lot of them tend to be anti-everything. Anti-nuclear, anti-airports, anti-new rail links, anti-new motorways etc. Makes a nice change for them to be pro-something. And they see these demos as a way to meet old mates, have a drink, put two fingers up to the establishment.'

'The Bus Boys,' Bakunin murmured to himself, tucking the precious scrap of yellow paper into his breast pocket. 'Yes, I think they could be very useful, thank you Edwin.' Then, as Newall watched, he gathered up the signed contract and put that in his briefcase.

'Rent-A-Mob,' Newall continued. 'Not to be scorned. Yes, they have a useful part to play. Incidentally you don't literally hire buses or coaches. Be a bit too obvious. CRVs, long-base Range Rovers, minibuses, people carriers, that sort of thing...'

'More covert,' Kovalenko said. 'Yes, I think we get the picture. Then the assassin seemed to flick a switch in his head, Newall thought.

'Do you know any good pole-dancing clubs, Ed?' he asked. 'Now we've wrapped things up here.'

*Ed? Ed!*

Dr Newall's immediate reaction was to tell them that those clubs exploited women and he wanted nothing to do with it, thank you very much. Then he thought maybe he could plead a prior engagement. He had the whole of Bolton city centre to re-plan by 10am tomorrow, maybe.

Finally he put his brain in gear. They were businessmen a long way from home. Bored. Lonely. And, yeah, long term his plan for the Purity Valley settlement desperately needed them. Gaia! he would have to bite the bullet to fulfil his long-term objective.

'Nearest lap-dancing places would be in Manchester,' he said, feigning disappointment. 'Good way from here.'

'Nonsense, that is fine. It's only about 30 minutes drive from here, correct? Less the way Arkady drives his Porsche.'

'Yes, I suppose so,' he said weakly. He had a depressing vision of his battered old 2CV leading a sort of automotive funeral procession back into Manchester with the Porsche and the Merc creeping along behind, mocking him. Then he'd have to find a hole-in-the-wall to supplement the fiver he had in his wallet. Money he resented spending on Manchester scrubbers. Bloody hell. The things he did for the planet.

He was resigning himself to a night from hell and trying to compose his face into a glee mask when the ever-threatening Arkady leaned over and playfully pinched his cheek. Physicality never far away, he thought resentfully, while pretending to smile.

'Now I understand. You think we will be dull dogs, don't you, Edwin. Boring Russian businessmen. But maybe we will surprise you, yes?'

The two Russians laughed uproariously at the thought of themselves being dull dogs. Newall seethed. That playful pinch had bloody well hurt. Still, he had manfully resisted the desire to yell or even to rub the spot.

'Not at all,' he managed to lie. 'It's just *I'm* rather a dull dog these days. My fiancee. Somehow I just want to spend all my time with her now.'

'Congratulations, Edwin. We didn't know. What is her name?'

'Penny,' he said, Gaia save him.

'As in Penny Black, yes,' Arkady roared, slapping his thigh in appreciation of his own wit. 'Or maybe she is Penny Red...'

'Penny Brunette actually...'

'Oh, very good, Edwin,' Ilya said. 'You capped our little joke.' Then he smiled what seemed a genuine smile. 'But I understand. You are a clever man, more of a dinner party sort of guy maybe? Good food and wine and conversation. You must bring Penny down to London - at Ursa's expense of course - and nominate a really nice fashionable restaurant. Arkady and I will bring our ladies.'

Doctor Newall's heart did a back flip. How was he, a provincial visionary, expected to know the current fashionable watering holes in London? He could always just plump for the Ritz of course and bullshit about the quintessential Englishness of it etc. Much worse was the idea of taking Penny to some such fashionable place with strange and confident people. She would clam up and maybe even die.

He remembered the time they'd been invited to a posh dinner party hosted by Dave Summit, the CEO of Woolton MBC. The stupid girl had drunk too much for Dutch courage beforehand and then sat like a rabbit in the headlights all night. She'd sat for hours being too timid to even ask where the loo was. So when they got out eventually he'd had to stop the car a mile away while Penny ran down an unlit ginnel, lowering her pants as she ran. Then she'd got back in the car and vomited with relief over both of them. No, he didn't want Penny anywhere near this. She was just too nervy. And he'd waited too long for this opportunity. He forced himself to smile.

'What am I thinking of?' he heard himself say. 'Where are my manners? Of course we must find a good club. We'll have a ball.'

As the old red 2CV strained up the hill out of Cloughgreen Doctor Newall saw blue smoke billowing away in his rear view mirror. Damnation. He really didn't want to waste money replacing it. But maybe he would have to.

By dint of will he put it out of his mind and concentrated on his meeting with Angela Snow, one of the planners he knew at Woolton MBC.

She was an old pupil of his, must be in her thirties now, couple of years since he'd seen her. Back then she'd been what his mother would have called "girl-mad". *Wonder if she's changed?*

He finally turned off the valley road and joined the road up to the tops. The road was narrow now and caked with mud from tractors and Land Rovers. It was bounded by black and mildewed dry stone walls with emerald green pasture and dirty sheep the other side. The 2CV was wheezing and straining. He pulled into a passing place to let an old red Defender and a trailer full of panicky sheep pass.

The arranged meeting place was just past the next farm. He passed the farmhouse with its array of dead tractors and cheap Eastern bloc lorries. He pulled over 200 yards further on at the end of an unmade lane next to a silver Mondeo and a pale green & black Kawasaki superbike.

He got out and ran his hand gently over the bike's streamlined wraparound fairing the way he had with Kovalenko's Porsche the previous day. He couldn't help himself. In spite of his feelings about carbon - and the Kawasaki must push it out like a jumbo jet - it was a quality object that resembled sculpture. Sometimes superb design enabled an object to transcend its function and attain a sculptural beauty. You wanted to touch it, like a Henry Moore.

He was musing on these mixed feelings when he heard raised voices coming from down the track near the ancient ruined cottage.

A man and woman in their early thirties, the owners of the Mondeo presumably, were remonstrating with a slender figure in green motorcycle leathers, waving their arms around. The blustery wind caught snatches of the ruckus: "crazy woman", "planning lunacy", "cunt".

He smiled grimly. He had a pretty fair idea now what was going on. Good girl. He'd taught her well.

The couple had left the motorcyclist and were coming back up the pitted, puddled track. Their gestures were slowly calming down, their arms dropping, defeated. Nonetheless, just to be out of the firing line he got back into the 2CV and looked away from the Mondeo.

'None of it makes any sense,' the bloke was saying.

'The in-house water well and the carved mantelpiece were to die for...and so old. Had to be fifteenth century.'

'I'm going to take it up with her superior, bloody snotty dyke.'

The bloke revved hard and the Mondeo bulleted away, showering the 2CV with dark-brown clods of mud.

'Tsk, tsk, temper, temper...' Doctor Newall remarked to himself as he got out.

Angie Stone was strolling up the lane looking cool as an ice maiden. Thick black tousled hair in a bob, thin face, no makeup, slim boyish body, no boobs. Allover green leathers with plenty of chains and green motorcycle boots. Yep, Angie looked just the same as last time he'd seen her. Tough lady.

He grinned as she came up and pointed his finger at her. 'They're going to report you.'

She grinned back. 'Won't make any difference.'

'The Unitary Development Plan.'

'You always were a smart ass...sir.'

'Wanted to renovate the cottage and put in a nice suburban garden, gnomes and stuff, in the middle of all this agricultural land?'

‘You got it.’

‘How old is it by the way?’

‘Fifteenth century. And it has got beautiful features inside.’

‘But...’

‘But.’

‘So what did you say to get them so riled?’

‘That we’d rather see it fall down than have the UDP contravened and the landscape debased.’

He looked at her, raised his eyebrows. *Tough titty. Rather see it fall down.*

‘Well, we would - as you damn well know. Unless you’ve gone soft in your old age.’

‘No danger of that. Just got bigger fish to fry. Renewables and sustainables offer a whole new ethical key to unlocking this landscape and making it work again.’ He tapped his nose. ‘If you know how.’

‘And you do know how of course.’

‘Naturally.’

‘No point in knowing the Regs if you can’t bend ‘em like Beckham, as you used to pound into us.’

‘It works for me. The end justifies the means. Also, it can be personally profitable.’

‘Meaning?’

‘Could you use some money for a little consultancy work?’

'You know me.' She eyed up her beautiful pale green and black racing machine. 'These don't come cheap. Even secondhand. Plus I've met the love of my life, Phyllida.'

'And?'

'Phyl's very high maintenance. But she's young, talented and drop-dead gorgeous.' She held her palms up, shrugged her shoulders, grinned. Hopeless case. What can you do when the lightning bolt strikes?

'What does she do for a living?'

'She's an opera singer.'

'I thought they made a bomb.'

'A young, struggling opera singer.'

'Oh,' Newall said, trying not to smile. *Not an opera singer at all then, really. Just young and drop dead gorgeous.* So you need the dosh...'

She nodded.

'"Else Phyllida doth flout me,"' he added.

'What?' Angie's eyes looked incomprehending at his Shakespearean whimsy.

'Never mind. Before our time.'

'So I already do freelance work.' She held a finger to her lips, 'Ssshhh, you know what they're like in the department. But hang on a minute, Dr Newall. If they've got you - the Machiavelli of all planners - why would they need little old me?'

'You see things I don't.'

'Ah.'

'Yes, ah,' he said. 'If you're interested, why not follow me up to The Leg of Mutton and we can talk in the warmth.'

'Okay,' she said, putting on her green helmet and swinging her leg over the big Kawi. 'I'm interested. But not in anything illegal.' As he watched she threaded the key in the ignition and fired the brute up in a great crackling roar. Then she throttled it back so he could hear himself talk.

'Wouldn't have to be. Just a few steers, a few words to the wise about the lie of the land.'

'Like I say, nothing illegal. But let's talk about it at the Mutton.' Will you do it or won't you, he wanted to say. Will you help the wind farm cause?

'You foll...' he started.

But Angie Snow was following no-one. She was already 20 yards down the road, tucked tight and low behind the fairing, snapping through the gears, the exhaust note like a banshee frightening the bejesus out of the sheep.

He smelled the burnt petrol left in her wake and got into the 2CV. He was right, as usual. The big old superbike was creating about as much carbon waste as a jumbo jet.

He started the 2CV and got it lurching up the road to the Leg of Mutton. Then he smiled gently to himself. Compassion was not an emotion he was much given to. But he'd always had a soft spot for Angie Snow who took life full on and cared not a jot for approval.

If she weren't gay he might make a play for her himself, he thought. If elephants were mice. If snowflakes were diamonds. If cabbages were orchids. *If.* Now in her thirties and smitten, Angie was still 'girl-mad'. Hers was never going to be an easy life but he somehow admired her. And now maybe they could help each other.

Doctor Newall rang Ilya Bakunin, Ursa Power's MD, next day. 'It occurred to me, this model of the proposed sites you're showing?'

'Yes, Edwin.'

'I think you should show it as briefly as possible. Give them a glimpse of it, to show willing, then whip it away quick before they get any ideas.' He could hear loud laughter at the other end of the phone.

'The Mushroom Principle, right?'

'Exactly. Don't give the peasants time to bother their little heads. Just pretend you're keeping them in the picture.'

'Except our picture shows midnight in a coal cellar.'

'Sounds good to me.'

'Okay, we'll have the model in Cloughgreen Library just one Friday and Saturday, not the whole fortnight. We'll say other people need to see it at other locations.'

'Perfect. I'll see you there on the Saturday, Ilya.'

'Look forward to it, Edwin.'

# 5

Sunday November 4th

Charley Fort was surprised to hear from Willie when he rang him. It had been about 10 years since they last spoke. But he listened patiently enough. He'd always liked the easy-going photographer.

'Look, Willie,' he said eventually, 'I'm just a jobbing hack. Sounds to me more like you need some campaigning journo like John Pilger or someone. Though by the sound of it he'd probably be on the other side. You guys sound like the bad guys to me.' Then came the sound of a guffaw. Willie ignored it.

'That's the point, I just don't know. I'd like you to do some digging for us, Charley. There's something doesn't feel right about all these new turbines they want to put in. We've got a whole lot already in our eyeline at a wind farm called The Delf. I thought that would be it, that we'd done our bit locally already. And if these things are as powerful as they're made out to be, surely we wouldn't need to have any more? Never mind another 78. I'm just a bit worried about where it's all going to end.'

There was a pause. 'Well, look, like you, I don't know enough about them. I mean, they're supposed to be good things aren't they, if you watch the Beeb and read the colour supps...'

'Well, come on up for the weekend and do a bit of burrowing. Bring your wellies and I'll take you walking with Nelson.'

'Who?'

'The dog. And I'll lay on some good single malt and Verity's finest cooking; no expense spared.' There was silence on the other end as Charley thought for a bit.

'When?'

'Ay-ess-ay-pee. I know it's short notice, but could you manage next weekend?' Another pause as Willie heard the wheels going round.

'Okay, Willie, for old times' sake. Have you got a computer?'

'No end of 'em,' Willie said proudly. 'Mac or PC. Mine or hers.'

Charley Fort turned up late on Friday night, the 9th, after a 6-hour drive from London. Willie heard the snarl of the of the classic red Porsche arriving in the courtyard. Like someone ripping silk. Charley revved it hard, brought the oil back up into the cylinders, then cut the engine. Willie checked it out through the window. Beautiful machine, but probably at the stage when it cost a bomb to maintain it. Then he went outside to greet his old mate. As Charley got out of the car, Willie realised he was one of those guys who never seemed to age.

He was about 5'10" with a square, tanned open face and washed-out sandy eyes. The faded gingery hair was close-cropped as it had been in his conscript South African police days. He was in good shape for his age and looked as though he still played veteran rugby. Although like a lot of older rugger buggers he'd lost his waist. Resembled a hard meaty rectangle now. Accent on the hard.

He cupped his hands behind his neck and stretched, doing a quick take on his surroundings.

'Hello, Golden Boy, you old bugger. You know this is really beautiful up here - in an arse-freezing sort of way.'

Willie Dee smiled. Long time since he'd been called Golden Boy. He'd been the Golden Boy all his life and knew it. Blond curls, an easy manner and effortless scholarships.

Later, photography awards, beautiful women and big money had followed effortlessly. But now the corn-blond curls were ash-blond with treacherous grey hairs amongst them.

'Beautiful only in an arse-freezing sort of way, hey?' he laughed. 'Still the same old smooth-talking colonial, I see.'

'Same old, same old, yeah. Wow,' Charley said as a gust of wind caught the long, pink-tissue-wrapped bouquet of flowers he was holding. 'It's windy up here.'

'Not today it isn't, Charley. Windy is when you struggle not to be blown over getting from the car to the back door. You'll see.'

Clutching the long paper cone of flowers Charley looked as embarrassed as a rugger bugger at the perfume counter.

'For Verity,' he said, glancing down.

'Bolly Dolly.'

'Hey?'

'You'll see.'

Like most men, Charley's eyes twinkled when he was introduced to Bolly, who was about his age.

The decision to really find out about wind farms had calmed Bolly down. And she seemed prepared to trust Charley's journo skills and listen to what he discovered with a good grace.

The two men exchanged pleasantries and news of shared acquaintances. But it was soon obvious everything and everyone had moved on. All they still had in common was a shared warmth that was a consequence of boozey good times. In view of the work to come they had an early night.

They did a short walk with Nelson after breakfast next day.

'Over there,' Willie said, pointing past the Storm-n-Shine chimney in the valley which was trailing a streamer of white smoke. He jabbed towards the high ridge on the opposite side of the valley. 'That's where they want to put the new wind farm, Cloughgreen Common.'

'Pretty dominant,' Charley said, laconically. 'In fact, pretty much in your face.'

'Have you any idea how high 410' is?'

'Bloody high.'

'Someone said you'll be able to see 'em for 30 miles.'

'I believe it.'

When they came back Charley immediately got down to it. He spurned Willie's silver Mac Pro in favour of Bolly's black Sony laptop. Watching him work for a moment, Willie marvelled at the younger man's complete speed and ease with the laptop.

He had quickly mastered PhotoShop on his Mac. Once he'd realised PhotoShop was a digital darkroom where he could employ all his photographic skills without smelly chemicals he'd been like a fish in water. But non-photographic applications left him hesitant. And his keyboard skills were lamentable.

They left Charley to see what he could find out. They'd agreed to call a halt at 7pm on Sunday when he would down tools and reveal all he'd discovered. In the interim Charley worked like a *Stakhanovite* on speed, even taking some meals in his room.

Sunday November 11th

At seven sharp they gathered together in the lounge. It looked like being a long chat, so they'd decided on the comfort of settees and armchairs. Willie had turned off the overhead lighting and turned on all the low-level table lamps in an effort to relax things and defuse a potentially explosive situation. He had no idea what Charley was going to say, but he certainly didn't want to fall out with Bolly again.

Bolly had laid on piles of cheese and pickle and roast beef sandwiches and there were open bottles of red and white wine. He and Charley helped themselves, but he could see Bolly was too wound up to eat. She sipped her trademark champagne. After they'd eaten a round of sandwiches she could contain herself no longer.

'So. What have you discovered?' she asked, her face taut with barely suppressed impatience. Charley stopped chewing and looked them both in the eyes.

'Well, there's a hell of a lot to tell. What you've got here is a tiger by the tail. This whole wind farm issue is a combination of the state, a powerful windfarm lobby run by the United Kingdom Wind Commission, developers backed by the financial muscle of merchant banks and various Green organisations.

'It's gobsmacking, this whole wind farm business they've generated in the UK over the past 5-10 years. It's a multi-multi-million pound industry that's been created by guaranteed government subsidies for 25 years from when the plant goes in. So far as I can see, though it's a very expensive con...'

'Hang on, you can't just say that,' Bolly said. 'Everyone knows wind farms are making an enormous contribution to renewables...surely that's right?'

'Let him finish, Bolly.'

'Okay, but...'

'Okay, I know you two disagree on this,' Charley said, making calm down motions with his hands. The old South African policeman first on the scene at a 'domestic'.

'So let me run through a few major facts first.' He waved a sheet of hard copy. 'I've made a shopping list of problems or issues that I'll run through with you. Let's call it Charley's List.' He paused.

'But first I have to say this has been an eye-opener to me, Bolly. Before running this little exercise I'd have agreed with you - "everyone knows wind farms are making an enormous contribution to renewables".

'Like you, I believed what the TV and the colour supps told me. I told Willie as much before I came here. Sadly, that's what the powers that be have spent a lot of money persuading us to think. But I think I was wrong and Willie was right to have misgivings. So please don't shoot the messenger. Okay?'

'Okay. Go on,' Bolly said warily. 'We asked you to come here, so we at least have to listen to you.'

'Okay if I just check off my list first and then go back to individual points later?'

'No probs, Charley,' Bolly said, 'I've got a pad and pen. Go for it.'

'Okay, first and worst, maybe,' Charley said, looking down at his list:

'One, they are hopelessly inefficient. The wind industry likes to talk about the "installed capacity" of a wind turbine. That is their optimum capability over a year if they were running 24/7. Theoretically that's what they are capable of. But it can never happen. If the wind blew 24/7 full volume people couldn't live in those places. Even on top of mountains there are still calm days.

'Yet all the official figures are based on these installed capacity figures being achieved. How much electricity they claim to generate, how many thousands of homes they could power etc All this bullshit is based on these misleading figures.

'But even the Government admits that few actually achieve 25% of that maximum figure. Some achieve only 8%! 'You can check out the actual performance figures, or "the load factor" for the last 12 months for every wind farm in the UK. These figures are on a site run by the Renewable Energy Foundation - www.ref.org.uk. The Delf, incidentally, is one of the best with 28%.'

For them to work at their quoted propaganda figures, the installed capacity, we would all have to be walking around in a howling gale every day.'

He paused, 'Thirsty work this. Don't suppose we've got a beer. Willie nodded and went off to get one. He handed it open to Charley who swigged it by the neck.

'I've waited for you to get back. The next shocker is - because they are so inefficient they could never replace coal-fired or nuclear power. No matter how many you put in. There just isn't enough space in the

whole of the UK.'

'Hang on a minute,' Bolly Dolly said. 'Let me just make a note of that. That can't be right surely?'

'I think you'll find it is. Part of the problem is they're so inefficient you would need tens of thousands of them. An energy expert calculates you would need to carpet an area 6 times the size of Wales to provide the energy required for our sustainables target.'

Charley made a moue.

'Are you sure? But that's crazy,' Willie said. 'They'd have to carpet bomb the whole countryside with these things.'

Bolly Dolly scribbled away furiously. 'I have to say I believed they were a lot more powerful.' She looked shocked.

'I sort of thought you had maybe a dozen around each town and that sorted its energy requirements.'

'Well, it's an easy mistake to make. One of the wheezes the UKWC uses to sell 'em through to the public is to highlight a wind farm and say "Look, this wind farm now supplies 4,000 local houses with clean Green electricity." And everyone goes wow.

'Even allowing for the fact that the figures will never amount to the potential figures they're sold in on, what no-one ever asks is how many units of 4,000 houses are there in Britain. So how many tens of thousands of wind turbines would you need to replace conventional power stations?'

'They're televisual, I suspect,' Willie said. 'They look great on telly. Big and seemingly powerful, gently thwacking away, gentle giants. They've become a sort of visual shorthand when any lazy TV producer wants to illustrate a green or sustainable story. Course they don't look so great to the poor sods off camera who have them in their faces.'

'Don't interrupt, Willie. Just 'cos you don't like the look of them. Let Charley get on with it,' Bolly Dolly said.

'Okay,' Charley said, 'Well, the next point is pretty obvious if you think about it. Like we said earlier, the wind doesn't blow consistently 24/7. So they can't help but be unreliable. The wind drops, the turbines stop, the electricity flow stops. It's essentially a flawed technology.

'What you may not know - I didn't - is that you have to keep ordinary coal-fired stations running on standby to cut in when the wind turbines cut out. Otherwise there'd be failures on the Grid, as has happened in Scandinavia.'

'On top of that they need the right sort of wind. If the wind is too light they can't operate. If the wind is too severe, they have to be turned off or the force of the wind would lever them out of the ground. Bit like the wrong sort of snow on the line on the railways down south.'

'But that surely makes a mockery of their Green credentials if you have to keep coal-fired stations running in reserve...' Bolly Dolly said, looking unhappy and confused. Charley just shrugged.

'None of this comes cheap, either,' he continued. 'In fact everything about them is hideously expensive. To persuade the wind farm developers to invest the Government guarantees them 25 year subsidies. That amounts currently to 1 billion pounds a year. This makes it some of the most expensive electricity in the world.'

'It's a bit of an irony that this supposedly free power costs so much to pluck out of thin air,' Willie laughed sardonically.

'The arithmetic is quite interesting,' Charley continued. 'A wind turbine apparently costs about £2 million to build and install and then they last for 25 years. A 2MW turbine - and they're now building bigger 3MW brutes like the ones they propose for Cloughgreen Common - generates £500,000 a year plus. So, allowing for ground rent to the landowners, the turbines should pay for themselves in say 4-5 years. All the rest is profit.'

'But they're still making a green contribution, you can't deny that,' Bolly said.

'Well, you might think so. But even then they're not as green as you'd think. According to some figures, before, during and after construction they contribute to the release of CO2 which may take up to 15 years in 'payback time'.

'If this is all so damning, why do so many green parties support them, then? Tell me that,' Bolly asked, looking both defiant and bewildered.

'Well, like you imply, there is a lot of heart-searching between the tree huggers that has gone on. Because to have wind turbines you have to accept some pretty nasty facts. The UK has a large amount of the planet's remaining rare peat bogs - like Cloughgreen Common, in fact. These rare peat bogs act as natural 'sinks' for CO2, absorbing it naturally. So when you rip up the peat to establish holes 17 metres deep by 17 metres wide and pour thousands of tonnes of concrete into it you're not only destroying rare flora and fauna but you're destroying a natural carbon sink.

'To get sustainable renewable electricity you have to destroy non-renewable peat bogs.'

'Save the planet - trash your local countryside,' Willie said.

Charley shook his head wearily, running a hand over his short brown hair and looking like the bamboozled defence lawyer in some Hollywood court drama.

‘I know, I know,’ he said. ‘What starts out looking like a great idea makes no sense once you start looking into the reality of it. It’s an obsolescent technology with dreadful side effects.’

‘I didn’t know that, about the peat,’ Bolly said, visibly shocked. ‘How can the environmental lobby allow that?’

‘It gets worse, I’m afraid. Taking the peat away increases water run off from the hills to properties on the slopes and in the valleys. And it goes without saying that rare ground-nesting birds like twite will be driven away once you get the heavy plant in.’

‘But that is terrible,’ Willie and Bolly said in unison. Ordinarily they might have laughed and said ‘Snap’ or some such, but neither was much in the mood for laughing.

‘I’m afraid the catalogue goes on. There are various instances of them killing colonies of rare bats. Obviously, migrating birds are easy meat. And raptors drawn to the high ridges. Then the strobing and light flicker frightens horses, so they panic and react unexpectedly with dire results. Generally speaking, wind farms are poor neighbours to just about any living thing.’

The damning details seemed to go on and on and Bolly sank back into her armchair, shocked and appalled.

Eventually Nelson got up off the carpet, extravagantly stretched himself and went and sat ostentatiously by the door.

‘Is he okay?’ Charley asked. Willie checked his watch: 10.25 pm.

‘Yeah. He’s telling us it’s bedtime. He goes to bed at 10.30. He’s probably telling us he needs a leak.’

‘Sorry, old fellow. Way to go yet.’

‘I’ll let him out for his wee. Then we may as well take a short break while I get us some more refreshments,’ Bolly said.

They broke off to replenish their glasses and Bolly Dolly went to the kitchen and brought out some cheesy biscuits and a plate of small cocktail pies. Plus more booze. Charley used the time to catch up on the eating and drinking. Hard to give a presentation and eat at the same time. Bolly drummed the arm of her chair lightly, impatient for more facts. She let Charley finish a cocktail pie and then resumed before he could fill his mouth again.

‘I notice you haven’t mentioned anything about how they affect people yet,’ she said.

‘I’m coming to that. Generally speaking, everyone except the wind fanatics seems to accept that having them too close to people is not a great idea. But the international community can’t agree on acceptable distances. The UK safe distance is shorter than some other places. But then we’re a small country, so it probably has to be to make these things viable at all.

‘There’s a pretty grim website about human health compiled by two academics called Frey & Hadden. The site address is www.windturbinenoisehealthhumanrights.com Their site provides details on the health problems these things can create.

'Various studies suggest all sorts of problems to do with low frequency and subsonic noise (which you can't hear) that can produce anxiety, stress, sleep problems etc.

'Other emissions distort light and create associated longstanding visual problems to people nearby. Some people have even needed respite care. Other people have been driven out of their homes, which then become unsaleable. Some developers acknowledge the problem and turn the turbines off for a few hours a day. Most ignore it. The wind farm lobby says these claims are as yet unproven. Or "a myth", as they like to say. But as someone else points out that's a bit like not stopping asbestos or thalidomide production because you strongly suspect it but can't conclusively prove it.

'Worst of all - and I feel for you two here - you have people who bought their homes in tranquil places who are now living a nightmare and can't even sell their houses. Plenty of evidence of that. Both in Britain and all over the world.'

'God, I don't think I can take any more of this,' Bolly said.

'I agree, it's a lot to take in. Unfortunately there is more.'

'How can it be any worse?'

'Well, sometimes they catch fire or lose blades ...Despite what the Greens would have you believe these things are whacking great industrial machines. They have bearings that burn out. They have electrics that can short-circuit.

Occasionally blades fly off over roads. You can see photos of it on the Net.'

'Eh? Why don't we ever hear about it then?' Bolly demanded. This was now straining the limits of her credulity. 'This is awful. They seem to be terrible things. In exchange for a very little energy we have to put up with all the many disadvantages you claim there are. And being swamped by them. But I just can't believe it. It doesn't add up. What I don't understand is why none of us have heard all this stuff you've been talking about.'

Charley gave a tight little smile.'What do you know about PR?'

'Makes celebs and products look good, yeah?' Bolly ventured.

'What else?'

'Dunno,' Bolly said, after a little silence.

'Well, making people look good is one thing,' Charley said. 'The even better part of the black art of PR is information suppression. Suppose the celebs you mentioned get caught in inappropriate situations in a public lavatory, for example. Or shoplifting. Or selling their granny. Well a good PR outfit can suppress that story and stop it hitting the media. The American military call it "running interference".

'Anyway with the UKWC's PR outfit you're up against one of the best practitioners in the UK, if not the world. Their PR has been brilliant from Day One. Right from the word go they've created this soft, fluffy pastoral image.

'Whichever PR guy dreamed up the phrase "wind farm" to describe an industrial site filled with massive steel turbines bedded into thousands of tonnes of concrete deserves some sort of PR Oscar. If it were Happy Families you'd have kindly Farmer Blow, ruddy cheeked, ambling along to harvest some lovely green energy for us all. Hey, it's a bit like scrumping apples from Nature, yeah?

'In reality rather than fluffy Farmer Blow and his free natural electricity it's more like developer Daddy Windquids and his cash cows. Over the next 25 years all the Daddy Windquids will be able to milk their cash cows for billions thanks to this government's guaranteed subsidies. What a racket.'

Willie looked horrified and glanced at Bolly Dolly. She was pale with rage beneath her freckles and Willie thought he'd best stay silent.

'I don't like being conned,' she said quietly. 'What you're saying Charley is these UKWC people, the wind farm lobby, can stop bad turbine news hitting the papers and TV screens, as well as promoting their own biased good views?'

Willie could almost see smoke coming out of her ears. 'UK...WC, at least they've got an appropriately shitty name.' Willie made eyes at Charley. *Ignore her. Carry on.*

'You got the idea It's called defensive PR and these guys are the best. They do a great job of preventing the British public finding out about anything remotely adverse about wind turbines. If one of them goes on fire, or a turbine blade comes spinning off, or a breakdown disrupts the Grid in Denmark, say, you won't hear about it. Similarly if people nearby are having trouble with blade flicker or blade rumble. It's shushed up.

'Anything to promote the fluffy myth that industrial wind turbines are hardly machines at all, really. Much less machines which emit distorted light and sound waves as exhaust emissions. Obviously if you told the great British public you wanted to industrialize all the beautiful high places in the countryside by stealth with these flawed machines, there'd be riots in the streets. So they don't.'

'Shit,' Bolly said.

'Yeah, I'm afraid so. But it's green shit. Sacred shit, therefore. And these vested interests have been doing all this for a long time. Since Day One in fact. So now they've got all their contacts in place and they're very good at it. Plus they have very deep pockets thanks to their members who are coining it from the subsidies.'

He paused and passed them an A4 sheet of paper. 'There's loads of stuff on the Net which tells you people's experiences living near them. But equally the pro wind farm sites will amaze you. The wind farm guys will tell you black is white and anything else is a nasty myth propagated by Nimbys.'

Bolly looked at the website names he'd passed her. They had names like www.yes2wind

Charley waited till she'd finished reading and smiled cynically. 'That last thing I said. They call anything critical of wind turbines, no matter how factual, "a myth". Which is a great way of calling any of their critics liars without actually libelling them. Like I said, some of these sites will tell you black is white and white is black, whatever suits their interests. They'll even tell you, despite all commercial evidence to the contrary, that house prices actually *rise* when you put a windfarm in front of them.'

Bolly bristled. 'How can they do that, tell lies? It's illegal surely?'

Charley spread his hands palm upwards. 'The Net is largely unregulated. You can say pretty much what you like. And some of it is judgemental. Some people want wind farms no matter what; they don't see them as coming with a price that has to be weighed up, either monetary or in terms of visual pollution or even health.

'A lot of the pro-wind farm propaganda is directed at gullible people who want to believe emotionally and don't want the hassle of actually thinking. Young mums who want nice things for their kids, rebels without a cause, people who wanna save the planet from their sofa without even putting low-energy bulbs in. And if you can point to it on the Net it must be true.' He paused.

'The terrible thing is that for a visual world that doesn't want to think too hard the turbines are very televisual. In fact, for the diehard wind farm fanatics they're possibly totemic. Just having them there to point to is really important. Even the pro wind farm sites themselves talk of their wonderful iconic symbolism.'

'But that's terrible,' Bolly yelled. 'It means loads of people are being conned so the green fanatics get what they want and the turbine manufacturers and developers have a licence to print money.'

Charley sighed and took a long draw on his whiskey. 'You could say that. Yeah.' He rubbed his hands over his gritty eyes.

'God you look completely knackered, Charley,' Bolly said.

'That's the trouble with all-nighters, you feel it this time next day,' Charley admitted wearily.

'Coffee anyone?' Bolly asked. The men silently nodded.

'So as a result of all this propaganda anyone who sticks their hands up to disagree is branded a selfish pariah,' Willie said.

'That's about the size of it,' Charley agreed. 'They don't want any dissent. These things are right and good. No argument. End of conversation. Let's keep cramming them in. Make ourselves rich before anyone rumbles the scam. Both the Greens and the developers are hell bent on whanging 'em in while the going is good. Too late then. The Government has signed up for 20 years.'

While Bolly was making the coffee, Charley got up to stretch his legs. He walked over to the mullion windows. It was pitch black outside except for a necklace of farmhouse lights twinkling along a contour opposite. He tossed back the last of his scotch and turned to face Willie.

'What's really evil about these people, fascist really, is how they brook no argument. The thing is, they've seized the moral high ground. What they say is "Wind farms are going to save the planet."

'How can you oppose that? If you do, then you're not just Nimbies, you're spawn of the devil. The propaganda has created a climate where saying you don't like wind farms in polite conversation is akin to admitting you eat babies.

'What the wind farm nutters particularly don't like are claims that the things don't actually work - that they are inherently flawed by a variable, fluctuating, unpredictable power source, ie wind. You're supposed to just accept they work and are worth the visual price you pay. Which mostly you'll find is not a cost the fanatics, being mostly metropolitan, pay. It's the poor sods who actually live near them.'

'Why do ordinary people buy all this?' Willie asked despairingly.

'Because, bless their cotton socks, most people want to do the right. thing. And it's been a great soft sell. Most people like the sexy idea of these gentle-looking things saving the planet.

'They don't know about the pitiful output, how they kill things and how much hassle they create. They're too busy with their everyday lives to look into the facts and figures.

And anyway the wind farm lobby do their best to keep the reality at bay in the media. You know, it's a shocking thing but really  Christopher Booker in the Sunday Telegraph is the only mainline newspaper columnist to have stood out against them.'

Bolly Dolly returned with the coffee.

'All of this you've found out about turbines is shocking, but surely it's now too late. There's no alternative.'

'Ah, Bolly, this is yet another aspect of the con they've sold you. The anti-wind farm critics call it Hollywoodisation. Like I say, the wind farm PR guys make a great emotional appeal to people and part of the story is the "We're at a minute to midnight" angle for saving the planet. A bit like that Hollywood cult movie "The Day The Earth Caught Fire". If we don't do something NOW, then we're all doomed.

'The reality is climate change has been going on forever. Climate change has always been a fact of life on planet Earth with Ice Ages, tropical times, rising and falling water levels, separating continents and consequent shortages and population migrations.

'How we deal - that's the challenge. Can we be civilized enough to take in peoples' whose homes are flooded, share scarce water in other areas, adapt to new crop growing and diets, ways of life? That's where it's going to get tough.' He sighed. 'The human record of generosity and care for other tribes isn't great.'

After all the talking and talking and concentrating, he suddenly yawned.

'Sorry, Charley, we've exhausted you,' Bolly Dolly said.

'What about one last nightcap,' Willie said. 'There's a clear sky and a beautiful moon out.'

'Help yourself.' The men did.

They all put on jackets and scarves and Willie led them, glass in hand outside. The lemony moonlight played on the plateau of the ridge that was Cloughgreen Common facing them.

Willie made them clink glasses and toasted them: 'A really useful evening when we've learned the cost of a few things.'

'I'll drink to that with you,' Charley said, then looked up at the stars. 'It is damned beautiful up here.'

'Although in an arse-freezing sort of way,' Willie said.

Charley looked sheepish. Then raised his eyes to the galleon moon sailing over the distant moor, collecting his thoughts. 'You know the really worst thing about these turbines is they have to be in spots like this, the UK's last remaining high, wild unspoilt places. Places for walkers, cyclists, horse-riders, climbers and photographers to go and escape the hordes in our overcrowded, over-concreted cities. If we can't get the truth out then in 5 or 10 years' time they'll be all over the high places. There'll be no beauty spots or places to escape the concrete or steel. It's a creeping industrialization of all rural Britain.'

'You said "We".'

'Sure, I'll carry on helping you if I can. What I've discovered has shocked the socks off me, too. The metropolitan bastards who are ordering it place no value on these places. Those supposedly green organizations who support it should die of shame.'

'They won't though,' Willie said mildly, looking at Bolly Dolly. She was an intelligent woman. He wasn't going to ask her tonight, but he knew she had changed her mind. Having heard the evidence, how could she not?

Bolly suddenly let out a small shriek. 'My God, look at the time. I'm sorry, Charley. We've been really mean to you, keeping you up till this hour of the night. Is that about it?'

Charley put down his glass, hardly touched, on a low stone wall and rubbed his eyes. 'Few more things, but you're right I'm bushed. It's been a steep learning curve. Maybe I could go back after lunch tomorrow, finish off tomorrow morning. Sleep in, maybe?'

'Of course,' Bolly said, taking his arm and shepherding him in out of the cold, starry night. Nobody noticed that Charley had left his half-empty glass on the wall.

Monday November 12th

The three of them came into the garden next day after breakfast and Bolly's eye fell on the abandoned glass from the night before.

'"A glass half full of wine left out

To the dark heaven all night, by dawn

Has dreamed a premonition

Of ice across its eye as if

The ice-age had begun its heave,"' Bolly Dolly said, retrieving the unfinished Glenfiddich.

'Don't tell me, Ted Hughes,' Charley said. Bolly nodded.

'It's not exactly right. The poem is called *October* Dawn. And the glass is supposed to contain wine.'

'Near enough, Scottish wine,' Charley said, looking at the rime-encrusted glass.

'While he's up here I promised Charley a little look-see at the countryside. Would you like to come with us, Bolly?'

Bolly frowned a little and rare lines appeared on her freckled brow. 'No thanks. I want to look into some of these websites Charley has earmarked for me. And go through Charley's List.'

'Okay then. Just 3 for the road,' Willie said. He went into the kitchen, filled his left trouser pocket with small brown gravybone biscuits, whistled Nelson and took his red lead from behind the door.

Charley had borrowed one of his old purple ski jackets and a green scarf and wellies with a red woolly top. He grinned inanely. Willie, snug in his Barbour, green flat hat, cords and expensive German walking boots surveyed his mate. Sartorially, the best you could say was he looked warm.

'Lead off, MacDuff,' Charley said. The black lab had already exited the courtyard facing the barn and headed on to the moor. But Willie called him back and strode off down the lane past Jumper's place, Black Rock Farm. No sign of him. Or Joanna Baillie or the Faas. Soon they came to the ancient Causeway Road. It was a rat run along the top of the valleys, so Nelson was put on his lead.

'The Ancient Brits, the Romans, the Celts when this place was part of Elmet, and then the Vikings all trod this road.'

'It has that sort of feel,' Charley agreed, 'commanding the valleys. Presumably down there would have been infested with wolves, bears and the bad lads, the psychos?'

'Dead right. We go down here,' Willie said, hanging a right and dropping down to a narrow lane past another farmhouse. Nelson was freed and wandered off to sniff at the long grass under the dry stone walls.

Suddenly the world spread out below them. Back in time, as Charley had intimated, the thickly wooded valley beneath would have frightened the ancestors, being filled with wild animals and wilder people. But those thick woods had been cleared up to a thousand years ago in places. Cultivation had moved up the valley sides. The history being recorded in some of the higher farm place names: Lower Intake, Middle Intake, Upper Intake. Where higher virgin slopes had been "taken in" as new pasture.

Today Willie looked down on a patchwork spread before him. High moors with dead brown bracken; dark blue hills beyond; dark green conifers on the upper slopes; emerald green pastures lower; small dense woods of black, silhouetted deciduous trees lining the valley bottoms.

'There's an old coffin trail through those woods,' Willie said, pointing.

'Eh?'

'Back in the seventeen, eighteen, nineteen hundreds, the hill was too steep for the horses to pull the hearse all the way up to the chapel. So they'd get it halfway up, then unload it onto the mourners' shoulders and relay it up a track through the trees.'

Charley whistled at the steepness of the land. 'Warm work. When men was men, eh? They must have taken turn about en route.'

'I guess so.'

Old stone-built barns and farmhouses were strung out along the contours. The architectural vernacular testament to four hundred years of slow change. Here and there stood odd, blasted trees tortured and killed by the wind and cold but still standing sentry along the tree line. And of course Cloughgreen itself on the valley bottom. Willie pointed out its fine Grecian-temple-style Town Hall spotlit by the sun.

'I see Clough's got it's own mini Parthenon. Like a lot of the old northern towns,' Charley said

'Sort of,' Willie laughed.

They stopped for a moment to take it all in and Nelson, expecting his master's camera to come out as usual, sat obediently next to him. The wind was getting up again, as always, blowing big girls' blouses of white cloud before it. The dark, fast-moving shapes of the cloud on the ground sent a nearby flock of sheep racing in panic.

'God, I'd hate to live their lives up here,' Charley remarked, watching them.

'Ted Hughes reckoned they were the dirtiest sheep in the world.'

'Well, they're hardly clinical conditions they live in, are they?'

'If durability meant sweetness they'd probably be the sweetest-tasting lamb in the world.'

Just past the farm called Stoney Intake they came off the tarmac and onto huge, broken stone flags, half submerged in puddles, the remains of a medieval packhorse trail. The road passed between green lichened stone walls. The pastures they enclosed soon gave on to the heather slopes of Thor Fell, another of the ancient places.

Nelson waited patiently as Willie wrestled with the dropped hinges and iron fastening of the five-barred gate. As he passed through and veered left to descend Thor Fell he moved into the teeth of the wind, his ash-blond curls whipping away backwards, the tears coming to his eyes. The eroded downward path was treacherous with slick, waterlogged grass and rocks loosened by rain. So they took their time, digging their heels in. This wasn't a place to twist an ankle, high, exposed and far from help.

Eventually they picked their way through the rocks and shale at the base of the fell and rejoined the large, broken-down slabs of the packhorse trail. Jumping the huge puddles in and around the smooth, tilted stones, Charley felt more as though he were negotiating a ford.

Keeping his eyes on the ground to check his footing, he was amused to see the racing clouds reflected in the water. Over it all came the bleating of the sheep, the crying of the crows, all playing in the light and shade of the big open skies. On a day like this it was a very heaven. He could see what Willie delighted in. Even if it was still arse-freezingly cold.

And this countryside was what the bastards wanted to ring around with concrete and steel... They never came here, they never wanted to come here. And so they were willing to sacrifice it. When of course for them it was no sacrifice at all. How often was that the way, he thought dryly, that those who cried out loudest for sacrifices were those who would be making no sacrifices at all. Politicians sending fresh-faced lads over the top. Politicians setting loud and whirling health hazards amongst ordinary people's homes. *Plus ca change.*

Willie gestured to Charley to stop. 'Back there you can see the wind farm outside Halifax. Over there in that direction is The Delf wind farm up the way from us. That way is a new one near Riddingley. Right ahead is where they want to put the Cloughgreen Common wind farm.' Charley swivelled his head, taking it all in.

'I can see your problem all right. You're going to be penned in by all these things wherever you lift up your eyes. Little Cloughgreen in the valley will be surrounded. In fact, what's to stop them putting another one right here where we're standing?'

'Exactly what bothers me. There seems to be no end to it all. Once they're in, they completely destroy the scale of the place. Everything else, the huge skies, the desolate moorland, the cries of the curlews becomes insignificant beneath the whirring, clanking, flickering turbines. And for what? Pitifully small amounts of expensive electricity. And once these peat bogs are gone, that's it. God is not making them any more.'

Charley shook his head. 'I agree with you. It's a tragedy. What's worse, the way it's being done by stealth, most people won't realise until it's too late.'

'I know,' Willie said sadly.

'Meanwhile, what I also meant to say last night, is that the Government is doing its best to slap down opposition. Have you heard of PPS22?'

'No.' Off the moor the walking was easier, following the old traders path between dry stone walls and lush sheep pasture.

'Well at any one time there seems to be about 150 wind farm protest groups on the go. There's a severe dichotomy between the people in London who will probably never see them but want them. And the people in the shires who have to live next to them and don't want them. Anyway thanks to our friends in the wind farm lobby, the Government even changed the planning laws to make it easier to steamroller the opposition. PPS22 was a set of new regs introduced by John Prescott to make it easier to get the planning applications through.'

'You're joking. You mean Prescott in effect just moved the goalposts?'

Nelson disappeared into some long grass near a ruined cottage to drink at a concealed spring. He emerged coughing. Gone down the wrong way.

'That's about the size of it. I don't know if it's right, but he allegedly said something about being happy to sign anything if it destroyed some Tory's view.' Willie smiled a smile that didn't reach his eyes. 'That's crazy as well. Hardly anyone in Cloughgreen votes Tory and the vast majority of people are not rich by any means.'

'You have to say it's not this Government's finest hour when it comes to democracy. If you don't think you're going to win, you just change the rules.' Charley shook his head.

'And they wonder why people don't vote,' Willie said. 'Between this government, the wind farm nutters and the fat cat developers we really are going to be up against it, aren't we?'

'Yeah. Like I said.'

'What I really don't understand is why the Government doesn't see how flawed these things are. They must have droves of scientific advisers to tell them, surely?'

'They do, yeah. A report by The Centre for Policy Studies written by a guy called Tony Lodge has told them that they should concentrate on nuclear and clean coal. That onshore wind farms had negative consequences for both the environment and local residents. He urged the development of tidal power to meet the renewables target which he said does not have the environmental impact of windmills on hills and was much more reliable than wind.'

'Wow, really?'

'Yeah, but whether the Government listens or not is another matter. Greenpeace naturally said it was simply "not credible" to suggest that wind power did not have a central role to play. They really like the symbolism of these things being in your face. Plus of course, there's the "N" word - nuclear is a big no, no, in British politics. Successive governments, both Labour and Tory, have shied away from doing what they both know is actually unavoidable.'

'Something else I don't understand,' Willie muttered. 'If nuclear is necessary, then nuclear is necessary.'

'That's the Frogs' pragmatic attitude. They've got loads of nuclear power stations over the Channel.'

Then Greenwood Royd came in sight and the conversation tapered off. They had only climbed about 200' to the valley ridge then dropped back down again. But because of the constantly undulating nature of the path Charley felt they'd walked much further.

They got out of their walking togs and Willie showed Charley his darkroom in the barn and the adjacent gallery where he'd hung his large black and white landscapes.

'These are beautiful, Willie.'

'Well, it's an artistic indulgence. There's no money in doing landscapes professionally unless you're very lucky. So I've never done any in my working life. But now I'm retired, I do it just for me. Take a Nikon with me every time I go out. It's a whole new ball game for me. Just fun.'

'I don't know about no market for 'em. I'd buy one, they really are beautiful.'

Willie looked slowly at him. Then he took down a fine tortured skyscape featuring the ragged edge and high plateau of Cloughgreen Common. 'Take this then, as a memento and as a thank you for all your help.'

'It's too much.' He hesitated, holding the photograph reverentially, 'but if you mean it...'

'Take it,' Willie urged. 'That landscape may not look like that much longer.'

After lunch Willie said 'I know you've done loads already and it's a bit of a cheek, but I was wondering whether you could pen the odd letter to the Cloughgreen Recorder for us. Try and get other people in town up to speed on what's going on. I 'm no good at writing. I'm just a visual guy.' He tried to look earnest. 'You must help us, Charley.'

Charley waved his hands and grinned broadly.

'At last some good news. You don't really need me, Willie. Now I've done the research. No, don't say anything,' he said, holding his right hand up like a traffic cop. 'Bolly can do just as good a job as me. She'd make a great advocate.'

'But...'

'Seriously, Willie. Verity let me have a peek at her draft manuscript on Ted Hughes. Your wife writes like an angel. Have you seen her stuff?'

Willie shook his head, blond curls flopping on his forehead. 'I didn't know she'd even started it. But then I've not read much lit crit lately, I doubt if I'd understand it...'

'Oh, yes, you would. Verity has a way of making things crystal clear. She's a natural writer. What do you say, Verity?'

Bolly Dolly's eyes were moist from the unexpected praise and she seemed to have risen an extra inch in her chair. 'Yes, if you think I could do it, then I'm up for it. We can't just stand by and see the whole of Ted Hughes's Elmet be industrialized by these things when they don't even work properly. It's gesture politics of the worst kind, shoving these ghastly things in our faces just to make a point.'

'Good for you,' Charley said, finishing his tea. 'I'll leave you all my notes and details of the websites.'

As they saw him to his car he said 'There's a story in this for me, too. If I can break it through UKWC's protective PR barrier, that is. If I hear anything else interesting I'll let you know. Good luck, you two.'

He had already turned the ancient red Porsche around and loaded his overnight bag. He got in, fired up the engine and revved hard. The sports car trembled, exhaust burbling, eager to be off. Then Charley waved and was gone. The Porsche started back up the pock-marked lane on its way back to the place where all the decisions were taken. The Metropolis. A messenger from the front line come and gone.

'You've no idea what else I've discovered,' Bolly Dolly said, taking Willie by the arm.

They watched the powerful car crawl all the way along the rutted track, Charley driving it slowly to preserve the sump. Past Jumper's farmhouse, Black Rock Farm. Past Joanna Baillie's three converted cottages. Past the Faa Brothers farmhouse and cowsheds. Until the vivid red Dinky toy breasted the rise that brought it out on to the Long Causeway. Willie could almost feel the sports car's relief as he watched it stretch its legs and barrel along the top road.

When it had disappeared Bolly turned to Willie, still linking his arm. 'You know, I never got my coffee in bed this morning.'

'Feel like it now?

'I do.' He smiled.

'You're a bad lot.'

'Probably.'

'My mother warned me against women like you, Mrs Dee.'

'Was she right?'

'Didn't know the half of it,' he laughed. 'At least I hope not.'

Later, after the bedside coffee had gone cold, he turned to her.

'So. Are we all right now?'

'What do you think?'

He smirked.

'We were always *all right*. I just felt you were being boorish. And alarmist.'

'And what do you think now?'

She laughed.

'I think, like your mother, we didn't know the half of it.'

She lay quietly against his shoulder for a while. 'Seriously, Willie, we are going to have to try and fight these awful things. Not just for us but for everyone else. Nobody should have these ghastly, useless things in their backyards. As Ruskin might have said, they are neither useful nor beautiful.'

She got out of bed and wrapped a dark green and white dragon kimono around her, highlighting her long red hair. Then she swished out downstairs.

She came back clutching a chilled bottle of Bolly and two champagne flutes. She handed the bottle to him and he started to untwine the wire around the neck.

'I'm going to try and do what Charley suggested,' she said. 'Be the voice of commonsense against the wind farms.' He popped and poured the champagne into the glasses she extended.

Then Willie raised his glass. 'Here's to the voice of commonsense against wind farms everywhere.'

Willie and Nelson followed one of the many sheep trails that criss-crossed the moors beneath the Hallow Stones. It was a favourite walk. The winding grass path meandered through knee-high moorland grasses, red-stemmed bog cotton and shallow muddy pools.

This morning it was clear, still and chilly. But Willie had been here in sleet, blizzard and fog. Even then he could see the half-concealed rocks, ledges and potholes at his feet. It would be a fool who came in the dark. All around them the huge black rocks, some weighing thousands of tons, tilted at crazy angles. Ten millennia of wind and rain had carved a freakish natural sculpture park up here. An eagle's head, a giant beaker, a joined up gallery of Easter Island heads, enormous cubes, ravines between overhangs, claustrophobic walls and rooms.

It was an edgy place. Some days static electricity crackled through the wet grass and numinous feelings raised the hairs on the back of his neck. Back in the 1920s they'd found a Bronze Age torc, daggers and spear heads around the base of some of the largest rocks.

It felt like a natural sacrifice spot. His mind's eye could easily see the ancient Celts of Elmet encasing sacrifices in wicker baskets, setting fire to them and pushing them off the tops of the giant boulders or into the enclosed spaces between them. You fell twenty feet down into one of those stony cells and there would be no way back. Broken back, neck or skull promised an agonizing, lonely death. He watched Nelson carefully, but the dog was not one of those labradors that career around the landscape; he was naturally cautious.

As he wandered through the enormous black boulders he thought how huge and concealing they were; natural ambush places. There was one narrow path through high overhanging rocks which Nelson balked at. If urged, he went through the passageway, his hackles raised, growling and looking miserably right and left and Willie had no doubt he saw ghosts. He was not ashamed to admit that on dark and foggy winter mornings there were plenty of places his own courage trembled.

Today, with chilly blue skies it was as welcoming as it could be. He stopped while Nelson sniffed at the calling cards of other dogs, resting his hand along the side of one of the huge blackened rocks. It was tough as coarse sandpaper beneath his fingertips. You could run your skin over its gritty surface and easily cause the blood to run. And yet in the winter the thick ice and frost sealed it over and made it treacherously smooth to any steadying hand leaned against it. Similarly the smooth rocks which lay underfoot.

The time and interest Nelson was devoting to his sniff could only mean a bitch in season, he thought, and he looked around for likely culprits. A light wind stirred the bog cotton.

400 yards away and 100' high he watched a kestrel doing its wingtip-fluttering sky dance above some small invisible mammal. He could see why old Yorkshiremen like Jumper called kestrels windhovers. Then a raven screeched and the windhover wheeled away as its intended prey went to ground.

Most days it was like this, no human sounds, just the old wilderness sounds the way it had been for millennia. Only wind. And rain. And the howling of the heavens as a big sky writhed and boiled like water in a cauldron, oblivious to what happened below, an impartial theatre for life and death.

The squawk of his mobile made him jump.

'Willie?'

'Yeah.'

'It's Charley. I heard something yesterday I thought would interest you.'

'Okay.'

'Right. I was over near the old Italian hospital in Holborn, behind Southampton Row.'

'I know where you mean.'

'I was in this pub when I heard a couple of kid journos talking at the bar. You're never going to believe this...'

'Go on.'

'Well the kids it seems have really got this climate change stuff between their teeth. The way they're talking they see it as the next big thing they can make a giant 'rep' with. It's become like a competition to see who can be most sensational and alarmist.'

'How do you mean?'

'Well, one was saying to the other one that they had to start coining new phrases to overcome apathy, frighten the horses. He was saying that "global warming" sounded far too cosy...'

'Eh?'

'He reckoned they should start calling it "global burning".

'Bloody hell...'

'And that's not all. They want to stop talking about problems with CO2, the gas we all exhale, and which plants need to live and push on again. They already now call it carbon pollution. Now they want to call it "black carbon". As in carbon causes global burning which creates even more filthy, dirty, black carbon.'

'Jesus wept, Charley...'

'I know. It's yet more Holl...'

And then the line went dead. Willie swore under his breath and dialled up Charley's number. But the signal was lost. He walked a few hundred yards and tried again. Still no joy. What the hell did "hol" mean? Hollow? Holocaust? Hologram? Who knows? It was irritating.

He took one last look at the giant Hallow Stones and set off homewards to tell Bolly about "global burning" and "black carbon". Maybe she'd know what "hol" was meant to mean?

As he turned the corner the hard blue sky revealed the brutal outlines of some enormous new turbines on the east Lancashire skyline. It soured his morning. The bloody things were closing in. And there seemed to be sod all he could do.

At that moment, though, he knew in his water they had to fight the proposed development on Cloughgreen Common. If they didn't, this area would become the dumping ground of the whole country for these ghastly things.

Ted Hughes's Elmet, as Bolly liked to think of it, would become an industrial wasteland. And pushed to its natural conclusion all the other wild places in Britain would be thrown away. For pitiful amounts of expensive unreliable electricity. It was not an option.

# 6

Monday November 12th

Dr Newall leapt out of his bed with relish for the day to come. He felt like Saint Paul coming off a Greek fishing boat on some Aegean wilderness island. There was fire in his loins as he prepared to preach to the unconverted. Watch this space, Ursa Power, Dr Newall is about to start delivering.

He took a cup of tea and a slice of Marmite toast on the run. 5 minutes later he fired up the Sony and fed his password in.

He'd written to newspapers before, but never when it crucially mattered like this. But how hard could it be? He'd written lots of general letters supporting green issues. And he'd delivered loads of papers to other academics, documents with pages and pages of footnotes, good meaty stuff. He'd even received standing applause at a conference in Brussels once.

After 20 minutes of bum glue applied to the seat of his pants the screen remained empty. Some large splashes of rain hit the window distracting him. He never normally noticed the weather. He had no interest whatsoever in outdoor activities. He thought of getting up and making a coffee, but resisted. Then he remembered out of the blue it would be his father's birthday next week. Too bad. Next his eye deviated to some unopened mail on the desk and his hand moved to start opening it. Then he caught himself. All this displacement activity, instead of thinking of the matter in hand. For heaven's sake, how hard could it be, writing a letter to the local rag?

Looking at the wall for inspiration, his eyes lighted on his three-face international wall clock. He could just as well be in London, New York or Moscow for all the weather or his father's birthday mattered to him. Inner space was what mattered, the life of the mind.

He massaged his temples with his knuckles, concentrate. The problem he decided was knowing too much. Where did he start selling the whole renewable wind farm argument to the peasants who read the Cloughgreen Recorder? Those people whose mouths moved as they read. How much could he safely assume they knew?

His mind drifted back to his fortunately brief days as a uni lecturer with the great unwashed, the first year students. He had to do what he did then. Assume they knew nowt. That was the way to tackle it, shouting now and again to keep them awake. After that it came out pretty easily:

Because of our distinctive geography Cloughgreen is in a unique position to become the wind farm capital for the whole of the UK and act as a beacon for more selfish communities elsewhere. Swift action now will earn us civic pride beyond measure and truly put Cloughgreen on the national map.

The barren, deserted uplands above our fair town, for so very long a home to pylons and a dumping ground for household waste and detritus, now have the chance to host a revolutionary cutting edge technology that will provide clean, carbon-free, renewable energy for decades.

For centuries these moorlands have been industrial land that served the community well, until those industries died. Now the revolutionary new wind turbine technology on offer can again bring them into useful harness. Our moors offer the precise locations that modern new wind farms need. They are high enough to capture wind throughout the year; they are sited well away from urban centres; and they are in other ways redundant, serving no useful purpose.

If we welcome the splendid initiative proffered by Ursa Power we can provide clean, renewable power not just for the whole of Cloughgreen but an excess that will help the whole country meet its renewables targets.

This golden opportunity is the sort rarely given to people to earn the thanks of generations to come, our children and grandchildren. Not only here but all over the world as we make our small contribution to prevent global warming and rising seas that stand to make millions homeless. The clock stands at 2 minutes to midnight to save the planet but it is still do-able, and I say we must do it whatever it takes.

Some very, very few people will doubtless say it will spoil their favourite walk or their horse ride. To those very, very few people I say we must make sacrifices for our children and our children's children. What is a stroll on the moor for a privileged few compared to saving the planet for the many? Nimbyism is unworthy of us all.

I urge everybody to go along and see the scale model Ursa Power is providing in the library this weekend. To see representations of these clean white blades moving peacefully in the sunlight providing safe, clean electricity for those in the valley below and others beyond will make you wish to embrace this clean Green future. Some will even see in these beautiful moving shapes representations of sculptural kinetic art within the landscape. That is however only a bonus. The renewables job the wind farms can do is something we must all support. The planet, Gaia, awaits our help. Let us not be found wanting.

Dr Edwin Newall

Back in the day, Humphrey Drumm, portly editor of the Cloughgreen Recorder, had been a crack crime reporter on Fleet Street.Even after Fleet Street decamped to Wapping. He had been a fully paid-up and popular member of the Wig & Pen club and the recipient of a very hefty salary.

Then one day when he'd got within spitting distance of exposing a major crime family he'd received a very explicit warning. One that, in accordance with the conditions of the warning, he never revealed to anyone least of all the police.

Most people sleep safe in their beds secure in the knowledge the British police are all-powerful. Humphrey had been around long enough to know that real crime wasn't like it was in 'The Bill' where cop cars came screaming up at the last minute and saved the day.

He knew of crime syndicates so powerful that even senior police officers feared them. Where some criminals were so psychotic they were literally beyond the law. In the mindset they inhabited the police were a minor inconvenience and murder merely a tool of their trade. Genuinely the people of nightmares.

He knew of retribution that went undetected for a decade. Men who had disappeared and been found ten years later with six-inch nails driven through their hands and feet into floorboards in derelict buildings; a moth-eaten gag now dropped from their skeletal skulls as testimony to their lonely death agonies.

A shaven-headed, broken-nosed minder had once pointed out a council flat in a Docklands tower block which had been equipped as a butcher shop to 'repackage' corpses. Once dismembered and removed of fingerprints and teeth, small bloody packages fed the Thames fish. He had no doubt there were similar places in Manchester, Birmingham, Glasgow etc. Nothing succeeds like a good idea.

So Humphrey had concluded he'd done as much as one man could sensibly do and sought other journalistic avenues. For a while he'd written Drumm Beat, a sort of commonsense non-PC opinion column that Libby Purves might have written. In which he'd been perfectly sound and professional; but not gilded and outstanding as before. And not as good as Libby Purves either. His salary ebbed away as his alcoholic intake rose. Until a friend had taken him to one side and told him it was once again time to seek pastures new.

The Cloughgreen Recorder was part of a large provincial newspaper group. And the idea of being an editor and having a comfortable, non-threatened life and being lynchpin of a small community, a big fish in a small pool, appealed to Humphrey. Apart from which he didn't think he was ready for the knacker's yard just yet.

The main men on the editorial board of the group took some convincing he was serious. Why would he want to be their man in the English equivalent of journo Siberia? He was a stellar name. What baggage did he bring with him? Rumours of his flirtation with the booze surfaced. Had he become a lush?

Eventually he charmed them, flattered their egos. And they assumed, rightly, that anyone who had been a heavyweight in London for 20 years, whatever their profession, knew the game inside out. Nonetheless there was no star salary and there had been veiled warnings that they would be keeping an eye on him. They wanted no glory-seeking crusades on their commercial watch. So Humphrey Drumm, wily old fox that he was, knew that whatever good he felt he could do had to seem to be balanced with an equal word for the bad guys. Good by stealth then. And 3 years on, being pretty extrovert, he found he liked being invited to all these social functions, being asked to open things or officiate or judge events. It furnished a very congenial social life.

Cloughgreen being a small town, he found he came into contact with Dr Newall at almost every remotely political gathering. Inevitably Newall was to be found lurking, low key, in the shadowy margins, like a pike waiting to snap up influence or contracts for some new planning opportunity.

It also irked Humphrey that in the whole of Cloughgreen probably only he and Newall affected lavish bow ties. More importantly he distrusted self-important ideologues on first whiff. No question, no matter what else he was, Dr Edwin Newall was an arrogant ideologue of the first water who liked the sound of his own voice. A chance meeting at a Christmas function where Newall had been asked to speak had been more than enough.

Now here upon his desk was a letter from the good Dr calling for a Green crusade and sacrifice. (The sacrifice to be from others of course, rather than himself). The prose was so windy and vainglorious it read as though the man were ranting from a soapbox. That being so, Humphrey felt duty bound to publish it for the further edification of Cloughgreen's citizens. If it didn't enlighten them about wind farms, it should at least enlighten them about the good Dr Newall. Humphry smiled, took a cigar from the case in his drawer, opened a window and lit up.

He puffed contentedly through the window into the street. Then, smiling, he passed Newall's letter through for publication without altering one word. Except for giving him a belter of a headline. Maybe he could still do some good in a small way. Give the prat enough rope.

Dr Newall read the article with smug satisfaction. 'The Fat Hack has misrepresented me with the headline: "God-given Wind a winner" indeed. Gaia! What superstition! As if I'd say that. But he's left the rest untouched. It reads pretty well,' he said modestly. Penny Wragg devoured it. My hero.

Dr Newall woke about 8 on Saturday morning after the usual Friday night binge. Not true, his precise mind said. It was quite often a Saturday night. Penny lay next to him on the pillow, her mouth wide open, snoring horribly. He nudged her with his elbow and she shifted slightly, the snoring subsiding. How ugly she looked with her mouth open like that. Someone should tell her.

Watching her with her mascara run, her cheeks and forehead greasy from booze, her hair cracked and dry he thought how terrible a thing sex was, to bring him to this. Some people's sex lives, eh? It isn't all Mills & Boon, is it?.

'Does you good to get your ashes raked once a week,' his father, Colonel "Nasty" Newall, that old romantic, had once told him. His token sex education chat. Sex education from the days of Empire when men were men. Flavoured strongly by the ash of long-dead house fires or dead steamship boilers, who knows? Not exactly balm to the soul. Heaven knows what his mother had endured.

Penny moved again on the pillow and he realized her breath stank like a drain. He recoiled, then stayed sitting up. In all fairness, he probably smelt no better. He got out and headed for the bathroom. The shower refreshed him and made him feel confident about the coming day. The toothpaste took the bad taste from his mouth.

Later, he told over toast and coffee he was going to show her the proposed turbine site on Cloughgreen Common so she knew what he was talking about.

She'd seemed absolutely thrilled. She truly was, reflecting that this was the  first time he had ever really involved her in his work. That had to mean something, didn't it.

The 2CV bounced along the narrow road on the floor of the valley. After a few miles they swung away from the parallel railway lines and canal on their left and started a gentle climb up another valley to the right. There was no ribbon development here and they drove through lowering wooded valleys on each side with only the occasional house. It was so dark it felt like early evening.

'Wouldn't like to live here,' Penny said, the gloom affecting her.

Something in the ancient 2CV was making an irritating rattle. Right from new the car had felt like it had a rough-running WW1 aero engine strapped inside a tubular pram. The noise level was spectacular, so to hear a bad rattle above it was disconcerting. Theoretically, you were supposed to be able to fix 98% of everyday problems on a 2CV with a piece of string, a wad of chewing gum or a woman's stocking. Hmmm... He had read somewhere that the 2CV had been designed to enable a French peasant to transport a pig to market. He glanced sideways at Penny who was wriggling in her safety belt. Plus ca change.

'I've never been up here before,' she said happily.

'Why would you want to? There's nothing here.'

'It is pretty, all these woods and downhill streams.' She thought for a moment. 'For a picnic, perhaps?' She visualized this scene from a future perfect life, a married idyll with the philanthropic Edwin. To her right the good doctor snorted.

'You'd need double layers of thermals to picnic up here. It's about 400' higher on the tops than down in the town where we live. Gets brass monkey weather.'

'I meant in the summer of course.'

'Don't think it makes much difference. This is the arsehole of Cloughgreen we're going to. High and nasty and bereft of anything. It's just made for industrial use. See all the pylons already here?' She nodded. Indeed she did.

Dr Newall made a laborious uphill right turn. Then the engine screamed in protest as it was forced up a cinder track on a 1 in 3.

About 200 yards uphill a steel barrier barred the way. A metal notice pinned to it read Road Closed. It was a shock to her after the green slopes and woods they'd passed through. Even the ubiquitous grazing sheep looked greyer and dirtier, somehow industrial. Old TVs and armchairs and computers and tyres and builders' detritus had been dumped at the entrance to the moor.

Dr Newall got out and beckoned to her to do the same. 'Not pretty, is it?' he said. 'This is all the locals think it's fit for.' He indicated the tipping and collection of broken household squalor.

'Some people, you gave them golden bowls to eat from they'd shit in them,' she said, quoting her long-gone father. Dr Newall gave her a look.

'Who told you that?'

‘My father.’ Gaia, he thought, she’d had one like he did. Maybe that was what brought them together.

‘This is what we’re up against,’ he said. ‘The wannabe rural fantasists.’ He strode over and indicated a display case with coloured pictures of birds and wild life and peat and wild flowers that were native to the moor: bog cotton, peregrine falcons, meadowsweet, brown twite.

To her art director/designer’s eye the board was both well laid out and nicely executed; it invited the eye in. Clean design, nice serif typeface, elegant illustrations, not too romanticized, sharply detailed in fact. She particularly liked the illustration of the twite. What her mother would have called an LBJ, “a little brown job”, indistinguishable to most people from other LBJs.

‘You listening?’

‘Sorry, yes. “Wannabe rural fantasists” you said.’

‘Look at that board and you’d think this was some rural idyll. Like Constable might have painted. Dedham Mill or some such. Once things kick off they’ll be claiming there are rare bandicoots up here and all sorts. Golden eagles, unicorns... you mark my words.’

‘Bandicoots are rats, I think, tropical ones. Shouldn’t think you’d get many of them up here.’

‘You know what I mean. They’ll invent stuff. Rare flora and fauna.’

‘Like twites, you mean.’

'If you say so.' With a slight jolt, Penny realized he'd no idea what a twite was, had obviously never even read the notice board. Didn't want to know. That wasn't like the man she knew. A man who accumulated knowledge the way most blokes accumulated dandruff.

'Anyway, now we're here you may as well see the whole site.'

They set off down a 10' wide semi-made road, good enough for a tractor or a Land Rover, but uneven, pocked with deep puddles and half-exposed bricks and setts. It looked like it had been repaired many times over the years. The road had been driven through the moor so there were 18" banks on either side. The land stretched away flat for a long way, tussocky grass, bog cotton, pools of water some historic-looking spoil heaps.

After about 5 minutes Dr Newall paused, waving his arm around him at the desolate winter moorland. 'Look at it, it's a shitty green desert. Nothing here. Nothing of any value at any rate. And back down there,' he pointed down towards Cloughgreen, 'is a shitty little town full of small-minded, ignorant, selfish people frightened of change. Knuckle-dragging Nimbys.' He pointed down in the direction of the town. 'That place died out about 40-50 years ago. They just don't know it yet. The place is all clapped out, wrong sort of buildings for modern industry; too narrow and cramped and liable to flooding. Too dirty and unhygienic. It needs completely reinventing.' He grinned his secret squirrel smile at Penny. 'It may just have to extend a few hundred feet up the valley sides to do it.'

Penny knew that smug secret squirrel smile. It meant he knew things other people didn't. She didn't know what he meant about moving the town, but she knew there was no point in asking.

After they'd tramped along the gently undulating road for a further five minutes, Dr Newall suddenly exclaimed and pointed to a spoil heap to their left.

'See! How beautiful is that! A slag heap from old mine workings. Loads of 'em all over the place. Not a beautiful moor at all.'

'Well, beauty is in the eye of the beholder.'

'Maybe. But that's not worth beholding.'

'Some people would get pleasure from watching the twites and the sky larks and the peewits and curlews. And bog cotton is pretty. Like cotton buds on long stems, near these pools. Then the stems go red.'

'A few birds are a small price to pay for this prime wind turbine site,' he said tramping on.

'Still, it might be very pleasant up here in the summer...'

'What summer? We're at over 1300' woman. This place draws snow and ice like a magnet. Easter snow is quite commonplace. Even in the summer it's ball-breakingly cold. The wind knifes through you. You can see we're well above the tree line.'

Now he mentioned it, there were no trees. Not even shrubs.

'There is a sort of wild, untouched-by-man grandeur about the place, though,' she ventured. He hooted with laughter at this.

'That's just because you don't know what to look for. A landscape detective would point out a score of things you wouldn't notice where man has intervened and engineered things.' He raised his arm and pointed. 'There are loads of drainage ditches, for example, even if overgrown.' He lowered his arm and went quiet.

'Don't be fooled. They've mined for lead and coal here and lime for fertilizer. And they've quarried stone for the mills and reservoirs and the town.'

'Wouldn't that be a worry if you were putting deep foundations in for the turbines? Underground mine galleries.'

'Well, yeah. If you put the foundations in the wrong place. But Ursa will have hydrologists swarming all over the place checking out things are sound.'

'Hydrologists?'

'Scientists who specialize in charting and understanding the properties of the earth's water, especially its movement in relation to land. Ursa are investing big bucks. They'll want to make sure their investment's safe.'

Penny suddenly felt a warm glow for Edwin. How incredibly clever he was. And committed. And worthy. How many women had their men engaged in trying to save the planet like he was? She thought of her sister and her bloke. Bernie, the banker, & Belle the Oxbridge cock-teaser/sellout. Bernie & Belle, the gruesome twosome. All they thought of was money. Well, Edwin was different. She linked her arm through his as they walked and he sort of grunted.

After about half an hour they came to a place where the land rose up dramatically like a frozen green tsunami. At its edge the land fell dramatically away in a succession of long slopes, hiding Cloughgreen at its base. But you could see for miles across the valley at the facing slopes.

'This plateau here is where the outermost of those big beautiful shiny turbines will go. But that's just the start, believe me. They're the key that will unlock many other opportunities.' His brown eyes gleamed wetly with passion and Penny felt proud to have witnessed this moment with him. In later years she might be able to recall it as a moment of destiny that marked the change in Cloughgreen's character. But then she turned back from the moorland plateau and looked out front, seeing it properly for the first time.

'What a view!' she exclaimed, clasping her hands together in front of her. 'You can see for miles. As far even as Waterloo Pike on the far horizon,' she said, naming the huge stone obelisk which served as a Napoleonic peace memorial.

'Look at the way all the farmhouses on the opposite side of the valley string together along the contours. Actually when you look closely there are some on this side of the hill and to the side which look pretty close. Won't they be affected?'

'No. They're well away. Way beyond the recommended safety limits.' Then he puffed his chest out and snorted. 'Anyway you don't want to let yourself get taken in by all that myth stuff the antis push out. That's all garbage. They'll be fine.'

Just then some fat rain drops fell and he took that as his cue to push her gently in the back and turn her round for the slog back to the car. 'Come on, Penny,' he said, 'let's get out of this godawful miserable place. It's depressing enough without getting soaked through as well.'

As they trudged back in silence she couldn't get her mind away from that last vista with all the farmhouses, converted barns and cottages along the contours. Made from the local millstone grit they tucked into the green and brown landscape with the trees and looked like they'd been there for ever, as natural as if they'd grown out of the ground. Some of them had been there for about 400 years she knew.

Those people looked to be living a peaceful rural idyll with their sheep and cattle, their dogs and their horses, not hurting anyone. Surely these new wind farms must affect them?

Then it occurred to her. Of course - up on those hillsides loads of them would have spring water.

'Will digging the foundations for these big turbines not disrupt peoples' spring water supplies?' she heard herself say.

'Naw. Most unlikely. In any case it will all be looked into, don't you worry. There will be plenty of time to investigate everything thoroughly. Here,' he said, reaching into his pocket, 'have one of these.' He passed her a bag of creamy toffees and she took one.

*That's right, stuff one of them in your gob and leave the brainwork to those better equipped.*

He took a toffee himself and sucked away happily. He had seen the future. And the future was Green.

# 7

Friday November 16th

Willie drew back the bedroom curtains and looked out. The land was grey and washed out, sodden and unkind. The world had turned to rain. For days now it hadn't stopped. People in the shops and markets were talking of nothing but the unceasing monsoon. Those in known flood areas were getting sandbags out. Even places not flooded had been overwhelmed by grey skies. It was like living under a rough grey blanket.

He watched as the gale rocked the hawthorn hedges. He turned around without saying a word.

Bolly looked at him and read his expression.

'"November, the month of the drowned dog"...Old Ted Hughes had this landscape and weather in his bones,' Bolly said.

Some days at this time of year the dog walk definitely felt like duty. He left Bolly in bed with her coffee, kitted up and set out over the moors from the back door.

The grassy tracks and lanes had been tramped into muddy conduits by the men and dogs and sheep and cattle and horses and foxes and rats and mice that all used them. A few species of moorland grass stood tall and red and gold in the murk, hanging on in hope of resurrection.

With his waterproof gear and hood tied tight it sounded as though he were in some Napoleonic sea battle. His knee-length coat rattled and cracked in the gale-driven rain. The hood resounded to massed volleys of hail as though it were musket shot. The plastic trousers flapped and crackled like torn-away sails.

Labradors glory in water but after five minutes Nelson was beaten and bedraggled. Instead of running off the top, the hard-driven rain had penetrated his oily coat. He looked done-in and sorry for himself.

The waterlogged turf and churned-up mud made for heavy going. When they came to the stream under the small stone bridge where he paddled the dog backed away, frightened by the roar of white water. The run-off from the hills had turned the stream into a deafening brown and white cataract rushing six inches beneath the arch of the bridge.

Any dog stepping in there would rapidly become the drowned dog of Hughes's poem. The surging mass of brown water would have swept a horse away as it plunged hundreds of feet through the flooded 4'-wide rocky channel to the valley bottom.

Willie shivered and quickly moved on, sensing the uneasy breath of Nelson's mortality.

Looking to the side of the valley opposite he could see about twenty parallel silver lines descending where normally no water flowed.

Floodwater found the quickest way off the tops.

They stuck it out for an hour then went back. Days like this between November and February were the price you paid for the ever-changing panoply of light and colour the rest of the year. You had to be philosophical.

Being next-door neighbours, Willie and Jumper, shared a cab down from the tops to the Hamlet as per usual. Instead of running into the Hamlet, Jumper stood by getting soaked while Willie paid off Ali, of Ali's Premier Cabs. Old gents' behaviour.

'You should have gone ahead,' Willie said. Jumper merely shrugged. Water off an old farmer's back.

They stepped off the street into the small vestibule at the front of the Hamlet and Jumper shook himself like a giant, purple-nosed dog. Willie ran his hands through his wet and wind-blasted blond curls, wiped his palms on the backs of his jeans. Then they went through the second door into the pub proper.

Wesley was behind the bar, idly polishing his thick, black-framed glasses when Willie and Jumper entered the Hamlet. This lunchtime Wes looked like Ronnie Corbett between sketches. Relaxed. The pub appeared comatose, dust mites being the most active form of life.

'Morning gents, the usual, pint of Black Sheep 'n' pint of Gweens?' Wes asked, stifling a yawn. The two nodded. Wesley looked towards the snug, his black specs sliding down his nose. 'Your partner in crime is already installed.'

Stretching up to his full 5'4" Wesley reached up and flicked two pint glasses from the shelf above his head so that they tumbled end over end to land one in each hand. These he stuck under the Black Sheep and Guinness taps, tapping them on nonchalantly.

'Cheap barmen's tricks, Wes,' Jumper muttered.

'Well, I'm a very cheap barman, Jumper, boom, boom,' Wes said, smiling. 'Seriously though, if you feel like livening the place up, playing at Led Zep on tour and wrecking the joint, then today's the day. The Gestapo has gone shopping in Leeds,' he chortled.

'Nothing inexpensive, I hope,' Willie said, smiling.

'Just replacement stuff, I think, new rubber hoses, castrating shears, you know the sort of thing...customer control gear.'

'But you're still entire, aren't you, Wes?' Jumper asked with fake sincerity.

'Certainly. I've been treated of course. Sensors down there,' Wes looked down at his flies significantly, 'automatically come on at birthdays, anniversaries and Christmas. Everything works like clockwork on special occasions...you know, when permission granted.'

'Poor Wes,' Willie said, shaking his head and measuring out the usual amount of cash on to the bar, before following Jumper into the small snug.

'Don't you believe it, he loves it. Nothing like a dominant woman to keep you on your toes. You should try it some time,' Jumper said. Willie just gave him a pitying look, no words necessary. Apart from sport and old sports cars, women were Jumper's specialist subject.

As advised, Gerry was wedged behind their usual round table near the fire.

'Greetings, wind warriors from the moors,' he declaimed, making a theatrical gesture with his hand. 'What news from the blasted heath?'

'You're not going to believe the half of this,' Willie said, sitting down and supping quickly.

'Try me.'

'Yeah, lay on MacDuff,' Jumper said.

'Hang on, first things first,' Gerry said. 'Have you sorted things out with the beauteous Bolly?'

'Oh, yeah, that's all fine again.'

'Not that he deserves it to be,' Jumper opined. 'Falling out with a goddess like that.'

'Goddesses can be fickle,' Willie muttered. He put his black leather jacket on the back of his chair and Jumper did the same with his Barbour. Then Willie got out Charley's list and passed copies around.

The two of them scanned it and made shocked noises.

'If all this is right, then why on earth do they say these things are worth having? They plain don't work.' Jumper said.

'Partly because of the n-word,' Gerry said. 'Nuclear. And partly because if you don't want nuclear and you don't want carbon-burning power stations there is no alternative.'

'But that's like wearing wellies on your hands because you don't have gloves,' Jumper said. 'The wrong solution. It makes no sense.' Willie and Gerry laughed 'It's plain not the right answer at all. It says here you'd need to cover an area six times the size of Wales with 'em to make any significant impact.'

'And even then you'd need a collection of coal-fired power stations on standby for when the wind drops and the turbines fail. Or when they go on fire and have to be turned off.'

'On fire!' Jumper looked shocked.

'I sort of knew a lot of this, I guess,' Gerry said. 'Just not the enormity of the figures. How pitifully inefficient they really are. I've seen these huge glossy 6-12 page supplements that the UKWC ...

'Who?' Jumper asked.

'...the UK Wind Commission. They pump out these glossy, confident brochures and stuff. But, being in the biz, I read between the lines. Gently lolloping white blades against a blue sky, sheep gently nuzzling the grass in the foreground. Wonderful natural Green renewable power - "and sheep may safely graze" ...cue cello.

'While the reality is,' Willie said. 'If you look behind the pillar of the turbine you'll find a whacking great heap of dead birds and bats that the poor old dogs-body of a photographer's assistant has swept away out of sight. And out of picture horses, eyes wide and panicked, stampeding in all directions for the horizon.'

'Yeah, I've read that,' Jumper said. 'About the horses, I mean. I don't compete any more, obviously. But I still read the horsey publications. And stuff from the RHS, the Royal Horse Society. There've been a lot warnings about how industrial turbines can frighten the horses.'

'Literally,' Willie said.

'The problem you'll have is convincing ordinary people of any of this,' Gerry said. 'The wind farm gang seized the moral high ground long ago. It'll be hard to get people to see the truth.'

‘Surely if you show these figures and just tell it the way it is, it’s obvious.’

‘It’s not as simple as that,’ Gerry said. ‘First off they’ll say you’re lying. But then they’ve been very clever in pushing people’s buttons and tapping into people’s needs. Between climate politics and frustrated spirituality the wind farm i*dea* - not necessarily the reality - appeals to a lot of people. The green lobby have been very clever in pushing the dream and hiding the reality. They’ve cleverly sold the sizzle and not the sausage. In a way what you’re up against now is overcoming this lovely warm emotional bath they’ve created with the hard, cold facts.

‘A lot of people want to believe in fluffy windmills because of the nuclear bogey and the totemic visual thing. Turbines seem very pretty on film if you don’t have the rumbling, flickering reality in your face and stopping you sleeping. Then again, the vast majority of people don’t want to be made to think and work it all out. Other day-to-day problems. Windmills will save the world? Great, we don’t have to worry about global warming or running out of oil, brilliant. So yeah, get the windmills in. And some people are gonna make a lot of dosh.’

‘What a terrible old cynic, you’ve become, Gerry.’

Gerry just shrugged and pursed his lips. ‘Haven’t I just?’ he said, slurping the last of his lager. ‘But you’re just saying that to divert attention from getting a round in.’

'He got 'em last time. I'll get 'em in,' Jumper said. As Jumper left to get the new round in, Gerry ran his fingers up through his dark brown jagged friar's beard.

'No, this semi-religious, spiritual thing the wind farm gang have got going, it's very clever. There are loads of younger people who don't believe in organized religion but still want something spiritual in their lives. Earth worship is their new neo-pagan religion. It's pure atavism...'

'Atavism?' Jumper snorted, raising his eyebrows. 'Steady on lads, humble farmer here.'

'Humble farmer who went to agri college.'

'Long time ago. Before atavism was invented probably,' Jumper said, winking broadly. Joke.

'Atavism means reversion to something ancient,' Willie said.

'Anyway the younger wind folk have taken up where the Gaia Theory left off and turned saving the planet into a pseudo religious crusade. Wind is the new god you can't dispute...'

'Aiolos,' Willie said.

'Eh?' Jumper looked baffled as he placed the next round on the table and sat back.

'Aiolos was a Greek god,' Willie explained. 'He was keeper of the winds. Zeus gave him an Aegean island topped by an unbreakable wall of bronze with cliffs above. His job was to contain all the mighty winds. When any of the deathless gods required a storm they called on Aiolos to release the winds and stir one up. Similarly, he could call 'em back in and calm the sea for heroes.'

'Perfect,' Gerry chortled. 'The turbines are his holy icons. The moving crosses of Aiolos. The physical manifestation of Aiolos's godhead. It's just too good. Helps explain why rubbishing the turbines produces such religious fervour.'

'Never heard of Aiolos,' said Jumper mildly, scratching his plume of white hair. 'Heard of Zeus...'

'There are loads of ancient myths about Aiolos,' Willie said.

'Odysseus got help from him on his trip back from Troy. Aiolos gave him a big leather bag made from a whole ox-hide. In it he had penned up every wind that blows, so that Odysseus could call up whichever wind he needed. The bag was tied tight with a silver cord and stowed in the hold. Unfortunately Odysseus was exhausted by a storm and fell asleep. His crew, thinking the god had given their leader treasures, opened the bag and let the winds escape. Their boat was blown back to Aiolos's island and Odysseus asked for another ox-hide bag. But Aiolos said no, it was obvious the gods did not want Odysseus to have help and he could not oppose the other gods.'

'It's another iconic way of thinking of the windmills. The Crosses of Aiolos. Ancient name for an ancient invention,' Gerry said. 'Love it.'

'I'm convinced the obtrusive visual appearance is definitely a big thing for the eco warriors,' Willie said. 'How much fuss do they make about geothermal heating or solar power? Not a lot.'

'You're dead right,' Gerry said.

'Yeah, I can see that, too,' Jumper said, lifting his Guinness. An angel flew over as they sipped at their pints. Silence. Then Gerry leaned forward.

'It's complicated. As if the pseudo-religious aspect isn't enough, Green has become the new Red. In other words all the misfits, disaffected and rebels-without-a-cause who're naturally unhappy with their lot and want to change the world - who would once have been communists - have become saviours of the planet. They really want something to feel righteous about and beat the rest of us over the head with. And now they've got it. Some of these guys, the fanatical fringe, are genuinely dangerous. There's a bloke hangs out with Newall, don't know his name, milkman, Kevin something...Duff? Bit of a saddo really, not very well educated, bit of a loner. But I heard him sounding off in the Bird i' The Hand one day. Some guy mentioned turbines being a scam and he nearly went for him. This Kevin bloke's face went white and his body bunched up for a bundle and he let out a stream of abuse...Anyway the other guy did the smart thing and bunked off.'

Someone suddenly opened the front door to the Hamlet and held it open. There was an icy blast of wind and a deafening racket of traffic noise. Sixty seconds later it abruptly stopped and the room went quiet again. Gerry carried on as if nothing had happened.

'For all these groups the industrial wind turbine is their holy cross, their icon, their symbol, their totem, whatever you want to call it. Cross of Aiolos fits. With 24-hour revolving news stations on a quiet news day the producer reaches for some green story as a "filler" and then presto, pics of gently swinging blades against optimistic blue skies. They are using this image as a club to batter the rest of us with. They never show stormy grey skies with still, turned-off turbines being powerless to generate anything. Cross of fuckin' Aiolos, being ancient and wind-powered, doesn't come with a 24-hour guarantee.'

Jumper excused himself and ambled off for a leak.

'Still, it's all pretty depressing,' Willie said.

'I know. But it's best you know you'll be up against Rent-A-Mob and the closed minds brigade. For loads of emotional reasons a lot of people don't want to hear this is an obsolescent flawed technology, however factual your arguments. You can talk till you're blue in the balls about there being different ways of addressing climate change but they won't want to know. Wind farms seem a big easy solution.'

The room went quiet for a moment until Gerry bethought himself.

'Of course the people around here whose quality of life and health are threatened by the in-your-face reality of wind farms will probably feel equally passionate, like you and Bolly. I don't know if that's a help or a hindrance. Don't want to seem just like Nimbys.' The sound of Jumper's heavy brogues broke in.

'Sorry I took so long. Wes is bored out of his brains out there. Nabbed me for a natter,' Jumper said. The old farmer looked thoughtful.

'No, the thing I was thinking,' he went on, 'is how ironic it all is. The people who live up here - and some who are still struggling to farm - do so in spite of the bloody, year-round destructive wind. It's a trade-off to live in a beautiful, tranquil place away from towns. And now the Metropolitan bastards in Westminster who hate the countryside want to use the wind as a stick to beat us with. Makes you want to spit.'

Willie laughed dryly. 'To think, when Bolly and I first moved up here, we used to think the wind was very romantic. Five minutes from Haworth as the crow flies. Very Wuthering Heights and Heathcliff and gothic, we thought.' He contorted his features and moaned: 'Cathy, Cathy,' scratching his nails against the table top. 'Ghostly fingers on window effects,' he explained. The three of them laughed.

'Bet all that Wuthering Heights nonsense lasted about ten minutes once you'd got up on the tops,' Gerry said, snorting through his spikey brown beard. 'Nineteenth century romanticism...'

‘Quickly quelled by the sheer bloody destructiveness of the wind. Houses, barns, stables, chimneys, guttering, roofs, trees, five-barred gates, cattle caught out in a storm, ewes lambing, you name it, they all suffer. Even decides what plants you can grow,’ Jumper added.

‘Yeah, Bolly discovered that soon enough. When we moved up here she brought a shed load of stuff from a nursery in Kent. Wind and cold killed the lot the first winter. Broke her heart. But then we discovered something truly wonderful.’ He smiled and raised his glass. ‘God bless tough old *berberis* in all its thorny variety. Saviour of the local garden centre.’

The other two laughed and clinked glasses: ‘To tough old *berberis*’.

‘The reality is that wind is a four letter word up here,’ Gerry said, ‘as in, “‘effin’ wind did it.”’ The other two laughed, but there was no mirth in it, just recognition of the truth.

‘Beats me why you two live up there on the tops.’

‘For an artistic sort of bloke, you’ve got no soul,’ Jumper said. ‘Anyway you can hardly see me farming sheep in Industrial Street, can you?’ Willie drained his glass and motioned to the others. The others drained theirs. Time to go.

‘If God exists,’ Gerry said, reaching for his jacket, ‘I think he must have a black sense of humour. We endure the wind for the beauty of this place and now it’s going to bring down all this creeping industrialization on us. It’s bloody ironic is all I can say.’

Willie and Jumper walked back from the Hamlet to the shack that was home to Ali's Cabs and went in. Ali had his feet up on the desk, reading a football magazine.

'You gents ready for the return trip?'

'Yes please, Ali,' Willie said.

They got into the much-loved pale green Rover, flagship of Ali's putative fleet. Strictly speaking, Ali's Premier Cabs comprised Ali's premier cab, but Ali was an optimist. As they settled down Willie's mobile rang. Jumper gave a look of distaste. He didn't approve of mobiles, a sort of electronic Canute. Willie answered it.

It was Charley Fort.

'I've just discovered something that will make you hoot.'

'I hope so.'

'Well, back in December '06 BBC South decided to show how cool and Green they were by doing a live radio broadcast from Green Park, Reading powered entirely by the local 2 megawatt wind turbine...'

'And?'

'And it was an unmitigated disaster. No wind on the day. They nearly never went out on air at all. Had to use a nasty petrol-fired emergency generator, belching out blue smoke into the atmosphere.'

'Seriously?'

'Absolutely. Instead of it highlighting the brave new world of renewables, it was a classic demo of the shortcomings of wind power. Unreliable. Unpredictable. Etc.' Charley hooted down the phone, causing Willie to flinch. 'They were probably glad of the blue smoke from the generator to hide their red faces.'

'How's it going otherwise?'

'Found tons of controversial material. Submitted a piece or two but damned if they weren't strangled at birth. There's some powerful voodoo at work behind the scenes to suppress anything that's not good news for wind farms. More than even I imagined. First time I've come up against this in my little world. Anyway,' he said, 'the Grocer calls out to me. New marmalade sensations to report on.' Then he laughed and was gone.

'Bad news?' Jumper asked.

'Not really,' Willie said. Then he told Jumper what had transpired and he rubbed his purple old hatchet nose and smoothed his blond mane back.

'If it wasn't such a terrible scam they're running, these UKWC people, you'd wet yourself laughing, wouldn't you? The dependability of wind power graphically demonstrated by a local radio station having to rely on a diesel generator to go on air? Good job it wasn't a small town.'

'I wonder if these new windmills will be good for business?' Ali speculated. 'Loads of people coming into Cloughgreen by train and wanting to be ferried up there to see them, maybe?'

'I doubt it, Ali,' Jumper said.

‘Why bother going to the trouble of coming here? The way things are going turbines may soon be rare as lampposts,’ Willie said.

‘You’re not serious?’ Ali asked, turning to face them and going through a red light he hadn’t even noticed. He didn’t even hear the blaring horn of startled White Van Man as he was forced to swerve.

‘No,’ he’s not,’ Jumper said, wincing and alarmed for their safety. ‘Just a joke, Ali. Concentrate.’

Ali turned round, slumped back in his seat and paid attention to the road.

Willie gave Jumper an old-fashioned look. ‘We hope I’m joking.’

# 8

Saturday, 24th November

The big redbrick library that the philanthropist Christian Greenwood had donated to the town in the 1870s was still materially good for another 100 years minimum. But it was cold as the grave. Every time the door squeaked and someone came in, Dr Newall winced as the icy east wind, fresh from Siberia, drove across the foyer like a bow-wave. Ilya Kovalenko took crafty nips of vodka from a silver hip flask. The building did have central heating but it wasn't up to modern standards.

Dr Newall and Kovalenko were standing a little way from the splendid architect's model with its lush green hillsides, miniature sheep and jaunty white turbines. Kovalenko was getting a little bored when the door squeaked and the next icy blast ushered in a threesome. He nudged Dr Newall.

'Who is that stunningly beautiful woman like a Russian snow leopard with the long red hair and all those tiny freckles?'

'Who?' said Dr Newall, who had been day-dreaming.

'Over there. Just come in. With the tall old hippy with curly blond hair and the fat guy with hair like a monk.' Dr Newall followed the Russian's gaze.

A tall redhead in a short dark-green wraparound coat, short black skirt and thigh-length black leather boots was standing next to Gerry Stansfield and some tall guy he didn't know.

'The guy with the bad haircut and scruffy beard is Gerry Stansfield, Penny's boss. Some third-rate adman.'

'Never mind him. What about the stunning woman in the fuck-me boots?'

'Hey?' Dr Newall was stunned. He disapproved of all this testosterone in the wind. 'I don't know.'

'If I lived in a small town like this, I'd find out,' Bakunin said. 'Be careful though. I bet she's got claws.'

As they watched from a distance, the trio approached the wind farm model.

'It's worse than I feared,' the tall guy with blond curly hair said.

'Bloody hell, you're right,' Gerry Stansfield said.

The redhead let out a long hiss of disbelief. 'My God,' she said. 'It's like a ring of steel sitting on Cloughgreen's shoulders.'

'The whole scheme extends much further than I imagined,' Gerry muttered.

'Yeah,' was all Willie Dee could manage. Before Dr Newall could stop him Ilya Bakunin had gone over and introduced himself to the woman and her companions.

'It is very impressive, is it not?' he said. 'It will put Cloughgreen on the map.'

'It will utterly destroy the landscape,' Willie said, his shoulders slumped. 'It will make us look like Runcorn or Port Talbot.'

'You exaggerate.' Dr Newall said.

'You will never get away with it, we will fight you,' Verity said, her freckle-kissed face pale beneath its usual swarthiness. 'Neither Cloughgreen nor Woolton councils will approve this monstrosity.' Dr Newall leaned forward, smiling smugly in their faces.

'The local councillors know nothing. But it doesn't matter, a big scheme like this, of national importance, will go over their heads. It will be passed on to the professionals in Bristol, the planning inspectorate. They will pass our appeal on the nod. You'll see.' Willie and Gerry had moved forward, seeing Verity's body language. She was leaning forward and looked as through she wanted to scratch Dr Newall's eyes out. They took an elbow each and pulled her away.

'Come on,' Willie said. 'He's not worth it.'

Dr Newall waited until they had got some distance away and opened the door before pronouncing loudly: 'Jonathan Porritt, onetime head of Friends of the Earth, said "The modern wind turbine is a mighty intrusive beast, it's not into nestling or blending"...' Then he cackled loudly, provocatively.

'You bastard,' Verity yelled as the two men hustled her through the door. Once outside she shook their hand off, green eyes flashing. 'Who is he, the little reptile in the bow tie?'

'That,' said Gerry Stansfield, 'is Dr Newall. Oozes charm doesn't he?'

Willie shivered. The wind brought tears to his eyes. It had shifted round to the north, coming fresh out of the Arctic. Now it was bloody cold. He looked up at Thor Fell, the giant hill that dominated the town. It was hidden by thick grey mist. Then he looked at Bolly Dolly. She had tears in her eyes too. But he thought they were tears of rage and frustration, not cold.

Ilya Bakunin turned to Dr Newall, as the old ladies behind them tutted away at the recent scene. 'That was unnecessarily brutal, wasn't it? That last bit to the woman, I mean.'

'The woman was being uppity. Needed to be told the way it is.'

'"Uppity",' Bakunin sniffed around the word. 'You know Edwin, I don't think you really like women.' Dr Newall stared at him. He didn't think he was a poof, did he?

'On the other hand, I confess to finding their views a little shocking. I know what you said, but...' Dr Newall appraised Bakunin. The Russian businessman was indeed looking shocked and surprised.

'I still don't understand it. Wind power is the way forward. With you behind it, it could make Cloughgreen very famous.' Dr Newall smiled his smug, secret squirrel smile, the one that had almost got his face raked by Verity Dee's nails.

'Don't worry about it, Ilya. Like I said, the peasants are revolting. Just knuckle-dragging Nimbys, that's all.' Then he stared up at the taller man. 'Provided we pay attention to detail we have nothing to worry about. The government wants this to happen to get their 10% of renewables. And if it's going to happen it will have to be away from places like the Lakes, The Peak district, The South Downs, Devon, Constable country, heritage country, and even,' and here he winked and pushed his finger gently into Bakunin's chest, 'seemingly ideal places like the Solway Firth. It will have to be precisely in scruffy little green deserts like this that nobody has heard about or cares about. We'll be fine, trust me.'

'I think you have made an enemy of that beautiful woman,' the Russian said. 'Like I told you, she is a snow leopard. Unusual dark complexion with those tiny freckles for a redhead,' he mused. Then he looked sternly at Newall. 'Beautiful, yes, but with claws.' Dr Newall just smiled and shrugged.

Ilya Bakunin hadn't become a colonel in the KGB by being obtuse. He suddenly had an insight into his new consultant. He seemed to breed enemies as easily as some men bred pigeons. His friend, Arkady Kovalenko, didn't like Newall. Now this woman, whoever she was, hated him. If Dr Newall walked steadily, it was only because he had a chip on both shoulders.

# 9

15th December

After Willie had brought Bolly Dolly her morning coffee he got dressed and went downstairs to let Nelson out for his morning pee; stage 2 of the daily ritual.

There was a pale lemony sunlight. More importantly, after six weeks of it there was no battering rain and, amazingly, no wind. He stretched his arms wide and breathed deep. The day felt like a gift from God. Without a wind it felt immeasurably warmer.

He walked along the garden path and looked down the green slopes of the hills to the tiny grey town in the valley. The Storm-n-Shine factory had the last working chimney in

Cloughgreen. Other blackened brick phalluses stood erect but useless, frozen in time along the sides of the valley. The factories they had served were long demolished as the textile trade imploded; but the ruined mill owners had found the chimneys too expensive to disassemble. So the blackened chimneys stood like financial tombstones, mute witness to a bygone life.

Storm-n-Shine was the town's biggest employer. They also provided about 80% of Gerry Stansfield's income with their spring and autumn catalogues, he reckoned. Dangerous; he'd known quite a few one-big-client ad agencies be brought down if the client hit problems. He'd told Gerry, but what the hell. Take a horse to water and all that.

To Willie the Storm-n-Shine chimney acted like a sort of redbrick windsock. This morning he could see a whisper of white smoke drifting straight up in a lazy spiral against the blue sky. No wind. He wondered if you'd see that a dozen times a year.

'Come on, Nelson,' he said. 'You're in luck this morning. We'll get a good walk in while the going's good.'

The ground was sodden and waterlogged, unable to absorb any more water.

Nelson, running, aquaplaned on the greasy green turf and shot one foot out as it went from under him. He looked furtively over one shoulder to see if master had noticed. He was a dog with appearances to maintain, didn't wish to lose face.

Willie wondered how having only one eye affected the dog and changed course to a route that would avoid hazardous downhill descents.

The days had been shortening dramatically as they headed up to the winter solstice. It lacked 10 days to Christmas and the land seemed battered and tired out. Today, with no wind, it seemed to be holding its breath, hanging on for spring resurrection.

It got him thinking. Even with electric light, a solid roof over your head and central heating, the weather and the time of year  depressed people's spirits. If you were out in it every day your face got reddened and raw from the constant wind and rain.

How the ancient peoples living in this landscape in caves and shelters must have yearned for the fire festivals and feasting of midwinter. Warmth and firelight and drunken ease and roast meat and pray to the goddess the sun comes up again soon; the priests knowing when the sun's nadir had passed. Even the Romans had celebrated 25th December with Sol Invictus, the Sun god victorious. God, how we all long for the sun to be victorious again, he thought.

As was often the case on his walks, his outer eye watched over Nelson while his inner eye pondered different things. The past 6 weeks had produced a lot to think about. The wind farm announcement in the Recorder. Charley's mind-boggling discoveries. Then Dr Newall's windy call to arms in the Recorder had produced a firestorm of response in the paper.

There had been a whole page given over to readers' letters. Most had been against Doctor Newall's decision to unilaterally declare Cloughgreen wind farm capital of the UK. But there was some support for him, too. These people were mostly emotional. *The need to save the planet. No alternative but to act. Anything better than doing nothing. How pretty they looked when you visited them* (but not if you lived near them). Many of them seemed to have been brainwashed into an almost hysterical pseudo-religious frame of mind, as predicted by both Charley & Gerry. Interestingly, and cynically maybe, looking at the postal codes almost all the pro-wind farm types seemed to live well away from the proposed sites and many of the antis lived near them.

The other general point was that the antis were far more factual. Like Bolly they seemed to have taken the time to acquaint themselves with data and not liked what they'd discovered. There were arguments about how much carbon was used in the manufacture of the turbines. Figures about how poorly they performed. How many you would need to replace a conventional power station. How much developers earned per year per turbine and so on.

The Recorder had printed a letter from one Verity Dee, which Willie, though biased, thought was a fine response to Dr Newall's rallying cry for sacrifice. Verity went in hard on how the technology was fatally flawed by the unpredictability of the wind. That despite the potential power generation figures quoted, the most they ever achieved was around 28%

of that. Nobody in their right mind would buy a car or a watch that performed only 28% of the time max, would they? Particularly when you couldn't even predict when the 28% of the working time would be. Interestingly it drew forth a phone call.

He had been looking at an auction house's catalogue of prints by Anselm Adams, one of the early masters of photography, wondering whether to go and have a look, when the house phone rang. Expensive but exquisite.

'I'd like to congratulate you on a fine letter,' the voice boomed, 'and to extend an invitation to come and meet up with us. My name is Carter Briggs and I'm president - for what it's worth - of The Friends of the Living Moorland. I suppose you'd call us the local anti-wind farm body.'

'I didn't write the letter,' he said.

'Did you not? Are you not V. Dee then?'

'It's my wife Verity you want. I'll get her for you.'

Verity took the call and it was arranged they would meet Carter Briggs and his number 2, Dr Phyllis Bentley, at Briggs's house, Knowle End, the following Saturday.

'One last thing,' Carter Briggs said, 'I'm 6'6", so don't be alarmed when you meet me.'

'I won't,' she said.

Verity insisted on driving, as it was her meeting. She had her new green Mini Cooper moving before he'd got his seat belt on. She whacked her theme tune up on the stereo -

Marianne Faithful singing The Ballad of Lucy Jordan - and settled into some serious sporting driving.

Her father had taught her to drive on their estate when she was about 13 and he'd taught her the old fashioned way. So she double declutched as she went, keeping the revs high. Slung low in the Mini, Willie felt like a pinball in play. Some of the narrow country lanes had dry stone walls so high you couldn't see what was coming towards you and there wasn't a lot of room for error on each side either. He felt unnaturally nervy, his feet pressing down on invisible brake pedals once or twice; but they reached their destination without incident.

Carter Briggs lived on the opposite side of Cloughgreen. His house looked out over a different valley towards the obelisk called Waterloo Pike standing high on The Pennine Way. Knowle End was a large detached house of the sort estate agents referred to as "a gentleman's country residence", circa 1850.

As they approached Bolly's mouth dropped open. 'Look at them,' she said, taking her right hand off the wheel to point beyond the house.

'He's got micro turbines. Two of them. That's a turn up for the book.'

'Actually they're okay, though, aren't they? They're no bigger than trees. They don't destroy the scale of the landscape like the big industrial ones, do they?'

'No they don't,' Willie said, as they drove in through high blackthorn hedges onto a circular gravel drive. 'Few bob here'.

'Makes Greenwood Royd look like a bungalow,' Bolly agreed, bringing the car to a halt and taking the ignition key out. The house was a grey stone country house with a pillared portico as an entrance.

'Don't forget he warned us he was enormous, so not to take fright,' Verity said. As she spoke a large man of about 50 with snowy white hair and broad shoulders appeared under the Palladian doorway.

'Crikey,' Willie said, 'He wasn't kidding.' Carter Briggs was every inch of 6'6" and looked not unlike a larger, younger version of Jumper Lonk. Viking stock such as you could see in all the playgrounds of Cloughgreen: blonde-haired, blue-eyed kids with apple-blush cheeks. Half close your eyes and you could see Carter wearing a wolfskin, wielding a double-handed axe and going berserk against a Saxon shield ring. All in the genes. Still, he seemed pleasant enough today, Willie thought.

Carter Briggs crunched over his manicured gravel wearing a sharp Prince of Wales check suit and expensive tan brogues, white shirt, blue tie. He was smiling broadly beneath a mop of blond hair and an all-year-round tan. Skiing and yachting, Willie guessed. He opened Verity's door and handed her out.

'Delighted to meet you, Verity,' he said. 'Carter Briggs at your service.' Then whizzing round the front of the car - he was one of those big men who was light on their feet - he grasped Willie's hand. 'And the famous Willie Dee.'

Willie looked puzzled. 'The photographer. I've read some of your books.'

'Really?' Willie said. He'd only published two. Both coffee table books. Look-at books, not read-me books.

They exchanged pleasantries and Carter Briggs took Verity's elbow. 'Come in and meet Dr Bentley, my number two at Friends of the Living Moorland' he said, sweeping her in along a maroon-carpeted entrance hall to a large entertaining room at the rear. Trailing behind, Willie was met by vast quantities of eau-de-nil furnishings and chintz. The Persian-looking carpets seemed a bit tatty but were probably worth a fortune, he decided. The furniture looked antique but well lived in and reminded him of Alan Clarke's comment about someone being the sort of man who'd had to buy his own furniture - no family heirlooms. In fact both the house and Carter's easy manners reminded him of a nobility shoot he'd once done for a Sunday supp. Carter wasn't nobility, but there were confident generations of money behind him that was clear. He was an officer and a gentleman, by way of old trade money.

In the centre of the room was a large, highly polished dining table. A small, slim woman with permed salt-and-pepper hair, round glasses and intense violet eyes rose and smiled as they entered.

Her dark blue suit was exquisitely cut and emphasized her trim figure. Moving to meet her, Willie guessed she had never had children.

They sat around the table, looking out through large French windows at the magnificent view over the valleys to the Pennine Way and Waterloo Pike.

Small talk was exchanged. Carter Briggs explained that the family were still successful hauliers, though the family had been mill owners and landowners locally for hundreds of years before that. Dr Phyllis Bentley, Miss Phyllis Bentley, explained that she had been a biophysicist, an academic. Though she, too, had come from a longstanding local family of mill owners. They both felt a sort of noblesse oblige towards their small town and had formed Friends of the Living Moorland ten years earlier to protect the surrounding moors from exploitation.

'We've fought off a quarry application and a plan to do open cast mining since then,' he said. 'So we know how the planners work.'

'Everything submitted in septuplicate,' Dr Bentley joked.

'And typed in Arial 12 pt minimum,' Carter added. Willie and Verity smiled in amusement. What a double act.

'Carter understands politics and is quite fearless about taking on corporations. And my academic background means I have an eye for detail and compiling reports and documents,' Phyllis said with a twinkle in her eye. Carter Briggs was making an aw-shucks ma'am gesture, but it was clear to both Willie and Verity that Dr Bentley, though about 15 years his senior, had a vast admiration for Carter.

'We thought you might like to join the Friends. Only costs a tenner a year. And we might be able to give you some background support. It was a wonderful letter, Verity. And with the coming battle we need as many people onside to try and spread the message about how inappropriate these turbines are. Keep bombarding the Cloughgreen Recorder and try and influence the general populace to influence their councillors before the planning app comes up before the council meeting.'

'We'll join, obviously. But what we would like to know is why the government and so many ordinary people seem to believe in these things when as soon as you look into them the figures don't seem to add up against all the negatives.'

'Ah well, our friends the UKWC, the UK Wind Commission, have been telling fairy tales for a good few years now,' Dr Bentley said, smiling wryly. 'They can count on big donations from the developers and manufacturers to spread the wind gospel.'

'And they also suppress all the bad news, about fires, accidents, health problems while massaging the figures and generally implying the planet will catch fire any time soon if we don't have wind farms,' said Carter Briggs.

'If you've got an enormous open country like America or Russia and you can tolerate such poor individual performance then wind farms are fine In countries like ourselves or Japan where land is at a premium, they make no sense. We're overcrowded already and have relatively little wild countryside. What we do have is an enormous coastline. We should be harnessing the totally predictable energy of tidal power or wave power. Neither of which violate our few remaining wild places,' Dr Bentley said.

'What would be really helpful to our understanding would be if you acted as devil's advocate,' Verity said. 'Take us through what the wind farm supporters believe and why.'

'Okay,' Carter said, as his housekeeper brought through tea and a heaped plate of biscuits. Bourbons, custard creams, ginger nuts, fig rolls, chocolate wholemeals, even jammy dodgers, the sort of biscuits Willie hadn't seen since he was in short trousers. People who laid on comfort food like this were surely people you could trust, he thought. Anyway this was really Verity's show, so he was free to help himself, leave the chat to Bolly Dolly.

'Fire away,' Dr Bentley said crisply, her violet eyes twinkling.

'Well, what is the general overall case for wind farms, 'cos we can't see any commonsense arguments that stand up?'

'Right,' Carter Briggs said, reaching into an orange folder he had in front of him, 'it will make life easier if I quote from a document supplied by an organization called Country

Guardian. First, not even the wind farm industry pretends that turbines produce electricity more cheaply or more efficiently than conventional power stations.'

'You would need to cover most of Wales to replace even one large conventional coal-fired power station,' Dr Bentley said.

'And, being both unpredictable and uncontrollable, the wind is a difficult energy source to work with.'

'You need the right type of wind. Too little and the turbines don't work. Too much and they have to be turned off before they blow over. And you need to run a conventional station on standby for when the turbines go down.'

'But, the wind farm supporters say, they have three great advantages. One, they provide energy without the problems associated with nuclear power - risk of accident and problems with waste storage.

'Two, they do not deplete fossil fuels, which are finite.

'Three, they produce energy without harmful chemical emissions, such as Co2, So2 and Nitrogen Oxides, gases associated with global warming and acid rain.' He paused. 'Those are the three main arguments for industrial wind turbines. For these arguments to be valid certain things must happen.

'If built in sufficient numbers they must be able to close down or replace nuclear power stations; that will never happen. Two, they need to be reliable; that will never happen either because nobody can predict either wind availability or wind strength. Three, they need to be economically viable; because of the subsidies, the electricity they generate is far more expensive to the householder.'

Carter shrugged and smiled wanly, held his hands palm up.

'They're not really proper turbines,' Dr Bentley, the physicist, said. 'Strictly speaking they are more accurately called an "airscrew generator". In effect they are bastard turbines. True turbines, be they water, steam or gas, have 3 things in common. They are encased, the casing being vital to their operation; they operate at very high revs per minute; and they produce enormous amounts of electricity relative to their size.' She paused and smiled wryly, fiddling with her cuff.

'One of the ironies of the thing is that if they were proper cylindrical hardworking, efficient turbines, they wouldn't have a fraction of the visual appeal for the wind farm nutters and the gullible public. It's that cute windmill look they go for.

'Even then when the TV producers and commercials producers show 'em on telly, they never show 'em against stormy skies, turned off to save 'em being uprooted.'

'Or limp with brewers droop on a calm day, sitting there doing nothing. Static and impotent,' Carter interjected.

'Anyway,' Phyllis went on, 'The airscrew generator, or so-called "wind turbine" is designed to produce power at low to moderate wind speeds, when the output is a trickle. As wind speed strengthens and real power becomes available they have to be shut down or they will blow over. A 200' high wind turbine of 500 kw capacity will on average - at their average output of 25% capacity - produce 125 kW, enough to boil 50 electric kettles.'

'I knew it,' Verity yelled, punching the air like a footballer, 'that's the fatal flaw. They're not even proper turbines. That's why they don't produce the goods.'

'Of course they are getting bigger now. The new ones they want to inflict on us will be 410' high. And they've got some over 600' high ones in Germany. They'll generate a bit more power but you can't get away from all the basic failings. And the bigger the turbine blades the louder the noise, the more obtrusive the blade flicker/strobing. Plus you need more concrete and even more acreage to stand them on.'

'Surely the Government must have experts who tell them how inefficient these things are? And they know how unpopular they are or they wouldn't have introduced PPS22 to move the planning goalposts and make it easier for planners to shoo them in.'

'Well, the only real answer to adequate amounts of clean power is nuclear energy. And the Government knows that okay. France, which is more pragmatic, now gets 90% of its power from nuclear sources, and are the experts on the new generation of safer plant.' Carter went thoughtful for a moment. 'There again, President Sarkozy came right out and said that flying over Europe he was appalled by the ugliness of wind farms and their effects on European landscape. He said it would only be possible in France on brown field sites. Governments in this country - and to be fair this includes the previous Tory ones - have for years been running scared of the N word, hoping another government would have to confront nuclear power and the anti-nuclear lobby. Talking up wind farms is both a sop to the Green faction and a smokescreen to hide behind regarding new energy sources. There are loads of alternatives for renewable power. Offshore wind, tidal, wave, hydro and obviously nuclear. The problem is none of them is either as cheap or immediately available.'

Phyllis suddenly spoke up. 'Eventually there will be breakthrough technology. Photovoltaics. Producing electricity from all the free light you see around us. Breakthroughs with quantum physics even.'

Verity thought for a moment. 'You have obviously read Frey & Hadden, the two academics, and their accusations of ill health and intrusion caused by noise and wind flicker. And there are similar stories from America, Australia, all over the world. How do they get away with denying this?'

Dr Bentley twinkled behind her glasses and smiled a quiet smile. 'They say scientifically none of these threats to health are proven. And scientifically speaking there is merit in a rigorous approach. However, what they don't say is the government unit charged with researching health and safety issues concerning noise spends proportionately far more on turbine noise than on any other subject. Nor do they say that when there is reasonable evidence to suggest something then it should be prioritized and looked into, not disregarded. People suspected something was unhealthy with asbestos and thalidomide long before it was proven and vested interests shushed things up. Whatever the problems or human cost, this Labour government has set its sights on having wind farms '

'But that's scandalous,' Verity said. Dr Bentley sighed deeply.

'In truth, the noise emissions are difficult to predict. As well as how close you are, so much seems to depend on the individual topography of the site. And then again, it is also dependent on local atmospheric conditions. You must notice that with the Delf wind farm near you?'

'We do,' Willie said. 'But fortunately we're shielded by an outcropping shoulder of land. We notice the same acoustics phenomenon far more with the railway on the floor of the valley. That's about 2 miles from us as the crow flies, and it's mostly barely a whisper. But on certain days it sounds as though it could be 20 yards away.' Dr Bentley nodded.

'Yes that is similar. The problem is there genuinely seems to be no computer model or such like that you can feed in geographical features and receive meaningful sound predictions back. Even if the developers cared. Which they don't. Neither do the Government. PPS22 specifically says that within the distance guidelines - which incidentally differ from country to country and are shorter in the UK - possible noise problems should be overlooked. They are happy to take these risks until there is proven medical evidence on the books. And they refuse to provide the proper research to get that evidence.'

'Meanwhile all the developers and their bosom pals in the Green movement do is sneer and say issues about noise and blade flicker are myths. Myths basically mean lies without being legally actionable and imply you're a bit of a moron as well as a Nimby,' Carter said.

'But surely there have been people driven out of their homes, needing respite care, by both noise and unceasing blade flicker,' Verity said.

'Myths, all myths, they'll tell you. Although there has now been a famous test case involving a woman called Jane Davis and her husband at a place called Deeping St. Nicolas. Their council tax was reduced.'

'And loads of people, including estate agents, who have either suffered price cuts in the valuations of their houses by 25/30% or been unable to sell at all when prospective buyers see the wind farm location and the interference,' Verity continued.

'Myths, just myths. There are sites you can go where the wind-wallahs actually have myth sections to rebut your opponents with. Try embracewind.com. Or yes2wind.com.'

"No evidence", they say to just about anything they don't like.'

'We on our side of the fence are more robust, Verity,' Dr Bentley said. 'We say they tell lies. Massive great whoppers. And where they are not outright lies they lie by omission or by false comparison. When it comes to the figures game they tell dreadful untruths. They were made to recant on some figures they'd put out by The Advertising Standards Authority where they were comparing state-of-the-art turbine figures with the oldest, obsolete coal-fired power station figures.

'They routinely deliberately mislead the public over turbines' theoretical maximum performance figures and the actual measured output over a year, or load factor.'

'The figures that make me laugh are those which say this wind farm or other will provide power for 4,000 homes. First they provide this boast on the theoretical maximum performance of the turbines working 24/7. And you want to say well, yeah, jolly good. Even if it did that, which it won't, how many lots of 4,000 homes are there within the UK? So how many thousands of turbines do you need to supply even 10% of them?'

'I know. If we had a landmass the size of Siberia, maybe,' Willie said. 'But Britain is a tight little island with so little wild country for people to go to spiritually renew themselves.'

'You hit the nail on the head,' Carter agreed.

'If these turbines were high tech and you had a giant one outside every town and maybe 50 outside every city then that would be different. But to my eye the sheer numbers of the things you need to make a significance and the sort of high wild places they inevitably have to be in makes them a disaster,' Willie went on. 'Why would all Cloughgreen's visitors who come from Sheffield and Doncaster and Manchester to run or walk or cycle on unspoiled moorland want to walk amidst whooshing, flickering steel and concrete? That's what they've come here to escape.

'As to these environmentalists who support these things, knowing they kill rare flora and fauna and literally frighten the horses, that's totally beyond me. "Trash your own backyard, save the planet," I don't get it.'

'The developers I can understand; they just want to get their noses into the trough. Fair enough, that's what developers do. But these environmentalists, who are supposedly guardians of our rare mosses, the birds, bats and butterflies, how they square this I just don't know,' Willie said, spilling his guts.

To his embarrassment the other three clapped and Verity and Dr Bentley said 'Hear, hear.'

Willie grinned self-consciously. 'There, that's my rant for the year,' he said, looking at his feet.

'No, you were quite right,' Carter said. Then he got his housekeeper to buy in a Szechuan takeaway and he and Carter drank whisky with it as though they were in a backroom in Chinatown. Verity and Dr Bentley sipped a small glass of Frascati each. *Driving.*

They arrived at 2pm and they left around 10pm, having spent a lot more time discussing wind farm issues. In particular the need to fight their battle on the individual merits of Cloughgreen Common. And not to attempt to fight the big, overall issues.

'This has just been the phoney war,' Carter concluded. 'It'll probably all go quiet till after Christmas now and then we'll have to start lobbying public opinion both in Cloughgreen and Woolton.' And that was how they left it.

They swapped email addresses, promising to stay in touch. Carter led them back down the hall and out to their parked cars. Phyllis pecked Carter on the cheek and got into her car. Then Carter pecked Bolly on the cheek and she got behind the wheel. Willie was just about to get in when Carter placed his hand on his arm.

'You know, Willie, if saturating the UK countryside in industrial turbines is the answer, we've been asking the wrong question.'

Bolly followed Dr Bentley's black Golf GTi with its fuel injection and oversized alloy wheels down the gravel drive. To Willie's amaze her red lights fast disappeared into the blackness of the unlit road.

Like she often did, Bolly caught his thought. 'I can catch her if you like, show you a bit of real driving.'

'It's okay,' he said quickly, laying his hand over hers on the gearstick. There were no streetlights. And there were long stretches of pitch-black moorland with no house lights.

Bolly went quiet, concentrating on the Cats-eyes in the bendy black void.

'I think Carter would be a bad man to cross,' Willie mused.

'Well, he's certainly a big lad...'

'No, I didn't mean that. I mean he's determined. And clever. And I get the feeling once he gets his teeth into something he doesn't let go.'

'You make him sound like a human Rottweiler,' Bolly chuckled.

'I'm glad he's on our side,' Willie said, 'he's worth ten of Newall's sort.'

'Well, let's hope so.'

Bolly half-opened the windows and the scented night air wafted its silence through the car.

Then suddenly out of nowhere, as though she'd been considering it, she said quietly 'I just hate to be conned, Willie. Totally sucked in and suckered. Like millions of others. I can see the appeal, but it just doesn't add up. Wind farms are a failed dream. Well, we'll see.' Then she flicked the Ballad of Lucy Jordan on to the CD again. Battle cry of Verity Dee, the song that changed her life.

The previous evening had given them plenty to think about, Willie thought, as Nelson stopped dead and went into his pointing stance, looking skyward. Willie checked to see what the dog was pointing at. It was a windhover, or kestrel. He watched as it teetered on the wind, fan-dancing at 100', flicking its wingtips this way and that. Then whatever it was hunting went to ground and it flew away.

When he looked back to earth his eye was caught by a large waterfilled puddle that seemed to be 3" deep. Some puffy white clouds reflected in it, shimmering against a blue backdrop in its grass-greeny depths. He told Nelson to sit and took the digital Nikon out of his backpack. One of his current projects was inspired by a book of primitive art. He was trying to make magical, abstract images. You needed a slightly fey image and then there was a way of digitally enhancing it that made it look like an art etching. This looked to be a promising image. Nelson regarded him soulfully, having dutifully sat and waited. Willie smiled and tossed him a biscuit.

Nine days to Christmas. He would be glad to take Bolly Dolly to her parents' home in Ireland and forget all about the 78 proposed pseudo turbines and the depressingly large tonnage of concrete they would bring with them to the moor. Some chestnuts roasting on an open fire, a blazing midwinter fire festival of any kind, a bit of wassailing. Indeed any diversion. That was what they both needed.

On the 21st December they packed Nelson in with the luggage and drove the Range Rover down to Croydon to collect Willie's father.

Dr David Dee, a retired GP, was now 80. But he was more extrovert than his son, genial, twinkly, and still *compos mentis.*

Having slept overnight in Croydon they packed Dr Dee in the back with Nelson and drove down to Pembroke in Wales. Then it was the ferry to Rosslare and a drive to the far south of Ireland. Past villages so slow-paced they could accommodate giant oak trees in the middle of the high street.

Verity's father and her mother, a still attractive former Scandinavian cabaret singer who'd passed on her tan complexion, lived in a small Elizabethan manor house attached to an ancient ruined castle. With no money for renovations Ballymallen Castle was the castle time had forgot in a part of Ireland time had forgot. The "mouldering heap" Willie called it. It was a gothic ruin that could have been painted by Caspar Friedrich on a stormy night. Health and safety issues now precluded tourists and much-needed income.

The money that enabled the handsome young aristocrat to race Bentleys, fly biplanes and wine and dine attractive women was long gone. Truth to tell, the money was starting to dribble away around the time they sent Verity to finishing school in Switzerland.

Before that Patrick and Inge Carbery had been a gilded young couple who lived life in the fast lane. They drank Singapore slings in Singapore, wore Bermuda shorts in Bermuda, sipped Manhattans in Manhattan, and sang the

Marseillaise in Marseilles. Their photo albums showed one hell of a life. But now they were frail.

They lived modestly but comfortably adjacent to the castle. Verity adored them and Willie loved them. But "quiet" was the watchword for how they now lived. A handyman/gardener/chauffeur and his wife as housekeeper were the remaining hired help. The occasional trip to Cork was now more daring than "hopping over to Paris for lunch" in a biplane had once been.

But they were generous hosts and they welcomed Dr Dee for the festive season. Willie had stipulated the one rule for the holiday. Nobody was to mention wind farms. He wanted a quiet and peaceful Christmas. Time to gather their strength for the coming struggle.

# Part II

# PROPHECIES

# 10

Willie and Bolly set off back to Croydon on January 2nd. Christmas had gone well. Bolly's parents, the Carberys, had kept an open house with county friends and Bolly's friend Grainne, also back home, dropping in. The two of them nattering away for hours and giggling like the schoolgirl chums they had been.

The blazing fire festival Willie had sought had been fulfilled by candle-lit nights in front of roaring log fires in the 12' by 12' fireplace in the mansion's living room. Sometimes her father got his guitar out and he accompanied his Scandinavian wife. The soft candle light was kind to their advancing years and despite his stiffening fingers and her ageing throat for a few magical hours they both sounded like the old pros they had once been.

The wassailing in the form of foamy black pints, shots of amber Bushmills and lethal fruit punch had everyone singing along in the evening. Then late into the night they told family tales gilded and embellished by time and distance.

Willie warmed to see how readily his father David had joined in the merriment and tale-telling. Sometimes he talked a little too much. But that was just the sign of an old man growing lonely in an empty house. He wondered whether he should ask him to come and live at Cloughgreen?

The winter days in the southwest of Ireland had been kind. The Gulf Stream drift flowed offshore promoting an almost spring-like climate. And Willie was amused to notice that many of the houses, including the Carberys', had the plumbing outside.

Willie's father was still a photo nut from all those years back when he'd taught him the basics. On their daily walks Willie let him use some of his pro kit. Dr Dee was like the proverbial kid at Christmas.

Back in the Fifties he had been the sort of keen amateur who belonged to a club. He'd vied with other members to see who could produce the sharpest, most detailed black and whites of icicles on trees or tree rings. That sort of amateur club stuff, anyway. Like most of his mates Dr Dee had been an equipment junkie, marvelling at the science of new cameras, faster lenses and faster films. Even though they could only afford to read about most of the new stuff coming out. Now he couldn't get over how much digital manipulation you could do inside the camera and how you could switch from ISO 100 to ISO 1200 at the touch of a button.

While he and his dad were playing around with his cameras Nelson romped with Misty and Magic, the house Labradors. And not for the first time Willie wondered if the world would not be a better place if it were run by easy-going Labradors. Plenty of food, a good walk, a play every day and affection, what more could any sensible being want?

When you took on a lab you got a loyal companion and a needy walker. Deal. If you welched on the walking that was when your trusty companion started to literally eat the furniture. Seemed reasonable.

The day before they left Balmally Castle he phoned Jumper to ask him to use the spare key and go and turn the central heating on. Jumper was happy to oblige - Black Rock Farm was only 400 yards up the lane - and offered to get in fresh milk, eggs, bacon and bread for their breakfast.

Jumper had been exercising Bushmills, Bolly's chestnut gelding, and reported he was fine. He also reported that snow which customarily fell like clockwork on New Year's Eve had fallen on the stroke of eight. Willie had groaned inwardly. Woolton Council were good at gritting and snow clearing the road between the tops and the valley bottom. But their small lane, if the hidden springs and snow iced over, was deadly. Even in a 4WD.

But here they were, rattling along the valley road, preparatory to swinging up the hairpinned 1 in 3 to the moorland tops and there was no trace of snow. The air was clear and still and the thermometer registered -2. The snow Jumper reported had melted while they were on the ferry. With exaggerated caution they crept up the winding road to the tops in low gear and then along their own narrow lane.

The world metamorphosed while they slept. By the following morning falling temperatures had generated black ice underfoot. When Willie stepped outside with Nelson freezing fog drifted around his ears. It felt cold enough to freeze his nose off. To see how cold it was he got into the Range Rover and started it up. According to the car's thermometer it was only -3. But small ice balls blew in flurries over the courtyard. With the wind chill it felt more like -10.

Despite the cold, Willie the photographer stood in awe of the brilliant white hoar frost. It knocked your eyes out. It was half an inch thick on trees, branches, gates and grass. Blades of grass had become five times their width. The frost jammed the blades up in regimented lines like soldiers shoulder to shoulder. Seed heads and husks resembled fabulously expensive crystal glass objects set on an icing sugar background; the dead black space between them like black jewellers' velvet. It was second nature to fetch the Nikon.

He rattled off a few picture postcard shots of Greenwood Royd amid its new white architectural framing. Then while he was waiting for Nelson to chomp his breakfast he played about with close-ups of the hoar frost. He got down on his hands and knees and angled the camera. He whacked off a few with available light, which was pretty murky. Then some with fill-in flash to be on the safe side. When he worked he went into a sort of focused trance. His eyes and fingers melded into one organism moving over the subject, making unconscious decisions about how to see it. What sort of focus, what depth of field, whether to crop tight or pull back and go wide, a sort of practiced empiricism, seeing what worked. He had a 24-200 mil zoom fitted to the Nikon which suited this opportunist sort of work perfectly. If you could see the shot in your mind's eye you could frame it perfectly in the camera. Not that he was averse to cropping on the Mac later. But as with film, the bigger the original image, the better the quality. He was so engrossed in the changed nature of hoar-frosted objects that Jumper marching up behind him in his work boots made him jump.

'Sorry,' Jumper said, genuine old-fashioned manners coming to the fore. Alongside his purple nose, his face was pink from cold and his blue eyes were watering. He wore his customary farming gear, purple boiler suit plus several holey old sweaters beneath it.

'It's okay. Not your fault.'

'Just thought I'd tell you I'm taking some of the "lads" down to Blackpool for their holidays. Well, near Blackpool, on the coast at any rate. It's much milder this time of year down there. Cold winds up here do 'em no good. Mastitis and worse...' He waved back down the lane to where he had his livestock trailer hitched up to his old Army Land Rover. 'Give them a month away from this cold snap.'

For some inexplicable reason Jumper always referred to the remaining 50 ewes he'd kept on as a hobby as "the lads". They were mightily pampered lads, Willie knew, going into Jumper's barn in inclement weather. Plus they all enjoyed food supplements, being sheared and vaccinated/dipped at the right times etc. And when they lambed they all scientifically produced twins, too. Oh, yes, no messing about there. Jumper took a pride in them. 50 had been the smallest number he could retain and still consider himself a farmer. Thinking on what Jumper had said, about going to the mild Fylde coast, Willie decided Jumper's sheep were probably the luckiest sheep in West Yorkshire, given all the other poor sods who had to live rough on the moors. Holidays on the coast indeed for their health!

'Might stay over the night for a chinwag with old Harry up near Blackpool,' Jumper was saying. 'So if Bolly wouldn't mind watering Big Ruth tomorow morning and giving her her feed?' he asked, referring to his horse. Big Ruth his mare was named after Big Ruth from Burnley, his long-time on/off lover.

'No problem,' Willie said, automatically clicking off the batteries on the Nikon to save juice. Jumper and Bolly shared horse duty when the other was indisposed. It was a given. 'You'd better get going, get your trailer out of the way for the postie.' Maybe Jumper's hearing was starting to go, he thought. He obviously hadn't heard the postie's red Land Rover careering up the lane head to head with his Land Rover.

'See you later,' he said, hurrying off. Then he checked and turned. 'I kept the Cloughgreen Recorder for you. But there's nothing new about the wind farms.'

'Thanks,' Willie said, deciding to wait for the postie. The postie's Land Rover crunched up, outrageously red against the stark white hoar frost. Steve wound down the window and passed him a bundle of mail, tied with a red elastic band.

'Cold enough for you?'

'Yeah. Beautiful though.'

Steve, young and fashionably shaven-headed, grinned under his black woolly top and pointed at the Nikon.

'Surprised you don't take it to bed with you.'

'How do you know?'

'Best not go there,' Steve laughed.

Willie took the red elastic band off the bundle and flicked through it. Mostly bills and junk mail. Except for an envelope from his small gallery in Covent Garden. Dave Swinburne, his old assistant, who ran the place for him had sent him the month's figures. Reading them he frowned. Poor for the third month running. Counting Dave's wages and the overheads he was just about breaking even. Dave wasn't the sort of guy to rip him off, but there was something badly wrong. He would have to look into it. He'd never expected to make a fortune selling framed prints from shots he'd taken all over the world, just a little extra income. But whatever Dave was doing managing the gallery wasn't working. Maybe Dave was the wrong guy. But he was a useless photographer and he had two kids. What else would he do? He'd have to think about it, maybe go down and have a chat with him. He couldn't afford to run the gallery as a Dave Swinburne charity.

Bolly Dolly was hard at work on her PC, trying to wake the locals up to the dangers of total encroachment of all their high places. 'Use that phrase "ring of steel" you came out with at the library,' he told her and she beamed.

'Your're right, that sums it up pretty well. The whole of Cloughgreen surrounded by a ring of steel.' Then she frowned. 'The trouble is, it's not just poor little Cloughgreen. It's the whole of Ted Hughes's ancient kingdom of Elmet that's going to be groaning under concrete and steel. If these bastards have their way they'll swamp the whole area with them. You remember what Newall said about us being in a unique position to make us wind farm capital of the UK?'

He nodded.

'Well, he's well on the way.'

Later, when Willie reviewed his hoar frost shots, he was disappointed. There were some perfectly okay chocolate box shots, but that was like shooting fish in a barrel. He rejected 99.5% shots these days. You got one shot that genuinely rocked you back, then that would definitely work for the punters, too. Didn't happen often though, if you were honest with yourself.

Dr Newall thought Oliver Cromwell had the right idea about Christmas: banish it. The mistake had been bringing it back. It just interfered with everything in an artificial sort of way. Stopped business. Promoted artificial expectations in people. Got people pissed and saying things they shouldn't have. Encouraged people to spend money they didn't have. Just generally got in the way.

It was hard to pinpoint where the last one had started going wrong. Christmas Eve wasn't too bad until Penny had drunkenly suggested they should maybe shack up together in the New Year. He had pretended not to hear that and gone to the loo - Gaia! What a prospect! Actually living with Penny Wragg.

But you couldn't claim that Christmas Day had been anything other than a disaster. He had given her a rather nice plaque of the Green Man for her flat. Which she'd loved. And a small bottle of Chanel. Then he had opened his suspiciously large prezzy - a portable TV.

Since he'd left uni and lived alone Planet Newall had been a TV-free zone. What did he want with all that reality crap and mental pollution? He had a perfectly good wireless anyway.

'There are some really good environmental programs on,' she said. 'I thought we could watch them together in the evenings.'

'It would interfere with my chess. Three nights a week I play a move in one of my three games, in London, New York or Moscow.' She just looked at him.

'But I don't play chess,' she said.

'But I bet you've got a wonderful telly already,' he'd pointed out and then she'd gone quiet. In the end she'd agreed to go and swap the wretched thing for a set of Beethoven symphonies conducted by Herbert von Karajan.

Then there was the turkey she'd insisted on buying "For our first proper Christmas together". Why she'd thought of doing this was beyond him since she could ruin boiled eggs. Must have been a sentimental rush of blood to the head. And everyone knew turkeys could be tricky to get right even for a good cook.

Presumably most people had an idea that some turkeys were bigger than others. When she'd come to put the turkey in his oven it simply wouldn't go. You'd have more chance getting an elephant into an eggcup.

'Oh, it's all ruined,' she howled. 'Now what am I going to do?'

Well, he wasn't Merlin the magician, was he? What could you do except hack it up and cook it a different way? He'd mentioned this and she'd burst into tears, grabbed her handbag and rushed off to the loo. Probably didn't have a recipe for turkey pieces.

When she returned 15 minutes later, she was more composed, though he thought he detected a whiff of gin.

'We'll just have to go out for lunch,' he said, taking control.

'We won't be able to get in anywhere now on Christmas Day,' she wailed.

'Well there's nothing in here,' he said reasonably. 'We can't have beans on toast on Christmas Day, can we?' Then he'd taken control and fetched the Yellow Pages and handed it to her. She'd ballsed things up, let her sort it out. 'Why don't you see if you can make amends, ring around, see if you can get a late cancellation.'

She'd made a bit of a moue, then realized that after all it was her who'd dropped them in it. It took her over an hour until she found somewhere, a pub over the border in Lancashire called The Quiet Woman.

'You're in luck,' the landlady had said. 'We've been fully booked for weeks. But we had two late unavoidable cancellations yesterday.'

The Quiet Woman was a big redbrick pub built between the wars with bow windows, several bars and lounges, a functions room upstairs and a big car park. Dr Newall noticed that most of the cars in the car park were of a similar age and condition to his old 2CV. Getting out and seeing the inn sign he nearly split his sides. The eponymous Quiet Woman was a woman in period dress, holding her head under her arm. Quiet? Positively silent. Penny harrumphed.

'Disgusting. What sort of misogyny is that in this day and age.'

'Go on, it is quite funny,' he said. 'In a non-PC sort of way, of course. And it is Christmas.'

Inquiring at the bar, they were directed to the dining room. They went through the frosted glass door into a large room containing crepe decorations, a Christmas tree and many trestle tables. It looked like a works Christmas do. For pensioners.

The landlady, having taken their money, shoved Dr Newall firmly in the back and propelled him to two empty places halfway down one side of the table. 'Come on, don't be shy, help yourself, the ale is part of your ticket price.'

Dr Newall noticed there were bottles of stout and big jugs of bitter spread down the table.

A blue-rinsed lady on his right patted the seat. 'Make yourself comfortable, lad. You're in Jimmy an' Vera's seats. They'll not begrudge you. Not where they've gone.'

'Where have they gone?' Newall asked innocently, thinking Bermuda, Lanzarote, Jamaica maybe.

'They've gone to meet the Lord. Hypothermia and pneumonia in that last cold snap.'

And so it went. Everyone was wearing their best suits and outfits. But there was a smell of elderly male sweat from ancient suits and talc and lilac water from the elderly ladies. Because of competing with Bing and his dreaming on the stereo and elderly voices shouting to make themselves heard the noise level was gale force. He had the feeling he was in the middle of a barely constrained sitting-down riot. There were a lot of pink cheeks and glistening eyes and pointing fingers. Penny had a swig from her flask and she was soon enjoying herself. The noise got louder as the booze went down. And good enough the stout and bitter kept on coming.

The soup was out of a can and slightly burned. The turkey was like dried-out cardboard, with congealed gravy. The overcooked, soggy sprouts smelt like rotten cabbage and poorly maintained geriatric care homes.

‘Right tasty, these sprouts,’ Dr Newall’s neighbour confided,‘ no problems with your dentures, are there?’ Everyone ate slowly, thoughtfully, savouring their Christmas treat, wondering if it might be their last. So when the Christmas pud came it was anchored fast in a moat of thickening custard.

Nonetheless, crackers were pulled, mottoes and riddles exchanged and most thought “it were a right good do”. As time stretched out Dr Newall desperately wanted to get stuck into the jugs of bitter or even Penny’s warm, illicit handbag gin. But he knew he had to drive home. He daren’t lose his licence.

They got home by six and by seven he’d drunk most of a bottle of Bell’s and blotted Christmas out. On Boxing Day the cheating bastard in New York beat him in their chess match. Had to be being coached by a Grand Master. So, another memorable Newall Christmas then.

But now, having got Christmas out of the way, was the time to start concentrating Cloughgreen’s minds on this wonderful opportunity for sustainable, renewable energy that Ursa Power offered.

He’d had plenty of time to prep his second letter and had decided to emphasize the need for real sacrifice not just doing simple little things like changing to long-life lightbulbs, recycling and stuff like that. He made a long list of things that in the great cosmic plan he considered to be trivial: long-life light bulbs, turning radiators down a degree, better insulation, only heating and lighting the part of the house you used, buying energy-efficient condensing boilers and washing machines and wind-up radios etc. It was all very well, but it wasn't heroic stuff like wind farms.

Humphrey Drumm smiled when he read Bolly's letter. Like most craftsmen he could appreciate other people's work. He liked the phrase "ring of steel". He would pinch it and use it in editorials for the Recorder and he would certainly print the letter. V. Dee, whoever you are, you can certainly turn a phrase.

Then he got out his copy of Ursa Power's proposals and compared them with the large area map on one of his office walls. By God, he thought, she is right, too. If they get their way there will be a ring of steel on all the high places around Cloughgreen. It will completely change the nature of the countryside.

There was more change being done to the English countryside, he thought, than at any time since the Enclosure Acts between 1750 and 1860. At that time there were over 5,000 individual Inclosure Acts, as they were then known, taking away common land from the ordinary people. In all about 21% of land in England was enclosed, amounting to nearly 7 million acres.

Humprey Drumm, opened his window, lit up a cigar, leaned out and exhaled. The difference then was that people realized the countryside was being drastically changed. This time, thanks to rogue planners like Newall, a government that favoured stealth and ruthless developers, it was all being done on the sly. One day people would wake up and find all the high and beautiful wild places where they went to recharge their batteries and stand and stare were occupied by whooshing, flickering piles of steel. And for not much in exchange it seemed to him. But then those quiet places were gone for all time. They would never be handed back. And God wasn't making replacement landscape.

He smiled absently at the ordinary people on the pavement below going about their business in this windy little town. After living in the south all his life he found the weather atrocious. Yet almost everyone here, women included, went bareheaded in most weathers. And it would be a brave man or a lunatic who took an umbrella into the rugby club. On the other hand, at the briefest sign of sunshine people stripped off and got into shorts and vests to make the most of it.

They were a quirky lot. But yes, he loved the people in this little Yorkshire town, stoical, hardy, down-to-earth and yes, occasionally belligerent. The dry local humour handled whatever life could throw at it, and he liked that. But some of these metropolitan bastards weren't playing the game. You can't fight what you can't see coming.

He puffed away, thinking be careful, Humphrey, be careful. Impartial at all times, remember. And if you believed that you'd never been a proper journo. Impartiality my eye. Little Cloughgreen was up against dark and powerful forces that wouldn't stand up to be fought, the sort of forces that preferred to come in by a back window and smother you in the night while you slept.

Well, we would see. It was all a matter of judgement, wasn't it? One man's impartiality was another man's bias. He stubbed out the end of his cigar against the outside wall and looked guiltily both ways before chucking it down on to the pavement. A small act of rebellion against the wowsers.

Then he closed the window and went through into the outer office with Verity's letter. 'Run this as the lead on the letters page. Sub it: "Town threatened by Ring of Steel,"' he told his assistant. Then he added 'Run it next to Dr Wind's latest effort.'

'Dr Newall?'

'Who else?'

The weeks between January and late April were golden ones for the Recorder. Circulation and Humphrey's mail bag rocketed as the pro and anti wind farm factions sought to influence the upcoming Cloughgreen council decision.

At one stage someone dug out a photo of what they termed "the gentle footprint of an industrial wind turbine". This turned out to be an enormous 17 metre diameter crater that was also 17 metres deep. About 56' in all directions.

It dwarfed the giant piece of plant next to it. Humphrey gleefully swamped most of the front page with it.

The following week someone ruminated on how many tonnes of concrete would be needed to fill these holes and how much carbon was generated making it. And how much carbon was expended making the turbines, transporting them and installing them and constructing the new roads needed to gain access to the site for the giant construction machines.

And so it went. People lamented the fact that all the rare peat - which in themselves acted as carbon sinks, absorbing carbon - would be ripped up.

V. Dee pointed out the scam of what the wind farm lobby claimed the turbines did and what they actually produced, together with a website to check the annual figures for all turbine sites. 'They don't do what they say on the tin,' she concluded. As the weeks went by Humphry came to admire V. Dee's turn of phrase.

There must have been well over 200 correspondents including local luminaries like Councillor Irene Vine. But the four most regular contributors because they were best-written or in the interests of balance were Carter Briggs (Chair of Friends of The Living Moorland), Dr Phyllis Bentley, V. Dee and Dr Edwin Newall. Dr Newall, furious at V. Dee, referred to 'him' in private as The Clap.

The first three contributors all wrote enormously factual criticisms stuffed with facts and figures. Dr Newall's messianic windy rants alleged "everyone" supported him and was on his side. Those who didn't were Nimbys, child-eaters, ignorant and spawn of the devil. Failure to make sacrifices would be frowned upon by stern-faced, unborn future generations huddled in the cold and dark after The Day The Earth Caught Fire.

Every factual argument the anti-wind farm people came up with Dr Newall sought to swat to the boundary. Myth, myth, myth, he lashed out. White was black, black was white. He even claimed an overlooking wind farm increased the value of your property. Many, many non-Nimby folk were queuing for the honour of buying next to them, he implied. Humphrey Drumm thought he was shameless. Still, in the interests of impartiality...

In a wonderful tease, V. Dee challenged Newall to establish a waiting list of these people and leave it behind the counter of a local estate agent. A fortnight later a gleeful estate agent confirmed they had no wind farm supporters yet queuing. Seemingly not enough Imbys close to the site.

Furious, Dr Newall swore to prove his point by establishing a wind farm supporters action group called Wind Will Win - WiWiWi.

'What?' Penny asked.

'WiWiWi - Wind Will Win,' Dr Newall had snapped.

Dr Newall knew he could always prove his point. Her duly convened the inaugural meeting of WiWiWi in a small room above a pub. As the meeting time approached he kept looking at his watch. He couldn't believe it when only 12 people turned up. 'Must be a big football match on telly,' he muttered to himself. He did a head count to be on the safe side. The 12 people included a micro turbine rep, 4 antis come to spy out the land, Kevin Duff, leader of the Bus Boys, Penny and a man and his dog. Putting on a brave face, Dr Newall sought the high ground.

'Let me begin by saying that contrary to myth and what you may have read in the Recorder I have it on good authority that house prices close to wind farms actually rise.'

'Hear, hear,' Penny yelled.

The man and his dog - a ginger, black and tan, 57-varieties dog - regarded Dr Newall thoughtfully.

'You'd lie that much for these things,' the man said quietly, shaking his head. Then he rose and led his dog through the ensuing silence to the door. The four antis took their lead from him and left in his wake. They had seen enough.

Defiant, Dr Newall rose again. 'Another collection of these myths is this health nonsense,' he said briskly. 'All totally unproven scientifically. Not a shred of evidence. No-one ever got ill by hearing a few whooshes of a wind turbine or seeing a few blade flickers. Not unless they weren't ill already.'

Strictly speaking, that wasn't quite right, Penny thought. The whooshes and the flickers did seem to go on day after day, week after week, year after year. And maybe that did wear you down. But she didn't say anything. That would have been disloyal.

At the next WiWiWi meeting there were two reps, Penny and Kevin. He adjourned the meeting downstairs to the snug and officially closed the organization.

Meanwhile, back in the pages of the Recorder, Dr Newall's few diehard supporters, while grudgingly admitting the turbines didn't always perform very well, maintained "Something Must Be Done". And wind farms were the only available something. So wind farms we must have.

All very well, thought Humphrey Drumm, but what really ought to be done? Ineffectual wind turbines weren't the only answer, never mind the right one. Even he could see the cost to the country's landscape for the minuscule electricity delivered was too high a price to pay.

Finally, V. Dee wrote a letter acknowledging that the scales had fallen from her eyes. Some people, obviously including Dr

Newall, would want to see industrial turbines erected wherever possible as a sort of Green icon or totem to beat the rest of us with and remind us daily of the Green cause. Because of this symbolic value, with them frowning down from all the high places around Cloughgreen, for some people it wouldn't even matter if the turbines were turned on or not. It would remind the rest of us that right-thinking people, including the government, were responding positively to global warming, so there, yah boo sucks. Up yours, if it offends you. A cheap, spiteful gesture.

Humphrey Drumm went further in his own mind. It seemed to him that people like Newall actually gloried in the fact that they were so ugly and obtrusive. Via the grapevine he'd heard of Dr Newall's scene at the library quoting Jonathan Porritt and how intrusive turbines were on the landscape. Shocking as it seemed, some people like Mr Porritt didn't want turbines to blend in. They positively gloried in the fact that they were in your face. Ideological reminder.

One Friday night in March Penny Wragg came over to Radical Road, clutching Chinese takeaway and wine, to be confronted by a grinning Dr Newall and a neurotic-looking sheepdog.

'It's called Bounder,' he said. 'For all sorts of reasons.'

'What's it doing here?' she asked, noticing an odd smell. 'And what's that awful pong?'

'He usually lives outside,' Dr Newall offered by way of explanation.

'Can't he go out in the garden now?'

'No, and we must be careful not to let him out without his lead.' As he spoke, the dog crept forward, cowed-looking. Hesitantly, he put one long-clawed paw up imploringly on Penny's brand new purple tights. As the fabric split into a hole he looked up soulfully at her. Please love me.

'Aaagghh,' Penny yelled and the dog fled back across the room and hid behind Newall.

'Poor Bounder,' Newall said sympathetically, before turning back to Penny. 'Don't worry. He's only borrowed. He's going back tomorrow afternoon.'

Next day was blustery but sunny. Dr Newall decanted the dog and Penny on the edge of Cloughgreen Common. He took the lead firmly and handed Penny the small point-n-shoot digital camera he used for reference pics.

'Right, follow me. This shouldn't take long.' He strode purposefully on until he came to a high point where one of the proposed giant turbines would stand. Then he looked at the great scuds of white cloud blowing along. 'Stand down there,' he commanded. 'Set the camera for "action". That should capture the photogenic clouds behind me.' Then he yanked Bounder tightly in on his lead, made him sit next to his knee, grabbed the back of his neck and held his face firmly to camera. 'Do it quick before the bugger moves,' he urged.

'Cheese,' Penny said blithely and snapped the happy scene. That would have done Dr Newall. But being a designer Penny fussed around and insisted on taking another half dozen. Sure enough, when played back one looked truly heroic. Dr Newall's pose was that of a Himalayan explorer with, inexplicably, a lost-looking, bug-eyed dog he'd discovered at the summit.

'Great,' he said when Penny showed him. 'I'll email this to that old windbag Drumm. Then let them dare say I want to sacrifice these foul green deserts because I never use them for recreation. What could be more recreational than this?' Penny smiled. Bounder whimpered. It's freezing up here.

Humphrey Drumm laughed so hard he nearly choked himself. A gift from the gods. By way of redressing the balance of the giant turbine footprint, he printed Dr Newall's pic equally large on the front page. He'd heard some colourful views in the pubs around town concerning Dr Newall's opinions. May as well let people see what the odious Newall looks like. For recognition purposes.

It was a bonus that the cowed dog also made him look like a dog-beater. On the Letters page inside he printed Dr Newall's refutation that he didn't personally enjoy the moors for recreation. Here he was with his dog on the very same moor he considered suitable for turbines. Later, when the turbines were installed, he would enjoy walks up here even more were it possible. By some oversight Humphrey Drumm "accidentally" printed Dr Newall's full address above the letter in the Recorder.

Shortly after the dog on the moors picture the first hate mail started arriving at Radical Road. Some of it was in red biro, some in green ink, some on purple notepaper, some in cutout letters from magazines. None of it was fan mail. Contrary to all environmental logic Cloughgreen overwhelmingly didn't want to be Wind Farm Central UK. Dr Newall was genuinely shocked. The iron entered his soul.

The following week he received a stout A4 manila envelope that clearly contained something semi-liquid. The smell told him it was excrement. Then overnight someone poured green paint through the letterbox of his front door and daubed ARSEHOLE on it.

The police were sympathetic but pointed out the dangers of petrol and how much bad feeling Dr Newall had stirred up. Petrol could be next. The only thing to do was fit an iron plate over the letterbox and have his mail redirected through the Post Office.

Okay, Dr Newall, thought. If that's the way you want it, but you neanderthals won't stop me. Just make me craftier. I was wrong to try and appeal to your better natures. Back to being a secret squirrel. Playing the long game. Applying the Mushroom Principle.

It was time to play his trump card against the despised V. Dee who seemed to have so influenced the arguments in the Recorder. His final letter, prior to the Cloughgreen Council meeting, stated that V. Dee was a global warming denier (how heinous was that?), loathed all wind power (how stupid was that?), supported only trivial ineffectual measures (how selfish was that?) and was a knuckle-dragging Nimby to boot.

Verity replied that in actual fact she was a climate change believer (there were anomalies about global warming); that she approved wind power turbines off-shore; embraced micro turbines which had only the footprint of a tree and made householders self-sufficient; that she embraced all manner of renewables and that the fact of the matter was that in smaller, highly populated countries both health issues and rare recreational land issues effectively made wind farms with their unpleasant side effects and demanding siting requirements totally unsuitable.

Humphrey Drumm printed this letter with a quiet smile. Verity Dee has got you again, Newall, he thought. You just seem to so underestimate people. After he'd put the letter in hand he decided to take an early lunch at the Crown Hotel. He walked over the canal bridge. The clean, fish-stocked water twinkled in the sunlight. Then he walked past the steam-cleaned creamy stone Town Hall and into the Crown Hotel. There were a few seedy-looking businessmen with scuffed, down-at-heel shoes already standing at the long bar. They turned to look when they heard the door snap shut but he looked right through them and proceeded to his corner, next to the ice bucket, at the other end of the bar.

One way or another, he supposed, the wind farm issue and the floods of correspondence would soon be over. Once the Council had made their planning decision. It had been his first big ongoing issue since he had been in the editor's chair and fantastic for circulation. People had been rushing to buy their copy of the Recorder as soon as it was published, in case they missed any new developments. What would be next?

The barmaid came up from the cellar and he smiled and pointed to the Black Sheep pump, his usual. He sipped the crystal pint and savoured it. They kept it well here. The whole wind farm correspondence had not been without amusement and some quirky points, he reflected. For some reason, for example, no women, apart from Penny Wragg, had written in support of the wind farms which surprised him. Then there was the guy who designed what he was pleased to call 'kinetic art'. These objects seemed to Humphrey to comprise giant-sized kiddy mobiles. Metal sculptures made out of 3-litre olive oil cans flattened out and welded together to make shiny tin sculptures which either moved in the wind or recycled water fountains. What was it with the olive oil cans? Was his ma frightened by a Spaniard chewing olives? Anyway this guy actually wanted an industrial turbine outside his farmhouse to swish "ever-changing, spontaneous light through the windows of his life" and bring him "the unheard music of the spheres" via subsonic sound. Loony tunes. The guy definitely needed to get out more, Humprey decided. However, he was the only person to categorically state he wanted to live near a wind farm.

One of the other high spots had been watching Dr Newall tie himself in knots over designating which moors around Cloughgreen were "good moors" or "bad moors". Good moors like those much loved at Waterloo Pike and the Hallow Stones he would designate too pretty to have wind farms. Bad moors, ie what he considered ugly ones, like Cloughgreen Common, were ideal for wind farms. One of V. Dee's letters alerting the populace to Dr Newall's far reaching vision of a wind farm on every hilltop, including the much-loved Hallow Stones and Waterloo Pike, had drawn a storm of disapproval. In seeking to deflect this very real ambition Dr Newall had unwittingly elected himself as a sort of wind czar for the whole of Elmet. Thus further antagonising the good folk of Cloughgreen who did not like the unloved and unelected setting themselves up to tell them what to do. Dr Newall's defining of the "good moors" and the "bad moors" had drawn even more fire for his arrogance and who was this planner to delineate suitable wind farm sites for the locals? Oh, how Humphrey had chortled at that, rubbing his hands and puffing on his cigar high above Water Street.

It amused Willie and Verity, too. 'Imagine relying on Dr Newall for aesthetic guidance,' he hooted. 'Like putting Attila the Hun in charge of nursery care.'

'I'm not sure I'd even trust him with recommending how far zebra crossings should be from schools or kerb heights. We've only his word he's any good at that.'

'The trouble is whatever he does there's always a hidden angle he wants to get away with.'

The pending council meeting to discuss the wind farm planning application galvanized Dr Newall into action. He'd met Ursa Power a few times over the weeks since his get together with Ilka

Bakunin at the library. It was getting close to Cloughgreen Council making their decision. April 21st was deadline day.

Bakunin and Kovalenko were in fine spirits, but became sombre and business-like when he said he had a checklist. He produced a typed list from his pocket which annotated specialist reports and tests that needed to be done.

'Most of these have been done, to some extent,' Bakunin said.

'But you should know we have specialist advice which has changed the way we are playing things,' Kovalenko said. 'We became a little uneasy with our legal advisers. They seemed too passive and had no real experience of wind farm situations. So we asked around and came up with a legal company that has made a name for itself getting wind turbine applications through.'

'You wouldn't like them, Edwin,' Bakunin said, smiling tightly.

'No?'

'Well, we don't. They are not nice people. Grandmothers, homicide and a quick buck come to mind.'

'Oh.'

'Frankly we find them pretty unspeakable. They are arrogant, extortionist and uncultured. But they are winners. And that is what we need.'

'We have changed our tactics a lot,' Kovalenko butted in. 'These people recommend deliberate obfuscation and diversionary tactics. Even some loose ends deliberately left undone, red herrings to chase. Anything to swamp the opposition and divert attention from some of the main issues.'

'Where we may have problems getting a satisfactory result they recommend not even raising the matter,' Bakunin said. 'So, for example, we will be deliberately vague with the hydrology report. We will say certain householders close to the site have deliberately refused access and to co-operate with sound checks...etc, etc. What do you think?'

'I agree,' Dr Newall said, smiling. 'Totally. Obfuscation sounds wonderful. What the eye doesn't see, the heart doesn't grieve over. Give 'em the old razzamatazz.'

'The Mushroom Principle again. Feed 'em shit, keep 'em in the dark,' Bakunin volunteered.

'You like that phrase, don't you?'

'A happy cow never sees its own backside,' Arkadiy Kovalenko added gnomically.

'I never heard that one before.'

'You wouldn't. I just made it up.' Kovalenko smiled wolfishly, teeth like enamel stilettos.

The three of them hooted with laughter and the vodka came out. No sign of the PR girl. Easy come, easy go. Self-service then. Still, these guys were okay. They were going to win. Which was all that mattered for the planet, for Cloughgreen, for Purity Valley and for Dr Edwin Newall, Numero Uno.

'Have you sounded out how things are with the planners at Woolton MBC, Edwin?' The blond MD was being earnest again.

'No, but I will. Tomorrow or the day after. As soon as I can get to see my contact. When I last spoke to her things seemed fine.'

'Her? Oh, Edwin, you dog.' Kovalenko the assassin and ladies man flashed his enamel stilettos again.

'She bats for the other side.'

'Excuse me?'

'She likes other women.'

'Oh,' Kovalenko said, disappointed. He helped himself to another consolatory drink and filled the other two glasses. Dr Newall lifted his glass and heaved it back in one, they way he knew he was supposed to. Time to leave while he could still drive. On the way out he had a thought. He turned and went back in, caught Bakunin closing his briefcase. 'One last thing,' he said. 'Call the Bus Boys. Get 'em out in force for the planning meeting. Show of support at the Town Hall.'

Bakunin grinned happily. 'Why not? They did a great deal handing out brochures around town. Then filling in all those pro-formaed letters of support - even if they do mostly live in Manchester and Oldham.'

He met Angela Snow at the same pub outside Cloughgreen as he had last time. The big green Kawasaki was warm to the touch as he passed. Here they were well away from inquisitive eyes and fellow planners in Woolton. It was a lunchtime Saturday. Just walkers and a few riders from the stables next door. The day was fresh and blowy, blue skies, a stiff breeze bending blue and yellow crocuses, laundry blowing on the washing lines behind the stable, good drying weather.

'So how's Ursa's app being viewed?'

'You know what Ernest is like.'

Dr Newall nodded. He did indeed know what Head Planner Ernest Maitland was like. Bachelor, tall, skeletal, pasty-faced vegetarian, late fifties, wore *pince-nez* and cardigans knitted by his mother, with whom he still lived. Smelled not too good, whether because of all the veggies, unwashed cardigans or plain lack of soap. Pillar of his Baptist chapel, though. What the Americans called a straight arrow. Through and through decent. By the book. Boring.

'Well, Ernest's a bit antsy about the hydrology and the old mine workings. Everything else seems more or less okay.'

'What about the environmental impact report?'

'Iffy but subjective.'

'And the peat, sound and sight line reports?'

'Well, he's implied they were a bit casual.'

'They're meant to be. Ursa are playing it that way. They deliberately don't want to raise any questions where they may look bad. If you don't want to hear the answer, don't ask is the line they're taking.' He sipped his gin and tonic and thought for a moment.

'It might be an idea if you implied it was because they were new to the game, a bit careless, before Ernest starts thinking it's anything more sinister.'

'Okay. Anything else? Am I earning my consultancy fee?'

'You're invaluable. But there is one other thing. The guy who's doing the Council's hydrology report?'

'Yeah.'

'Might he be up for reconsidering?'

Dr Newall frowned, put his head on one side. 'You know, conscientiously going back and ever so slightly amending his report more favourably if this is giving Ernest cause for concern.'

'Well, he's certainly no straight arrow, like Ernest. Bit of a Flash Harry, a joy boy, likes the good things in life. He might be up for it. But if he's going to stick his neck out then he'll really want looking after. I'm not putting anything in writing, just giving you a little inside info. But he really is risking his professional rep by putting things on paper. You must understand that.'

Dr Newall looked her straight in the eye. 'Money won't be a problem, I promise you.' He felt like James Bond or some undercover operative sanctioning a black op.

'He likes his motorcars. He's a petrolhead like me. Was admiring a new Jag coupe when I last saw him. Would that be within reach? They're not cheap.'

'I'd have to ask. But I would have thought so. What's a Jag between friends? When there are multi-millions at stake over the next 25 years.' Angie Snow laughed, hoydenish.

'You don't seriously think they'll take the turbines down then, do you? After 25 years? They'll just put in new bigger, better earners. Mark my words.' Angie Snow smiled her version of the planner's secret squirrel smile.

'Gotcha!' she pointed an imaginary gun at him with her fingers. 'Probably for the first and only time.' She laughed triumphantly. 'You really hadn't thought of that, had you?'

'You're right. It hadn't occurred to me. Been thinking of other things.' It surprised him he hadn't thought of it. But of course it was a natch. It was one up his sleeve for Ursa. Angie was right. The battle would have been won. Later it would be a breeze to get bigger, better new turbines in. Bigger, better profits ergo. The locals would have no stomach for a new fight. The council would have no cash to fight it all over again. Interesting.

Then he switched back to the matter in hand. 'Will you sound your hydrologist out then? About a revised opinion. Subtly.'

'Sure.'

Later that night he phoned Bakunin at Ursa Power. He outlined the possible deal. There was only the barest hesitation.

'That's it? A one-off bonus? Just a new Jag?'

'Well, a Jag coupe, that's what my contact thinks will get him salivating. We might get the report rewritten for less, of course, if you want to haggle.'

'No, no. If he's happy with that, that's fine. He's sticking his neck out after all. Let's try and get that hydrology report finessed.'

"Finessed". Dr Newall liked that word. Maybe these guys had more style than he'd given them credit for. He sat quietly for 20 minutes, listening to the tick, whirr and click of the 3 different wall clocks in his study: Moscow time, New York time, London time. Then he forgot all about chess and phoned Councillor Irene Vine.

Irene Vine had been a librarian most of her life until her greengrocer husband had a heart attack and drove his van into a 50-ton truck one starry January morning. Fresh veg rolling around him in the gutter, he was dead before most people's alarm clocks went off.

The insurance money and the money from selling the business had changed her life. She had been able to give up her job, pursue her interest in local politics and take foreign holidays. Young Greek and Spanish waiters had introduced her to a form of physical love which she found wonderfully pleasuring and satisfying with none of the messiness of penetrative sex. It had an ugly long Latin name but was absolutely delightful. Dr Newall seemed to find it equally appealing. Which suited both of them. And if she could further a younger man's career, then why not?

It was a casual arrangement that suited both of them, she thought, as she placed an A4 envelope on the dining table. It contained advance news of various council contracts she'd heard of and tendering details.

Dr Newall sometimes wondered what he was doing seeing Irene Vine, a small, plain middle-aged woman, romantically like this. But at the end of the day it was realpolitik. Irene Vine was very useful, knew all sorts of people, was aware of upcoming contracts and what they were looking for, opened all sorts of back doors for him.

After they had conducted their sexual affairs upstairs they usually came downstairs and drank a glass or two of wine together to put a civilized veneer on things. Tonight it was sweet sherry in thimbles, but what the hell?

'How do you think public opinion is, regarding the wind farm apps?'

'Since the antis circulated those brochures around town depicting the scale of the turbines *vis-a-vis* Blackpool Tower, Waterloo Pike, Woolton Cathedral etc and the map with where they would all go, then feeling has been very high. Most people don't have great imagination. But now they've been shown how colossal the turbines are and how they will dominate the landscape ordinary people just don't want them. They hate you as much as they hate Ursa Power, thanks to your letters in the Recorder.' Dr Newall smiled a tight little smile, thinking of his closed-up letterbox. He knew that all right.

'But the councillors know better surely. They will vote for a renewable sustainable future?'

'I will of course. But I don't know about the others. Some people are genuinely worried it will kill a successful tourist initiative. Over the past few years the tourist centre and its work has brought loads of people into the town. They eat and drink at the pubs and cafes, buy cheap shirts and trainers in the market. They browse the other shops and buy souvenirs and stuff.'

'What? They come here to see our played-out green deserts?'

'In droves. You'd be surprised. Lots of people come to walk. A lot more come to run the fells. Some come mountain biking. And the town's actually on some 5-day horse riding tours.' Dr Newall swatted an invisible fly.

'What about the other councillors?'

'Well, some reflect local feeling, they're traders themselves. One or two are sympathetic to sustainables. But others are plain nervous of re-election next year.'

'But they must vote the turbines through, surely?'

'Well, we'll see,' Irene Vine said, 'But don't bet your house on it. There are a lot of twitchy councillors out there.'

'But they must,' Dr Newall said, his voice rising.

'The voice of reason says we should have them, Edwin. And doubtless your planner chums and people in academe agree. But ordinary people plain don't like them. Not if they are going to interfere with their enjoyment of the landscape or overlook their homes. In theory they're a great idea, but the reality is they're often hideous eyesores. If they could be hidden away it'd be alright.'

Dr Newall looked as if he had a bad smell under his nose.

'No,' he placed a clenched fist on the table, 'they have to be here, standing high and proud. Erect.'

'Never mind.' Councillor Vine patted the manila envelope on the table, 'There are some wonderful opportunities coming up in Olderroyd and Reddingley for a man of your talents.'

'Right now these wind farms are more important than anything else.'

'I don't want to upset you, Edwin. I know how high-minded you are and how much this means to you. But we live in a democracy. Part of me feels it's wrong that people living far away should be able to impose these things on the people living next to them. Politicians in particular. No matter how good the cause. That would be a sort of green fascism.'

'Whatever,' Dr Newall snarled.

# 11

The gang were all there on April 21st at 7pm. Inside Cloughgreen Town Hall the audience was gathered for the council vote on the Ursa wind farm application. Every councillor was up on the platform sitting behind a long table and looking suitably grave. No apologies for absence. Local feeling was so high they knew they would have been expected to attend on deathbed stretchers if need be.

Willie and Bolly were there. Carter Briggs and Dr Bentley were there. And Dr Newall and Penny. And the Ursa Power guys. And Gerry and Jumper. And Kevin Duff, the diehard leader of the Bus Boys, with 40 of his lads. And the loony tune who wanted an industrial turbine blasting flicker and ultrasonic noise through his house so he could hear the music of the spheres. And so many of the locals that another hundred extra chairs had to be found and brought in. Many of the audience wore "No to the Wind Farm" badges. The Bus Boys all had lookalike green tee-shirts saying Yes 2 Wind.

The place was buzzing. A couple of bobbies leaned against the rear wall watching it all with bemused amazement.

'Bet this old place hasn't seen such commotion since 1847,' Jumper said.

'What happened then?' Bolly asked.

'The council met up to discuss the enactment of the new Ten Hour Bill.' The other three looked blank.

'The new Act limited the working day of children in the mills to ten hours. Plus the mill owners had to agree to contain and eradicate contagion. And to provide at least one hour's Christian education every Sunday. There was uproar. It was all deemed very onerous, catastrophic even. Many mill owners prophesied economic ruin.'

'But a ten hour day... that must still have been terrible for the kids....' Bolly said

'Remember it well, do you, Jumper?' Gerry asked, grinning.

'Those who can read can still read about it,' Jumper said sniffily.

'The mill owners scraped through, of course,' Willie observed.

'Bet the profits took a hit, though,' Gerry said.

'Gerr-y-y-y...' Bolly began, when the Chairperson's gavel smashed down and there were cries for hush.

Eventually the Chairperson settled them all down and they heard planning applications for a loft extension, a two-car garage and some illuminated advertising signs. They were discussed somewhat brusquely Willie thought, as he watched proceedings. They all went through on the nod.

Dr Newall's eyes were on Councillor Vine. She didn't look happy, he thought. Her round face showed bags under her eyes as though she'd slept badly, her short black hair seemed greasy. And the mid-blue suit she'd favoured, tied tight around the waist, made her look like two sacks of potatoes on top of two stumpy legs. She suddenly looked her age. Her air was one of beaten resignation and Dr Newall suddenly knew, despite all his efforts, they were going to lose.

The Chairperson formally announced the Ursa Power wind farm application and made a brief introduction and mention of the issues. Then each of the councillors made a short statement of their views. It was plain which way the vote was going to go.

After each of the councillors had their say the Chairperson called for a show of hands. The Cloughgreen planning application for Ursa Power was rejected unanimously.

Suddenly the staid old Victorian town hall with its impractical high pale blue vaulted ceiling and chocolate marble columns was transformed into a football stadium. Cheer after cheer rang through the fusty Victorian space. The people had spoken. And been listened to by their elected representatives. Democracy had triumphed over the greed of the few and the dogma of the distant: there would be no ring of steel towering over little Cloughgreen. The people had won!

'We did it!' Bolly yelled, eyes glistening and on her feet like the rest of the assembled audience. Willie smiled wanly. It wasn't over yet. The councillors beamed down benignly into the hall - See, we came through for you. What a crowd pleaser we delivered!

Up on the platform, only Irene Vine, smoothing her two potato sacks down with red, wrinkled fingers, looked dismayed. She sought out Dr Newall's eyes and shrugged slightly - I tried.

The anti-wind farm supporters were chattering happily, the release of tension after all these nerve-racking months was palpable.

Dr Newall and the two Ursa directors strode briskly to the door with a couple of heavily-built men in attendance, scanning the crowd.

Then the two coppers moved gently forward. 'Right, let's be having you please, ladies and gents. Can we clear the hall, please. The caretaker still has work to do. Give the man a break.'

Bolly, Willie, Gerry and Jumper exited the fake Greek temple between the pillars, beneath the frieze of long-dead

Cloughgreen worthies in fake Greek cloaks. As they came down the steps Newall caught their eye. Their ignorant joy enraged him.

'You haven't won yet,' he yelled. 'This will be kicked out by the real people. The people who understand stuff like this, the planners in Woolton. They won't be a pushover like these nobodies.'

'God that man makes me mad,' Bolly said. 'He is just so hateful.'

'Don't let him get to you,' Gerry said, deliberately looking straight ahead, away from the little Ursa clique.

Willie looked past Dr Newall to Rent-A-Mob. 'Who's the short fat guy with the red face and greasy black hair, giving me the hard eye? What's his problem?'

'That's Newall's first lieutenant, Kevin Duff, the other poison dwarf,' Gerry said.

'He's staring at you like that 'cos you're everything he's not,' Bolly said. 'Tall. Clever. Good-looking. Successful. You fighting the wind farms gives him a reason to hate you.'

'He's the bloke I was telling you about. Not very bright. But bordering on alkie and very resentful. Bad news.'

'The trouble is, Newall may well be right,' Willie said. 'After all, there's nothing in it for Woolton for supporting us. If they don't put these bloody awful things here the government will force them to put them somewhere else in the borough. If they put 'em here, it's out of sight, out of mind, it's a long way from Woolton and Woolton voters.'

'He's right, lass,' Jumper said. 'I've lived here seventy years and Woolton's never been a friend to little Cloughgreen. No, the fat lady hasn't sung yet.'

The foursome went to the Happy Dragon for a Chinese banquet. But Newall's outburst had rained on their parade. The feast turned to ashes in their mouths and they felt guilty leaving wonderful food on the table.

'Food no good?' a worried waiter asked, wringing his hands.

'It was wonderful,' Bolly reassured him, 'just no appetite.' They exchanged sad smiles and he started to pile the plates up.

It came on to rain while they were eating so they had the waiter order Ali's cab. They dropped Gerry off half a mile up the road at his place in town.

Then they settled into the 5-mile drive back up to the tops and the moors, the streetlights vanishing and darkness descending.

'Theoretically Woolton should take our Council's view into account,' Willie said. 'But as that smug bastard Newall implied, the real decision in Woolton will be taken by planners, people just like him. Could be his mates for all we know. And the other thing is, we're effectively in the hands of strangers again. People who don't care two hoots for Cloughgreen. People with a different agenda and for whom the decision will have no personal impact whatsoever. That's what's so wrong about how all this works.'

That killed the conversation in the darkened car. Just the sound of the engine and the regular clunk-clunk of the wipers. No-one said another word till they let Jumper out in the lane at

Black Rock Farm and bade him goodnight. After he got out he turned round and Willie wound the window down.

'He wouldn't have lasted, you know,' Jumper said.

'Who wouldn't?'

'Gerry. If he'd been one of those mill kids back then. They'd have broken his fingers. Then they'd have broken his heart.' That said, he turned around and disappeared into the darkness of the path to his farmhouse.

Ali drove on 50 yards. Then turned the mist-green Rover around in the cobbled courtyard that separated Greenwood Royd from its barn/gallery. The tyres made squelchy rubbery noises in the quiet night air, as Willie fumbled for his wallet.

Once inside Bolly could see Willie was feeling down. 'Come on, Gerry's right. We shouldn't let Newall get to us. Let's drink to tonight's victory and enjoy that. There's still time to stage a few things to try and get Woolton on side.'

Then she took two champagne flutes off the top of the white grand piano and a bottle of Bolly from the fridge.

Willie petted the ever-enthusiastic Nelson while they sipped the champagne. They could have drunk all night and never got drunk. At the end of the bottle Willie got up and took Nelson outside for his late night pee. Bolly climbed the creaky oak stairs to bed.

She wiped her makeup off and brushed her teeth. Then she flossed out the stubborn particles of sweet and sour pork. Why was it that pork stuck to your teeth?

She hadn't really known Willie when she'd married him 6 years ago. Like many marriages it had been a bit of a gamble. She had known him as a kind, slightly taciturn man with fierce attention to detail who was a hugely successful photographer. He was confident and knew his way about town. He had access to the best restaurants, clubs, wine bars, good-looking models and hard-to-get tickets. He even knew how to get cabs on a rainy day in London. He made life look easy.

Only later did she realize how vulnerable he was to depression on the rare occasions when he felt he had failed or that something beyond his immediate control made him feel impotent. Maybe all successful men were like that; she didn't know.

What she did know was what she could bring to the marriage. Not just happiness when things were going right, but solace and warmth when they weren't. If he couldn't sort some things, then it was down to her.

She flushed the loo and walked into the bedroom, hearing the backdoor slam downstairs as Willie brought Nelson back in from his late night pee.

She took her "special" perfume from the dressing table and squirted some on her neck, cleavage and a little lower.

Then she got into bed and waited for him, listened to him going though his ablutions in the bathroom the way Nelson did.

While she waited she ran over his conversation-stopping remarks in the car. She could understand his dismay. It was the futility of the gesture politics the government wanted to enact and being made to feel helpless by distant strangers who cared nothing for what they would destroy. The prime minister was like some Caesar catching on to the fact that part of the populace liked watching Christians being sacrificed. He had found a crowd-pleaser. So, go grab some Christians and make a big show of feeding 'em to the lions. It was an unpleasant feeling, being these latter-day Christians forced to make an unwilling sacrifice to appease the Green mob. Kill the Nimbys so the rest of us can feel good! They're only Nimbys, what the hell. Nimbys are untermenschen.

Finally she heard the bathroom door click open. She leapt out of bed to the window and twitched the curtain open a little at the top to let moonlight flood in on the bed. She knew he liked to look at her. Then she flicked the light off and got back into bed.

He undressed slowly without turning the light on. By the light of the moon he looked morose, even the famous Golden Boy curls seemed to hang heavy.

As he got under the duvet she said 'Look Willie, like Newall said, it's not over yet. We'll come up with something they can't foresee and can't possibly ignore. You'll see.'

'Will we?' he said miserably.

'Yes,' she said, pushing her warm breasts up into his face. 'Come inside.'

Moving her breasts over his face aroused him quickly and she soon felt urgent stirrings against her thigh. He was a big man in every way. She waited until he'd entered her then she raised her bottom and did that little half twist with her hips that let him slide all the way in. Then he was moving inside her. His phallus was so enormous it kept on advancing until it felt as though the whole penis glans was inside her womb.

And yet for her it felt satisfying, the perfect fit. Tonight wasn't about a performance or making demands. It was comfort sex.

Even at 55 he was built like a stickleback under his denims, no flab. She held onto his jutting hipbones as he plunged and soared above her, occasionally making circles. Like most guys she'd known he had his own style. She let him go at the pace he wanted, move her as he wished, and her mind drifted...

Wouldn't it be amusing if all the romantic outpourings of the poets and songwriters in the end came down to just plain good old human geometry? A basic, enduring sexual attraction that was made satisfying by a perfectly sized carnal male/female coupling. That really it was all about sexual geometry and getting your angles right and having a good fit. Just fleshy plumbing, really. How prosaic was that?

Then her mind drifted to the old Beautiful South song, Perfect 10.

If he's extra large, well I'm in charge
I can work this thing on top
If he's XXL, well what the hell
Every penny don't fit the slot

She smiled as another irony occurred to her. The Beautiful South was an ironic name dreamed up by a band from the north. Hull was it? As a joke about how southerners perceived the south. The joke was, the southerners didn't know it was ironic.

Willie came with a mighty surge and a groan and she touched his shoulder lightly. 'Stay inside for a little while,' she said. And he did, falling asleep, emotionally and physically spent.

Dr Newall and the lads from Ursa Power tied one on in a Cloughgreen hotel, vowing for better things in the council which had the final say, Woolton MBC. Angela Snow would see them right.

He'd taken Kevin Duff along as a treat. The leader of the Bus Boys often seemed to sport frayed collars and thin, holey shoes. On his milkman's wages Dr Newall didn't think he enjoyed too many meals out. Besides he liked the way Kevin referred to him as "Boss".

With the exception of Kevin the party was sanguine. They all expected they would get the app passed by the bigger, more distant council. If not they'd appeal to the Planning Inspectorate. Kevin didn't say much during the meal, perhaps overawed by the two powerful Russians. But like a faithful dog he could sense his master's mood. As they were paying the bill he leaned forward towards Dr Newall.

'Burn 'em out boss, that Verity Dee and her bloke? Know where they live. Big place on the tops. Torch 'em, boss?'

Dr Newall was horrified. Kevin had taken the Nasty Newall route his father would have ventured. Raw violence. The two Russians also looked aghast, although Kovalenko then grinned.

'No need for that, Kevin, we're gonna win anyway,' he said, leaning forward and squeezing Kevin's bicep gently. Manly stuff.

'No, no, not at all. Leave them be,' Dr Newall belatedly managed. Kevin's chest deflated, he looked at the table. Only wanted to be of service.

Looking at him, Dr Newall felt pangs of sorrow. The wind farm crusade had become Kevin's religion, his vocation, his whole life. Saving the planet made him feel important. It beat getting up at four in the morning and trundling milk bottles around. But it led to him losing judgement. The wind farms, he suspected, had become so important because there was nothing else in his life. Kevin was useful, and he would use him; but it was sad for him to have nothing else.

Kovalenko was pressing another large brandy on Kevin. 'For you, please,' he said, grinning, 'the hero's drink.' Then he poured himself another large one. 'Here,' he said, linking arms, 'we drink it like this.' Kevin smiled again, pleased to feel valued. The two men of violence knocked their drinks back.

Eventually the bodyguards drove Bakunin and Kovalenko's cars back to their hotel in Manchester. After handshakes all round, Kevin Duff trudged off to his flat the other side of the park. Probably no cash for a cab, Newall thought. Masochistically he decided he'd walk the half mile home in the heavy rain from the hotel. He saw the coloured haloes of the street lights through wet lashes and watched the water gurgling along the gutters and down the grids. He liked the feeling of the rain coming through his shirt and suit. He'd failed, been beaten, he should feel pain, suffer. If nothing else, his public school had taught him that.

Deep down he knew he hadn't been beaten, not really. They'd win the all-important next round in Woolton when the planners at Woolton MBC, the pros, got involved. So nobody had won tonight, not really. It was immaterial what Cloughgreen Council thought. In the end it had to be passed up to the bigger metropolitan borough for yea or nay. And even then Ursa could appeal further to the planning directorate in Bristol.

But he'd hated listening to the, selfish, ignorant, know-nothing Nimby mob cheering and thinking they'd won. Throwing their sweaty nightcaps in the air, as Shakespeare might have said. The mob. He loathed and hated the mob. Potential dwarf-throwers all of them. Seek out anyone different and do them down. But one clever individual could always outwit them. Oh, yes. Ultimately Dr Newall would triumph.

He was surprised at how upset he felt. Normally with any slight reverse he went home, turned on some soothing Bach, had a large gin and tonic, and felt better within minutes. Forgot about the moral pygmies.

Tonight he didn't bother with any of that. Just hung his wet clothes up, dried his hair and face and started to brush his teeth. The smell was revolting, curdling on his gums so he dropped the toothbrush. Shit, what was that? He peered drunkenly at the toothpaste tube he'd picked up. Screwing his eyes up, he made out the words "female depilatory". Gaia! The silly cow had left her leg smoothing kit next to his toothbrush. She would have to go.

Around 4am his eyelids started to flicker like panicking butterflies.

The music was bouncing off the walls of a big house in Cheshire's stockbroker belt. Some early Stones stuff with that heavy, clanking, metallic rhythm. The lighting was dim and it was that time of the party when most people were so pissed and self-absorbed they didn't care what anyone else was doing. The whole house smelled of spilt ale, spliffs, cheap red wine and the excited sweat of both sexes. Manchester jeunesse en fete. Someone's rich parents had been foolish enough to go on holiday without their student offspring.

He didn't know anyone there. They weren't his techie crowd. But he'd heard about the party in the pub earlier and sidled along later. By which time whoever opened the door was too pissed to care whether they knew him or not.

And within half an hour he'd got lucky. He didn't know who she was, though he'd seen her around the campus. By the way she looked and carried herself he guessed she was an arts type.

The lights were low and couples were pairing off. The woman he was with said she was called Frances Hunter. She was a large raven-haired beauty with violet eyes and pouty red lips. Slightly overweight, to be honest, with huge matronly bosoms and hips. And generous calves bowed slightly from too much horse-riding. She was rich and classy. His insides turned to water at the thought of burying his face in all that warm soft flesh. He had a hard-on that felt like it could push walls over. He was lost for words. Felt he could barely speak for lust anyway. Didn't trust himself.

She was smiling at him lasciviously. Then she made it easy for him. She grabbed his hand. 'Come on,' she said, 'What are we waiting for?'

With that she led him from the room, her happy prisoner. As she led him off upstairs, the jangly early Stones music receded.

Eventually they found an empty bedroom and she closed the door behind them as she dragged him onto the bed. 'Come here, you beautiful man,' she said, pulling his head down towards her.

Up close her hair smelt wonderfully like a wood after rain, fragrant but pungent, warm and animal. Her lips were soft and seeking and he thought his heart would burst.

At first he thought it was a streetlight, but then he realized the traffic was just a distant hum. So it must have been an outside security light that gave the room just enough light to see by, a soft, intimate light. Enough to peek by, but not inhibit.

As things progressed, she spoke softly in his ear. 'Hang on a moment'. She moved away a little and wriggled so that her tight purple dress rode up around her hips, then she quickly dragged her tights down, revealing acres of plump, luscious white thigh.

He caressed them and she started to moan a little, eyes closed. He reached behind her and gently moved her zip down to her waist. He was rewarded by the sight of the most enormous piece of female support he'd ever seen. But it was black and lacy at the top and it contained the sort of curves he'd only dreamed about. An airbrush artist's wet dream. Fumbling with excitement he slipped the strap down over her shoulder and scooped one breast out. It was alabaster, heavy in his hand and surmounted with a giant red strawberry-sized nipple. He assayed a gentle kiss and it became darker, warmer and bigger. The world was closing in on him. It was just her warmth, her smell, her lips and his urgent cock. He could feel his blood pounding around him.

'Get your pants down, quick, I can't wait,' she whispered.

Now he was clumsy, fumbling with excitement. But he managed to drag his pants down and with them his jockeys.

Slowly she opened her eyes and looked at him dreamily, with heavy lids. Then she opened them further.

'My God! she said. 'Is that it? It's only 3" long. You're deformed. Get away from me. I can't do anything with that.'

His erection started to wilt, but then as he got hold of it to put it back in his pants it shamed him by shooting semen into his jockeys.

'Just take it away,' she yelled, pointing. 'Go. Now.'

He took the stairs down two at a time, his cheeks on fire, and charged out into the concealing darkness. Stickiness marring his groin, he ran and ran until he got a stitch in his side. But some things you can't outrun. No distance was too far. And there was the rub. No distance would ever be far enough again.

Gaia, it was like yesterday, he thought as he came shaking awake. Shit, he even had a hard-on, he realized, remembering the enormous ripe strawberry nipples and the luxuriant black bush. To his shame the lust burned as bright in his brain as the humiliation. That sight of her offering herself tormented him even when awake.

I'd kill her if I met her again, he thought. Either that or go ahead and fuck her anyway. Then he looked down at his hands, they were subconsciously held palm up, ready to cup her wondrous arse. To his everlasting shame he knew killing her wouldn't be an option.

The sheets were sodden, the sweat ran down his face and his heart raced. That bloody Frances Hunter. Met her once for an hour and he'd never forget her name as long as he lived. Every time he thought about going with a new woman he remembered bloody Frances Hunter. Putting his manhood up for judgement and being found lacking. That was her legacy. That was his ongoing torment. Why hadn't Colonel "Nasty" Newall, macho man, bequeathed him more? Betrayed again by the bastard.

Staying with Penny Wragg, although he knew she wasn't his fighting weight, was a sort of insurance against it happening again.

He knew he wouldn't sleep, so he got up, dressed and went across to his study. He placed Bach's Sonata no.6 on the music system, went to the concealed wall safe and took out a thick folder. The label on the front read: The Purity Valley Project. And there was a logo he had designed. The word Purity was laid along the top of a white picket fence, which in turn sat upon the word Valley.

After an hour of perusing the folder his equanimity was restored. It was fine imaginative work, even if he did say so himself. It encompassed all the latest green thinking plus the basis for a whole revolutionary new community with rules you signed up to. The Purity Valley Living Contract. A whole different unselfish, renewable, sustainable way of living which would include every sustainable device. Purpose-built houses would all have solar panels, micro turbines, stream turbines to channel water runoff from storm rain, underground geothermal pumps for heating and inbuilt recycling bays, spring water, cisterns, grey water recycling and a sewage system which produced fertilizer for the community allotments. There would be single-storey roll-in earth houses for those in wheelchairs. He wouldn't just build it and take the money. He would head it up and oversee the whole community of course.

Smokers would be banned. And he thought of banning alcohol to stop binge drinking, but he would be living there, so maybe not. Maybe it would be rationed for members. Birth control would be mandatory after the concessionary first child. Gambling would be banned. Red meat strictly restricted. Car ownership totally banned, except for the electric community car. All employment would be on site and within walking distance - mandatory. The use of electricity would be rationed and strictly metered - except for the executive, naturally. And there would be compulsory community gatherings to sustain the Purity Valley spirit and discuss new purchases and the ethics behind them. The whole site would be contained by the trademark Purity

Valley gleaming white picket fences which residents would be required to paint once a year. Again mandatory.

Cloughgreen, the site of the first Purity Valley project, would be the model for other green projects like it all over the world. He just had to get all the wind farms in and around Cloughgreen first. Then later, once he'd effectively changed the landscape, he'd go for the new land re-zoning he thought he could wangle. That would enable the Purity Valley community high on these green deserts. The wind was a tool which would open many doors still undreamed of. He just needed to have faith in The Long View and the mushroom principle, do good by stealth.

He even had the big property developer James Delahanty slavering in the wings. Yes, he was playing a long game none of the peasants out there could even guess at. And it would bring him fame and fortune. See if they were still so full of themselves then.

# 12

April 25th

Since their first meeting at Carter Briggs's house Willie and Verity had spoken to both Carter and Dr Phyllis Bentley several times by phone and email. But April 25th, 4 days after the Cloughgreen Council meeting, was the next time they had agreed to meet up again.

They had decided to meet at Dr Bentley's home. Her house was a large converted barn on the same side of the valley as Carter's house, out along the North Road. Willie drove the Range Rover.

Billowy white clouds gambolled over clear blue skies and it was warm for the time of year. Clouds of bilberries lined the sunken banks of the moors and farmers were turning their cattle out from the barns to pasture. A sign the really bad weather had passed. God was now in his Yorkshire heaven. Official.

'Should see the first house martins and swallows arriving soon,' Willie said. Bolly harrumphed, her thoughts elsewhere.

After about 4 miles Willie turned off the road onto an asphalted parking place surrounded by flower beds. Dr Bentley's rorty black Golf GTi stood at rest. A big silver Merc sports saloon gently nuzzled its hatchback.

'Carter obviously favours a businessman's express,' Willie murmured, as he nudged the range Rover in gently behind the Merc.

A small path led away from the parking area to the side of the barn. Halfway down the end wall of the barn was an entrance. The cheery red-painted door was open so Willie rapped it with his knuckles and walked in...to a big surprise.

Far from the traditional interior they had been expecting, the inside looked like an ad for loft living. The whole bottom floor was open plan with a seating area and small bathroom at one end and large kitchen and dining area at the other. A polished pine central staircase led up to a minstrel's gallery with bedrooms and a larger bathroom off it.

The huge wagon doors of the barn had been replaced with a massive arched pane of toughened glass. The view fell away over the valleys and rose to the ridge opposite with the giant grey obelisk of Waterloo Pike. At this distance it looked as big as a girl's finger.

Carter and Phyllis had been seated at the far end of the barn around the long occasional table. Now Phyllis rose from the settees and strode quickly to meet them, while Carter politely rose and nodded.

'Hi, Bolly and Willie, come on in,' Phyllis trilled.

Despite being around 65, Phyllis's sprightly manner continued to amaze Willie. Today she was wearing an oyster coloured roll top sweater with pearls above oatmeal slacks and tan leather mules. She had the trim, elegant figure of a woman who had exercised all her life. She looked vital and even sexy, Willie thought, and guessed there had been a fair few discreet affairs over the years.

Carter Briggs, wearing a double-breasted blazer and grey slacks, still seemed eye-poppingly large, like some genial front row rugby forward.

After the welcomes had been made, Dr Bentley ushered them to the dining table. They agreed that the Cloughgreen decision was great news, but only the first step. Newall had still to be watched for some dirty trick. Woolton MBC was a whole different thing to win.

'How are things going over there?' Bolly asked. 'Have you heard anything?'

'Difficult to say. The chief planner at Woolton is a dry old stick and is playing it straight down the line. Not giving anything away. But the planner at Reddingley is on our side. He told me that the joint landscape report they commissioned dealing with visual amenity and general environmental issues had been negative. He also said that Ursa Power had been very sloppy and casual about doing other tests such as hydrology, sound and ecology.'

'It's Ursa's first wind farm app isn't it?' Bolly said. 'Maybe they're just not up to speed yet and are under-rating us and the opposition.'

'Could be, but there's something a bit fishy about it,' Phyllis said, bringing food to the table. 'We've heard via the grapevine that Ursa fired their lawyers and have hired these specialist lawyers who specialize in wind farm apps and have a very heavy reputation.'

'Heavy?' Willie asked.

'The new guys seem to win a lot. They appear to be win-at-all costs, if you know what I mean. Heavy boots brigade.' Carter made a face.

'They definitely seem like the bad guys. Somehow, being naive and being in bed with this lot doesn't seem to add up,' Phyllis said, plonking down the last of the food.

She had served up a Ploughman's Lunch. Simple, but, Willie noted, everything was of excellent quality: sharp Cheddar, sweet homemade pickle, crisp lettuce, firm cherry tomatoes etc Served with bottled ale from the local micro brewery for the gents and a chilled bottle of Chardonnay for the ladies.

Phyllis was coming to the table to finally sit down when Carter stopped her.

'Sorry to be a pest, Phyllis, but you haven't got any of that excellent fig jam have you?'

'In the fridge. No problem.' She turned around and went back for it, returning with a squat round jar. Carter noticed their bemused glances.

'Have you not tried it? Concentrated fig jam, especially made to complement hard cheese. You must try it,' Carter said. So they did.

Bolly kicked off the conversation proper. 'Newall is forever prattling on about the cost to the planet if we don't have wind farms. And some people point to the increasing cost to the taxpayer of this expensive wind farm electricity. But the real cost is to all our wilderness places. Because wind technology is so inherently flawed you'd have to obliterate the whole landscape with turbines to achieve their stated aims. Who is going to explain to the next generations that we polluted all their quiet and beautiful places in exchange for gesture politics and obsolescent machinery we knew couldn't function unaided even when we erected them?'

Willie smiled. Attagirl. He was proud of the campaigner his wife had become. He only wished he could be more like her. But he would always be a watcher not a doer - until someone sought his help. Tell me what you want and I'll do it. That was his limitation and knowing it irked him. It seemed like he was leaving too much of the real work to Bolly.

'Well said,' Carter boomed. 'Which politician will ever take credit for destroying all our wilderness places?' He smiled ruefully.'I think we all know the answer to that one.' He paused for a moment. 'And in actual fact there are some new figures that make the damn things more expensive in every way to the taxpayer. I'll show you them when we've finished eating.'

'First things first,' Dr Bentley said. 'There is a lot more documentation I can supply to the planners at Woolton, which I'm working on now. But the question is what more can we do to influence popular opinion in Woolton and bring pressure to bear on the councillors? Left to their own devices you know the idiot planners will recommend Ursa's app go through, not least because of the government pressure to meet renewables targets.'

'We need some sort of PR stunt like you two did here in Cloughgreen with the ad agency chappie...' Carter mentally searched his contacts list.

'Gerry Stansfield,' Willie volunteered.

'That's the chappie. Anyway those two leaflets you did - the comparison chart with the giant turbines and the dwarfed local buildings. And the photo simulations of how they would dominate different local landscapes. They completely educated people and got them on side. "Raised awareness" I think is the current lingo. Well we need something similar for the people of Woolton. But closer to home. Nudge them where it hurts.'

Bolly beamed.

'I think I may have just the thing, but we'd need some technical help. From someone who knows a little physics.' Now it was Phyllis's turn to beam.

'That can be arranged. If it's not my sort of physics I have a lot of good friends in the physics faculty back in Liverpool Uni. Tell me what you had in mind.'

So Bolly told them and the other three clapped and hooted with laughter. If this didn't make the point to the good people of Woolton, nothing would. It felt good to be fighting back and taking the offensive. Instead of sitting mute and letting UKWC pump out its pernicious propaganda of gently revolving white blades and idyllic summer skies.

'Do you really think it can be done?' Bolly asked.

'I don't see why not. Physics dons are very clever people. And I should think the mischievousness of the idea will appeal to some of the younger element, too. you know, sticking it to pompous local government and authority. Although it's making some very pertinent points it could well be a bit like a rag stunt,' she chortled.

'We can use the Range Rover and I'm sure Jumper will lend us his trailer to accommodate the gizmo they come up with,' Willie said. 'Gerry will help me and Bolly to do some leaflets to hand out in Woolton, explaining what we're doing.' Willie was in his element now he'd got the brief and knew what was required. Doing things made you feel good. He also felt he had the smartest wife in Cloughgreen.

At the mention of Jumper's trailer, Phyllis's eyes lit up and she pressed both hands together and exclaimed 'Not Jumper Lonk?'

'Yes, he's our next door neighbour. You don't know him, do you?' Willie said.

'Oh, I know him well, from years back.' Bolly gave her a searching look.

'Not that well,' she said, laughing. 'He's the sort of man mothers used to warn their daughters about getting into taxis with. Or riding to hunt with, for that matter. There used to be a famous jockey who people said you should never leave in a closed room with any female you liked. Lock up your wives and daughters. That's Jumper.'

Then she broke into a broad smile. 'He's a force of nature. Mind, he's such a nice man. You can't help but like him.'

'Mmmm,' Bolly smiled. She shared Phyllis's views on allowing Jumper unrestricted female contact.

'He was a really good international horseman, you know, represented England many times at eventing. Big strong wrists. But it was the class thing that did for him, I think. The sport used to be very toffee-nosed then. And you know Jumper. He's pretty outspoken. Tells it like it is. It didn't go down too well in that company, in those times. Then there were other peoples' women, talk of caddish behaviour...'

'But he really was good? As a horseman, I mean.'

'Oh, definitely, he captained Great Britain a few times, I think. He was fearless. You'd meet him on the hills around here when he was younger and he'd like as not take a five-barred gate in his stride to avoid having to stop and open it.' She smiled quietly. 'And to impress the ladies, of course, if any were watching.'

'We're going to help him with his lambing any day now,' Bolly said.

'Yeah, I think this is the first year he's admitted he might need a little help,' Willie said. 'I've also noticed he's started using those old stone mounting steps in his yard to get up on to Ruth.'

'Well he may be a tough old bird, but he's not immortal,' Phyllis said.

'No, he isn't. Even that nip of Bells in his morning tea can't make him that,' Willie said.

After lunch they decamped with their coffee to the other end of the barn and sat on the settees and armchairs arranged around the long low table. Willie noticed a number of black and white photos on the walls in slim black frames. Phyllis back in the day. Skiing, riding, swimming and posing near sunny villas, smiling confidently in them all. They could have been Vogue front covers. Oh yes, once upon a time Dr Phyllis Bentley had led a few young men a merry dance, Willie guessed.

Carter fiddled inside his jacket and produced a warm, crumpled clipping from The Sunday Times.

'This is what I was telling you about,' he said. 'Written by their Environment Editor and quite a turn about. It seems people are at last getting the message, it just may not be in time for us. It's an even bigger eye-opener on the financial rip-off.'

'It seems that as the developers whack in ever more monstrous turbines the rake-off becomes ever-more bloated,' Phyllis said.

Carter waved his arms gently, calm down. 'I know, I know, but this is where this chap Leake starts to get to what matters. I quote "So far renewable power companies have erected 2390 turbines at 200 onshore sites. Another 5,000 odd are planned, with many more to follow. The power generated will be carried away by lines of pylons crossing Snowdonia National Park and areas of outstanding natural beauty in Anglesey, Kent, Lincolnshire and Somerset. For enthusiasts like Ed Miliband this destruction is the price England must pay..."'

'Who says?' Bolly demanded. Willie gave her a look.

'No, she's right,' Phyllis said. 'Who asked the people of England? The trouble is, like Newall, Miliband won't even see it as destruction and visual pollution.'

Carter nodded firmly. 'You're right, a short service commission and a real job for 3 years in the big wide world would soon knock some of our politicians into shape,' Carter said.

'Anyway, Mr Leake goes on "Alas, it's not the only price. A quick calculation shows just how lucrative wind farms can be for the lucky few. Take the output of a 3-megawatt turbine standing about 550'. In a good wind it can generate enough power to meet the annual needs of about 1600 households. The owner of such a turbine could expect to sell the 9,200MW of power generated in a year for about £331,000. Not bad, but the real profit lies elsewhere, in the form of little bits of paper known as Renewable

Obligation Certificates or Rocs. Under a government scheme, the wind farmer is allowed to "create" one Roc for each megawatt hour of electricity generated - and to charge the consumer for doing so.

'Currently each Roc is worth £48, so our 3MW turbine is creating an additional £441,600 each year, simply from the sale of Rocs. Add this all together and this one machine will earn £772,600 a year, or just under £20m over a typical 25-year lifetime - assuming the subsidies continue at the same rate. And it will have cost only £3-4m to build."'

Willie thought he was going to explode. 'Jesus, does that stink! Over three quarters of a million quid from just one turbine per year. And all for a minuscule amount of electricity and trashing what little countryside we still have left.'

Dr Bentley raised her eyes. 'He makes another good point which often gets forgotten. As well as the dratted turbines you need legions of pylons marching off across the beautiful places as well to deliver the juice.'

Carter Briggs raised his finger. 'It's good stuff, isn't it? Can I carry on?' The other three nodded.

'Mr Leake continues with a little how-they-work lesson for those who don't know. "The problem is this: wind does not blow all the time, so if Britain is to keep the lights on when the breeze slackens, wind power needs support from other forms of power. This means that for every wind farm we build there must be a coal or gas-fired power station waiting in the wings to take over..."'

'He might have mentioned that it's not just when the breeze slackens you need conventional power stations to take over. It's when it reaches gale force and they have to turn them off for fear of them being uprooted,' Bolly said, grinning. 'Useless bloody things.'

'Anyway,' Carter continued, 'Mr Leake points out that all these extra turbines in the wings will inevitably require the building of more conventional power stations to back them up and take over when the wind drops and they fail. Or they have to be turned off for gales.

'Finally, he concludes, "A couple of years ago, Ofgem, the energy regulator warned the government that the renewable obligations system was handing wind farm operators windfall profits that could provoke a consumer backlash - perhaps one as angry as the fuel tax protests of 2000.

'The fact that we're paying through the nose for this so-called green electricity is another problem with wind farms,' Phyllis said. 'But it will only raise its head when the great British public realises what a scam onshore wind farms are. In the interim, I'm with Country Guardian: the electricity yield is negligible, the price we pay is all our wilderness country.'

'Brandy anybody?'

Willie looked at Bolly.

'I'll drive. You go ahead.'

Willie and Carter opted for the brandy and the ladies had more coffee.

Carter visibly settled back into the settee.

'What gets me is the total inability of the politicians to say they got it wrong. I mean, fair enough, at first glance wind power seemed like a great idea. Some guys were even designing wind-assisted supertankers, but they were soon dropped because they didn't work.

'Industrial wind turbines simply aren't fit for purpose. You can write in seven words all their benefits.'

Bolly smiled. 'Okay, I'll buy it. Knock, knock. What are the seven words?'

Carter spoke slowly and deliberately: 'Wind farms. Produce. Minuscule. Amounts. Of. Carbon-free. Electricity'. On the other hand, you can fill two sides of A4 with the disadvantages and harmful side effects. No contest.'

'We've noticed you've got loads of micro turbines in the farms and barns around you. Like Carter's,' Phyllis said, turning to Willie and Bolly.'

'Yeah. Willie and I quite like them. They make people self-sufficient in electricity which is great. Like people in hot countries with solar power. And their footprint is no bigger than that of a tree. Eat your heart out Jonathan Porrit, micro turbines do nestle into the countryside - unlike industrial wind turbines.'

'That's where the government should be putting the subsidies - into micro turbines. Loads of people would go for that,' Carter said. 'One big snag, though...' he raised his hands as though to conduct them...

'...no big gestures for the government to show off,' Willie said.

‘It seems to me if you could plant them somewhere sterile like the Atacama Desert where there are no precious bogs or wild flowers or bats or birds or horses or people then they’d be fine,’ Bolly said.

‘Exactly,’ Carter said. ‘But in the here and now our written submission has to fight them on the specifics that exist on Cloughgreen Common. Which apart from special landscape considerations which are very subjective there are genuine real problems with the hydrology. Regarding the surface water run-off and possible flooding from the denuded tops. Plus the inability to pinpoint all the ancient mining galleries. Plus the fact that disturbing the lay of the water table will almost certainly cut off peoples’ spring water which most people up there depend on.

‘Obviously we will be putting in all the supporting stuff about the rare mosses and the nesting twites. And to support the health issue and problems caused by strobing, blade flicker and noise we’ve located Mrs Jane Davis who is happy to make a witness statement on our behalf.’

Phyllis waved gently at Carter who now took the lead. ‘I don’t know if you know about this, you two, but Mrs Davis made legal history when her local council near Spalding accepted the fact that the wind farm had degraded her property and so they reduced her council tax bill. Naturally the actual value of her farm has also been reduced. Well, no, let’s get real, not just “reduced”. Her local estate agent has declared it unsalable. Despite what Newall and yes2wind say. It’s common sense, isn’t it...’

Phyllis took up the tale again. 'Of course the Davises were driven out by the noise and blade flicker. They rent somewhere else to live and sleep and go back to work their farm during the day.'

'God that's just awful,' Bolly said. 'Why don't they print that on the front pages of the national newspapers?'

'Because UK Wind Commission's PR guys mostly smother it, as Charley Fort told us. It has been in the national press, just not big news. Whereas it should be a national scandal, people being driven out of their own homes like that.'

Willie shook his head and turned to Carter and Phyllis. 'Do you know in all the time since Charley Fort looked into this for us he hasn't managed to get a single adverse wind farm story accepted.'

'With those monster subsidies, it's mega business for developers in the wind industry. With, as we were just discussing, mega profits. They're gonna fight tooth and nail to keep the gravy trough full.'

Phyllis drained her coffee. 'I'll ring those guys at Liverpool Uni about producing your gizmo for the Woolton demo. I'll ask them to ring you two tomorrow if that's okay.'

'Sooner the better.'

Later that evening, as Willie took Nelson out for his late-night leg lift, he saw the first bats of the season exiting his barn. 'Wonderful,' he sighed, as they strung out into a long zig-zagging necklace against the moonlit sky. They moved so swiftly it was as if they were recklessly spending all the hibernated energy they'd accumulated. For Christ's sake steer clear of The Delf, he thought.

They were such gentle, elegant creatures. He fell asleep with his arm around Verity figuring out how best to photograph them. High-speed flash, obviously. But what special techniques...?

# 13

Overnight it poured down hard enough to fill the black rock basins on top of the Hallow Stones to overflowing. Nelson waded in, lapping greedily, the noise carrying in the early-morning stillness.

Gusts of wind raced in long lines through the lush, fresh grass. Maybe it was because the grass was wet but he discerned an almost electrical hum, as though the wind and water were generating an electrical current. He didn't dare reach his fingertips down in case he got a shock. One of his old mates would have put it down to ley lines. Whatever it was, Willie had experienced the sensation before and found it very unsettling. It was as though the static electricity field upset his own neural connections. Whatever, on days like this the feeling was both physical and unnerving.

The mega-ton black millstone grit boulders scattered over this big open moorland were monstrously grand. You couldn't survey them without being aware of mighty forces back in the last Ice Age hurling these colossal rocks around like dice and being in awe of that.

A Bronze Age torc had been found on the brow of this rise, where many of the giant boulders stood shoulder to shoulder thrusting themselves at the windy skies. Even on a sunny-blue-sky-day like today, this place had the stink of death about it. Legend had it the ancient fire-worshipping peoples had sent their sacrifices off this brow, rolling burning wicker baskets with their human cargo downhill to their deaths.

Distant race memories? He could believe it.

Whatever it was, there was a strange numinous feel about the place; but it had nothing to do with Christianity or peace. It was more to do with primitive power and awe. On foggy days up here with Nelson he found it downright creepy. This strange electric current racing through the grass made the hairs on the back of his neck stand up.

Not for the first time, he reflected, it was also wild and remote enough to have been a good murder location down the ages, too. There was a natural ambush place where Nelson's hackles rose and he hesitated. He felt it, too. God knows how many poor souls had been done in up here and their bodies dropped into the gaps and crevices of the giant rocks for the ravens to gorge on.

He shook himself and shivered and called Nelson away from his sniff. They strode briskly down from the high places onto the lower moors. Then they came to the pastures that had been taken in from the moors over the centuries, the intakes.

From afar off he could see Bolly was waiting at the back door . She saw him and waved madly. He speeded up. When he got to the garden gate, she could wait no longer and yelled to him.

'Dr Freddy Mount rang. From Liverpool Uni. He said Phyllis had spoken to him and he'd like us to go over now and meet him for lunch.'

'Today? Sunday?'

'He said Sunday was a good day for him.'

'Okay, let's go. What is it, about and hour and a half run?'

'Yep. I'll take the Mini-Cooper if you like and you can have a few pints. The run will do her good.'

'Suits me.'

They were out on the road within an hour. Bolly borrowed Willie's sat-nav and followed it to the motorway.

'Doctor Mount asked how we'd recognise each other.'

'And? Green carnations? Sunday Times in my breast pocket? What?'

'I just told him I'm a tall redhead with an unusual tanned freckly complexion and you look like a lanky old hippy in denims with curly blond hair.' Willie grinned, recognizing one version of himself.

'You're right. Not many combos like that around.'

'You been to Liverpool before?'

'Never. You?'

'Loads of times. While ago now though. When I was a kid we used to visit Dad's uncle Fergal.'

'What was he like?'

'Very Irish. Black sheep of the family and wonderful fun. He was disinherited when he was 18 and came over here on a cattle boat from Dublin, made his own fortune. Total reprobate.'

'Uncle Fergal sounds quite a lad.'

'He was that alright. I think he was a bit of a wild man when he first came over. Used to pull faces at policemen, get them to chase him and throw their truncheons at him. Then he'd duck, collect the truncheon on the run and drop it down a grid. Knowing they'd be embarrassed and have to pay for new kit.' Willie laughed.

'He must have led a charmed life.'

'Oh, he did that. He had lots of tales. But he was a very old guy when I knew him. Like a lot of Irish guys he came here and stopped. Never went back. Became a Scouser.' She paused and turned to look at Willie for effect, a habit he found unsettling when she was driving.

'He used to laugh about Liverpool being the alternative capital of Ireland. But he also had a theory which amused him.'

'Yeah?'

'Yeah. You know about Liverpool being famous for music...'

'The Beatles and all that...'

'And for drinking and good craik...'

'Yeah.

'And for being a rough old, violent place...'

'Of course.'

'Well, great Uncle Fergal, said that all these things, music, the talk, the arts, drinking and violence were just the things that made the Celts famous. More than that he said it wasn't only all the Irish, it was all the Scots and Welsh who've settled there, too. Hardly any English. He used to say all his drinking mates were called Finnegan, MacNamara, Mullaney or Monaghan. And some of the others were McLennan, Campbell or MacDonald. And the rest were Williams, Jones or Hughes.

Anyway he used to say Liverpool was the Celts' revenge on the English; a bolshie celtic city in the heart of England and more or less ungovernable.' She thought for a moment. 'He said they did a lot of keening, too.'

'What do you mean, keening?'

'Well, literally wailing in grief for a dead person. But metaphorically put, some people say Scousers whinge a lot. All part of the Celtic package.'

Willie hooted. 'Bet they love that. Did you ever go to a football match up here?'

'Funny enough I did, a few with Uncle Fergal, watching Everton. He had shares in the club or something and he could always get tickets in one of the stands.'

'Not Liverpool FC, then.'

She laughed. 'Good grief, no. It was a religious thing when he started going. If you were Protestant, you supported Liverpool. If you were Catholic Irish you supported Everton. Apparently there were nuns at the gates then with collecting boxes. And Irish priests on the terraces.'

'Division of labour? Nuns collect, priests watch the game.'

Bolly smiled. 'They were different times then.'

'Yeah, so was it good craik?'

'Excellent. Night matches at Goodison were so atmospheric. It was back in the days when everyone smoked. So the stadium was cloaked in a fog of mist off the Mersey mixed with blue cigarette smoke. You'd see cigarette lighters glowing briefly on the Gwladys Street end like fireflies as people lit up. Everton played in blue shirts, white pants and blue and white socks. When I watched them they weren't very good. So there was a lot of very funny Scouse black humour, which made it fun. But the older guys talked about the glory days when they won the championship in the sixties. They had this Scottish international centre forward called The Golden Vision.'

'The Golden Vision?'

'He was called Alec Young. Small for a striker, only about 5'8", but fantastically skilful. Could head into the top corner of the net from the edge of the penalty area. Sell dummies. Score from acute angles. Uncle Fergal showed me a video of him once. He really was something special.'

'Really?'

'Oh yeah, he became a sort of football god to the Evertonians. And then someone wrote a telly play about him called The Golden Vision. Anyway the atmosphere for night games was fantastic. Floodlights causing the mist to swirl, then there'd be maybe 50,000 chanting "Ev-er-ton, Ev-er-ton, Ev-er-ton." Exactly that rhythm. Like a blue and white zulu impi. Exciting stuff. Then if the opposition were southerners they would chant "All cockneys are bastards".

'Really?' was all Willie could manage. He had long thought of himself as an honorary northerner, but he suddenly wasn't sure it would count for much up here.

'Nothing personal. Just economic politics. The south has always ripped the north off. Just their way of showing they know it.'

She glanced at a road sign. 'Coming to the end of the East Lancs road. Nearly there.' She muttered and did an emergency stop at a set of lights.

'It's a strange city. It could be the most macho city in England. And yet it's got more listed buildings than any other city in the UK after London, which obviously is so much bigger.'

'How come?'

'Well in early days it was the major port of the British Empire. Part of the slave triangle. With a lot of very rich merchants and a hell of a lot of civic pride. The Victorians built some wonderful buildings on the colossal Greek model. If you like little Cloughgreen Town Hall, wait till you see St George's Hall. It's like a mega Parthenon.'

Eventually they drove in through the suburbs along long shopping streets that seemed to Willie to be entirely made up of closed shops with full-length steel shutters. It was Sunday-morning silent. Loads of people still in bed. Just all this shining steel with graffiti on it and litter blowing. And deprived-looking people. Depressing.

'Forgive me for saying so, but this looks like my idea of Beirut.'

Bolly sighed. 'Well, it's not the soft and prosperous south, Willie.

It's had hard times these past 40 years. People like us we take a lot for granted. One way and another we've been really privileged...'

'I know, but...'

'No buts. If you're down among the disheartened, you see people on telly with all this stuff, you want to have it, too. There's a big temptation to go help yourself.'

'A famous photographer called Bill Brandt did these wonderful photo essays of Liverpool, Glasgow and the North East in the Forties and Fifties. Harsh, gritty black and whites, of course. He showed the grinding poverty in our big northern cities. But also the humanity. Somehow you wonder if much has changed.'

'Come on, Willie, you know that's not true. It's a different sort of poverty. It's not starving-to-death poverty and kids with rickets. Or kids-with-no-shoes poverty.'

'Maybe. But it's still poverty. If people feel they're poor, they probably are.'

Bolly sighed. 'When Uncle Fergal had had a few and got serious he would say Scousers were good people who'd been let down by their own. He said the city had been ruined by the middle classes abdicating their responsibility and moving out.

'No social cement to hold everything together, he said. For a long time, he said, after the offices let out the middle classes scuttled back across the Mersey at 5 o'clock to the gentility of the Wirral. Or fled by train to the far outer suburbs on the way to Southport. Uncle Fergal used to say that Liverpool was effectively one big working class city. With the middle class having abandoned them and looking on from a safe distance.'

`Doesn't sound very PC.'

'Well, he wasn't, was he? He was an old Irish scoundrel, self-made businessman who lived near Southport and died long before PC came about. He told it the way he saw it.'

They both fell silent after that and Bolly put an Annie Lennox CD on.

Eventually they came to the city centre. Willie was stunned by St George's Hall and the nearby Walker Art Gallery. Then they drove down Rodney Street and he was enchanted by the tall, elegant Georgian terraces.

'These are beautiful,' he said.

'Doctors and solicitors places. Or used to be anyway. Wait till you see the Phil where we're meeting Dr Mount.'

'The Fill?'

'The Philharmonic pub. Opposite the Philharmonic Hall. It's world famous for its brown marble urinals and art deco mirrors and design.'

'Okay.'

They parked the car and walked down Hope Street. Willie was tickled to find that, as the song said, there was a cathedral at either end of Hope Street: "If yer want a cathedral, we've got one to spare...'

Dr Freddy Mount had said that the uni campus was not far from the Phil and therefore a good place to meet.

They reached the pub just after opening time, but Willie was distracted.

'Wow, look at that,' he said, pointing to the Philharmonic Hall opposite, a massive red sandstone Art Deco masterpiece with tall chamfered towers.

Bolly eventually dragged him away and over the tiled floors of the Philharmonic pub.

Shafts of sunlight beamed down through stained glass windows as they went through a door into the partitioned-off round central bar.

The place felt sleepy. Singletons waited patiently for their first pint to be served, some with the Sunday papers under their arm. Too early for couples or groups.

Willie and Bolly stood at the circular bar, not far from the entrance to two satellite rooms with green leather armchairs and small black wrought iron tables.

The barmaids moved slowly, yawning, getting over a good night. Willie and Bollie were waiting their turn as people were slowly served when someone tugged Bolly's sleeve from behind.

'Verity Dee?' Just two words in a thick Scouse accent. The speaker was a wiry man of medium height, mid thirties, with sparse, crinkly ginger hair and moustache and a bony, white face pinched around a beaky nose. But the intelligent brown eyes spoke volumes.

'That's me.'

'I'm Dr Freddy Mount. Dr Bentley's friend.' To Willie he looked as though he'd come straight from central casting for uni lecturers. He wore an old green-check sports coat with leather patches, grey flannels and brown Hush Puppies with an open-neck cream shirt.

But he had a pinched look about him and Willie, the anthropology graduate, surmised Dr Freddy Mount was a Scouser who had come from a poor background, been a bright lad who'd gone to grammar school and made something of himself. But he was one of those guys you couldn't uproot, like Gerry Stansfield who had tried and failed to leave Yorkshire. Dr Mount's taproot was deep in Liverpool, it nurtured him. He was born here. He liked it here. He was valued here. He would die here. It would be impossible for him to leave.

'How's Phyllis? Dr Bentley.'

'In splendid form, Dr Mount, and fit as a fiddle,' Bolly said, half-turning. 'This is my husband, Willie.'

The two men shook hands and then he pecked Bolly on the cheek.

'Glad to meet you both. Call me Freddy. Phyllis's a great old bird. Bit too sparky for some of the stuffed shirts when she was here, if you know what I mean. Born before her time. She was a feminist before there were any. And she was a great teacher for those blokes who were prepared to listen. Knew her stuff.'

Willie had ordered up the drinks and they took them through to one of the quieter small rooms off the main bar. As they sat in their green leather armchairs sipping their drinks, Willie suddenly noticed Freddy Mount had a roll-up behind his left ear. A man of the people.

'Left-handed, right?' Willie suddenly blurted.

Freddy looked astonished. 'Not "Shoot lefties" day, is it?' he asked. Then he grinned. 'Okay, how d'you guess?'

'Roll-up behind the left ear.'

'Observant. Any idea what I had for breakfast?'

It was Willie's turn to grin. 'Not yet. But I'm working on it.' He liked the look of Freddy Mount. He looked as though he might be a hands-on sort of guy, which was just what they needed.

'Okay, you two, let's get down to business,' Bolly said. 'Freddy, did Phyllis tell you it's an anti-wind farm demo?'

'Yep. And she outlined the idea. Sounds a hoot. But best you tell me again, make sure I've got the right end of the stick.'

'It's a sort of industrial *son et lumiere*,' Bolly said. Then she ran through exactly what they wanted and Freddy grinned broadly.

'Love it, I'm sure we can do that. What sort of place is this all planned to go off in?'

'Well, it's Woolton's main city square. The prime target is the Council office building. Cutting edge when the council architect designed it in the Sixties. Now it's a concrete and glass tower where you fry in summer and freeze in winter.'

'Better and better. We can really make an impact with all that glass,' Freddy said, rubbing his hands.

'The cream concrete has discoloured badly,' Willie added irrelevantly. 'It looks like shit, with all the streaks and water marks you get.'

'Anyway there's no problems with what you want to do. One simulated giant wind turbine coming up.' Dr Mount smiled as though it were a great joke. 'No problems with that at all. I can tell you exactly how we can fake it up - though you might not understand it, so I won't bother. How are we going to mount it and get it there?'

'10' by 4'6" trailer, pulled by Range Rover.'

Freddy Mount took the archetypal fag packet from his sports jacket and made a biro note of the dimensions. 'Should be no problem.'

'Like a lot of Scousers I guess I'm anti-authority on principle. Retarded adolescence, I guess. I like the idea of supporting the underdogs and sticking it to authority, giving the know-all planners a dose of their own medicine.'

'We weren't sure how you'd feel, given it's the sainted wind farms that everyone's been promised will save the planet.'

The physicist leaned forward and laughed so hard he nearly fell off his chair.

'Look, anyone who knows anything about science or engineering knows industrial wind turbines are crap: they're nothing like up to the job. In the 21st century, if it wasn't for the wind farm hype, who is going to tolerate any machine that at best works to 30% of its potential capacity? And even then it's completely unpredictable as to when it's going to cut out altogether. What sort of technology is it when you need a weather forecast to see if you can generate electricity? Bronze Age technology, that's what.' He took a swig of bitter and reflected. 'As you probably know, they're not even real turbines as such. Properly speaking...'

'...they're airscrew generators,' Bolly finished.

'That's right. The Net is full of engineers and physicists who are appalled by these things, saying they are not the right answer. I was having a look last night. I don't know if you have seen this one. It's from some Sheffield physicist. He pulled out a wad of inkjet paper from his pocket and handed it over the table. Bolly looked down and read "For comparison purposes, and taking into account capacity (or load factors), the land area covered by a wind power station of the same energy output as a nuclear power station would be about 2000 times as great (or an area of land 20km by 25km would be covered by wind turbines to produce the same electrical output as one nuclear power station occupying an area of land 500m square). Furthermore, the wind turbines are of greater height and rotate so that their visual impact is amplified. A considerable infrastructure in terms of possibly improved roads and access tracks is required for wind turbines." She handed it back to him, shaking her head.

'Powerful stuff, isn't it?' Freddy Mount said. "Why should we plaster over what's left of the countryside with crap engineering? What's the point? Get the nuclear plants in and have done with it. It'll have to happen sooner or later. Better sooner before we have third world style power cuts. The French are way ahead of us. 90% of their energy comes from about 30 nuclear plants. No nonsense.' He looked thoughtful then spoke again.

'The public are being sold this soft dream without being told the scale of the thing and how much land they take up. A Scottish power generation engineer on the Net reckons a conventional power station takes up 0.03 hectares of land per MW while the equivalent wind farm would occupy 9 hectares per MW. Big difference. He also reckons that if existing plans go through you won't be able to stand on any one of the Munros without seeing a wind farm. So much for Scotland's wilderness country.'

Like your style, thought Willie. 'Another one? Goes down pretty well, this bitter.'

'And then as a bonus you'll be able to sample our flash brown marble loos,' Freddy said, waving expansively behind him.

Willie looked at him.

'Seriously. Over the years they've had camera crews in there doing documentaries about them.'

'You're pulling my plonker...'

'You'll be amazed.'

A few pints later, Willie was duly amazed by the stylish urinals. When he came back from the loo Freddy was telling Bolly about the Moorsyde Wind Farm Action Group site on the Net.

'It's incredibly professionally done. Lots of pics. You can see headless raptors dead on the ground in Spain. And any number of industrial wind turbines on fire or with blades snapped off.' He started ticking them off on his fingers: 'One at Sheffield University broke twice in 15 months, fire in one at the Nissan plant near Sunderland, one collapsed into the school playground at Raasay in the Scottish isles...there's loads of accidents. See for yourself. You wonder why they never make the national press or telly.'

Bolly told him about UKWC and Charley Fort's experience. He shook his head.

'With so many multi-millions at stake, big business, I suppose it figures.'

People were now standing around their room. Somebody bumped their table and Freddy leapt forward, steadying the two pint pots. 'Mind the ale,' he said, gruffly. Bolly looked a bit taken aback. The noise level had risen appreciably since they'd arrived and it was getting harder to hear themselves speak. 'Anything else you need to know?'

'No, I've got a pretty fair idea.'

Things were starting to get really boisterous at the Phil as they walked out around two o'clock.

'Ring us when the gizmo's good to go,' Bolly said.

'Ciaou,' Freddy said, hoisting his right thumb. As he lowered it he put his left thumb and forefinger behind his ear for his roll-up, dragged a Bic from his pocket and lit up. They watched as he sauntered off down Hope Street, thin puffs of blue smoke marking his wake.

'Ciaou, Freddy,' Bolly said to herself. 'You are a one-off.'

'That is one singular Scouser physicist,' Willie said. 'Can't wait to see what him and his mates come up with.'

'Just so long as it rattles the air waves like the real thing.'

# 14

The bouquet lay conspicuous among the pint pots on the table. Suddenly Hilda glided up. She was a smooth mover for a large woman. Today she was magnificent in bombazine. Her buxom figure was tightly sheathed from a mandarin collar below the chin to below the knee in shimmering emerald green. The fabric cried out to be touched. She pointed at the flowers.

'The wages of sin, I presume? Payment in advance.'

'I'm visiting a lady friend, Hilda, if that's what you mean.'

Hilda made a face, her lips compressing.

'Well, I don't approve. A gentleman of your age and station in life. Still, we can't let these poor innocent things die of alcoholic poisoning, can we? With you lot breathing fumes all over them. I'll put them in water for you.' She leaned forward to pick them up and Willie prayed that Jumper wouldn't reach out and pat her temptingly tight-encased bottom as it heaved into his sightline. But he didn't. There was no dreaded black moment. And Hilda swept the flowers out through the door and back to her domain.

'I'll leave them on the bar,' she yelled over her shoulder. Then she took a cream-coloured whiskey manufacturer's jug, filled it with water and plonked the flowers in. Her lacquered blonde cockatoo perm never quivered.

'Amazing woman, Hilda, makes a favour sound like a threat,' Gerry said.

'Big Ruth is it, the lucky lady?' Willie opined.

'Big Ruth from Burnley? A queen among women. But no. Someone I know over Reddingley way. Builder's widow. One of my occasionals. She rings me when the fancy takes her. As a few of 'em do.'

Gerry snorted. 'Hilda was right about one thing though. All this womanizing will be the death of you, Jumper. Bloke at your station in life,' he mimicked.

'At least I'm still at the station. It's being parked in the sidings worries me. You could do worse than follow my example, he said,' nodding at Gerry. Jumper finished his Guinness and held a giant red paw up. 'Look, I ask nothing more than to die in the saddle. A horseman's death. Like a Viking with his sword in his hand.' Willie laughed.

'You're incorrigible. But look, I have to update you on this wind farm scam and recent developments.'

'Best get some refills in before you get started,' Jumper said, looking significantly at Gerry.

'Oh, alright,' Gerry agreed and shambled off to the bar.

'He's getting worse,' Jumper said.

'It's part of his professional Yorkie act.' Willie put a broad accent on: "'I'm tighter than a shrew's arsehole, tha' knows...No bugger gets any more use out a anythin' I discard. Not a shirt. Not a pair o' kecks, nothin'.'"

'Maybe,' Jumper said, 'I think he's just tight.' His cool blue eyes twinkled. When the ale was replenished, Willie started.

'We took a trip over to Liverpool yesterday, Bolly and me...'

'Still got the Range Rover then, have you? With all its wheels and everything? Nothing gone missing?' Willie looked abashed at the two grinning faces.

'Is it really as bad as all that?' The other two nodded. Yes.

'Well, yeah the Range Rover's fine. But we were there to discuss the next stage of the campaign. Bolly's great idea is to go right into the centre of Woolton and show the planners and the people in the city centre just what industrial wind turbines are all about. The guys in the Physics Dept at Liverpool Uni have arranged to produce this gizmo for us which simulates the effect of an industrial wind turbine close to.'

'Yaahooo, go get 'em, cowboy. I like it,' Gerry whooped.

'So do I,' Jumper said, his eyes twinkling. 'All these buggers in suits making these decisions when they've never been near a wind farm in their life, nor ever likely to be. You show 'em, Willie.'

'I'm glad you feel like that because I'm here to ask favours. I'd like to borrow your trailer, Jumper, to transport the gizmo. And I'd like you to help us design a flyer to hand out, Gerry.'

'Help yourself, I'll even drive the Range Rover if you're worried about the towing,' Jumper volunteered.

'How about you, Gerry?'

'Well, I'm a bit busy at the moment doing the set-up for Storm-n-Shine's next catalogue, but sure. It's not going to be a big job, is it?'

'No, just a standard sheet of A4, second colour, printed on one side, use existing artwork for the turbine pic.'

'Piece of piss then. It's just a layout and a bit of typo. The Mac will eat it for breakfast. Same typefaces as last time for headers and body copy?'

'Yep.'

'It's a doddle.'

'Great. This is Bolly's copy and rough,' he said, handing over a sheet of A4 to Gerry.

Gerry looked at Jumper. 'Read it aloud? Save you getting out your reading specs, Jumper.'

'You're a gent.'

'Let's not go over the top,' Willie said and Gerry grinned coyly, like a naughty schoolboy caught doing a good turn. He inclined his friar's pate down over the sheet and began to read:

THIS IS WHAT WIND FARMS DO
IF YOU'RE TOO CLOSE TO THEM
(pic of giant turbine blades in your face)

To help you understand the resistance to wind farms we have devised a machine that replicates a small cluster of just four wind turbines that are at the current recommended distance from people's homes.

1. THAT CONSTANT SWISHING ACROSS YOUR EYES IS CAUSED BY BLADE FLICKER. IT IS VERY DISORIENTATING, ISN'T IT? IT CAN MAKE IT HARD TO CONCENTRATE, CAN'T IT? IF YOU HAVE TO LIVE WITH IT ALL THE TIME YOU CAN'T EVEN WATCH THE TV IN PEACE OR READ THE PAPER, YOU HAVE TO DRAW THE CURTAINS EVEN IN THE DAY TIME. IT MAKES IT HARD TO SLEEP. AND IT LITERALLY FRIGHTENS HORSES.

2. THAT WHOOSHING NOISE YOU HEAR IS THE SOUND OF THE BLADES GOING AROUND. IT CAN GET LOUDER OR DIE DOWN DEPENDING ON THE WEATHER AND THE LIE OF THE LAND. BUT IT CAN EASILY PENETRATE YOUR WINDOWS AND DOORS. EVEN DOUBLE GLAZING. HOW WOULD YOU LIKE IT DAY IN, DAY OUT? EVEN AT NIGHT. IT DRIVES YOU BARMY.

3. THAT OCCASIONAL CLANKING NOISE IS THE SOUND OF THE MECHANICAL DRIVE INSIDE THE TURBINE. YOU NEVER KNOW WHEN YOU'RE GOING TO HEAR THAT EITHER.

4. WORST OF ALL IS THE SOUND YOU CAN'T HEAR. THIS IS CALLED SUBSONIC NOISE AND IS OUTSIDE THE RANGE OF HUMAN HEARING. SCIENTISTS CALL IT "WHITE NOISE". IT'S HOW CIVILISED NATIONS TORTURE THEIR ENEMIES. LEAVES NO MARKS BUT HURTS YOUR MIND. SOME GPS BELIEVE WIND FARMS GENERATE THIS "WHITE NOISE". YOUR BODY FEELS IT RATHER THAN HEARING IT.

5. FACT: PEOPLE HAVE BEEN DRIVEN OUT OF THEIR HOMES BY THESE SIDE EFFECTS. OTHERS HAVE BEEN DRIVEN AWAY FOR RESPITE CARE. ALL HAVE SUFFERED A LOSS OF VALUE IN THEIR HOMES, SOME HAVE BEEN UNABLE TO SELL THEM.

6. WHAT'S IT ALL FOR? WIND FARMS GENERATE PITIFUL AMOUNTS OF EXPENSIVE ELECTRICITY, MAKE FORTUNES FOR FAT CAT DEVELOPERS AND RUIN OUR BEAUTIFUL REMAINING WILD PLACES.

STOP THE CLOUGHGREEN WIND FARM APPLICATION - TELL YOUR COUNCILLOR 'NO!'

Not In My Back Yard - Not in Your Back Yard - Not In Anyone's Back Yard

Issued by the Friends of The Living Moorland, Cloughgreen

There was a brief silence. Then Jumper said 'Bloody hell!' and rubbed a large red hand over his purple hatchet nose and ruddy cheeks. 'That's strong stuff.'

'She can write, Bolly can,' Gerry said, pursing his lips.

'That's what Charley Fort, the journo, said.'

'No, that really is strong stuff. You'd pay a fortune for a London ad writer to do that.'

'She's trying to write a book on Ted Hughes, the poet.'

'Blow that, she could make a fortune in London adland. I'd give her a job tomorrow.'

'I'll tell her, but I think she prefers writing about Ted Hughes.'

'Whatever, it's great stuff. If that doesn't make 'em sit up and listen, nothing will.'

'We just have to hope the gizmo is half as good.'

'I think it will be. Dr Freddy Mount seems a real can-do guy. Industrial wind turbines offend his professional sense of what is real technology. I'm sure he won't let us down.'

Willie went off to get a new round in and when he returned, the topic had changed.

'Like I said earlier, I'm off on a flying visit to Reddingley and then I expect lambing to start in the next few days. You and Bolly still up for it?'

‘Of course.’

‘Right, I’ll give you a ring when things start moving. Theoretically it’s all supposed to kick off May 1st. Late this year, but now it’s more hobby farming I thought I’d let ‘em come in better weather. Still, Mother Nature, you never know.’ He took a deep draw on the Guinness and Gerry did the same to his pint of lager. It was as though someone had blown a silent whistle, Willie thought, as the other two raced their pints down.

They finished together and Gerry said ‘You’ll be okay finishing yours on your own, won’t you? Storm-n-Shine waits for no man. Take care.’

‘I promised I’d be over to see her by three,’ Jumper said.

‘Don’t forget to reclaim your flowers.’

‘Right. I nearly did. See you soon for the lambing.”

Then he’d gone around to the front bar and was thanking Wesley for looking after his flowers.

Still, mission accomplished. The demo leaflet was in hand and the gizmo’s carriage awaited. Bolly would be pleased.

He drained his Black Sheep and walked out into the spring sunshine.

# 15

Dr Newall turned off his computer and rubbed his eyes. It had been a sod of a day with one of his clients. The man was obtuse and also frightened of his own shadow, wondering what other people would think if he okayed Newall's radical traffic calming plans.

In the end he'd made him accept the plans, but it had been hard work. Sometimes selling the job through was much harder than doing the job.

He had already made his weekly chess move for the Moscow game and emailed it. He had a few days grace before the London game. Time to reflect. After a little while his mind wandered. It was rare for him to make a mistake, but now it occurred to him that he had.

After his upfront crusading for the turbines in the Cloughgreen Recorder he had been wrong to allow himself to be seen around town with Ursa. It might suggest he was their employee and taking money for his help. Not that he was doing anything illegal. But it wasn't smart.

He was a *bona fide* independent planner, he was free to take anyone's shilling. But being seen to do so somehow seemed to detract from his independence. Also it made him vulnerable. The hate mail and other worse substances that had come through his letterbox had shocked him more than he had allowed himself to show.

Above all, he had exposed himself to the mob. Show yourself in anyway different and the mob would kill you. At 5'6" he was not his father, Colonel 'Nasty' Newall, able to tie one hand behind his back and still kick six bells out of the bad guys. He didn't mind standing up as the great wind farm prophet. But if things weren't going to play that way then he had no intention of being the wind farm whipping boy. Let Ursa take the flak. No, he would stay in the shadows when the Woolton planning application meeting came up.

'And so, the appointed day arrives,' Bolly said. 'May 1st, official lambing day at Jumper Lonk's place. I'm surprised you're not more nervous,' Bolly said.

'Why should I be?'

'Because you're so squeamish.'

'I asked Jumper if I could do a photo essay of the process...'

'The process!' Bolly mocked. 'Much you know.'

'And he said, yeah, so long as I gave a hand when necessary.'

'It's a good job I'm coming too, Willie. But look, because I love you dearly let me just put you in the picture before we go next door.'

'Okay.'

Bolly held aloft a thin tan paperback.

'"Moortown Diary". Written when Ted Hughes was livestock farming with his father-in-law down in Devon. Just so you know what to expect, let me read you one of his notes.'

She took a deep breath and started to read: '"All sheep, lambs and calves are patients; something in them all is making a steady effort to die. That is the farmer's impression...."'

'Okay, I'm prepared,' Willie said. Bolly laughed.

'You're not. But I tried.' She waved the little book. 'There are some wonderful pieces in this. But I warn you a lot are pretty visceral.'

'I've seen stuff over the years,' Willie said, gruffly, knowing he sounded macho and ridiculous. He picked up his camera bag. 'Come on,' he said, 'let's go.'

They marched up the lane, hand in hand, and in through Jumper's five-bar gate. It was chilly, but sunny and they could hear lapwings down the lane. Willie loved the crested, stubby-winged lapwings. They were the stunt pilots of the moorland birds, performing barrel rolls and aerobatics. Curlews, with their long protruding bills, and aggressive low flying were the fighter boys.

There were already several small lambs on Jumper's front field. In the modern fashion, Jumper had numbered them with blue dye: 1, 1A, 2,2A, through to 7 and 7A, annotating who their mothers were. Bolly nudged Willie and pointed out one particular lamb. Instead of a number it had a blue query: ?

'I think Jumper's losing it,' Bolly said, giggling.

Jumper heard their laughter. 'I can hear you. I'm in the barn,' he yelled. 'We're off and running already.'

'We noticed,' Bolly said.

'Anyway what's so funny?'

Bolly told him and he smiled.

'Oh, that. I reckon that's a foreigner strayed off from some place else. That or I really am losing my marbles.'

'Okay if I start?' Willie asked, fitting his flashgun to the Nikon's hot shoe.

'Go ahead.'

Jumper finished with the ewe he was helping and came over to Bolly.

'They all seem to be twins so far,' Bolly said.

'That's right, Bolly, and with any luck they all will be. It's all so much more scientific these days, twins, timings, supplements. But of course, it's still Nature, things can go wrong...

'I've only got 50 ewes nowadays. Just a hobby really, something to keep me busy and self-sufficient in lamb for the table. Any less and I'd just be playing at it...'

Willie was clicking away.

'Jumper could you just lean over that last one...'

Jumper obliged. 'I'll expect a set of these then, when you've finished.'

'Naturally.'

To Willie's relief and Bolly's surprise everything went well until the afternoon when they heard a commotion outside in the lane. Jumper sized it up at a glance.

'Some of Ted Bates's breakouts.'

Then, 'Oh, shit, we can't let that go. Come on Willie,' Jumper said, lurching off towards the gate. Willie handed the camera to Bolly and followed him at a trot. He saw immediately what had upset Jumper.

There was a group of six woebegone sheep in the lane, just outside his gate, looking enviously in at the rich, well-dressed pasture. Their ribs were thin, they were lame and all had strands of raggedy fleece hanging off them. One of the ewes, bleating piteously, had a lamb's head and forelegs projecting from her rear end. The lamb's head was dusty dry and had been there maybe 6-8 hours, Jumper guessed. It was obviously long dead.

'Just hold her head tight,' Jumper bellowed, grabbing the ewe in one massive hand. Willie did as he was told, clamping the sheep's head between his knees. Jumper went to the rear and after some vigorous, educated tugging he had the dead lamb out and onto the road. He moved it to the grass next to the wall.

'Drive the rest of them to me,' he said. 'Yell and clap your hands.' He went on ahead and opened another gate and between them they got the runaways in. 'I'll put them in a trailer and take them back later.'

He shook his head. 'It's a scandal, really, the way Ted treats his sheep. He should give it up. He can't make it pay.' Then he waved his arms. 'But who am I to tell him?' On the way back he picked up the dead lamb and placed it behind the dry stone wall.

'I'll sort it out later,' he said, looking over at it. 'It's been dead a while. Bad business. With luck we've saved the ewe. I'll look at her later.'

'Let's go and have a brew,' Bolly said.

As she poured the tea into mugs from a big shiny brown pot, Jumper indicated the bottle of Bells on the table.

'Anyone join me?' he asked, sloshing a measure into his mug. Willie joined him. Bolly had been right. He wasn't ready for sheep rearing realities. It had been hard not to gag.

'That really upsets me,' Jumper said after a long swig.

'Not the ewe,' he said quickly. 'There's worse things happen than that. But the fact is them poor sheep have been wandering round half-starved and ailing for weeks. Breaks my heart to see that.'

I bet it does, Willie thought. This, after all, was the farmer who took his "lads" away on holiday to mild, coastal Fylde during the bleak winter.

'I've rung Ted a few times and told him but he's too rushed off his feet to care. I don't want to fall out over it. The poor bugger's got enough on his plate trying to survive. I've known him 20-odd years.'

'There's nothing you can do,' Bolly said, 'other than what you have done.' Jumper smiled a thin, bitter smile.

'I live the life of Riley by comparison with poor Ted Bates. Financially secure, retired, just 50 ewes. I'm in clover. Poor Ted has three jobs. Sheep farmer, supposedly. Works for Yorkshire Water during the week, tending reservoirs. Then does part-time bar work Saturday and Sunday nights. Poor bugger's run off his feet trying to make ends meet.' He drained his cup and refilled his mug, sloshing a smaller measure of Bells in.

'This government and the EU have just about done for the hill farmers. The government hates us. Thinks we're all aristocracy with thousands of acres who spend all week fox-hunting. Bahh! They know nothing. Think we can all have farm shops. Imagine farm shops in the backwaters of these hills. Lucky if you see a rambler. No idea of real life, the way ordinary people live, this government. Not up here at any road.' He reflected.

'Didn't do hill farm management at their public schools, I shouldn't think. Nor much else to do with real life, come to that.'

'Is it really that bad?' Willie asked quietly.

'People like Ted Bates? Worse than you can imagine,' Jumper said. The whisky had brought tears to his eyes and purpled up his hatchet nose. He ran a hand through his wavy white hair.

'You know, some of the lads up here, hill farmers, they had to wait 6 months for the government to pay 'em the subsidies they owed 'em this year. Call 'emselves socialists. They've no idea how ordinary people live any more. They really don't. They think farming's all caviar on toast. Not clapped-out Land Rovers and baling twine.'

Bolly was shocked and was about to ask more about it, when a sheep noise from outside demanded attention.

'I tell you one thing, though the Greens have got right. If fuel is running out and carbon from transport is damaging the planet then we should all eat local food. Much better than wasting precious fuel and polluting the atmosphere at the same time. More goodness in it, too. The problem is, when the numbskulls in this government finally realize it, it will be too late. All the people who can grow our food will have been driven off the land. You can't just plug in trained, experienced farmers by Act of Parliament, when you've seen the writing on the wall. Too late then. Interfere with everything, understand nothing, this lot.'

'You're right,' Bolly said, 'the biggest problem with this government is it doesn't do joined-up or long-term thinking.'

'If Gerry was here he'd say it was because all that concerns them is short term staying in power,' Willie said.

'And who's to say he's wrong?' Bolly asked.

After that things went quiet and they drifted back to Greenwood Royd in the late afternoon with a promise to come back later if needed. But the call never came. Jumper coped on his own, as he had done this last fifty years.

After supper they settled down in the music room listening to some Burt Bacharach and having a glass or two, as was their wont.

The experience with the dead lamb had made Willie philosophical.

'You know, we both lived in London a good few years. How often did you see death in that time?'

'I can't say I did.'

'I know. A city of 13 million people, near as damn it, and I only remember two dead people. One was a very much loved chairman of a PR agency who had a heart attack. The other time I had this dreadful trip to make across London and so I went on the Circle Line. There are some very busy stations on the Circle Line. On the way to my meeting, the carriages emptied out and I suddenly realised this guy in the next carriage hadn't moved since I got on half an hour ago. So I got off and moved a carriage back to check him out. He was dead. So I grabbed a porter and we got him off. I often wonder how many times he'd been around the Circle Line while people sat next to him or opposite him and hadn't even noticed.'

'And the point is?'

'Well, about six months ago I watched a crow battered to death against the outside of our house by the wind while I was making your morning coffee.'

'Don't blame me,' Bolly laughed, throwing up her hands. 'Anyway, I remember. It upset you.'

'No-o-o, I didn't mean that. But most days Nelson and I go out walking we see something dead. A rabbit, a mole, a field mouse, a rat, a badger, a sparrow, a sheep, a fox in a hedge where it's gone to die, once even a sparrow hawk lying on its back behind a wall, its great chrome yellow talons turned up to heaven.'

'And again, the point is?'

'It's healthier, Bolly, to remind ourselves on a daily basis of our mortality. The countryside does that. Helps you appreciate life.'

'The closer the grave, the sweeter the roses smell, you mean.'

'Something like that. It reminds you we're just natural things like everything around us out here. We're not enduring like concrete or toughened glass or gravel or millstone grit. Sooner or later we all perish. Like a worn-out inner tube.'

'Well, while we're having heavy thoughts, let me tell you right now I no way want to be reincarnated as a Pennine sheep.' Willie had to laugh. Him neither.

Dr Newall finished his G & T and reached for his mobile. Angela Snow answered immediately.

'What news of our hydrology consultant, Angie?'

'Paul Vennis? It was a pretty disgusting sight actually, when I outlined the sweetener for him to reconsider his findings.'

'Oh?'

'He practically salivated all over me. He so wants a Jag coupe. He'd like me thrown in, on the back seat preferably; but that's another story.' She hummed a brief snatch of the Stones' "You cain't always get what you want."

Newall sniggered. 'No, I could see that wouldn't appeal. But that apart he's going to come through for us?'

'No probs. He outlined a scenario that had made him reconsider. Sounded quite plausible. So as to let our upright chief planner off the hook. Ernest's getting quite twitchy at the moment, wanting to do the right thing. You know what a straight arrow he is. He's actually come out in that nervous flaky rash he gets in his eyebrows and on his forehead.'

'Seborrheic dermatitis. What's brought that on?'

'Dave Summit, our glorious CEO, has been taking an interest.'

'Yeah?'

'Most definitely.'

'And?'

'He's got the idea that we may recommend turning the app down. Which, other considerations apart, we would have done. But from Dave's point of view this is not great news. Seeing as he's got a Government requirement for Woolton to get in a sizeable amount of renewables. Up until recently he hasn't even thought of anything except dumping them out of sight and out of mind in Cloughgreen...'

'And Dave's very ambitious...'

'Most definitely. He sees Woolton as a stepping stone to greater things, does our glorious leader...'

'So he's been bending Maitland's ear with a reminder that apart from saving the planet this could well be an issue of national importance.'

'Exactly.'

'"Just so long as you don't expose Cloughgreen to any real danger, of course, Ernest "...he'll have said, being the nasty weasel he is.'

'He'll have said something like that.'

'But the pressure has still been put on Maitland to try and find it so?'

'You got it.'

'I almost feel sorry for the dry old stick. Almost.'

'It's his poor old mum I feel sorry for. I bet she's getting her ear bent rotten while Maitland wrestles with the issues,' Angela Snow said, laughing.

'Ah well, the end definitely justifies the means, hey, Angie? How is Phyllida?'

'Phyllida is absolutely gorgeous. Bosoms to die for,' she giggled. 'And so appreciative. She likes a girlfriend who can show her the good things in life.' (As do you you, Newall thought archly.)

'So everyone lives happily ever after.'

'I don't see why not, Dr Newall,' Angela Snow said.

'Bye Angie.'

Willie had early May down in his Nature notebook for the arrival of the first foals of the season. So they'd decided to take Nelson in the Range Rover for a walk over to Cherry Tree Stud.

They drove as far as they could and parked the Range Rover in the car park of a closed down pub. The plan was to ascend the summit of the Common for the view before going in search of foals. It was a stiff trek up a muddy trail to the crest of the Common. But the view was magnificent. It looked out over myriad cottages and farmhouses in a green and pleasant landscape. On the far side of the valley, about 2 miles as the crow flies, they could see Greenwood Royd.

'There are so many farms and cottages that would be directly beneath the turbines here,' Willie said.

Bolly just shook her head and muttered something under her breath Willie didn't catch. This spring should have been idyllic but they felt the looming threat of the wind farm and the malign influence of Newall. Despite having won the first round in their anti- wind farm battle neither underestimated Dr Newall.

Even though he'd said nothing about it in the Recorder, they had no doubts he was in cahoots with Ursa Power, feeding them every last bit of advantage he could summon. That oily grin and pigeon-chested strut concealed a furtive nature.

Glumly they retraced their steps down to the hamlet where they'd left the car in the closed-down pub car park.

'Shame about this place,' Willie said, jerking a thumb at the long, low pub with its boarded windows. 'We've had some good pub grub here.'

'Happening to country pubs all over, isn't it? Combination of pub booze being too expensive for ordinary people and supermarket booze on special offer. No contest.'

They rounded the end of the pub and spotted the Cherry Tree Stud about half a mile away. It was sandwiched between several richly pastured sheep farms.

There was a large farmhouse with several big barns and stables. The buildings lay at the centre of several large paddocks. Cherry trees studded the development.

'Cherry Tree Stables, hey? Well, I don't think much of the eponymous trees,' Bolly said.

'They must just about form the tree line. Beyond which no tree grows. They can't help but be such scraggy sad specimens.'

The two of them looked at the cherry trees. They were bird cherries, no good for eating. They stood leggy and spindly in the wind. Sad.

'They will still look good in blossom, though,' Willie said.

'You,' she said, nudging him. "You always see the best side of things.'

They stood still at their vantage point. And there, bang on cue, they saw their first chestnut foal of the season. Legs braced uncertainly, it gleamed satin wet with its mother licking and fussing over it. Behind the white picket fence a man looked fondly on, his arms locked over the rail.

'You know, us being here it's a bit like some people in the Thirties felt the approaching shadow of the war and how it would change everyone's lives,' Willie said, looking down over the lush emerald fields and the big cherry-coloured metal barns.

'Wind farms throw a long shadow.'

'We should go down and warn the guy whose business this is. Sell it now while the going is good. Just in case Newall gets this wind farm in.' He nodded to the bloke watching the foal. 'He'd never sell a horse stud then.'

'Not to anyone who knew about horses. Not with all the strobing and blade flicker that would come down on his poor frightened horses. Actually it quite worries me on Bushmills, he can be a bit nervy at the best of times.'

Then they looked further over to the paddock area and the riding school. A small girl in riding gear and red-ribboned pigtails bestrode a feisty white pony. She was being led around in circles and instructed by a bossy, busty blonde in a worn brown check jacket, jodhpurs and boots. They could hear her raised voice from here.

'Can you imagine little kids on their ponies having to cope with blade flicker this close up. They couldn't do it. It would be impossible.'

'End of riding school. Kaput. In actual fact, this poor sod would be hard pushed to sell his farmhouse, never mind the whole thing as a business - the distance he'd be from all the whooshing and flickering.'

Bolly pointed her finger at him. 'Now, now, you're being what Dr Newall would call "alarmist".'

Willie clowned around, raising his hands in horror. 'Heaven forfend. Don't want that, do we? Mustn't alarm anyone. Must keep all the ducks sitting quietly in a row while he blasts away.'

He thought a moment. 'Tell you what though, let's just go and warn this guy anyway...someone could still have a sheep farm here. But the turbines would kill his stables business for sure. Horses would hate it. It's only fair to try and tip him off.'

'Right then,' said Bolly, striding out. They came off the hill trail and walked through the five-bar gate and down the broken-surfaced road towards Cherry Tree Stables. There were spindly rowans in the fields. More rowans cowered amongst the barns and outbuildings. They watched as the man left the foal and its mother and went back into the house.

When they came to the right turn to the stables the dirt road changed into tarmac. The picket fences leading to the farmhouse were white-painted and pristine. Willie opened the five-bar gate and held it for Bolly to pass through before closing it. The farmhouse doors, Willie noted ironically, were of a deep cherry hue gloss. Several coats deep to resist the wearing, wearing wind and rain.

Bolly stepped forward to the cherry-coloured door and banged loudly on the heavy brass lion's head doorknocker.

Close up, the man who answered the door was of middle height and middle age, pink-faced and prematurely bald except for blonde wings over his ears. He had red patches of colour high on his cheekbones suggestive of a choleric temperament.

'Name your business,' he said.

Willie felt suddenly awkward. 'We wondered if you knew there might be a wind farm coming up there?' He indicated over his shoulder.

'Could be next year,' he added.

The man seemed strangely belligerent.

'What of it?'

'Well, the horses wouldn't like it,' Bolly said. 'It could be terrible for business, particularly the riding school.'

'You an authority on wind farms, then?'

Bolly hesitated. 'Well, we know a bit about them... The riding school. Big, flickering, swooshing, turbine blades won't go well with nervous little girls on skittish ponies, that's for sure.'

'Hah,' the man sneered. 'You're Nimbys. Look, if it's good enough for the government and the greens, it's good enough for me.'

With that he slammed the door in their faces. If the government and the telly people all seemed to think wind farms were alright, who was he to object? What harm could they possibly do?

By June 6th Willie reckoned the first bog cotton should have appeared. He and Bollie drove up to Cloughgreen Common again. This time Willie took his Hasselbald and heavy steel Gitzo tripod. He rarely took the Hasselblad out now he had to pay for film and processing himself, as opposed to charging it to his clients. The camera took large format, fine grain transparency film and gave quality second to none. Today, he felt, could be a matter of historical record. How the moor looked with its rare bog cotton in situ before the bulldozers ripped it up.

As he walked, he leaned the heavy Gitzo tripod over his shoulder. It was a pain to haul it all the way up to the plateau of the moorland, but necessary. It was early and the crisp morning air made his hands ache on the naked steel. Clear skies, the temperature had dropped like a stone over night.

Bolly looked at the tripod.

'This is valedictory, isn't it? You're saying goodbye to it. You don't think you will see the bog cotton up here again, do you?'

'We won't if Ursa Power get their way. If bloody Newall plays his dirty tricks.'

'Christ, don't say that.'

He just looked at her and his boots slid in the shale as he took his eyes off the water-eroded path. Then she looked at his cold knuckles wrapped around the steel tripod and giggled.

'For your sake, I do hope the bog cotton isn't running late. Not now you've lugged that thing all the way up here.'

'You little minx,' he said, smiling. She ran on ahead, dancing up the path in her lightweight girly boots while he trudged on behind in his German, pro-level, made-to-take-crampons, incredibly serious, dead expensive, bloke's walking boots. It made him smile wryly.

‘Wahooooo,’ she yelled when she’d got to the summit and looked around. ‘Loads of it here, bang on schedule.’

And there it was. Great drifts of it. *Eriophorum angustifolium,* bog cotton or cotton grass - looking for all the world like cotton bolls on 10” curved green stems. When the gentle breeze stirred them they streamed out like strippers’ white tassles. Later in the year the stems would go a startling red.

At a distance he could see great white patches of bog cotton. In many cases surrounding deep blue moorland pools. Water, they just loved it.

It was a glorious morning. Blue skies, sunlight, puffy white clouds. The overwhelming blue of the skies turning all the shallow bog pools a deep blue. Dead yellow and reddy grasses from the previous year highlighted the new bog cotton. A treat for the eye, he thought.

Willie quickly had the tripod and cable release connected to the chunky, grey, cube-shaped Hasselblad. Then he set to work methodically making small aperture, slow, time exposures on the fine grained transparency film. One from the heart for posterity. Quality second to none, eat your heart out digital. Working naturally as a pro, he was shooting close up, medium and long, bracketing exposures, working the tripod, slightly varying the angles, when he suddenly remembered he would be paying for all the processing himself. Whoa, steady the buffs. This was an expensive way to work unless it was for a job and you could charge it. Have to be a bit more selective, even if it was for posterity.

Bolly had her binoculars on the warbling sky larks. Watching them fluttering up to a great height and flaunting themselves. Deliberately making themselves visible and vulnerable and singing fit to bust, trying to distract her away from the nest. It was the same tactic they had used to attract the females to mate. In effect, saying to the females "Look at me, look at me! Look how brave I am up here all on my own. Any old kestrel could just swoop down and get me! What a great, courageous chap I'd be to mate with!"

Factually, sky larks who maintained their singing under attack from kestrels were almost always so fit and strong they could evade the predator and crash dive to earth. But it impressed the ladies.

Bolly smiled to herself. Sex could be the death of you, ho, ho, ho. Then a chill fell across her. Or wind turbines, she thought, if you're that small and you choose to live here. And you lose your bearings in fog.

Using her binoculars, she looked hard for the twite. He was the archetypal LBJ or little brown job. Being both small and brown, he was not an easy bird to spot. But eventually she spotted a distant pair nesting in the heather.

'Twite!' she hissed, pointing, but Willie merely grunted over his tripod so she ignored him, too. She'd read up on the twite before they left. It was also called the Pennine finch or moor finch. She'd discovered it is unique in that it feeds its nestlings on seeds regurgitated as a kind of mash. Once it had been widespread throughout these Pennine valleys flying up in clouds of hundreds during the breeding season. Now you would be lucky if you saw thirty, the book had said. But here on Cloughgreen Common Bolly settled for two. And this was one of its few remaining breeding sites. If Ursa Power got their way it was *Gotterdammerung* for the twite and the bog, she thought.

Jesus, it made her angry. You can't build a twite out of spit and string. You can't build a bog out of kitchen peelings. Once they're gone, they're gone. God isn't making them any more.

Later in June the birds in their garden brought forth their young. Blue tits, great tits, collar doves, sparrows, chaffinches, green finches, most of the corvids and two shy young woodpeckers.

Gloopy, tentative, unsure even about being birds, the baby birds bumbled into the feeders and the tall, thick protective hawthorn hedge. Some of them waited to be fed by their mothers next to the feeders, others got into the big protected cage to feed themselves off all the provided seed and then suddenly panicked about how to fly out.

And then the hard-eyed sparrow hawks came. Eyes big as orangey-yellow headlights. The smaller male on the Thursday. His mate the following Saturday. Let the babies relax and let their ruffled feathers settle. Then hit 'em again. Professional assassins.

Their *modus operandi* was similar. They zoomed in low, hard and fast over the five-barred gate. Death on the wing.

Down-turned ripping beak, yellow talons like surgical steel scalpels. Accelerating fast down the acre and rising to shoulder height before pulling a handbrake-turn into the dense, thickly spiked hawthorn hedge. There was a commotion as the smaller birds squealed and dove for cover. Some fled out the other side. Some froze with fear. Some sat gloopy and uncomprehending.

Willie and Bolly watched as the male sparrow hawk emerged at high speed from the other side of the hedge. He had flown straight through it without slowing. They glimpsed blood on his chest feathers and something in his talons. Then he dipped out of their eye line. The hedge fell silent.

'Natural selection,' was all Willie could mutter at the time, stunned by the speed and savagery of the attack.

'Nature, red in tooth and claw,' Bolly murmured.

They had seen it every year since they had lived there and come to accept it. The suddenness and finality of the attack still took their breath away.

But they had come to accept the deadly encounters as a culling of the slower or weaker-minded among the avian gene pools. And despite everything they found the hawks impressive.

After the hawk had gone, they drifted off into a summer reverie, sitting around the wooden table and listening to the roar of the bees in the honeysuckle.

Next day, twenty yards into the moor, Nelson nosed over a small pile of downy, brown sparrow feathers. It marked the spot where the hawk had stripped its prey clean. Though really he knew better, it still saddened Willie.

Instinctively he averted his eyes. Looked instead at a long, meandering stand of 4'-high pinky-purple and cream foxgloves with their mottled bell-like flowers.

Then he thought about it. What the heck? Gloopy or frozen with fear, the baby sparrow wouldn't have known what hit it. New life had been pumped into baby sparrow hawks.

# 16

June 30th

The day before the planned Woolton demo there were torrents of summer storm rain. Bolly and Willie looked fretful and prayed for dry weather, mindful of the electronics in the gizmo. Willie set the alarm for five and fell out of bed when it went off. Nelson was rushed off on an abbreviated walk over the moors. The weather gods had favoured them. July 1st was warm and fine.

When they got back Bolly had ready a monster ration of scrambled egg on toast with coffee. They sailed out of Cloughgreen bang on 6 with Jumper's trailer hooked up and a black tarp in the back in case of downpours.

The plan was to go over to Liverpool to collect Dr Freddy Mount and Dave Dean, the DJ who was going to operate the sound part of the gizmo.

Then they would rendezvous on the outskirts of Woolton with a minibus hired from Pennine Garages containing Carter, Phyllis and another 10 Friends of the Living Moorland.

They pulled up on the tarmac outside a red sandstone mansion opposite Sefton Park in Liverpool. It had obviously been converted into flats. But they seemed pretty ritzy flats. This was Freddy Mount's place. He leaned out of a raised first-floor sash window and waved as they pulled up.

He was a skinny guy and he raced down the big curved mansion house staircase to greet them. His ginger moustache was quivering with excitement. He seemed positively high.

'Great to see you, Willie, Bollie. Any chance of a hand with the gizmo, Willie?'

'Sure, lead on.'

Upstairs in Freddy's room there wasn't much to see of the Gizmo. It had been encased in a large metal cabinet and painted green. It had slats on the front and leads for two 12-volt batteries. Someone had painted the words "Moaning Green Gizmo" on the side in a fine red fairground italic.

Freddy caught Willie looking and said 'One of the arts types did that. We couldn't resist the ironic green paint.'

'Why Moaning Green Gizmo?'

Freddy Mount's mouth stretched wide as a banana in what the Americans call a shit-eating grin.

'Just wait till you hear it, Willie! It's ace.'

'It looks evil,' Bolly said, having traipsed upstairs to join them.

'Yeah, but just wait till you see it in action and hear it. Awesome. Does both the whump, whump, whump of turbine noise and the silent subsonic stuff that gets into your bones.'

They turned around to see who had spoken. Freddy threw out a hand.

'This is Dave Dean, aka Deano, proprietor of Deano's Dazzling Disco. Deano's not a student,' Freddy said.

'Was once though. About 15 years ago.'

'Not a very good one.'

'Don't be cheeky, Freddy. If this thing gives trouble I can give it a bollocking in good Gauloise French.'

Dr Freddy Mount shrugged and grinned. 'What did I tell you?'

Deano was a stocky lad in his late 30s with a gelled forward-looking black haystack of hair. The round red face beneath had been so ravaged by acute acne that he looked like a small pox survivor. His blobby red nose had pocks you could store rice in. Bolly's heart immediately went out to him. But then considering his bearing she felt she didn't need to feel sorry for him. He was pure-bred Liverpool scally.

His cheeky chappy demeanour suggested he didn't trust mirrors much and knew his own worth wasn't skin-deep. Any woman that didn't agree with him wasn't worth it. Her tough luck. He indicated the other side of Freddy's capacious living room

'We've got two whacking great speakers here,' he said, 'fill a disco usually. They'll whistle up a storm. The CD we've put together is a killer. Loads of blade whoosh, overlaid with mechanical drive clank and unheard - but definitely there - some real torture chamber 'White Noise' which Freddy supplied. It's funny, the white noise, you can't hear it, but you can sort of feel it in your body and your bones.'

'Excellent,' Bolly said.

'Come again?'

'Sounds like Freddy has got it bang on. That's exactly what the health reports say it feels like. Why it makes you ill. Gets inside you.'

'I wouldn't have believed it unless I'd listened myself. I mean, it's spooky - sound you can't even hear but it makes you feel bad.'

'Believe it, it does.'

'Oh I do now, yeah, that's what I'm saying. White noise, him powerful juju, boss,' Deano said, affecting a Hollywood African accent

Having let Deano have his say, Freddy Mount stepped forward and rested his left hand on the Moaning Green Gizmo.

'Like I said, I've simulated the blade flicker of a small cluster of four industrial wind turbines overlapping slightly with one in front, the others receding. The simulation uses low-level lasers behind a cut-metal whirling array.' At the word "lasers" both Willie and Bollie shuffled their feet and took a deep breath, looked at each other.

Freddy smiled. 'Don't worry, folks. No actual planners will be blinded during the showing of this demo.' He patted the cabinet once more.

'Wait till you hear it go, it's the stuff of your worst nightmares. Deano's done a great job.' He paused and looked significantly at Willie.

'You're a photographer, right? Point this at a glass tower and we should have some extraordinary visual displays. You should get some great snaps. In fact we wouldn't mind a few of the whole thing as a memento.'

'Least we could do.'

'Send 'em via the Physics faculty. So I can show 'em to the lads who helped me.'

'You will have plenty of nice glossy 10 x 8s of the Woolton Council *son et lumiere*.'

Freddy chuckled. ' "*Son et lumiere*"; I wonder if that's what they'll call it.'

'Hell on wheels, I hope,' Bolly said.

They lodged the Gizmo safely in the trailer with Deano's sound equipment and at Deano's insistence lashed the tarp down over it. Then the two Scousers climbed into the back seat of the Range Rover.

'Sound, issn't it, this?' Deano pronounced. Freddy just smiled, like an indulgent parent.

After a while Bolly noticed that every time they stopped for traffic lights or at roundabouts Deano half swivelled and looked anxiously out the back window.

'Trailer okay, still?'

'Yeah. You gorra keep an eye out,' Deano said. 'Tealeaves everywhere. Terrible, isn't it?' He spoke as though the infestation of thieves was a native condition of the territory like blackwater fever. Bolly suddenly realized the tarp was there for security as much as protection from rain.

'That's half his livelihood out there,' Freddy said quietly, fiddling with his ginger moustache.

'Half?' Willie queried, changing down for the motorway filter road.

'Me vinyls an' me tapes an' me CDs are at home.' It came out as a low nasal whine. But Bolly suddenly realized what a generous gesture this rough and ready Scouser was making of his equipment and time. To her it had just been sound equipment, but as Freddy had pointed out Deano was actually risking his livelihood. She made a mental note to go on the Net and see him alright with some rare piece of vinyl when this was done and dusted. Something rare and tasty.

The purple minibus was waiting as inconspicuously as a purple minibus can wait, just where they'd arranged.

'I bet that's what Irish undercover agents use,' Deano joked.

'Careful,' Bolly said, 'Be a shame to lose one of the demonstrators before we even start.'

'You posh Irish then?' he said doubtfully, a concept that had never occurred to him before. Posh and Irish together.

Carter Briggs's sheer size stunned the loquacious Deano into silence as he pumped the hands of the fellow demonstrators. Bolly guessed he reminded him of police.

Willie looked at his watch: 10-45. They'd made good time.

'We need to kick off by 11.30 before people start drifting off to lunch,' Carter said.

That left time for Phyllis to unveil mounds of fresh sandwiches acquired at the Cloughgreen Deli Bar en route and flasks of coffee. In to battle on a full stomach.

The main Woolton square had a landscaped island in the centre of it with trim hedges and flowerbeds and park benches. There were mature trees every 20 yards on the pavements opposite. They parked the Range Rover up on the kerb with the minibus in the next gap behind.

Dr Mount had engineered the Gizmo so that it stood on a universal joint like that on a camera tripod. They whipped the tarp off and he quickly swiveled the Gizmo to face the Woolton Council building. He aimed the cone of the light at a point midway up to allow it to radiate outwards over the whole face of the glass building.

'Quick as you can, Deano, before some traffic warden or copper comes along.' He seemed to have assumed control of operations so Willie dithered on the edge idly watching them. They worked quickly, setting the kit up and connecting the batteries.

Bolly paced up and down with a big grin on her face. Willie could see she was enjoying herself massively. Until this wind farm stuff had kicked off he hadn't realized how aggressive she could be. All that Norman blood way back in her Dad's family.

At 11.25 Dr Mount sidled up to Bolly. Deano was seated at the controls in the trailer. 'All set to go, Bolly. Say the word.'

Bolly marched up to the trailer, red hair lifting in the slight breeze, like Boudicca next to her war chariot. *'Fiat Lux,'* she said. Then she pointed at Deano - 'cue Deano' - and brought her hand down. 'Let there be wind farm.'

Deano flicked the switches and all hell broke loose. Waves of golden light rotated slowly over the broad face of the glass building twinkling like fireflies. At the same time this amazing bass whooshing noise washed over the building. Intermittently, as promised, and realistically, the mechanical sound of the drive train cut in. The whole thing sounded like a banshee dragging its manacles and chains.

The effect was instantaneous. People in the Council buildings were rushing to the windows to see where all this was coming from. People getting in and out of their cars, ditto.

'What the hell is it?' a bystander asked. She had Gerry's explanatory leaflet thrust into her hand. Carter Briggs and Dr Phyllis Bentley were striding purposefully over to the main entrance of the Council building clutching handfuls of leaflets.

'Just going to educate the planners on what industrial turbines do,' Carter said gleefully.

'Mind you, I think they're already getting the message,' Dr Bentley chortled.

Willie Dee was shooting off image after image as they entered. He got some wonderful close ups of angry faces leaning out of office windows with light beams tracking across blinking eyes.

Dr Freddy Mount was leaning against the Range Rover smoking a roll-up. 'Pretty cool, huh. Suck that you planning bastards.' Bolly had to stop herself from kissing him. It was perfect.

The Friends of the Living Moorland, leaflets in hand, were working the square as keen as a team of Jehova's Witnesses. Some of them had brought very professional-looking placards - "Save the planet - trash your own backyard", "Save the planet - foul your own nest", "Save the planet - kill the bogs-n-birds-n-bats". There was even one directed at good old Dr Newall - "Think Green - plant a planner".

In amongst the leaflet distributors Bolly thought she recognised a few large members of the Cloughgreen rugby team. Good thinking, Carter, just in case it gets ugly.

'It actually sounds worse than the real thing,' Willie said. 'Because it's got that reverberating echo on it as the sound bounces all round the square.'

'It figures,' Bolly said. 'It's another manifestation of the whole noise problem the turbines have. It is so unpredictably bound up with the local topography. Here it's created an echo, as though the turbine were set up in a canyon. Anyway they're only getting it for half an hour, let 'em suffer.'

Meanwhile the Moaning Green Gizmo boomed on, its light array rotating arcs across the front of the building.

As they talked, Freddy lightly touched his sleeve and pointed. Behind them irate shopkeepers were gathered in a bunch and pointing angrily at them. Raised voices drifted over. 'I think we've had our fun, Willie. Best get those big lads back to protect the trailer.'

Willie rattled off a few shots of Freddy in front of the array and Deano at the controls. Then he looked at his watch. 'Ten minutes,' he said to Bolly. 'They could only stand it for ten minutes.' As he spoke he could see a delegation heading towards them from the Council ofices.

'Can you turn it up any more, Deano?'

'Sure thing, boss,' the Hollywood African said, rotating the volume switch. The booming-swooshing noise suddenly became unbearable, the clanking like metal spikes in the brain. God knows what the white noise felt like over in the Council offices.

Willie strode over to the other side of the square and spoke to the Cloughgreen rugby team's gorillas. They nodded and fell in behind him. They knew what they were there for. He suddenly realised they were dressed in their green and navy club blazers and ties.

By the time he got back Bolly was fending off the irate shopkeepers who said the noise was ruining their business, driving people out of their shops.

The three lads from the rugby team formed a loose ring around the trailer. There they lurked like semi-official security. Big lads looking serious.

'Ten minutes of wind farm noise that's all you've had. How would you like a lifetime of it? That's what people out in the country are getting.'

'That's the whole point, we're not in the country. Let them keep this racket out there,' an angry little guy with a white spikey haircut was saying. He was only about 5'8" but he was broad and stocky and looked as though he could handle himself.

Willie tuned out the angry comments and looked around hoping to see Carter Briggs returning to handle the Angry Brigade from the shops. Encouragingly, while the shopkeepers were ranting, various passers-by were giving thumbs up and yelling "Good on you, get rid of the hideous things" and stuff like that. The usual split Willie thought cynically. Also as usual those closest wanted them turned off and vanished.

The Moaning Green Gizmo droned on. He looked at his watch. They'd managed 15 minutes now. It was only a matter of time before the police arrived and moved them on, but so far, so good. There had been plenty of time to make their point. He had pictures for the Cloughgreen Recorder and the Woolton Times. Who knows, he might crawl under UKWC radar and even make the nationals.

Whilst he was musing on the impact the demo might make on the media the short spiky-haired guy made a lunge for the trailer. He would not have believed it had he not seen it, but

Chris Head, the massive 6'7" rugby team captain stepped smartly forward and intercepted the stocky guy. He extended both arms forward and caught the guy firmly around the throat. Then, grinning broadly, he gently lifted him about six inches off the ground, kicking and struggling, and carried him about ten feet backwards before depositing him gently on the pavement. It was an amazing display of colossal upper body strength. The short guy was red-faced with impotence and anger. But he wasn't going back for more. He stormed off back to his shop. 'I'm calling the fuckin' police,' he yelled over his shoulder.

Chris Head shrugged his massive shoulders and his two team mates grinned their solidarity.

'Bloody 'ell,' said an awed Scouse voice from the trailer, stunned by the feat he'd just witnessed.

'It had to happen sooner or later,' Bolly said, 'the police, I mean.'

'Quite,' said Carter Briggs striding into the proceedings.

The Moaning Green Gizmo whooshed on. 'Shall we disassemble it and pack up then?' Freddy Mount asked, having to raise his voice.

'Yes, please,' Carter said. 'We've made our point. Any more will I think be counterproductive.'

Dr Mount drew his forefinger across his throat in a cut-throat gesture and Deano killed the Moaning Green Gizmo dead.

Suddenly the roar of the town traffic seemed eerily quiet. The Council Buildings had ceased to be part of a startling light show and reverted to being a water-stained concrete and glass sixties tower block.

'So endeth the Woolton *son et lumiere,*' Bolly said. 'Pity really, only 20 minutes from this wonderful little Gizmo.'

'Sometimes, Bolly, you have to quit when you're ahead,' Carter said, and Willie was glad it was him who'd said it. That was when they heard the siren.

Two police cars came screaming into the square, blues and twos in action.

'Best round the troops up, Phyllis,' Carter said.

'Yes, sir,' she said, snapping off an ironic salute.

'Okay if we disappear, Mr Briggs?' Chris Head asked.

'Yes, and thanks for your help, lads. That little chap could have got nasty.'

'No probs,' Chris Head said and the heavy brigade sidled back to their minibus. No unnecessary confrontation with the law.

Carter Briggs strode confidently to the front of the Gizmo as the police officers approached. This is what his expensive public school and 3 years as an officer in a top drawer regiment had prepared him for: natural leadership.

'Morning officers, how can I help you? Carter Briggs at your service.'

Though it irked part of him to be so impressed, Willie admitted he was. With his plummy tones, easy stance and confidence, Carter Briggs oozed authority. Hands behind his back, legs akimbo, he could have been on the square at Wellington Barracks greeting his NCOs.

'We've had a complaint from the council offices about some machine bombarding them with noise and light rays, Mr Briggs,' the sergeant said, subconsciously deferring to greater authority.

'Light rays, Sergeant?' Carter chuckled. 'You mean like Flash Gordon or Dan Dare? Sci-fi? Death rays? That sort of thing?'

'I don't know about that,' the sergeant said, realizing how far-fetched it sounded. 'It's just what they said.'

'Well we've had a little *son et lumiere*, Sergeant, by way of a wind farm demo. But we haven't been using death rays, I can assure you. If we had something like that we'd be talking to the Pentagon. Not,' he rolled his eyes, 'trying to take out Woolton Council.'

'No, I suppose not,' the sergeant said, looking doubtful. 'When you put it like that.'

Best finish this quick. Everything from this guy's two hundred and fifty quid brogues to the way his haircut had that little duck's tail flick up at the back spoke authority.

'Anyway, you're finished then, you're moving on?'

Carter Briggs raised his hands, palms up, and lowered his voice, a reasonable man explaining. 'As you observe, Sergeant, no noise, no death rays. We have had our little demo and made our point. Now we're off home. We don't want to rip the arse out of it.'

'Well, if you are sure you are going now.'

'Just as soon as we've got the tarp on.'

'In case of further developments, I'll need your details, sir.' *Sir.*

'Here you are, Sergeant,' Carter said, handing him a business card.

Willie watched the sergeant take the card then write his Range Rover's reg on the back of it and the minibus's reg. Groan.

'If your superiors have any further questions, this leaflet may answer them. And of course you can always phone me,' Carter was saying, the epitome of reasonableness. He passed the leaflet over.

'Right you are, sir. Sorry to bother you. We'll just wait and see you off. Leave it at that.'

'Very decent of you, Sergeant,' Carter said. Dismissed. The sergeant waved his men back into the cars.

'Works every time,' Carter said, grinning. 'Let's go folks, while the going is good. Job well done. See if they can ignore this at Woolton Council.'

In the event, they couldn't. Humphrey Drumm ran one of Willie's pics under the title "What wind farms really feel like". In the text he promoted them to "activists", Willie noted.

The Woolton Times ran a front page piece under the header "20 minute demo hell", telling about the amazing effects and how it had brought traffic to a standstill with people rubber-necking and municipal anger.

The letters page next day was split about 50/50 pro and against the demo. Many ordinary people who had read the leaflet confessed themselves amazed that fluffy green wind farms could have such anti-social aspects. On the other hand, there was quite a backlash from some people more or less saying why couldn't these yokels just stay over in their hole in the ground in darkest Cloughgreen and leave the city folk to go about their business.

'Why can't you inbred bastards try and save the planet and leave smart Woolton in peace,' is pretty much the line, Willie said.

'Spread your legs and think of Woolton,' Bolly said. 'Your sacrifice hurts us just as much, I don't think.'

Best of all the Sunday Telegraph ran a pic and a very thoughtful piece entitled "Wind farm demo raises serious health issues". In it they reproduced stories from Frey & Hadden's website. And they mentioned the dual difficulties of measuring and predicting sound nuisance and of foreseeing the problems of noise and blade flicker vis a vis topography. And the fact that different countries had minimum distances to place wind farms from habitations. Inevitably, because the UK was already so crowded, the distances were shorter and sometimes fudged. The countryside was really too small to accommodate the vast amounts of space wind farms needed. They also raised the issue of how much renewable wind farm electricity was costing overall: subsidies, loss of the wild spaces and rare flora and fauna and now health problems for innocent people. If there was the slightest risk to anyone's health they argued, the wind farm should not proceed. Not the other way around as it was now where you had to trust to luck.

Bolly presented both Freddy and Deano with magnums of her favourite champagne as thanks for their part. Both seemed impressed.

'Stylish,' Freddy observed. 'If you need any more help, just give us a shout.'

'We will,' Bolly said. 'And as for you, Deano, it was amazing you should risk your kit for us. I'm going to see if I can find you an interesting piece of vinyl for your collection.'

'Ace,' Deano said, 'I'm really chuffed to have helped. It was, like, an adventure.'

Ten days later he was the proud owner of two vintage 45s by Blondie: "Kidnapper" and "Rip her to shreds". A good thirty quids' worth of anyone's money.

Dr Freddy Mount rang to thank them for Willie's photos and to say Deano was "over the moon" with his vinyl. Good. She was pretty sure Deano would have loved the energy and edginess of Blondie. She'd have sent Debby Harry herself, gift-wrapped, if she could.

When the adrenaline had stopped running and she and Willie had sat down with a quiet glass or two they'd agreed they could never have made the last-minute impact on the upcoming vote at Woolton Council without the help of Freddy and Deano.

'We even made one of the nationals. And that's finally it, now, Bolly. We, you and I, can finally do no more. We have to acknowledge that so far as we're concerned we really can do no more.'

'I wish there was something else, though. I mean, there must be something still which we haven't thought of.'

'No, Bolly, I know it's hard but we have to let go now and stop tormenting ourselves. There really is nothing else we can do.'

'It just seems so irrevocable. And what if that sneaky bastard Newall somehow tricks it through?'

'Bolly, our only hope now is Carter and Phyllis. Carter tells me Phyllis is a genius at putting well thought-out documents together and there are expert witness statements. But really and truly it seems our best chance is the genuine unknowability of the hydrology status. And Ursa's slackness. Some guy at Cloughgreen Antiquarian Society has come up with ancient maps and sketches which purport to show the extent and whereabouts of some of the earlier mine workings. Whether they'll accept them as evidence or not, we don't know. Plus there is the threat of flooding anyway if you strip off the peat from Cloughgreen Moor. And of course, the likelihood of so many farms' spring water being affected and their herds deprived of water.'

'Much Ursa Power will care about that.'

'Not a jot. But that's not the issue. It's how much Woolton's planners can ignore it.'

'If they put these things in all over Cloughgreen and ancient Elmet I'll never forgive myself.'

'Look, Bolly,' Willie said, getting up from his armchair and crossing the room to put his hands on her shoulders, 'I know how passionately you care about this. So do I. But I meant what I said. It's out of our hands now. We can do no more.'

'You say that, Willie. But I can't believe it. There must be something else we can do.'

'We must draw a line now, Bolly, for our own peace of mind. There comes a time when you have to let things go or they will go inside and destroy you.'

Bolly started ever so gently to weep. 'I have a bad feeling about this, Willie. Call it women's intuition.'

'Bolly, for a very long time we've fought the good fight. We've researched this thing, written letters, designed leaflets, phoned people, emailed people, done stuff to raise funds for the Friends of the Living Moorland, canvassed people, more or less lived and dreamed it. And the Moaning Green Gizmo was a great, successful climax. Now we have to try and get back to how our lives were before.'

'I don't know that I can, Willie.'

Willie sat down on the settee next to her, put his arms around her and kissed her forehead gently, hating the powerlessness.

'You must, Verity. You must.'

'If we lose, I'll never accept it. Never.' Willie sighed. She sounded like a little girl who was in danger of losing her pony. Then he offered up a silent prayer for the outcome on August 1st in two weeks' time.

'Hand on heart,' he said, 'whatever happens, Verity, we have nothing to reproach ourselves with. We could have done no more.

# 17

That July would be one the people of Cloughgreen remembered for many years. It was full of steamy early morning mists and humid, hot days.

Willie looked out of the window around seven when he was making Bolly's coffee and saw streamers of long wispy cloud against a blue sky. By the time he'd served the coffee and come downstairs the early-morning sun had heated the dewy moors up and generated thick mists. Another hour or two and the mists were burned off. Same almost everyday for a month.

Older people talked of it being like an old-fashioned Spitfire summer with blue skies and vapour trails in the sky. Nature was rampant. There were 6' stands of purple rosebay willow herb waving gently. The lacey white cow parsley was shoulder-high. And Nelson with his thick black coat drank and drank and drank. As the hot sun shrank the streams, he discovered springs hidden behind lofty ferns and in ruined cottages.

Day after day, Willie and Nelson walked across moors vibrant with purple heather. The bees were so drunk with nectar they were rolling around on the ground. Nelson had to be warned off playing with them.

One day they encountered a dense black cloud of horseflies that clung to everything. Willie's head and arms and legs were covered in them as he frantically swatted.

Getting home, he suddenly realised Nelson was bumping into table legs and chairs. He hadn't been able to close his good eye and now it was swollen with dead black flies that had feasted off the moisture of his eyeball. He appeared to be blind.

Willie panicked, got him into the Range Rover and took off down to the vets in Cloughgreen.

The vet washed the eye out and treated it, said it was sore and infected. He said it should recover but would require three days rest and eye drops. He covered the eye with a patch that fitted over one of Nelson's ears. And then this big, plastic, dunce's-cap-shaped collar which stopped him scratching the patch off and whacked into everything as he walked.

Nelson hated it. He whimpered, bumping into things and was generally miserable. It was painful to watch. For 3 days the dog was wretched. And over it all Willie fretted. What if Nelson stayed blind? At five, it would be too cruel. He was still a young dog.

It broke Bolly's heart watching them. Willie trying to anticipate the dog's needs and be his eyes, shoving him in the right direction. Telling him "This way, Nelson" and the dog trying to follow his directions but still bumping into the door or a chair leg.

Willie's anxiety, love and concern were palpable. Watching them she knew full well why she loved this man.

Three days later the patch came off and things were fine. Nelson could see perfectly again out of his one eye. He tried desperately to lick and lick the skin off Willie's hand to thank him. Finally Willie took the big white plastic collar off and Nelson did three high-speed victory laps of the garden for sheer joie de vivre, trampling some fiery red *crocosmias* in a final handbrake turn.

Then suddenly the black cloud that had hung invisibly over that perfect July materialized.

The calendar showed August 1st. The day of reckoning down at Woolton Town Hall. The sun shone brightly and swallows swooped. The field beyond the garden at Greenwood Royd was filled with waist-high, purple-topped thistles and Bolly breathed in deep draughts of their sweet scent. She had never realized they had scent before. Maybe it was the hot sun.

All day Bolly and Willie were nervous around each other. It felt like a very serious trip to the hospital for something feared and dreaded but not openly acknowledged. Neither of them wanted to talk about it, hoping for the best.

'Let's take the Mini Cooper,' Bolly suggested. 'Then you can go and have a few beers with Carter and the lads when we win.'

'Suits me,' Willy said.

Woolton town centre was a nightmare place to park, jam-packed with prohibitory signs and one-way systems: home of the borough planners. And they had flexed their muscles. Bolly parked half a mile away in a pay and display and they started to walk. Even though they were both in short sleeves and shorts it was still warm enough to sweat.

Woolton Town Hall was pretty much like Cloughgreen Town Hall in that it was a mock Greek temple, Willie thought. But it was much bigger. And unlike Cloughgreen which had been sandblasted white, its soot-encrusted exterior made it resemble one of the old satanic mills.

'Look out,' Willie said, 'Ursa have got Rent-A-Mob out.'

he pointed to about 100 youngish people in green t-shirts that proclaimed in white letters WE WANT WIND POWER. They were chanting their t-shirt front and seemed to have come for a party. Arkadiy Kovalenko, sharp-suited as ever, was chatting to a very pretty blonde in a white ra-ra skirt and bonny brown thighs. Willie noticed and smiled, and silently wished him well. No hard feelings.

‘If I were a puritan, I’d say drink has been taken,’ he said.

‘And folding stuff pocketed,’ Bolly added.

Slowly the Friends of the Living Moorland debussed from their minibuses. Apart from the same three rugby club minders who had been at the demo, they were predominantly middle-aged and soberly dressed. They passed through the massed chanting ranks with their modest “No to Wind Farms” lapel badges and an air of bewilderment. Where had this lot sprung from?

‘They don’t even have local accents,’ Bolly said with disgust as they passed into the massive hall. She looked around the hall. Most people were still standing around. ‘No sign of Newall.’

‘Don’t worry, the demon king will be lurking somewhere,’ Willie said.

The meeting started at 7 prompt with Dave Summit the fortyish CEO of Woolton Council on his feet explaining the procedure. He looked tanned, fit, immaculately groomed and at his ease, every inch the successful chief executive on the upward path.

‘Chief Planner Ernest Maitland will outline the expert view his department has presented to Woolton Council. Then Mr Ilya Bakunin, the MD of Ursa Power, will represent Ursa Power’s view. Then there will be five selected representatives of The Friends of the Living Moorland who will each be allowed five minutes to present their views. Followed by five speakers for the applicant, Ursa Power.’

His manner was gravely serious, but confident: “Trust us, we have excellent planners; we know about these things.”

‘So, to initiate proceedings I hand you over to Mr Ernest Maitland, our Chief Planner, he said, ‘a professional of many years experience.’ He gestured for Ernest to come forward.

Ernest Maitland rose stiffly and ambulated his tall, gaunt frame to the podium, clutching his notes. If there had been any wind his clothes would have flapped about him. He wore a slightly shiny, but immaculately pressed brown suit, which may have been made forty years earlier, rather as some grand aristocrat favoured well-made vintage clothing. Milk bottle white flesh emerged from apertures in the brown twill in a way suggestive of a cadaver.

Willie, who was about fifty feet from the platform, was shocked. ‘Jesus, he’s so ghastly white and anaemic he barely seems alive.’

‘And that suit looks like his dad’s. I bet Dave Summit’s haircut cost more.’

‘Well maybe not when the suit was new, when Ted Heath was prime minister.

Ernest Maitland favoured the delivery he had used for 30 years as a lay preacher. He leaned back and declaimed from his notes. His naturally reedy voice rose shrilly loud at unexpected points in a way designed to keep the congregation awake.

His audience on this evening found it slightly unnerving. But he was a meticulous man and he droned on for a good long while, startling them from time to time, conscientiously covering all the aspects the council was required by law to consider.

By way of introduction, he started by saying what a strategically important location Woolton Borough occupied, being sited midway between two areas of outstanding natural beauty, the Peak District national park and the Lake District national park. And that therefore the borough had especial duties to government, as well as the developer, to give careful consideration to this application for energy renewables in this part of the country.

'Hang on,' Bolly said. 'That's just why they want to knock us over as an easy target. He should be saying we must resist being seen as an easy sacrifice, just because we are where we are. Not saying open your legs and think of England.'

'Bloody hell. It doesn't give you confidence, does it?'

'Well, from their point of view, what he's really saying I guess is that central government is sitting on their heads. If they don't meet their renewables target in this part of the world, then dark and terrible things will happen to them. Withdrawal of agreed funding, fines, the lot. Play ball with us or we use the baseball bat on you. That's the way this government works. No persuasion or carrot. It's all bully boy stuff.'

'Shit,' Willie said. 'But surely they must listen to real local specific problems, not just the usual, dogmatic "we must make sacrifices rubbish?"'

'Don't bank on it. There seems to be a lot of enlightened self-interest at work here. Sssshhh, anyway, people are giving us looks.'

Willie and Bolly listened carefully to discover what Ernest Maitland had to say about the hydrology report. But he made no particular points.

He concluded: 'There have been attempts made recently of a reckless, almost lawless kind, to influence this council's decision.' He paused, before moving into Old Testament fire and brimstone mood. 'The good people of Woolton Council were subjected to a very nasty attack involving lasers and white noise which could have injured innocent local government employees. Public servants. That will not work. That cannot be allowed to work. Rather the opposite. We will judge this application entirely on its merits.'

Bolly nudged Willie, 'Freddy's gizmo didn't impress him. The old bugger's got totally the wrong end of the stick.'

'Yeah, he just doesn't get it, does he? The planners can condemn ordinary people to a lifetime of misery. But try and subject the planners to just 20 simulated minutes of it and the world falls in.'

After Ernest Maitland's impassioned plea that people power should be ignored, Ursa Power's MD was like a warm bath.

Ilya Bakunin was like a smoother, Russian Dave Summit, Bolly thought, but with more gravitas. Apart from confirming what an absolutely purpose built site Cloughgreen was for the delivery of vast quantities of wind power, Bakunin's speech was predictable.

Need to save the planet...renewables, blah...sustainables, blah,...future generations thank us, blah...clean, green electricity, blah. No mention of mazuma, moola, big bucks or roubles. He took a fraction of the time Maitland took and was obviously relying on his expert witnesses.

Both Carter Briggs and Dr Phyllis Bentley spoke eloquently against the application. Carter hammered home the risks posed by faulty hydrology. Dr Phyllis Bentley spoke of health risks. But finished with an analysis of letters to the council which revealed that support for the wind farm came almost exclusively from post codes outside the borough. The Bus Boys in other words, Rent-A-Mob. As usual, all the local correspondence was against it.

'More dirty tricks,' Bolly said. Willie shrugged.

*'Quel surprise.'*

Ursa's expert witnesses appeared to be all professionals and arrogant southerners. There was none of the self-deprecation that went down well in these parts. Willie could feel the resentment stirring among those in the hall as they felt they were being patronized. What was it Bolly said the Scouse football fans used to sing? All cockneys are bastards. Substitute southern for cockneys and you wouldn't be far out. Himself excluded of course.

Eventually Dave Summers came back and said it was time for the councillors to retire and consider what they had heard. They would return in 30 minutes.

The councillors filed back in at the appointed hour and were seated. The mayor went clockwise around the long table. One after another the arms went up in support for the application. It was passed unanimously. The councillors were acutely aware of the local feeling in the hall, so they looked very sober.

The mayor confirmed the result and there was a loud gasp of disbelief from the hall. Then there was a football supporters' type cheer from the Rent-A-Mob t-shirt brigade and Ilya Bakunin and Arkadiy Kovalenko stood like Cup-winning players supporting each other's arm. Result. Let the millions roll into our Cayman Islands bank accounts. A cool seven hundred grand for every turbine for the next 25 years. All 40 of them. Yahoooooooo!!!!

Bolly had gone pale under her usually swarthy skin colour and Willie thought she was going to faint.

'What happened to all the hydrology issues? How could we possibly lose?' she asked.

Willie was speechless. He felt like when he was nine and he'd spent a month building a rubber-band-powered, balsa wood and tissue aeroplane. It crashed into a blackthorn hedge and smashed itself to pieces on its maiden flight. He was near tears. He didn't trust himself to speak. Sorry, twites, we did our best.

Over the other side of the room Carter Briggs and Dr Bentley and the other people they knew from Friends of the Living Moorland waved wanly, also too choked to talk.

Bolly thought of what Gerry and Jumper had said.

Woolton have never done Cloughgreen any favours. But now the Fat Lady really had sung.

She looked over to where Dave Summers stood grinning with a group of councillors. Got almost all your renewables quota in, eh, Dave, and well away from Woolton and the people who matter to you. Sod Cloughgreen. And, oh, how those people in Westminster you want to impress will love you. You cocky, uncaring, selfish bastard.

'Come on home, Willie,' she said. 'There's nothing here for us. Thank god, I brought the Mini, I couldn't bear the post-mortems they are going to be having in the minibuses going home.'

'Are you going to be okay to drive?' he asked, dreading she'd feel over-emotional, put her foot down and kill them both.

'Yeahhh,' she did her brave smile. 'No-one died, did they? We just lost a wind farm application which will change a huge block of ancient countryside and what we have to live with everyday.'

'No,' he said, 'no-one died, Bolly,' putting his arm around her and steering her back to where they'd left the car.

She unlocked the Mini and they got in. 'I'm okay to drive now. I dunno how I'm going to feel tomorrow though. Or when they start putting the bloody things up in our faces.'

'No,' he said. Maniacally, he thought of that last line in Gone With The Wind: "Tomorrow is another day". He just about kept his mouth shut.

Yeah, tomorrow was another day, okay. But what sort of another day? He knew he should say something. But what? He was plain no good with words and feelings. He just wished he could photograph stuff and pass it over - This is how I feel.

In the ad business the writers had a funny saying. "If you find your art director can spell, get shut of him. Because he can't be a proper art director." He felt the same way about the spoken word and feelings and being able to control things. But he sensed one thing. The longer this wind farm issue went on the more he felt Bolly was moving away from him.

Two weeks later Reddingley Borough Council vetoed Ursa's app for the last 20 turbines on their patch. Ursa immediately appealed to the Planning Inspectorate in Bristol. Dr Newall and Ursa's legal team were confident they'd get the last turbines through eventually. The encirclement and occupation of Ted Hughes's ancient kingdom, Elmet, would be completed. And Ursa would then rake in another £14 million a year. To go with the £42 million per annum they would take from Cloughgreen.

Besides, so far as Dr Newall was concerned, the important turbines at Cloughgreen had been okayed. This was another step down the road to his Purity Valley development.

# 18

Humphrey Drumm, completely impartial editor of the Cloughgreen Recorder, felt as thunderstruck and downcast as the rest of Cloughgreen when his cub reporter phoned back the Woolton MBC turbines decision.

Why did the bastards of this world always seem to win he wondered angrily. More measured reflections over a pint of Black Sheep overturned this conviction. It just wasn't true. The good guys did win some times. Of course they did. And it was all relative. Noughties Britain still wasn't quite Stalin's Russia. Even though this over-mighty, constantly interfering government sometimes made it feel like Stalinism without the shooting; with its targets and quotas and 10-year-plans and great clunking fist.

Round about the third pint Humphrey calmed down. In his heart he felt it was a disaster for Cloughgreen and he also felt the decision opened the floodgates. If not 40 wind turbines to go with the 20 already in at the Delf, why not more? Where's the visual amenity to save, would be the planning reason? He could see that. You've got this lot already, what difference will another 20 or 80 or 360 matter? You'll be saving some other town from making a sacrifice. Oh yeah, his experience of life was that once people got the knife in it was hard to stop them twisting it.

Verity Dee, the most eloquent of the anti-windfarm campaigners on his letters page, had written in one letter, in mock religious mode, "I shall lift up mine eyes unto the turbines on the hills." And she was right, as usual. The very nature of Cloughgreen as a low-lying, valley route centre was it was surrounded by high hills. The turbines on Cloughgreen Moor and at the Delf, effectively half completed the "ring of steel" around the town that Verity Dee had predicted. Now Ursa Power and Newall had the taste of blood why would they stop? They would think the townspeople and the council had run out of the will and wherewithal to fight. And they were probably right.

The third letter he read next day had him cracking up. The previous night in the pub he had been thinking he wouldn't like to be anywhere near Verity Dee's house following the Woolton decision. But the woman was indomitable. Her letter was hilarious. Totally disrespectful, but hilarious. He knew he shouldn't print it. And it wouldn't change anything, so maybe he really shouldn't. But what the hell. That nauseating, puffed-up self-righteous git, Newall, needed his *amour propre* pricking. Why not? Most of the town would get a good laugh out of it. The bugger had won. If he was any sort of a bloke he'd take the letter like a man and see the funny side of it. Publish and be damned then.

Dr Edwin Newall blew his top when he read the letters page of the Cloughgreen Recorder. He didn't know who to blame most. That ghastly bloody VD woman or that stupid grinning windbag Humphrey Drumm.

'Look at it,' he yelled, shaking the newspaper like a flag at Penny, who was with him in Radical Road (it being Friday night).

'What does it say?'

'What does it say?' he fairly exploded. 'That bloody VD woman says "In tribute to all the hard work put in by Dr Edwin Newall in promoting the new wind turbines, I propose they should be known in perpetuity as Newall's Erections".'

'Well that's good, isn't it?' Penny said, as she mentally weighed up Chinese or Indian takeaway or maybe the new pizza place Gerry Stansfield had mentioned.

'"Newall's Erections,' indeed!' he yelled Poor Edwin seemed apoplectic; she couldn't see the problem. 'Who are these pygmies to ridicule a visionary working to influence the future of the planet?'

'It would be good, though, surely, to have all your efforts recognised?' she said. 'Newall's Erections. Wow! Everyone in town would look at them and think of you.'

'That's what I'm afraid of. Being a bloody laughing stock. I think I'd prefer to keep my erections private down here in Radical Road, thank you very much...'

'Oh, yes, I see what you mean,' Penny said, suddenly giggling, 'I never thought of it that way. That's pretty naughty of Verity Dee and Humphrey Drumm, I think. Very naughty indeed.' But she couldn't help laughing. She held out her hands to take the paper and read it for herself. But he pushed past her screwing it up like old chip paper and marched out through the back door. He made as tight a ball of it as he could and hurled it with all his strength. It landed in the pool of his Buddhist meditation garden and floated there, defiant. *Good fuckin' karma, right?*

'Bloody rag,' he yelled, coming in and slamming the back door so hard the glass shook and the key fell out.

It wasn't just the Lucky Dragon Banquet for Two Penny was sent out for. She was commanded to replace the gin and tonic supplies as well.

She hated to see him upset like this. She just couldn't figure out why people were so mean to Edwin.

# 19

The 8th of August marked a change in the weather. After all the heat of June and July it suddenly gave way to a fortnight of stormy showers. Around the moorland pools the stems of the bog cotton had gone fiery red. And the rain stimulated an outbreak of midges. After the showers washed the skies, the skies stayed blue and cold. The evening chills presaged an early autumn.

On the 14th Bolly and Willie lit an early fire. As they sat around the warm yellow flames Willie suspected the cold was psychological as much as real. Tomorrow, the 15th, was when the wind farm started to become concrete reality.

'How's it going, "Moorland, Mist & Myth", the next Ted Hughes crit you're writing ?'

'Don't know about crit. It's more of an *hommage*, like your photo book with all the wide angle nudes and giant pebbles is an *hommage* to Bill Brandt and Edward Weston. Moorland, Mist & Myth is more an unabashed paean to Ted's greatness.' She paused and stretched. She looked worn out. 'To tell the truth, I haven't written much for a while. The wind farm nonsense seems to have drained me. Can't seem to get going again. You know what it's like, winners get new energy. Losers just feel beat.'

Bolly was right in what she said, he thought. You slog hard for something and you win, you rise up on new wings reinforced and refreshed.

But the opposite was true. You slog hard, you throw your heart into something absolutely believing the innate truth of the campaign and how that truth once revealed is self evident. Then you lose. And the unfairness of it hurts so much. You feel knackered and doubt things you actually knew before.

But it was more than that, Willie sensed. To begin with they'd fought this for Elmet, to save a whole wonderful historic landscape being turned into an industrial estate. Then they'd fought it for themselves, to save their own immediate landscape. Now they knew so much about the Great Wind Farm Scam, as they'd come to know it, they didn't see why anyone should have industrial wind turbines forced on them or why Britain should lose an inch more of its precious wilderness. Wind farms just seemed to devour whole tracts of wilderness land in return for sparks in the darkness.

In short, their campaign had become a cause.

Bolly, he knew, felt it even more than he did. She couldn't seem to settle to anything. On her own admission the book wasn't going anywhere. Her gardening had become lackadaisical and half-hearted. On two recent trips to Harvey Nicks with Grainne, her dangerous shopaholic school chum, she'd come home empty-handed.

It seemed she could neither accept the Woolton decision nor let go. She was dangerously close to becoming an activist. And he felt he might be unable to stop her, only counsel caution. He didn't want her to go tomorrow, but he couldn't stop her.

'You know what day it is tomorrow, don't you?' she said, her wonderful red hair highlighted by the flickering flames.

'I know.'

'Well, then,' she said, 'We need an early night. Early start tomorrow to beat them up there. See you later in bed.' Then she got up and went upstairs.

He wished he could tie her up and keep her in the cellar for 24 hours. But that wasn't the way their relationship worked. Wasn't the way any relationship worked unless you were the Marquis de Sade.

'Come on, Nelson,' he said. Nelson obediently dragged himself up and off they went outside for evening ablutions. If only all life could be conducted with Labradors, he wished.

He knew he wouldn't sleep easy and he didn't. Nelson was snoring lustily and Bolly was sighing in her sleep. He listened to the soft soughing of the night breeze and the occasional patter of large rain splats on the window.

What shocked The Friends of the Living Moorland was the abrupt speed with which Ursa had announced their plan of action.

They intended to start the construction work just two weeks after their app was approved - tomorrow on August 15th. They must have it all planned and ready to go. Turbines ordered, plant hire booked, concrete mixers ready, the lot. He was dreading it.

Willie and Bolly and a contingent of the Friends of the Living Moorland were up on Cloughgreen Common by 7am.

'Notice anything?' Bolly asked. He nodded.

'And no birds sing,' he said.

'Wasn't that what someone said about the Nazi death camps?'

'Yeah.'

Cloughgreen Common lay deathly quiet under grey skies and the sort of drizzle often experienced at funerals. Except for a downcast gathering of protesters, all the living things seemed to have fled, as though sensing the approaching ecological calamity.

It was as if the ancient moorland had accepted its sacrificial role and was quietly baring its neck for the gouges and deep wounds to be inflicted by the chrome yellow mechanical diggers. The moor's backbone would endure as it had for millennia. The developers' machinery would just strip away its living skin and veins, the increasingly rare bog and mosses and wild plants that supported the endangered birds and buzzing and burrowing things. Just about everything that made it the unique living wilderness place it was.

'How can Friends of the Earth and Greenpeace support this sort of barbarity?' Bolly muttered to Willie.

'Bigger fish to fry than Cloughgreen Common, they're saving the planet, remember. Our bog and twite are expendable.'

'"Expendable". A soldier's word. Well, I hope they're proud of themselves. Because even Gaia won't be able to replace what they kill off here.'

'I don't wish to be cynical. But remember all those peaceful white blades waving happily to viewers on the telly? Well, our bogs and twites don't do such nice waves to the masses.'

'The trouble is, I know you're right.' She nudged him. 'Don't look now, but here they come.'

Following the success of the Woolton Gizmo demo there had been plans to get representatives of every anti-wind farm group there had ever been in the UK, around 250 plus in all.

Carter and Phyllis had taken it in hand. 'The trouble is,' Carter had reported back, 'they're all too middle-aged and middleclass.'

'They don't want to frighten the horses. What they don't appreciate is to get the politicians' attention you have to overturn the applecart. To do that you have to set wild dogs beneath the horses attached to the applecart and stand well back.

'But being middleclass most of us are law-abiding and want to try and work with the system. Even if the government is constantly trying to fiddle the system with changes to outflank us and get its own way. We get embarrassed confronting the law.

'Essentially, the sort of people we are, we lack that rebellious instinct to take to the streets, yelling wind farms Out, Out, Out and get ourselves on the telly. We should be ripping up paving stones and charging through the streets...'

'We expect the law to be reasonable and take care of us,' Willie agreed sadly.

'Well, I'm going to damn well demonstrate against the bulldozers and all the plant. Along with whoever else I can round up locally,' Bolly said. 'And you're going to take the pics for the national press,' she added, giving him no choice, he saw. And that was how that conversation had ended up.

Now in the early morning drizzle they watched as the giant chrome yellow plant came lumbering up, clouds of blue diesel smoke rising in the air. The noise reminded him of a wartime movie where a concealed German Panzer regiment suddenly started up in the Falaise Gap or somewhere. Deafening. Inexorable. Even at a distance the protesters on the hilltop could see dry stone walls that had stood for hundreds of years being shouldered aside as the huge yellow machines tried 3-point turns across the narrow lanes leading up to the moor and failed.

The leading yellow long-loader demolished Saint Ethelburga's 400-year-old lych gate in one careless side swipe. The crack of ancient wood was sickening. They had their PR girl, Victoria Flowers, riding shotgun in a girly pink Suzuki 4WD with a couple of heavies for security. Every time one of these unfortunate incidents happened she leapt out in her yellow
Day-Glo vest, Barbour, jeans and Hunter wellies, waving a cheque book to compensate and calm things down, taking peoples' names and addresses.

But of course not everything is that easy. Willie could see Bolly's colour rising and her fists clenching in impotent fury. He felt unmanned by his inability to help, so looked down and checked the settings on the Nikon for the tenth time.

Looking around he saw that Carter's misgivings about middleclass anti-wind farm solidarity were spot on. About 50 protesters had turned up, most of whom he knew by sight. There were a few amateur banners: "Support wind farms, murder the wildlife", that sort of thing. But nothing to worry the big money. He whacked a few record shots off anyway.

Bolly, red hair flaring, was wearing a green puffa jacket, a tight red mini and black knee-length boots. She was, of course, front and centre of the thin picket line at the entrance to the site. Carter and Phyllis had been drained dry by their efforts prior to the hearing and wisely gone on holiday to the Highlands and Biarritz respectively.

There were three navy blue police coaches in convoy busting a gut up the lane to the summit where the protesters waited.

Each coach was weighed down with about 30-40 policemen, all in full riot gear.

As they debussed, Willie caught the accent: Manchester. The powers that be on the Yorkshire side of the border had panicked and called for outside assistance. Watching them, big, beefy, red-faced city lads shivering on this windy Yorkshire hilltop Willie had a bad feeling. They wanted the overtime, but they really didn't want to be here, had no feeling of sympathy for the locals or what the problem was. Nobody had put wind farms in the city right up their noses, after all. They just wanted to get the gig sorted pronto and go home. Then they could get out of the cold and wind and go back to their warm local in Manchester and spend their "ovies" getting slaughtered.

The age old refrain when weekend trouble happened in Cloughgreen came into his head: "They came from over the border". Meaning the Yorkshire/Lancashire border. What had seemed amusing to him as a southerner 6 years ago didn't seem amusing any more. There were undoubtedly issues between the red rose and the white that still festered. Only today it wouldn't be licentious behaviour it would be fully licensed by the weight of the law.

A lot of the coppers looked very young. Sign of age, he mused to himself. Most of them looked pretty fit and sporty. He wondered how they'd feel if someone in Cloughgreen started erecting wind turbines on their playing fields? Because that was another part of the problem, it seemed to him. It was yet another metropolitan vs country issue with the metropolitans having sway over matters that did not directly affect them. Like erecting dog fouling signs in country lanes that were regularly fouled by sheep, cattle and horses. The law being made to look an ass.

Jumper Lonk had once shown him what had happened when a fox had dug its way into a friend's hen coop. One hen taken and twenty hens left bloodied with their heads or wings ripped off, some still running around. All just killed for sport. He had near been physically sick at the sight. But you couldn't explain fox hunting to townies. They saw it as toffs on a "jolly", not ordinary country folk defending their poultry.

At the sight of the Manchester coppers he wanted to rush over to Bolly and try and tell her to stay cool. But he had deliberately positioned himself on the edge of the action to get a good overall view. Both Nikons, with different lenses mounted, were equipped with motor drive to freeze any action sequences.

As the coppers fanned out to form a protective welcome line for the advancing yellow plant, he saw a few of them eyeing Bolly in her red mini and black knee boots and muttering obviously lewd comments.

In reality the fight was now all over bar the shouting. And there was precious little of that in the raw morning drizzle. This was pointless. The battle had been fought and lost. As usual big money and big government had steamrollered the little guys. So why on earth had he let her come up here? Because you couldn't stop her, Willie, he told himself. And that is the truth.

He had told her that whatever she did she must give the plant plenty of space. They were big, heavy machines, difficult to drive, tricky to manoeuvre, and slow to stop. Plus the ordinary guys driving them were well aware of the controversy and bound to be nervous. They weren't wind farm fanatics, they were just doing their jobs. But they'd be twitchy. They didn't want confrontation.

A friendly middle-aged sergeant, his riot helmet under his arm, approached Bolly. 'Give it up, love, the developers have got the law on their side. We're just here to protect the plant. No-one wants any trouble. If they want to breed pink fairies up here now they can do it.' He smiled and waited for her response.

Bolly looked hard at him. Patronizing git. Getting no response, he just shrugged and shook himself. 'Brrr, nasty, cold, wet place. I dunno why you're bothering,' he said, as much to himself and walked away back to his troops. Made the effort. Tried to tell her. Okay, you can't tell some people.

Bolly looked at his back as he walked away. Yeah, green desert, that's what you think, isn't it? Another peasant like Newall. And to show your contempt you're gonna put up these massive steel erections like two V-shaped fingers that will be in everyone's faces for 30 miles. Over my dead body you will.

Looking down the road as the heavily laden convoy chugged and growled its way up the hill Willie's eye was taken by a small, beat-up red saloon bringing up the rear. For a moment he couldn't place where he knew it from. Then the penny dropped. Newall. The bastard hadn't been able to resist the opportunity to come up and gloat. He hoped Bolly Dolly hadn't seen him.

Some hope. He could see her shaking her fist at the vehicle. Then she marched off towards the thin line of policemen. He had the digital Nikon raised to his eye on 200mil zoom and auto focus. As Bolly went to pass through the spaced-out picket line one of the coppers stretched out his baton to block her. She turned her head and said something to him. Then the copper seemed to change his mind and followed through with the baton, hitting her lower arm.

She screamed and fell to the muddy ground, clutching the arm. He knew she must be really hurt. Verity Dee was not the sort of woman who screamed easily.

Running on instinct he had the whole thing in sequence on the Nikon. Only now did he think, what on earth are you doing filming someone hitting your wife instead of stopping it? The classic war photographer's dilemma: prevent or record? Except this wasn't a war zone, it was a pretty redundant demo after the battle had been lost. The only person there who didn't know it, he thought miserably, was Verity.

He felt numb as he hurried over to where Bolly was still sitting on the ground. 'Are you hurt?' he asked stupidly, knowing from her body language that of course she was hurt. Her face was pinched white with the pain.

'I think it's broken,' she said, wincing.

The older sergeant who she'd spoken to earlier had bustled over, portly in his riot gear. He had his radio lifted to his mouth 'Ambulance, quickly. Suspected broken arm. Wind farm demo up on Cloughgreen Common.' He turned to the man who'd swung the baton. 'Talk to you later.'

'She should have stopped,' the young constable said, sullen, defiant, but chastened by what he'd done. Wasn't meant to happen like that.

'Let's get you up,' the sergeant said, taking her good arm and hoisting her. Feeling clumsy with the two cameras slung round his neck, Willie watched, slightly embarrassed.

'You Press?' the sergeant asked.

'No, I'm her husband.' Willie hesitated, then said 'Look I think I could get her to casualty quicker than the ambulance. I've got the Range Rover down there,' he pointed beyond the toiling, roaring mass of yellow tractor units slowly climbing the moorland road amidst the cloud of dark blue smoke.

The sergeant considered for a moment. 'Okay, help me get her into the police Land Rover and I'll run you down to your car.'

Bolly's injury seemed to have cowed the already quiet group of orderly protesters. They muttered and shuffled their feet but stayed well clear. Willie thought back to some demos he'd been at when he was a student. Something like this would have been inflammatory. The lads would have rushed the police and tried to tear their heads off. But now we're all older and wiser and beaten, he thought sadly. We just stand and regret.

When they got to Willie's Range Rover the sergeant turned to him and said 'Stupid accident. The officer just meant to bar her way.'

'He did not,' Bolly said loudly. 'He meant it alright.'

‘I’m quite sure he didn’t intend to break your arm, madam,’ the sergeant said. Then he turned to Willie. ‘Look, I’ll cancel the ambulance. And I’ll give you an escort to clear your way direct to Woolton General? Probably be a lot quicker than hanging around here with her in pain.’

‘That would be very helpful, Sergeant. You’re obviously in a lot of pain, aren’t you, Bolly?’

Bolly, ashen-faced, with tears brimming her lower lids, making her mascara run just nodded, yes.

The sergeant yelled at an officer who was lounging against a marked squad car. ‘PC Cartwright. Escort these people to Woolton General. Fast as you can. The lady’s in pain.’

The rest of the journey passed pretty much in a blur for both of them as they clung to the coat tails of the police car which was being driven by an advanced driver. Except for one small exchange they had.

‘Did you say anything to the guy who hit you?’

‘When he went to stop me I called him a fascist pig.’

‘Ah,’ Willie said, thoughtfully. ‘That’ll be it then, why he followed through.’

‘Just get those images to the press a-s-a-p, Willie.’

‘Okay, if that’s what you want.’

‘It is.’

So that was just what Willie did and it made front page in some local editions. But not in the nationals. Small war in a faraway land. Just a few wind turbines most people would never see. Minor disturbance, no-one died. Anyone here speak English and been raped? No. End of.

The long hot summer returned and stretched on and on. August turned into September, September shone into October. Throughout the country, rain was hard to come by. Even up in West Yorkshire the levels in the reservoirs dropped, exposing black stone setts at the edges or, amazingly, stretches of scruffy sandy beach the ducks patrolled.

The peat tracks and paths on the moors lost their springiness under foot and developed deep cracks. October brought a little overnight rain and heavier dews, but the Indian summer stretched on through November and into December. Right up until December 10th. When a pent-up weather front rolled in from the grey Atlantic, causing semi flash floods that sent torrents rushing over the stripped moors and into the town.

For everyone within a 10-mile radius of Cloughgreen Common it was a relief from the thick clouds of red dust the heavy plant had churned up. The dust had stung their eyes and choked their throats, staining the washing on their lines. For month after month the prevailing south west wind had carried the reddy dust off the high Common miles away onto car windscreens and gardens. It's like living near a Spanish beach or the Sahara, the locals had joked. The wind had carried the harsh growl of the diesels, too, to those people living on the tops. After centuries of the song of the sky lark and the bleat of the sheep the tranquillity of the moorland had been shattered.

Better get used to it, Willie thought to himself.

Sometimes, after the heat of the day had subsided and the growl of the diesels had ceased, Willie would go out into the velvety darkness of his garden and look over towards the escarpment of Cloughgreen Common. His eyes would fall on the amber glowing necklaces of the lights from farm houses strung out along two parallel contours of the hill. One by one they'd be extinguished as the owners went to bed, leaving just the darkness and the shark's back outline of the crest of the Common. Except that the lighting would once have been oil lamps nothing much would have changed in about 3-400 years, he mused.

Meanwhile Cloughgreen Tourist Office reported that foot traffic had fallen disturbingly. Far fewer people were dropping in for walkers' books or postcards or books about the town. The pubs and tea rooms and market traders had noticed the same. *Word of mouth.*

"Walk somewhere else."

"Clouds of red dust everywhere."

"The racket of heavy plant pounding over the hills."

"Like a whacking great building site."

Walk somewhere else. Spend your money somewhere else. Live somewhere else. That was the message going out.

What sort of neighbour would the new wind farm be to the town and those living near it? Willie had a pretty good idea.

# Part III

# APOCALYPSE

# 20

On 31st January Ursa Power's first wind farm site, up on Cloughgreen Common, was officially opened by a government minister.

As with the two mornings previous the sun had risen from a cloudless blue sky like some giant, ominous blood orange. At 1300' the North wind was bitingly cold, bringing tears to the eyes of all assembled. The minister wore a heavy dark blue topcoat, but nobody had thought to warn him of the icy blasts that would assail his ears and cheeks. His cheekbones felt slashed by razor blades. Ursa's two Russian executives had thoughtfully brought along a spare Russian fur cap with earflaps such as they wore themselves. After briefly weighing up dignity versus hypothermia the minister had plumped for the cap and survival. Looking around he saw everyone had streaming eyes and red or purple faces. So he edited his speech to the bare minimum. Least said, best chance of survival. Electronic flashes went off as the press recorded the event.

He raced through his bog standard Green-must-win dictum. Then he turned and hastily unveiled Ursa's somewhat embarrassing jolly dancing red bear ensign on the site flagstaff. A band struck up some stirring Russian anthem about the glorious wind off the steppes of the motherland and everyone who mattered hustled back into the warmth of the official limos.

In the back of the lead vehicle the minister removed his Cossack headgear and gratefully accepted a thimble of 60 proof vodka before turning to Ilya Bakunin, Ursa's MD, and remarking 'Very impressive. But wouldn't it have been better if the turbines had been turning behind me? They always look super on the telly.'

The two Russians looked at each other. We're developers, not bloody magicians.

'Well, minister, we would have liked them to, of course,' Bakunin said smoothly. 'You're right, they are very telegenic. But the wind this morning was just too high. We had to close them down for safety's sake.'

'Ah,' the minister said, reflecting. He'd heard they sometimes had to do that. 'Still, pretty impressive. Jolly well dominates the landscape for miles around. Sends out a strong renewables message, eh, convert the unbelievers?'

The two Russian executives smiled and offered some more vodka as they drove back to the hotel for breakfast.

The limo's powerful heaters pumped out a toasty warmth and the gorgeous smell of expensive leather was seductive. Why not? Another quick one to take the chill away.

The minister slammed the 60 proof vodka back in one, as he'd been instructed. 'You know,' he said, 'the way that huge orange sun rose up from behind the horizon was fantastically dramatic. Like a movie, almost. Pity really, you chaps aren't Japanese. Would have been truly symbolic then, wouldn't it? The Rising Sun and all that.'

The two Russians exchanged glances and smiled politely, said nothing. Just grin and bear it. Think of all those millions being pumped into our offshore account for the next 25 years, Arkadiy Kovalenko thought. It would buy a few dachas, a lot of vodka and a life of luxury.

Less than a mile away Joe Stansfield was having real problems. 'There's no water, Mary,' he yelled. 'Christ, what have they done to the water table and our spring. This never used to happen.'

'Yeah, we've got none. But Harry Gilbert's now got two flooded pastures where the water's just oozing up from a new spring that shouldn't be there.'

'He must got have our water then,' Joe said. 'Which I don't count right neighbourly.'

'Think, on, Joe. He doesn't want to have it there any more than we want to lose it.'

'But the cattle,' Joe said urgently. 'They need water...'

'You'll have to take the water tanker over to Jumper Lonk's like last time the spring stopped running.'

'Christ, we can't keep doing this.'

'Jumper's alright. He's got loads of water.'

'Yeah, but it's not practical. Apart from taking his water, it's inconveniencing him. And it's costing me time and diesel money to go over there. We can't go on like this.'

'You'll have to write to Ursa again, explaining what's been happening since they put the windmills in.'

'And no doubt they'll write back saying we have no proof it's anything to do with them. Like they did last time. Carter Briggs and the Friends of the Living Moorland warned this might happen.'

'We're not on our own. It's everyone this side of the hill has been affected.'

'That's no comfort, is it? The fact that just about everyone on spring water this side of the Common's suffering.'

'Joe, right now, you're gonna have to get the tanker out, take the Land Rover and go over to Jumper's place.'

'It's a lousy icy morning and the Land Rover's got balding tyres...we haven't got money to burn.'

'You're gonna have to risk it.'

'I know, but Christ I resent having to do it so the Russkis can get fat at our expense,' he said, grumbling.

'Joe?'

'Be careful.'

'Yeah.'

'We'll just have to get a borehole put in.'

'Right. And who'se gonna pay for that? We're not getting subsidized by the government, like the Russkis. We're struggling hill farmers. Just in case you'd forgotten.'

Mary sighed. 'We're gonna have to have a meeting with the other folk who are affected. See what we can do. Ursa can't just go on denying it for ever.'

'You don't think so? They don't care about us, Mary,' he said, banging the back door. 'Why should they? They don't even live round here. Crap all over us, churn up the landscape. Fuck up our water supplies. Steal the wind. Then go back to London or Vladdy-fuckin-vostock or wherever...they don't bloody care.'

There had been spring water problems right since they started digging out the massive 50' deep pits for the concrete they needed to anchor the turbines. The locals had complained and the contractors had just said they were teething problems that would be sorted out.

And that wasn't all of it by any means. Folks living on the road off the tops to the town had been reporting enormous amounts of run-off water from the denuded moors. After heavy rain they were having torrents storming downhill, flooding their front gardens and coming in under the doors. The council had supplied sandbags, but that wasn't really it, was it? Were they just supposed to accept that now that's just the way things were?

Jumper was sympathetic to Joe Stansfield. But all he could suggest was contacting Carter Briggs to see if he had any new ideas how to proceed. Now the locals could see how the turbines dominated the town and the effects they'd had on the moorland and the spring water no-one liked the bloody things. Apart from Dr Newall, of course.

On February 1st, the day after the official opening, Humphrey Drumm got an anonymous phone call telling him to take a photographer and get himself up to their great new Green showpiece.

Intrigued, he fell into his secondhand black Audi with the staff photographer.

'What are we looking for?' the photographer asked.

'No idea,' he said truthfully.

From a distance, as the car wound its way up from the valley and climbed the hills, there was nothing much to be seen. The weather had changed. In the still, misty air, the heavy turbine blades weren't even shivering. Not an inch of movement. No wind.

They left the Audi at the five-barred gate near the site entrance and went in. It immediately him them in the eye.

In large, dribbly green letters someone had daubed the words GREEN SHIT on the nearest five towers. The snapper scurried forward with his camera. Humphrey stood back and tried not to laugh. Then he walked forward and touched the 6'-

high lettering. The green paint was still tacky in the damp air. Hold the front page.

It's a pity nobody had claimed responsibility, Humphrey thought. There again there was no lack of suspects. When the wind farm application had been passed he thought the whole issue would die the death and he'd been actively giving thought to generating another hot topic for the Recorder. Got to keep the circulation up.

In fact the opposite had happened. People had started to use their local newspaper as a sort of social services agency. A place where they could report in their problems. Late night clanking from diesel pumps on the site. The never-ending clouds of red dust everywhere, getting in eyes and fouling washing and windscreens. Months of traffic problems with large loads and locals having to leave an hour earlier to get to work. Getting home an hour later. Most of all, the problems people were having with their spring water - or lack of. And the damned things hadn't even been turned on till yesterday.

He smiled again. Properly speaking, because of the gales yesterday when they'd been closed down and the dead calm this morning when they weren't able to turn, they hadn't yet started at all. Once they actually got going they would doubtless create more problems for those who were either close or visually exposed to them.

When he got back to the office, he found a handwritten note waiting for him. "If the Green movement is a living entity then these turbines are its turds..."

Oh, dear, he thought. Striking gesture, shame about the prose. No, he didn't think the note would be making the front page. He ran close-ups of the graffiti under the headline "Protesters deface new turbines".

It intrigued him as to who had done it. The language of the note was literate if somewhat uncouth. That was the odd thing. The language was educated, the sentiment crude. The combination seemed to rule out most people he could think of.

It certainly wasn't Carter Briggs' style. And it wasn't Verity Dee's style. The laddish action could be down to some of Carter's young buddies from the rugby club, but the note wasn't rugger-buggers style. In the end, he concluded, he had no idea who the culprit was.

And neither, when Arkadiy Kovalenko spoke to them, did the police.

The graffiti was the first subject Kovalenko brought up at his next meeting with Dr Newall. It was February 2nd, the day after the graffiti was discovered.

'The old woman at the Recorder, Humphrey Drumm is he called?'

Dr Newall nodded.

'Drumm rang me to ask what I thought, who was responsible. What comment I had to make. I had to tell him I had no idea. I felt a complete fool.' The ex-special forces man's face was white with anger and Dr Newall had to force himself to keep a straight face. Not nice to be made to feel impotent, is it, macho man?

Kovalenko looked him straight in the eye and lowered his voice. 'Who do you think was responsible, Edwin?'

'Teenage drunks, probably. Louts. Nothing worth worrying about. Get somebody up there with paint remover and clean it up. Then forget about it. Move on. That's why I'm here.'

Kovalenko shot his immaculate white cuffs, showing the gold cufflinks and then snapped the knuckles of his left hand. Abruptly, like the sun coming from behind a cloud, he smiled. 'You're right. We forget about it. But I tell you,' he said, his smile becoming toothy as a carnivore, 'nothing like this will ever happen again. Anyone else touches them, we'll know about it.'

Total control, Dr Newall marvelled, remembering his own anger at the Newall's Erections jibe in the Recorder. He had the feeling this former elite soldier could probably command his own heartbeat if he wanted to. A frightening man.

'Anyway, we're sorry Ilya cannot be here, he had to fly back to Moscow to see some of the main investors. But what did you want to discuss?'

'Well, it seems to me that now the Cloughgreen Common site is up and running you should consider extending your holdings in the area.'

'Yes?'

'Yes. You may remember some nonsense in the Recorder last year about so-called "nasty moors", like Cloughgreen Common, and "pretty moors".

Kovalenko made a face. '"Nasty moors" and "pretty moors?" Who is to say?'

'You've got the point exactly. They're all redundant moors waiting to be exploited and developed properly. Those terms really mean which moors people currently use for recreation such as walking, mountain-biking, running or riding and which they don't. You put a few turbines in and there's nothing to stop them doing any of those things, as you well know. Thor Fell, Waterloo Pike and the Hallow Stones all have excellent wind generation potential. They are all high ridges in isolated locations where they will attract the wind like a magnet does iron filings. People are forever being blown off the Pike ridge or getting hypothermia sleeping in tents.' Kovalenko laughed.

'Hypothermia I can believe. I nearly had that one day going between my car and the hotel. It's not so cold up here by Russian standards, but the wind chill factor is incredible.'

'The wind, yes. Because of the Pennines it rarely stops blowing. And I'm telling you these are 3 more prime sites ready for development.'

'But think all of the fuss last time, Edwin. And you say the locals say they think these are prettier, more popular moors to put the turbines on...'

'Ah, but, you are missing the point, Arkadiy. First, the locals are still exhausted from the last fight. Second, the councils will have no money left to resist you, even if they want to. And third, a lot of the steam has gone out of the planning objections based on special landscape appeal. With Cloughgreen Moor up and running, there is now on a good day intervisibility between that site, the site at Goose Hee and the one at the Delf. Effectively you could argue that any special landscape is already ruined.' Kovalenko crossed his legs, rested his chin on his right fist and smiled wryly.

'You make it sound so easy, Edwin.'

'Not easy, no. But opportune. The enemy is on his back with his legs spread wide.'

'You paint a pretty picture.'

Dr Newall shrugged. 'I am a visionary, not an artist.'

'Well, I will report this back to Ilya. Tell me again the names of these proposed new sites.'

'Thor Fell, Waterloo Pike and the Hallow Stones.' Arkadiy Kovalenko noted the names in a small black leather notebook which he replaced in his inside pocket.

'Okay, like I say, I will report this back to Ilya. However, I must warn you our present capital is now already tied up in future developments in Scotland and Wales.'

Shit, Dr Newall thought, he didn't want any stalling in his plans to enable Purity Valley. He needed these new sites to work his flanker with the re-zoning.

'I'm sure you could easily generate more capital now you've got a track record with one site already up and running.'

'Well, yes. You would think so. Even if it meant using unorthodox capital.'

Dr Newall didn't even ask. Decided he didn't want to know.

Ursa Power's Finance Director rose effortlessly to cross the room and extract an envelope from his open briefcase. 'Ilya and I were very pleased with the strings you pulled with the hydrology report. Someone at our fearsome lawyers said it was probably crucial. So we have awarded you a special bonus. Now that things are finally secured, up and running.'

He handed the open envelope to Dr Newall who took the cheque out and marvelled at it.

'I hope you find us not ungenerous.'

Dr Newall was flabbergasted. 'No, this is princely,' he said. 'Thank you both very much.'

Next day Dr Newall awarded himself a day off. He had been working hard on one of Irene Vine's leads which she'd handed him on a plate. The project was both lucrative and intellectually demanding. It was for a pedestrianization scheme for the centre of a small town called Olderroyd. He was using it as the template for something he hoped to do in Purity Valley, seeing how far he could force the car to the extremity of an urbanization. Literally marginalizing it if possible.

There was a spring in his step as he strode down Radical Road on the way to the station and his connection to the London train.

He smiled as he contemplated his finery. He was off to do a little posh shopping. And if you were flashing the plastic it always paid to look the part.

For lunch he had a sumptuous meal in Soho's oldest Italian restaurant, a place known to the cognoscenti not the tourists. Having ordered the steak, hunter style, he indulged himself in a fine bottle of Barolo, savouring the exquisite bouquet. Then he finished with some fresh figs, amaretto and coffee. Finally he caught the last train back with a status bag containing six shirts woven from the finest Egyptian yarn by the best Italian weavers. Plus three dashing new silk bow ties from Harrods. He liked nice things. One day Purity Valley would make him famous, but it was very nice just being successful for now.

# 21

February

Willie and Bolly smirked with amusement at the early February weather. Fierce, tumultuous storm wind with gusts rising to 70 mph and then icy calm within days of one another. Both types of 'the wrong sort of wind'. Both typical of the time of year.

They had watched all the triumphalism of Ursa's January 31st launch ceremony from their side of the valley. Distant figures and limos toy-like amid the giant turbines. And then the small red rag being hoisted.

'What a joke,' Bolly said. 'All that fuss and a government minister and the bloody things aren't even going around.' She broke into a bitter laugh. 'You sort of have to laugh.'

'Well, that's Newall for you. Not blowing hard enough when he needs to. Bit of his windy rhetoric would have soon got the blades turning. The team needs him and he's not there.'

'Yeah, but realistically it's not going to last forever,' Bollie said. 'The buggers will start whizzing around in our faces any day now. What are we going to do?'

'What would you like to do, Mrs Dee?'

'Move, obviously.'

'Shouldn't we give it a month to see how awful it's actually going to be?'

'Hey? We have these five giant turbines in our face, looking down at us, ruining the landscape every time we look up. How more awful can it get?'

'The emissions I meant. The sound and light exhaust stuff they push out. So at least we know what to tell people we sell the house to.'

'Are you crackers?'

'No. Honest. Anyway, chances are potential buyers will see and hear it for themselves. We just need to know how awful it will be.'

'Okay, we give it a month's trial.'

On the 3rd March they got together after Nelson's walk and solemnly declared the month over.

He sat in his lounge armchair next to their landline phone.

'We don't need to even discuss it, do we?'

'No. It's just as bad as we thought it would be. The sheer physical height is bad enough, the way they dwarf the landscape and throw everything out of scale.'

‘The sound nuisance is much worse some days than others, depending on local weather conditions, wind direction, humidity etc.’

‘I just overlooked the fact the noise would go on through the night and wake us up.’

‘And the more daylight and sunshine, the worse the blade flicker and strobing will be. Imagine a July heatwave. We’ll have to sit with our backs to the sun in the garden and get triple-backed curtains to close over when we’re in the house.’

‘Much as we love this part of the country and the people, we need to move, don’t we? We don’t need another 20 years of our lives, if we’re spared, living with this in our faces. It’ll make us ill.’

‘Right we’ve decided.’ Willie picked up the phone, dialled the number and spoke briefly.

‘She’ll be here at 3 this afternoon. Manager of their local regional office. Caroline Blunt.’

Willie looked at his watch as Caroline Blunt drew up in front of Greenwood Royd. Bang on three o’clock.

She drove a sporty little Peugeot, which, being a big girl, seemed to be wrapped around her like a metallic sari.

She eased her long legs and broad hips out and Willie saw she was a tall, big-boned blonde with wide orange lips and unshockable blue eyes. He’d known women like her who’d played women’s rugby at uni. They fucked you, not you them. She wore a biscuit-coloured blouse and a long-skirted pale blue suit with an enormous slit up the back.

Willie glanced at Bolly and knew she hadn't taken to her. The introductions were made and Caroline pronounced the location "idyllic" and first impressions "to die for".

Willie gestured her towards the front door and they followed behind her. Bolly nodded her head at the long slit up the back of Caroline's dress which was revealing acreage of white calf and dimpled white thigh. She rolled her eyes. 'Looks like twelve stone of uncooked tripe,' she whispered.

Caroline paused going through the house to examine the huge old open stone fireplace and the handmade, historically-authentic mullioned windows that were double-glazed. 'Serious wow factor, in here,' she cooed.

'Let's go outside first, before we see the rest of the house,' Willie said, ushering her out through the back door.

There was a sharp intake of breath and the estate agent wailed 'Oh-my-Gawddd. Shit, look at that!'

'Yeah, that might be a problem,' Bolly said quietly. 'What do you think?'.

Caroline Blunt looked embarrassed. 'I had no idea. I mean, I knew they were there, but...they're right in your face.' She dug little patterns in the white gravel with her big white shoes and looked down at them.

Willie and Bolly blanched and looked back at the house.

'Well, tell the truth and shame the devil,' she said, looking up after a small lifetime. 'The reality is you may never sell this place. I mean, the things are monstrous...' She looked embarrassed again. 'I mean, just look at them,' she gestured expansively. 'There's a whole wide landscape out there and you can't look at anything else.'

Willie felt like crying. Bolly felt like knifing her.

The turbines were still today. Not enough wind. They looked back at the three people in silent reproach. Bolly suddenly remembered that John Betjeman poem "Come friendly bombs and fall on Slough". For the past month she had entertained fantasies about buying a secondhand artillery piece from e-bay and and a secondhand artillery major to pound them into nothingness.

Willie was the first to rally.

'Supposing we can sell, how do you think the turbines would affect the price?'

Caroline got her orange mouth together and essayed a small, not very encouraging smile.

'Well, you've got three problems,' she began.

'Only three...?' Bolly interjected. The irony bounced off Caroline's thick skin.

'Yes, first it's a big, expensive house anyway. So there are fewer people able to afford it.' She raised a hand and checked off finger number two.

'Second, people who want a house like this in the country and are willing to pay top dollar want everything just so. They can afford to be picky.

'Third, if they want to live in the country they don't want to look at industrial installations.'

'Fourth, in the current economic climate it's hard to buy or sell anyway.'

'You said three problems,' Bolly said.

'Assuming we could sell,' Willie persisted. 'How would the turbines affect the price.'

'Could be anywhere between 25 and 50%.'

'You must be joking,'

Caroline swung around and pointed. 'Look at them,' she repeated, awe-struck. 'Like I said, people at this end of the market can afford to be picky.'

Willie found himself absently looking at the acres of white goosebumps through the long slit in Caroline's skirt. Her milk-white thighs stuck themselves together above the knee, he registered absently, his mind seeking retreat in harmless pornography, imagining the 'shlup' sound as the flesh parted. He heard Bolly talking.

'Before they were built,' she said, 'Dr Newall assured us all that everyone found them enormously attractive and that house prices next to wind farms actually went up.'

'The little shit tells lies. The whole town knows that.'

Bolly smiled acidly. 'I think you'll find he refutes myths.'

Willie had to smile as he saw a small lightbulb go on in Caroline Blunt's mind.

'Hang on a minute you're that Dee, aren't you, the one who challenged all the wind farm propaganda in the Recorder...'

'Verity Dee, yes. Guilty as charged,' Bolly acknowledged.

'My boyfriend talks about you. He plays for the rugby team,' she beamed proudly.

'Well then, you being Verity Dee,' Caroline went on, 'you never believed that rubbish about prices actually increasing, did you? Not for one minute. And neither did anybody else but his nutty mates. In actual fact you've now got what we call a "wind farm negative".

'Despite Dr Newall's logic of the asylum, real people, the sort of people who want to live in the contryside with beautiful views don't want swirling, rumbling 410' steel turbines in their faces.'

'But 25/50%?'

'Just look at them,' Caroline repeated. 'That's the trouble alright. You can't not look at them.'

Willie sighed deeply. 'The final part of the prophecy falls into place.'

The estate agent looked confused and unhappy, not sure what to say.

Finally Caroline said, 'You know that phrase "Location, location, location" and selling houses?'

They nodded.

'Well, Ursa Power just nuked two out of three of your "locations". Your only location now is your post code.' She shrugged, apologetic.

'It's okay. Don't worry, Caroline, it's not your fault,' he said. 'It's just no-one has wanted to listen and yet the whole thing has been quite predictable. You go on the Net and you can find examples of this sort of thing all over the world. We knew this would happen, yet through no fault of our own we've been stuffed.'

'You're right. You go on the Net you can see what's happened to house prices in America, Australia wherever. I'm an estate agent not a political activist like Dr Newall.' She stopped and spread her hands in a reasonable but candid gesture. 'Look, you know Dr Newall tells lies. If you can find this mythical buyer who wants to push the price up because of those things,' she jabbed her thumb in the direction of the turbines, 'don't bother telling me. You just bite his hand off.' She gathered herself up, making leaving gestures, then hesitated and stood back on one foot.

'It seems to me people who live near wind farms are getting the rough end of the stick from this government. If your house was blighted by a new motorway they'd have to pay compensation. With wind farms they pretend there's no problem. At the very least you should get free electricity from the things as some sort of compo.'

'Hear, hear,' Bolly said, clapping. 'We'll vote for you.' The estate agent gave her a funny look.

'Yeah, I know. The problem is, that's just what I think. Is there anything else you wanted to say?'

'Just how do you save the planet by trashing your own backyard?' Willie asked.

'I meant about the house sale.' The estate agent looked embarrassed again.

'Don't mind us,' Bolly said. 'We're just feeling battered and bitter.'

'Okay,' Caroline said, 'I'll keep your details on file. It seems you two need to talk about how desperate you are to get out. If you still want to take things further give me a ring and I'll send someone round to measure up. But really now isn't a good time. With the economy and everything people get even more picky.' That picky word again, Bolly thought.

Caroline smiled and moved surprisingly quickly for a big woman back through the house. After they'd heard her car draw away Willie digged Bolly in the ribs and did his girly imitation "But really now isn't a good time."'

Bolly smiled wanly. 'And when will be a good time?'

'In 25 years when they take them down?'

'Don't kid yourself, Willie. They won't ever be coming down.'

They took themselves back into the house.

'Nobody will ever be saying that again,' Bolly said.

'What?'

'You know, the usual visitor stuff people used to say when they first came here.' Bolly affected a precious, ladylike voice "What clever people, to have found such an idyllic spot".' She paused. 'Now they'll get out of the car, look past the house to those terrible whooshing steel erections and utter the words "My God" or similar.' Bolly turned and looked out the window. 'I mean, just look at the height of them. Given the location they're in they literally dominate our world.'

Willie said nothing. He knew she was right.

'Willie,' she said, 'What are we going to do?' He looked away to see where Nelson was. He had no idea what they were going to do.

'There is that one last thing she said.'

'Yeah?'

'How desperate to move are we?'

'Desperate enough. But not desperate enough to want to give away 50% of our house.'

Bolly just sighed.

Next day Willie took Nelson up to the Hallow Stones for his walk. In just ten days the bog cotton had become an immense sea surrounding the huge black boulders and the shallow moorland pools. The breeze blew tides through the fluffy white bolls, bending their white caps over their 6" stalks..

There was a low mist and rain in the wind. And nothing but the cry of the curlew and the song of the skylark. The tranquillity was almost other-worldly. He sat for a little with his back against the rough millstone grit, just savouring the moment. A curlew came power-gliding past him just a hundred yards to his right. The long, curved beak protruding, the scimitar wings outstretched, the long feet pulled high up and back. It was one of those rare moments when you can look back and think how perfect the world can be.

For a little while the loudest thing after the birdsong was the sound of his heartbeat. And that was full to bursting. Maybe this was the intensity with which Ted Hughes had seen this landscape?

Then the rain grew heavy and the wind got up and it felt more like wind in the rain than rain in the wind. It was time to move on.

# 22

June 3rd was a morning when lots of low cloud hung around the tops. For a change it was abnormally still. Barely a breath of wind at this height. Within the time he left the house and walked around the corner to Big Ruth's stable in the barn, Jumper could feel the heavy moisture settling on his eyebrows and hair.

These particular weather conditions did strange magnifying things to sound. He could hear the purple 3-car rail unit shuttling along the bottom of the valley a few miles away as though it were in the next field. Similarly there was a rumbling whump-whump-whump from the giant turbine blades on the hill opposite. So there was obviously wind movement higher up. It happened. It was why the old schooners had small sails higher up the masts. Just 50' could make an enormous difference to the air movement. And there was probably two hundred feet between here and Cloughgreen Common.

The people facing Cloughgreen Common had learned all about the effects of weather on sound when they put the smaller turbines in at The Delf, a couple of miles away. Of course with the new turbines being two and a half times bigger, sited directly opposite and above him these sounds were very much louder.

When the wind was gale-high and the turbines were struggling to cope, the sound was different. Then it sounded like aircraft noise. Not modern jet whine, but the deep thrumming roar of a heavily laden, piston-engined craft struggling for takeoff, deep down lungy and powerful. You could feel it in your body. Plus on stormy days, sporadically, you got the loud mechanical clank of the transmissions drive.

Jumper looked down into the valley. The town was obliterated by low grey cloud. It would be a grim morning down there, hemmed in by damp fog. There were blue skies up here and a weak tangerine sun. But strands of cloud hovered in the air above the ends of the field. A large slowly drifting band of it was stretched across the centre section of the turbines above and opposite, so that the whole centre section was blocked out. Only the tops and bottoms of the blades were visible as they turned in the lightish air.

Big Ruth staggered to her feet as she heard him coming, ready to greet him as usual. She seemed tired or sluggish, reluctant to face the new day. But she whinnied when she saw him and ambled to the open half door to be patted.

'What's up, old girl? Feeling your age this morning? It'll just be the damp air. Gets all of us like that,' Jumper said, as he reached into his pocket for the Polo mints and fed her one, thinking of the twinges in his knees that had woken him. Still, the customary dram of Bells in his early morning tea had soon sorted that. Elixir of life.

Big Ruth's eyes sparkled as she happily crunched her first Polo mint and Jumper grinned, twisting another from the circular green and white pack and placing it on her leathery tongue. She took it gently and crunched as usual. Then she leaned forward and butted him gently in the chest. More, please.

'They don't last long enough with you. That's the trouble,' he said, patting her neck. Two Polos later, which was her daily ration, he took the red bridle down off its hook in the barn and slipped it over her head. Then the saddle and stirrups.

He led her out into the cobbled yard and heaved himself into the saddle, eyeing the ancient stone mounting steps in the corner of the 300-year-old yard. Christ, I'll be needing them every day soon, he thought. Not just occasionally. How sad would that be?

'Come on, Ruth, old girl, just twice around the meadow before breakfast,' he said.

The horse moved heavily forward and they moved off into the field, both old warriors, at a stately pace.

The dampness in the air seemed to accentuate the odours as they ambled gently down the field away from the wind farm on the hill opposite and behind them. Whump-whump-whump went the turbines, overlaying the sound of Big Ruth's massive feet.

Apart from the noise, this was the routine Jumper had enacted for years. The horse being gentle and undemanding, his mind drifted off, letting him ride on auto. He was worried about how Verity was adjusting to life with the turbines in her face. She was a sensitive, highly strung woman who had fought hard and lost. And she hadn't come to terms with it. Her arm wasn't healing as quickly as it should and the pain was getting her down, he thought. He thought Willie should help her more. But part of Willie was naturally so diffident; Jumper wished he would be more passionate and show his feelings. But seemingly it wasn't in him. Ah well, nothing much he, Jumper, could do about it.

As he and Big Ruth came to the end of the field, his mind switched to groceries. He had run out of Colman's English mustard and also mint sauce, two things essential to his traditional English gent's cuisine.

Big Ruth, also on auto, turned left at the end of the field and ambled along inside the old hawthorn hedge which bounded the lane. Needed lopping, Jumper thought. And the drainage this end of the field could stand sorting out. It still hadn't drained properly after all the awful rain and the sheep had churned it up.

Then his mind drifted back to what seasonal fruit and veggies the market might have when he went down to buy the mustard and mint sauce. The Healey 3000 needed filling up, too. But a damp day like today wasn't the time to risk the old beauty's bodywork. Use the old Land Rover.

Soon enough they came to the end of the field and Ruth made a right, back up towards the farmhouse and into the direction of the turbines.

The whump-whump-whump sounded louder and Jumper raised his eyes towards the turbines, still half covered by a long streamer of grey cloud. As he did so, the early morning sunrise shone red on one of the giant swishing blades and flashed into his eyes. Big Ruth caught the same flash in her eyes and whinnied, frightened. Panicked, she reared up, taking Jumper unawares and throwing him backwards. Then she lost her footing in the sheep-trampled, waterlogged field and fell heavily backwards on top of Jumper where he lay.

He never felt a thing. Falling backwards from a height his skull had been smashed against one of the black rocks which were constantly working their way to the surface in these Pennine fields.

Big Ruth was not so lucky. One of her massive rear hooves had snagged in the mud and tangled roots from the hedge as she slipped. So she fell badly at an angle. Her front right leg was torn from its socket and smashed on impact. She screamed and lay where she had fallen on her master, whimpering with the sudden terrible pain. Unable to understand why she could no longer move. Why didn't Jumper, her lifelong friend, help her?

A pilot joyriding in his veteran red and white monoplane saw the whole thing. Flying low, to see what he could see in the countryside, he too had been momentarily blinded by the strobing and knew exactly what had happened. He had come up directly behind the rider and had seen the whole thing enacted as he approached. The man wasn't moving and the horse was writhing with one leg at a funny angle. It looked bad. He reached for his radio and phoned the coordinates in for an ambulance. But in his heart of hearts he knew it was too late. The man still wasn't moving.

Four hundred yards away, up at his own farmhouse, Willie had been letting Nelson out for his morning leg-lift. He heard Big Ruth's terrible scream as her leg shattered. The sound was high and piercing, carried on the damp air.

He put Nelson back in the kitchen and closed the door behind him. Then he jogged as fast as he could back up the lane to Jumper's place, cursing the fact he could no longer run as quickly as he used to.

He followed the horse's cries and took in the scene at a glance, rushing fast as he could to drag Jumper clear. But Jumper's clear blue eyes, those eyes hungry for female beauty, were now dulled. He stared unseeing at the moorland skies, all life gone. Willie knelt and checked his friend's pulse. But Jumper was gone. As he had known really. The gory mess at the back of his head with white bone protruding told its own story.

The sight of Jumper's body forced truckloads of adrenaline into him. Later he remembered it had been like coming out of a trance. He was suddenly aware of Big Ruth's cries. One glance at the angle of the horse's broken leg was enough. There was nothing to be done for her except to put her out of her misery.

Willie strode across the field and back into Jumper's house. Then he went into the kitchen and took a key from the knife drawer. He knew that was where Jumper kept the key to his gun cupboard. Oddly aware of his muddy boots he went into the chintzy eau de nil and rose patterned lounge. He put the key in the padlock that secured the mahogany gun cupboard, slipped the padlock off the hasp and opened the cabinet. Then he took out Jumper's favourite shotgun and slipped in some cartridges from the bottom of the cabinet.

He had the feeling that he was working instinctively, which he remembered, from other crises in his life. He had no doubt he was doing the right thing, repugnant as it was. He'd come to love the big gentle good-natured horse almost as much as he loved Nelson. From the angle of her leg he knew she was doomed. No more Polos for you, Ruth.

He kept the gun broken and put it in the crook of his arm, striding gingerly back across the waterlogged, treacherous field, conscious he could blow his own legs off if he slipped. He didn't like guns, but this just had to be done.

Nearing the horse, he could see the pain and incomprehension in her bloodshot eyes. 'Be alright soon, Ruth,' he said. 'Soon be with old Jumper'. Then he snapped the gun shut, laid the barrel against the side of her head and pulled the trigger quickly, not giving himself time to think. He was shocked by the recoil and the blood on his Barbour.

One barrel had done the job. He broke the gun open again and put it down on the grass. He took hold of Jumper's nearest arm and tried to pull him out from under. But it was hopeless and he was worried he might just harm the corpse by dragging his arm out of its socket. He took one last look at the scene and twitched his eyes shut, mentally photographing the scene the way he had since he'd first started taking pictures aged 12. It was an unconscious reflex.

He picked the shotgun up and started to walk back across the field to Black Rock Farm. 1/250th at f8, on Tri-X Pan, he murmured. Where the hell did that come from?

It was only when he got home that he broke down and wept. The last time he'd done that was when he was 11 and had broken a balsa glider he'd built on its maiden flight. When he'd brushed the tears away and steadied himself he called the police. An ambulance had already been called, they said. 'Bit late for that,' he said laconically, then proceeded to calmly tell the police what he believed had happened. 'You'll need some sort of hoist to get the horse off,' he added. Then he went back to the field at Black Rock Farm and sat with his friend, covering his head and shoulders with his jacket, to wait for the emergency services.

Alerted by the police, a middle-aged doctor came with the ambulance. And a fire tender came with the police. They were all calm and surprisingly sensitive, he thought.

'Was he a friend of yours?' the young constable asked, notebook out, taking details, as the fire-crew winched Big Ruth off Jumper.

'Yes, he was my friend.'

'Sorry.'

The doctor lifted Jumper's head gently and looked at the bashed-in skull and the large black rock on which it rested. 'Pure bad luck,' he said. 'If he'd fallen anywhere else in this water-sodden field he'd have probably been alright, maybe just a few broken ribs from the horse sliding on him.'

'Yeah,' Willie said. Death had already started to change Jumper. The great purple prow of his conk had dimmed and the wiry virile blond hair looked softer, more cotton-like, lifeless. In fact now the rampaging life force had gone out of him, Jumper looked remarkably like a mild old gent. Which he had never been. Willie had never thought of him as old. He had thought of him as a force of nature and forces of nature never get old. They simply cease to be. Please don't say he looks like he's had a good innings, he thought. The doctor didn't.

He turned calmly to the young police constable and said 'Nothing suspicious here, officer. It's just one of those wretched accidents that come out of nowhere.'

He signed to the waiting ambulance men and they lifted Jumper gently on to the stretcher as though he were still alive, covered him and took him off to the ambulance. The gentleness with which they handled him somehow pleased Willie. Force of habit, he supposed, they mostly deal with live people after all. But still.

'We can dispose of the horse if you wish,' one of the firemen said. 'Probably easiest.'

'Yes, please do,' Willie heard himself say, even then thinking he was betraying Big Ruth. She and Jumper should have gone out in some sort of equine Valhalla-like blaze of glory with fiery brands lobbed into her stable. But he was too upset to do anything else. Even if he could have physically handled the horse he didn't know what you did with dead horses.

'We'll have to come back for it,' the fireman said.

'Her,' Willie corrected him, but he'd already gone.

The policeman pumped him gently for the remaining details including next of kin and then quietly disappeared. Leaving him with a dead horse and a bloodstained patch in a sodden field, his hair damp from the low cloud. Silence now but for the whump-whump-whump of the wind farm.

'Best lock up if you can,' the policeman had said and he had nodded. Suddenly feeling exhausted, he trudged back to the big wooden tub next to the front door where the giant red peonies grew and extracted the spare house key from under it. He locked the door, put the key in his pocket and went home. Going through the back door into the kitchen he glanced at his watch. Not quite 10.30 in the morning yet.

That evening he told Bolly Dolly he had no idea how he had performed so correctly and dispassionately.

'We do what we have to do,' Verity said, folding him to her bosom. The atmosphere at Greenwood Royd was sombre.

Neither of them felt like cooking. They opted to heat up some stuff from the freezer - a thing they only ever did if they were ill or late back from a trip. But then they pushed the stuff around the plates before rejecting it and taking it back to the kitchen hardly touched.

After the sun went down they lit a fire in the Music Room. As much for the emotional comfort as for the warmth. Here we are - warm in our cave. The log fire roared in the big black stove with its tall 12" wide chimney disappearing up into the huge old fireplace. Warm shadows flickered around the white Sandtexed stone work and off the silent white grand piano with its cases of Bollinger on top. Bolly drank Jack Daniels on ice and Willie was drinking Laphroaigh and spring water. Nelson, who had picked up on the upset, lay pretending to sleep along the side of Willie's armchair, his one good eye flickering fearfully open from time to time.

Mnemosyne, a CD featuring the virtuoso saxophonist Jan Garbarek and the Hilliard Ensemble provided some emotional balm, but not enough. Eventually, Bolly managed to say what they'd both been thinking and choking on.

'Can't think how he came to come off. After all these years the two of them were glued together like a centaur. Do you think the bloody wind farm caused it?'

'We'll never know will we? Because there's no smoking gun. But if you weigh up the evidence, an old docile mare with a man on top who rode her every day for nearly 20 years and who'd been good enough to ride for his country, then you suspect some extra factor. Strobing or blade flicker directly into Big Ruth's eyes would have frightened her, for sure. But we'll never be able to prove it. That's how the bastards who run these things get away with so much.' He took a long swig of the single malt. 'No concrete evidence, but enough circumstantial evidence often to bury a small town. Allows them to call things "myths". The bottom line is, wind turbines are not good neighbours to man or beast.'

Bolly shook her head with the disbelief of recent death. 'I still can't believe it. I was talking to Jumper only yesterday. Now just like that he's gone for ever. I can't believe we'll never talk to him again.'

'I can't believe I went and cold-bloodedly shot Big Ruth. Me, the big softie who leaves it to you to poison the mice.'

Bolly got up and came and sat down on the floor on the other side of Willie's armchair from Nelson and stroked his hand. 'Like I said earlier, you do what you have to do. Big Ruth was in terrible pain and fear. She wouldn't have known what was happening to her. You put her out of her misery.'

'I know, but...'

'Ssshhh,' Bolly said, putting a finger to his lips. She drained her drink and went and refilled it. Sitting down next to him again she said 'The trouble people have had with their spring water and the blade flicker and noise these last few months have been like an overture, a setting of the scene in some ghastly opera. This is the start of it. Ever since you got Charley Fort up here, and we found out about wind farms it's been like a car crash happening in slow motion, something we couldn't prevent, but knew was coming. Now it's really happening...the wind farm up on Cloughgreen Common is starting to make its presence felt, like some dreadful monster flexing its muscles and affecting everyday life. Christ knows where it's all going to end.'

Nelson looked up mournfully, every nerve end in his body in sync with the miserable vibes of his owners. Willie looked down at the dog and smiled wanly at Bolly Dolly. He nodded pointedly at Nelson.

'What do you think?'

'Pack huddle?'

'That's what I thought.'

Willie let Nelson out for a last leg lift then locked up. When they went upstairs Bolly Dolly was already in bed, makeup un-removed, teeth un-cleaned. He ignored his teeth, too, had a quick leak in the bathroom, stripped and jumped into bed. Misery is never a pretty sight.

Bolly eased her way onto his left shoulder, careful of her damaged arm, now without its sling. He patted the other side of the bed and Nelson jumped gratefully up and nuzzled hard into his right shoulder: pack huddle complete.

The booze and emotional exhaustion had them all asleep within minutes.

He woke her in the early hours. Taking her hand and guiding it on to his erection. He was a big man, but it felt monstrous and inhumanly rigid to her, almost like one of those carved wooden phalluses you see in anthropology museums.

She was frightened she wouldn't be ready for him. But he put his fingers in his mouth to moisten them and then gently opened her up. He had big hands for a man who was so deft with camera controls. She raised her bottom and did that little half twist with her hips that let him slide in. Then he was moving inside her. His phallus was so enormous it kept on advancing until it felt as though the whole penis glans was inside her womb. He had wombed her many times before, but this was different, much deeper, it felt as though there was no room for movement from either of them. But then he'd taken the globes of her arse and was moving them around in slow circles. She could feel how tense he was, trying to hold himself back and his face in the pale chink of moonlight looked almost contorted with he effort.

'Don't worry about me,' she said, 'Just go for it.' Sex as relief. Soon enough he shuddered deeply and she felt sad he would slip away. But then her innards started to contract around him and to her amazement she too came in an amazingly wet rush, almost as if she'd wet herself. Her contractions were so strong and he was still so big, they lay locked together like dogs.

'Stay in,' she heard herself say. He stopped moving and lay still, except to take his hands away and stroke her cheek.

'Sorry for the urgency. Death affects me like that. It's almost as if...'

'Yes, I know.' Strains of the Stones raced through her mind - "This could be the Last Time"...After a brush with death, anyone's death, it was almost as if you had to demonstrate you were still alive and vital. It was a horrible thing to say but it seemed to revivify you. She'd felt that in the past herself. Her eyes were adjusting to the very weak moonlight through the chink in the curtain and she could see he was smiling.

'What's funny?'

'Nothing really,' he said, looking suddenly serious. Then he smiled again. 'No, I was just thinking. That was one for Jumper. A memorial fuck. He'd have liked that.'

'You bet he would,' she said, laughing, thinking of the indomitable life force that had been Jumper Lonk. 'Probably have liked it even better without your assist...'

He had to laugh at that. And that was good. There had been nothing much about love with that coupling she thought. More about absolving pain. It seemed as though his penis was so over-engorged it actually hurt him. So maybe there was love in that part of the act, after all. In just accommodating him and giving him relief. She'd last seen that desperate look in young men who'd been made to wait too long. Not really pleasure, just relief.

He shifted off her and moved her onto his shoulder.

‘Actually, feeling like that is quite a well-known reaction to sudden bereavement,’ he said.

‘Ah, the rational anthropology graduate, now we’re calmer...’

He laughed again and shut up. Somehow they would get through these difficult coming weeks with the funeral and no Jumper or Big Ruth. They would just have to.

# 23

It was a slow news day and Humphrey Drumm was perusing a mailing he had received from an up-market Highlands estate advertising its game and venison products.

It was a lavish, well-produced mailing and his first reaction was to salivate at some of the food shots. His second was to get real and calculate what percentage of his weekly pay a side of venison represented  His third reaction was to  quietly consider which of the town's worthies would be good company for a gourmet lunch built around venison.

The phone startled him and he grabbed for it. 'Drumm.' he said severely.

'Is that the editor of the Cloughgreen Recorder?' The voice was thin and reedy, hesitant.

'It is. To whom am I speaking?'

'Curtiss Wright.'

'Curtiss Wright,' Humphrey repeated, reaching for his pad and pen and scribbling it down. There was a nervous giggle down the phone.

'Yeah, I know, it's like a joke. Curtiss Wright was a company that made veteran aeroplanes and engines and my dad was a aircraft buff; so he called me Curtiss. I'm lucky he didn't call me P-47, I guess.'

'Hey?'

'The P-47 was a famous fighter plane they made.'

'Oh, right, I get it,' Humphrey said, managing a conspiratorial chuckle. 'So, Curtiss, what can I do for you?'

'I think I might have an angle on a guy who was thrown from his horse and killed yesterday up on the tops.'

'Yes?'

'Yep, I was the guy who called in the ambulance from my mobile. I saw the whole thing.'

'Where were you and what exactly did you see?'

'Well, the thing is I was joyriding in my little plane. Low wing monoplane, nothing fancy. Beautiful day, blue skies and low-lying white clouds, so I was right down in height checking out life on the farms. I was coming in opposite the new wind farm at Cloughgreen Common just right behind this guy and his horse. Then suddenly I was momentarily dazzled by strobing from the sun on the turbine blades. When I looked again the horse was rearing up and the rider, looked like an old guy with a mass of white hair, was being thrown backwards off the horse's back. I circled around to see if they were okay. But they were laying entangled and the guy was still. Didn't look good. So I made a real low sweep over them and he didn't seem to be moving at all. That was when I phoned the ambulance. I phoned later to see if he was okay and the ambulance guys said he'd died at the scene.'

'So your point is?'

'Well, Mr Drumm. I think it was the turbine spooked the horse and got him killed.'

'I see. You say it dazzled you.'

'It definitely did. And I was right in line behind the guy on the horse. The blade flicker must have hit the horse right between the eyes, too.'

'That would explain it. The man was a very experienced horseman who used to compete for his country. And the horse was a docile old mare he'd had from a foal. His friends are puzzled as to why the accident occurred.'

'No doubt in my mind.'

'It would be difficult to prove.'

'Impossible probably. I don't even know why I'm talking to you. Except maybe about his friends. To explain what happened. It was all so quick. It startled the hell out of me. But I'm a human being, I could see what caused it. To a poor dumb animal...'

'...It would have reacted out of sheer fright...'

'Yep.'

'It potentially explains a lot.'

'What was the poor guy's name? You say he'd been famous. I could maybe Google him.'

'He was called Sam Lonk. But most people called him Jumper Lonk. The horse was called Big Ruth.'

'It's something I'll never forget. Just a quick sequence. Seeing the guy. The dazzling strobe. Then seeing the horse and guy rise up in almost slow motion. It was like something out of an old movie. Big white-haired guy in a faded red hunting jacket and shiny black boots on a big black horse falling backwards. I'll never forget it.'

'Well thanks for calling, Curtiss,' Humphrey said. He paused. 'It's been kind of you to take an interest, both with the ambulance and now. But you mustn't beat yourself up about it. He had a good, long life and he went the way he wanted to. With his boots on in the saddle.'

Humphrey heard a slight reedy chuckle at the other end of the line. 'Kind of like an old cowboy, hey?'

'Yes, Curtiss, some folks round here would definitely say that.'

He put down the phone and filed Curtiss Wright's details. Then he became thoughtful and phoned Carter Briggs. Carter

Briggs confirmed what he thought and Humphrey flicked the laptop on.

The headline just about wrote itself:

PILOT FINGERS WIND FARM
FOR LOCAL RIDER'S DEATH

Dr Newall tossed the latest copy of the Cloughgreen Recorder across the kitchen to Penny Wragg.

'Look at what that wanker Drumm is saying now, Penny. It's incredible.'

Penny took up the paper and looked at the lead article which was all about that old lecher Jumper Lonk's accident. She had come to regret the fact that the Cloughgreen Recorder came out on Fridays, one of the days she saw Edwin. It meant that if anything in it upset him then she took the full blast of his disapproval. Even though it had nothing to do with her.

'I don't know how they can be so sure it was the turbine frightened the horse,' she said craftily.

'You see!' he raised his right index finger aloft. 'You saw it immediately. It's that obvious, isn't it? Could have been anything frightened the old nag. Could just have put her manky old hoof in a rabbit hole and thrown the old git. But oh, no, they have to blame the wind turbines.'

'No proof, though, is there?' Penny said, playing the game. She felt in the mood for Singapore noodles tonight.

'Exactly, that's the whole problem with the anti-turbine brigade. They whinge and shout and bleat. Yet there is never any definitive proof. This Curtiss Wright bloke sounds like a right geek. Probably the noise of his plane roaring up behind it frightened the horse in the first place, truth to tell.'

'Well spotted,' Penny said. 'Those little old propeller planes make a heck of a racket. Particularly when they're low.' On the other hand, the deep fried king prawns in honey sauce were a real treat. You couldn't afford those every day. And Edwin was paying.

'You're right,' Dr Newall pronounced. 'Well, he's jolly well not getting away with this. It really is too much.' He wrote his protest note to Humphry Drumm there and then while Penny was out getting the Chinese takeaway.

Dr Newall hand-delivered his letter to the Recorder next morning on his way to the post office and the girl on the front desk took it straight through to Humphrey. He recognized the giant "look at me" scrawl that passed for Dr Newall's handwriting, like a sort of earthquake calligraphy. Gawd, what's he got to say now, he said aloud.

He read it and frowned. He'd have to publish it. Newall had a point. It could easily have been the sound of the small plane roaring up behind it that made Jumper Lonk's horse panic and rear up. He passed it into the folder for next week's Letters Page. Then he had a thought and picked up the phone. He'd ring young

P47, as he'd mischievously come to think of him, Curtiss Wright, the joyrider.

He had to leave a message.

Next week Bolly pointed the letter out to Willie.

'Newall defending the indefensible again,' she said.

'Well, for a change,' Willie said, 'he might have a point. Those little single-seater jobs can sometimes sound like angry wasps.'

'I don't think so. I think that young pilot was pretty convinced of what he saw.'

'It could have been the plane roaring up behind them, Bolly,' Willie said, hating to have to defend Newall.

'No.'

'How can you be so positive?'

Bolly smiled a tight little smile. 'I used to ride Bushmills out with Big Ruth, remember.'

'So?'

'Big Ruth has been deaf as a post in both ears for the past 3 years.'

'I didn't know.'

'You ask Jumper,' she said, then burst into tears.

The following week Curtiss rang Humphrey back. It turned out he was an IT consultant. Probably aged about 16 1/2 by the sound of him. 'Sorry to have taken so long to get back to you, Mr Drumm. Been out of the country on business.'

Humphrey described Newall's letter.

'No, I don't think so, I'm pretty sure it wasn't the plane,' Curtiss said. 'Firstly, I was right behind them and the strobing startled me. Secondly, neither of them looked over their shoulder like frightened sheep do before they run. Thirdly, the little plane I fly has an engine the size of a motor mower. It just quietly putters along in a straight line. I'm not flying a stunt machine or a Stuka dive-bomber. Believe me, Mr Drumm, I'm no helldiver.' He laughed his nervous little laugh. 'No, it was definitely the strobing that upset the horse. And me, too. I'd stake my life on it.'

'Just no definite proof,' Humphrey said gently.

'Not court of law proof, no. But I know, Mr Drumm, believe me.'

Humphrey defused the situation with a few pleasantries and rang off. He was very much inclined to believe young P47, Curtiss Wright. He sounded like a very serious, conscientious young man. But like the turbine people always insisted "No definite, 100%, Doubting Thomas, put-your-fist-in-the-hole-in-his-side proof.

Following Jumper's death Willie had contacted Colin Combes, one of Cloughgreen's main solicitors. He then ferried Jumper's grey steel document box down to the solicitor's offices in town.

Combes was a slight, mild-mannered man with wavy black hair, a persistently threatening seven o'clock shadow and black framed spectacles which seemed to occupy most of his face.

Surrounded by piles of dusty cardboard folders and red legal ribbon, the old-fashioned tools of his trade, Combes seemed genuinely saddened by Jumper's passing.

'Good old Jumper, he said, taking the box. 'Organized to the end. He told me to expect this. I wish they were all like him.'

'Yes. He had his head screwed on.'

'I shall miss him.' Willie looked surprised.

'Down at the cricket club. He was the life and soul of the off-field activities. Marvellous memory for past seasons and a very dry sense of humour.'

'He had that alright,' Willie agreed.

'You know you're a beneficiary, I suppose?'

'No,' Willie, said, surprised.

'Yes. Quite a substantial beneficiary. And there's a keepsake for your wife. Then the rest of the estate is spread around his interests. He had no family, you know.'

Willie nodded.

'He always said this town was his family. And he though of you as his little brother...'

Willie laughed. 'I'd have been the quiet little brother.'

It was Combes's turn to laugh. His dark features broke out into a shy smile. 'Yes, he was a bit of a hell-raiser when he was a lad.'

Only when he was a lad? Willie thought wryly.

'Anyway, everything is very well organized, including the hymns for the ceremony and the pall-bearers he'd like, health permitting.'

Willie looked at him. 'You're one of the pall-bearers, and there are some strapping lads from the rugby and cricket clubs. But some of the other gentlemen are quite old.'

'I see. Well I suppose I'd better see if they feel up to it,' Willie said.

'Would you? That would be a kindness. If you wait a moment I'll give you the list. The undertaker will see the Reverend Andrew Shattock, about the other arrangements. One of his rugby club mates, I understand,' Combes said, smiling again. 'Jumper was pretty well connected in this little town. I shouldn't really say this, but he even got a good deal from one of his mates who is an undertaker.'

Willie grinned. 'Well that was Jumper. A true Yorkshireman to the end.'

Willie took the list and duly did the rounds. Health on the day permitting, everyone was determined to give Jumper a good send off.

After he'd been to the solicitors, Willie suddenly realized the only suits he possessed were denim ones. And Bolly suddenly decided her black suit wasn't up to scratch. So they took a trip into Manchester and sorted themselves out.

Willie took another trip down to see Colin Combes and it was decided they would approach Joe Stansfield, the farmer who had been begging water from Jumper for his livestock, to look after Jumper's sheep until they could be disposed of. The money would come in handy, Joe Stansfield said, and anyway he was grateful to Jumper for the water.

# 24

June 13th

The day of Jumper's funeral was one of those days when ironically it felt good to be alive, Willie thought. There was a warm wind from the South West and mares' tails skittering over a blue sky. In Jumper's fields clumps of lilac dead-nettle overgrown with tiny blue forget-me-nots gave off a faint sweet aroma.

Despite the sombre occasion, Bolly felt full of *joie de vivre.*

'"It's a warm wind, the west wind, full of birds cries,"' she quoted.

'The blessed Ted?' Willie queried. Bolly gave him such a look of scorn it made him want to smile.

'Hardly. John Masefield.'

The parish church of Cloughgreen, Saint Nicholas's, was as English as you could get. It had a square bell tower with a large gilded clock face, showing eleven. Atop the tower St. George's flag flew at half mast and the bell tolled discordantly. The church's blackened stonework had recently been steam-blasted so that it shone creamily in the gentle sunlight. Down in town the south west wind had dropped and Willie felt hot wearing the unaccustomed collar and black tie. Thinking about it he felt a small trickle of sweat run down his spine.

As he formed up with the other pall-bearers he took in the large crowd of people gathered outside of St. Nick's.

All the nominated bearers bar one had felt up to the task. So he now stood along with T.C. Ruggles, president of Cloughgreen Cricket Club, one-time demon bowler, now frail old gent; Buster Baines, president of Cloughgreen Rugby Club, one-time front row forward, now a very large gent; Terry Dixon, the current Aussie cricket pro; Chris Head, current rugby club captain and wind farm demonstrator; and, looking slightly scruffy with his friar's long hair and scissor-cut beard, Gerry, who was substitute for the unwell gent.

It had been agreed with the undertaker that the two elderly gents should be positioned amidships with the heavy lifting being done at the corners. Some burly undertaker's lads were on standby to step in if old TC or Buster were unable to continue.

They hoisted Jumper well enough. Then the undertaker stepped forward and placed Jumper's hunting pink jacket and polished, folded riding boots on top. To Willie's relief the undertaker stayed close to the coffin in case they looked like slipping. After what seemed an eternity of bumpy, slow marching the vicar hove into view.

Willie had seen the vicar often enough around town or in the pages of the Cloughgreen Recorder at fetes and weddings, but he didn't know him to talk to.

Close up the Reverend Andrew Shattock looked precisely what he was: a man's man. Broad shouldered, around 5'10" tall, brown-eyed, clean-shaven with thick grey hair close-cropped along a slide rule parting, Shattock had served 20 years as a padre with the Royal Marines. He was a friend of Jumper's from the rugby club.

Willie felt an immediate warmth towards him and a trust in the open-faced, head-on manner he affected. He felt his friend was in good hands for the last farewell.

The Reverend Shattock, or Andy as he was universally known, thanked everyone for coming and told them he'd only known Sam Lonk, Jumper, 10 years, but had known him well.

He was one of the sporting rocks upon which a small community like Cloughgreen rested. Always ready to help with his experience or enliven things with his wit. A chronicle of bygone sporting deeds.

Famous in his day as one of the pre-eminent horsemen of his generation who had represented his country on many occasions, he had worn his celebrity lightly. The congregation might note they had some famous horsemen from bygone days in their midst today who had made long journeys to be here.

But of all the roles he had played, horseman for his country, opening bat, full back, the one he had relished most was citizen of Cloughgreen, never leaving the town except to serve his country.

The Reverend Andy then went on to tell the sad tale of how immediately postwar, when a young Sam Lonk had been packed off to agricultural college, there had been a tragic accident. A former Battle of Britain pilot had been joyriding in an ancient biplane when its control wires had snapped. He had come down in an uncontrollable dive on Sam's family farmhouse, killing him and the seven Lonks inside who were gathered for a meal. At a stroke Sam lost his entire family.

After that, Sam told him, he regarded the town of Cloughgreen as his family. Now he had passed he had made generous donations to various of the town's institutions, including the church. The last act of a fine, civic-minded man. A good man by any standards.

But that may give too serious a view of the man. Many looked upon him as a life-force. He was the last of a certain sort of bachelor. He liked his drink but never fell over; he liked his women too much to ever marry one; he liked his cricket, but carried his bat at 58; he liked his rugby but stopped while he could still walk. Etc, etc

There were various titters while the vicar spoke and when he mentioned the women, Bolly looked around and became aware of an elderly, but well turned-out, female fan club. She knew none of them, but one statuesque woman stood out. It had to be Big Ruth.

Big Ruth stood about 5'10" with raven-coloured shoulder length hair behind a 40s roll at the front with a Roman nose and a bust like a ship's figurehead. She had flashing brown eyes and stood proud as a Hebrew queen.

'It's her. Big Ruth. It has to be. She was the love of his life, I think, Willie,' Bolly whispered.

'If you don't count the other 50,' Willie said.

'No, this lasted on and off 20 years, I think...'

The Reverend Shattock was quite happy to dovetail the ceremony to the individual. So the tape recorder blasted out Swing Low Sweet Chariot, Test Match special, Abide with me and then, when they were leaving the church, When the saints go marchin' in. It seemed to Willie a fair enough snapshot of the man's life. As Jumper used to say, "Saturday is for sportin', Sunday is for churchin'".

As he threw the clod of earth down on the coffin, Willie thought that for the first time ever the ritual of a funeral was working for him. Andy Shattock had got it just right with the tone about celebrating Jumper's life and then Bolly nudging him about Big Ruth had reminded him of who Jumper had been.

Some people are just so full of life you never want them to die. Maybe because it seems impossible. Maybe it's because if even they can die, then so can you; and it's an unwelcome reminder. But enough theorising. What mattered was the life Jumper had had, not the sudden violent way he'd gone. He had lived life in abundance. What more could you ask?

After Jumper had died so suddenly he hadn't wanted to hear the cliche about him having had a good run. But in truth that was the reality of it. And he would have liked to die in the saddle, as he said himself. So farewell, Jumper, old mate. They'd organized with Wes Douglas that they'd have the reception back at the Hamlet. It was a Tuesday so he was glad of the extra trade.

He'd laid on a large buffet of the traditional ham sandwich variety with some quiches and salads for the veggies. Colin Combes had funded the bar.

Bolly had thought that it would be nice for the three musketeers as she called the lunchtime pals to have their usual table one last time. So she'd brought Jumper's old red riding jacket from the church to further the illusion. The red riding jacket was draped over Jumper's chair and Gerry had put a pint of Guinness in front of it.

'Well, it went well, didn't it?' Gerry said.

'It was a good send off,' Willie agreed.

'Great turn out.'

'The church was packed. As it is in here.'

The first few pints went down quickly, Willie thought. Release from tension probably. Duty performed. No-one dropped the coffin. No-one fainted. No-one drunk in church. No-one slipped into the grave.

Lots of people knew each other. The lads from the rugby club, who looked very different from the lads from the cricket club, were mingling. It struck Willie that the lads from the rugby club could do you a lot of mischief if their blood was up. The lads from the cricket club had a different sort of hardness. They looked as though they could do you a lot of mischief with bat and ball in cold blood. Scarier types if anything.

The three old equestrians had been adopted by the other veteran sportsmen, T.C. Ruggles and Buster Baines. They were seated at a long table in a corner being looked after by younger club members. Anecdotes and tales of a younger Jumper's sporting prowess were being shared.

He saw Bolly had buttonholed Chris Head, the rugger captain.

She held her hand lightly on his sleeve. 'I've been dying to ask you. It was you, wasn't it, who painted Green Shit on the turbine?'

'It might have been,' he said grinning.

'Knew it,' she said.

'On the other hand it might not have been. Could have been a lot of people. They're not top of the pops round here, are they?'

'You're right there.'

'Could have been you even.'

'No. I think it was you and your lads.'

'Well,' he said, grinning again, 'you might be right.' Then he drifted off. When she looked around for Willie she saw the woman she thought was Big Ruth was standing at the table with them, looking at Jumper's riding jacket.

As Bolly watched the woman took the pint of Guinness from the table and took a sip from it, leaving red lipstick near the rim. She looked at it and then she made a deliberate impression with her lips on the glass itself.

A stout blonde approached with an angular redhead in tow, clutching her arm. 'I'm Sue and this is Vicky. We both knew old Jumper a long time. Would it be okay if we had a sip, too.' She looked at Willie and Gerry but she asked Ruth, Bolly noticed. Ruth nodded assent. Of course. The new women sipped one after another.

Sue deliberately left Big Ruth's lipstick bow on the rim and planted an orange smacker further down. Vicky followed suit with a bright pink one on the other side of the glass.

Three other ladies took their cue and edged shyly forward. A coral kiss, a crimson kiss, a peach kiss. Willie wished he had brought his camera. But it was a funeral not a wedding, after all.

'Wherever Jumper is I hope he can see this,' Bolly said, edging forward and adding an "Evening's Promise" coloured lip mark near the bottom. 'God rest, Jumper.'

She sidled over to Ruth and introduced herself. Up close she was a striking woman. She had olive colouring to go with the dark hair and the big amber eyes of a teddy bear. Unforgettable.

'How long did you know him, Ruth?' she ventured.

'About twenty years. He was a wonderful man.'

'Did you not think...'

'Of making it more permanent?' She smiled. 'No, like the vicar hinted he loved women too much to settle for any one of us. He was a bit of a wild boy. Besides he had a farm to run and I had a horse stud.'

'He talked about you, you know.'

'Yeah, I know. And about that nag of his.'

'You know what he called her?'

'Oh, yes. Big Ruth. He thought it were a great joke. I daren't repeat some of the comments he made about that,' she said laughing. 'He could be a dreadful coarse man sometimes. But you couldn't help loving him, he was so full of life.' She sipped at her rum and blackcurrant. 'All these ladies loved him at one time or another. We formed an unofficial fan club over the years, I suppose. Jumper's groupies,' she chortled.

'Do you have anything to remember him by?'

'Just a lot of happy memories.'

'Well would you like his old riding coat? He left it to me. But it would probably mean more to you.'

Big Ruth looked at the coat, eyes gleaming, then she looked taken aback. 'Well,' she said, 'if you don't want it...'

'No, Bolly,' said. 'It's not that. I'd like you to have it.'

Big Ruth picked the coat up and stroked the lapel thoughtfully between finger and thumb. 'Then thank you so much. You're a very generous woman, Verity. We weren't married, but I loved him. In fact he was a much-loved man altogether,' she said, smiling.

'Let me introduce you to some of the other ladies.' The dark-haired woman turned and made the introductions.

Then she suddenly raised a forefinger aloft as though she had decided something.

'I know what he would have wanted.' Bolly watched as Big Ruth took hold of one of the jacket cuffs and quickly wrenched the four brass buttons off. Strong, horsewoman's wrists, Bolly thought.

'There,' she said, pressing a button into the palms of the other four ladies. 'A remembrance of him for each of you.'

The ladies twittered their thanks and Bolly thought what a generous nature Big Ruth had. Jumper should have married her. But then he wouldn't have had the other ladies, would he, the old rascal.

Out of the corner of her eye she saw Hilda bustling forward, her cockatoo blonde crest sharp and shiny. She actually looked slightly tearful.

'He was an old lech,' she was saying, 'But in spite of that we'll miss him. He was part of the fixtures and fittings of this town.' Bolly watched as Hilda had a sip of the girls' Guinness and applied her smudge of "Midnight Mystery" to the pint pot.

She had seen Dr Phyllis Bentley at some stage in the proceedings but she noted she took no part in the Guinness ritual. Like Hilda formerly, she was maybe wary of Jumper even at this stage. Fearful he might suddenly leap out from behind the arras and grab her. But no, she thought sadly. That was now beyond even Jumper.

Willie drifted up to her. 'Bet I don't get a send off like this,' he said.

She punched him lightly on the arm. 'You better not,' she said. 'I'd be might upset if a load of ancient dancing girls appeared out of the closet.'

They read the Will a few days later. Colin Combes had tipped the vicar the wink about the roof and Bolly about the coat. But it turned out there were four equal financial bequests: to Willie, to the church roofing fund, to the cricket club and to the rugby club. Bolly was left his ancient riding pinks, his boots and all his tack. Gerry, to his amazement, was left the old Healey 3000 sports car which Jumper had rebuilt, chrome-plated underneath and never took out in the rain. 'He knew you respected old motors and would look after it,' Colin Combes told him.

# 25

'There's been a big drop off in demand. People simply aren't coming any more,' Mrs Collins said. 'I spoke to a minibus full of walkers from Sheffield whose leader was appalled at how the landscape had changed.

'"Why would we want to keep coming to Cloughgreen. We have more than enough steel structures to look at in Sheffield. This is supposed to be the countryside,"' he said.

Mrs Collins paused on her end of the phone for breath and Humphrey Drumm took a breather before she was off again.

'"The government talks of increasing biodiversity and encouraging farmers to be stewards of the countryside - how does all that fit in with this?' he said Or are you just the dumping ground for government wind turbine targets? 'Cos we don't want this. We've got enough steel and concrete in Sheffield, Scunny, Doncaster. We come to see beautiful hills rolling away into the horizon with wild flowers and sky larks. These things kill the views and everything that flies anywhere near them. As for the racket... we come hear to hear birdsong not turbine rumble..." and on and on he went. Quite an educated man he was, but very angry. Accused us of being apathetic about defending our countryside and I had to tell him that just wasn't so. No, indeed. We had no choice. And I'm afraid he was typical. So,' she said finally, 'we're going to have to close our doors.'

'That's sad.'

'It's worse than that, Mr Drumm. It will hit trade in the town. Such walkers who are still coming won't get the support and the guides to new walks. So they'll drop off further and so will the trade for the pubs and tea shops and the market.'

'It's a crying shame,' Humphrey said, at a bit of a loss. 'After the years of sterling work you've put in building the tourism up,' he said, trying to mollify her.

'Yes,' said Mrs Collins, sniffing. She sounded tearful, Humphrey decided. 'Anyway,' she concluded, 'I just thought you should tell everyone. The locals also buy notelets and Christmas cards and calendars from us, as well as maps. They should know to go elsewhere this Christmas.'

'Yes, thank you, Mrs Collins that was thoughtful. I'll do that.'

Humphrey put the phone down and sighed. The wind farm correspondence dragged on. People whose property now had no spring water. People whose tv reception didn't work properly anymore. People who claimed to be suffering from the noise or blade flicker. People who claimed to have had similar frightening experiences on horseback to Jumper Lonk.

Whenever he phoned Ursa for comment he received a perfectly polite stonewall from their PR woman, Victoria Flowers. The MD Ilya Bakunin refused to take his phone calls anymore. Following Dr Newall's advice, Ursa admitted nothing and refuted everything on the grounds that the claims were not scientifically proven. The people complaining were hysterics. The criticisms were myths. There was no demonstrable proof to any of it. It was all coincidence. Pigs might fly.

Humphrey had spoken to the practice manager of the Cloughgreen Health Centre who said there had been a significant rise in people living nearby complaining of headaches, lack of concentration, difficulty sleeping etc. But she said she didn't want to be quoted, because, like Ursa said, there was no concrete scientific proof. Just a mighty great coincidence. And she daren't risk offending the powers that be. Funding, you understand.

What it came down to was that everyone knew these things had adverse effects but no-one could prove it. Ursa just drew up the drawbridge and hid behind that lack of proof. It was like when people suspected asbestos had nasty effects but couldn't prove it. The asbestos manufacturers just kept on making it and exposing people to it.

He'd spoken to Dr Phyllis Bentley about it and she'd agreed that getting scientific proof was a very real problem. What she did say though was that under Health & Safety Regs the biggest number of industrial noise nuisance complaints investigated by government inspectors concerned industrial wind turbines. The problem was there was no reliable agreed way of measuring the noise. And the whole thing was exacerbated by the changing atmospherics which worked with the topography to affect the acoustics. Nonetheless, she said, there was now a name for this cluster of health symptoms. It was called Wind Farm Syndrome. And she referred him to a book by an American doctor called Nina Pierpont which was called just that.

The whole wind farm thing bugged him. It rumbled on in a low key way producing more and more human misery. But like Carter Briggs, Dr Bentley and Verity Dee he had no solution. He felt uneasy, but there was really nothing he could do without playing into Ursa's hands and risking looking a crank. He settled down to opening fetes and attending club suppers and, most entertainingly, starting the annual Rotary duck race for charity. His was the hand that launched a thousand yellow plastic ducks from Cloughgreen Weir.

Dr Newall had turned the lights on and was wrestling with his smart-arse chess opponent in New York who he suspected of cheating.

This latest backs-to-the-wall situation he found himself in had to have been dreamed up by a Grand Master.

When the phone rang he jumped. He glanced up at the GMT clock on the wall: 10-15.

The caller had a West Country burr which he recognized as a wind farm mate down in Devon. The voice was excited.

'You'll never guess what?'

'No, what?' Dr Newall said, playing along.

'You know James Lovelock lives around here now? Well, I've just heard in the pub that he has a new book coming out. It's going to be reviewed in the Sunday papers.'

Now it was Dr Newall's turn to be electrified. James Lovelock, green guru, founder of the Gaia Theory/Principle, was his hero.

'That's fantastic,' he said. 'What's it called?'

'The Vanishing Face of Gaia: A Final Warning.'

'Wonderful!' Dr Newall exploded. 'Stick it to the buggers. Tell it the way it is.'

'Exactly,' his mate said. 'It sounds strong meat, doesn't it? I can't wait.'

Nor could Dr Newall. It was only Tuesday. He ticked off the days till Sunday like a kid waiting for Christmas.

Sunday morning he fell out of bed first thing. Penny was at some school chum's wedding in Wales. It was just after six when he started the car up. The fumes from the bloody thing smelled terrible. It was only 400 yards to walk to the newsagents, but he was in too much of a hurry. They were still sorting the deliveries on the front counter when he walked in and bought three of the broadsheets.

He exceeded the speed limit getting his precious cargo back home. Then he ripped through the review sections. Nothing. Anxiously he looked at the front covers and found the stuff he wanted had been flagged up in a different news section with interviews with his hero.

The sub heads were like a blow to his solar plexus. Lovelock believes renewable energy is an elaborate scam, made possible by enormous subsidies. He loathes the ugliness of wind farms ...and believes they will be remembered as one of the great follies of the 21st century. Surely, it could not be. It wasn't April 1st, was it? His long-time hero, the high priest of the Gaia theory had turned out to be a closet Nimby! He could feel his blood pressure rising as he re-read the heads and sub heads.

Greens hijacked his Gaia theory, but he's in favour of nuclear energy and thinks wind farms are a con.

It's not enough to hold meetings before that religious symbol of spin, the giant white wind turbine and chant hymns of salvation for the planet. Furious, Dr Newall threw the paper aside and opened the next one. Gaia! Bloody Gaia! It was true! James Lovelock was a Devon Nimby. He actually said "I am proud to be called a Nimby, for my backyard is the countryside and I see that land as the face of Gaia."

The only good thing was that penny Wragg was marooned in central Wales somewhere dancing around a standing stone at some Celtic wedding. He was in no mood for asinine remarks or attempts to justify this man. He kicked out at his waste basket a couple of times, before fly-kicking it down the stairs. Then he fell into a black pool of despond and waited for opening time and liquid consolation. There was no doubt about it. Lovelock, his hero, was an apostate. He felt the bitter rancour towards Lovelock that all revolutionaries felt when the revolution moved on and their former leaders didn't. The fact that the famous scientist might have been hijacked to a cause he didn't believe in, wind farms, would never have occurred to him.

Three hours later, across town and high on the moors, Verity Dee discovered the same articles. She simply hooted. How deliciously ironic. The man who inspired all the pseudo-religious wind farm worship with his Gaia Principle/Theory turns out to be a proud self-confessed Nimby. With views on wind farms very little different from her own, or so it seemed. She rubbed her eyes and re-read the articles, paying particular attention to the quotes from the new book.

Next day she drove into Manchester and bought The Vanishing Face of Gaia. She was still nervous when she came to open it. She didn't know quite what to expect. Loads of airy-fairy mysticism, maybe, such as the save-the-planet brigade spouted? Or dry technical prose she couldn't understand. Finally, she was fearful she had dreamed the reviews. Or that they were simply wishful thinking.

In the event she was pleasantly surprised. There they were, the views they shared. He decried wind farms and advocated nuclear energy. The crisp, direct prose was a delight to read. There were amusing, self-deprecating anecdotes of how Lovelock and his wife had set out to live a greener life and the pitfalls they had encountered. As well as some very sensible observations on climate change. Indeed if she hadn't long since accepted climate change the book would have convinced her.

The wind farm supporters were big on linkage. Anyone who disagreed with wind farms was automatically dubbed "a climate change denier", a Nimby or a knuckle-dragging Neanderthal. During her long correspondence dual with Dr Newall in the Recorder he had called her all of these things. You weren't allowed to say there may be better ways to deal with climate change than wind farms.

Interestingly, Lovelock admitted that if wind farms were truly efficient and capable of resolving our power needs he would grit his teeth and ignore their ugly intrusion, "but they are almost useless as a source of energy." Which was pretty much what she and Willie had come to think.

He went on to say that it would need a 1,000 square miles of countryside to provide enough land for a 1 gigawatt wind farm. Plus a near full-sized fossil fuel power station to provide the back-up. By comparison, a coal or nuclear power station could be accommodated in a space no bigger than 6 football pitches.

He dealt very credibly with the objections to nuclear. The green lobbies and political parties, he said, owed their very existence to the unending flow of good stories about environmental disaster, starting with Rachel Carson's Silent

Spring via Three Mile Island and Chernobyl. Nobody died at Three Mile Island. And even though Chernobyl was terrible only 75 people died. In 50 years of the nuclear industry only 100 people had died. The risks and fears were exaggerated, he said.

He went on to say that although it is often said that nuclear waste is uniquely deadly and will persist for millions of years, the same is true of many chemical pollutants. Lead, mercury, arsenic, cadmium and thallium are all toxic elements that are permanently with us. What is different is that nuclear waste fades away. In 600 years it will be be no more toxic than the uranium ore from which it was mined. The yearly output from a 1000 MW nuclear power station is enough to fill a London taxi. Which is why, he said, he would welcome its burial at his home in Devon. And there was a colour picture of an idyllic Devon landscape above a tight-packed wind farm in Scotland. Compare and contrast.

She read the slim book at a sitting and started to go back over it with a marker pen. She waited impatiently for Willie to return from the print auction in Newcastle he'd gone to.

Finally just after ten o'clock he returned and she blurted out her news. And the views which had excited her. He sat down in the music room and listened patiently, sipping at his nightcap.

'I can't see how declarations from such an eminent voice won't change things,' she concluded happily.

'Well, I'm glad it's so cheered you up. But you mustn't let yourself get too carried away,' Willie said.

'How can you say that?'

‘Well, it’s quite highbrow, isn’t it? And it’s been reviewed in the broadsheets...’

‘It isn’t highbrow at all...’

‘But the perception probably is...’

‘It’s still in the national press...’

‘Yeah, but it’s not on telly, is it? Most people don’t read these days...you know that.’

Bolly looked hurt.

‘I’m sorry, but that’s just the way it is. Take that bit about how much space a nuclear power station occupies by comparison with the equivalent generating power of wind turbines. If it was a telly programme they’d have got some famous ex-footballer like Kevin Keegan walking around the equivalent of six football pitches. Then they’d cut to some famous Welsh rock star like Cerys Matthews driving around the 1,000 square miles of Wales you’d need to cover in giant turbines to equal the nuclear station’s output. Finally, to rub the point in, you’d have some self-important wanker walk on, wave at the landscape behind him, and say “Ultimately, it’s all about the price. Would you be prepared to give away so much of our beautiful wild places, and the creatures in them, for small amounts of expensive electricity?” People would actually see the enormity of it and be shocked. Six football pitches versus vast tracts of Wales, no contest. You see what I mean? Televisual age.’

‘You’re in the wrong job,’ she said sourly.

‘Don’t think so. Couldn’t hack all the Tristrams and Ruperts in TV production,’ he said. But she wasn’t listening.

Bloody hell, he's right. Most people won't even notice.

And as days went by, so it came to pass. Mr Lovelock was far more famous with the wind farm lobby and the Greens than he was with the general public.

Developers hard-charging to get their wallets upholstered with subsidies ignored the book. Government wheeled out their pet scientists to nay say it. The wind farm priesthood simply rewrote Lovelock out of their liturgy.

Verity felt deeply let down. Resentment festered. If Newall and his fellow travellers wouldn't listen to reason then something else had to be done.

# 26

Even before reading James Lovelock's book, Curtiss Wright's assertions had lit a flame within Verity Dee. The likely cause of Jumper's death incensed her. Months of noting all the letters of complaint in the Recorder which Ursa brushed off, as well as looking into the swirling, whooshing blades on a daily basis had led her into despair and depression.

It was all very well fretting about the impact these ghastly things were having. But if Curtiss Wright was correct - and, given the mare's deafness, it made good sense to her - then it was high time to do something, to make public the feelings of the suffering majority.

Ten days after Jumper's funeral, on the evening of 23rd June, Bolly went and sat outside the house in her Mini Cooper and rang Dr Freddy Mount on her mobile. 'Freddy,' she said, 'How would you kill an industrial wind turbine?'

There was silence for about 30 seconds.

'You realize that would be against the law?'

'I'm not asking you to do it. Just how to do it.'

'What does Willie think about it?'

'I haven't asked him.'

'Why not?'

'You know why not.'

'He'll say "no".'

'Yeah.'

'Okay, I'll give it some thought.'

'Thanks, Freddy. I knew I could depend on you.'

'One last thing.'

'What?'

'You should think about it, too. If you go ahead with this you cross a line you know. You criminalize yourself.'

'What if the law is a bad law. That it's been so stacked against the people it's not representative.'

'You still cross the line, Bolly.'

'But like I say, what if?'

'You still cross the line. But I suppose you can call yourself a political activist rather than a criminal.'

'There, you see Dr Mount.'

'They'll still call you a criminal though.'

'What do you think?'

'It doesn't matter what I think.'

'No, but what do you think?'

'I'm with you, God help me. I don't like the way this government has continually moved the goalposts with the planning regs and leaned on local government to bully people. All for a load of shitty technology that doesn't work properly.'

'So you'll help me?'

'Yeah, I'll think about it. Dr Mount - the rebel, God help me,' he laughed. 'I thought I'd outgrown all that.' Then the phone went down.

24 hours later, Bolly's mobile rang. The caller ID was clear enough. She took the phone out of the room where Willie was playing with Nelson and into the garden. She felt guilty, as though she were having an affair.

'So?'

'Okay. I know how to do it.'

'How?'

'Well, unless you have artillery you need to ask a physicist.'

'Stop teasing, what does the physicist think?'

'This physicist thinks he has a pretty elegant way to get the thing to self-destruct.'

'So, stop holding out on me, how do we do it?'

'Well, the thinking is like jiu-jitsu. You use the turbine's physical bulk to turn it in on itself and do a wrecking job.'

'Sounds ironic and a perfect solution. How much?'

'Not too much. Should be possible for under a ton.'

'A hundred quid?'

'Yeah.'

'That's fine. No problem.'

'I can't make any financial contribution, I'm afraid. The Child Support Agency has me by the short and curlies. But I'll come over and do it for you.'

'Hey, Freddie. I wouldn't have asked you for money. Your help is invaluable. And your discretion is also much appreciated. What Willie doesn't know he won't worry about.'

'If we get away with it he won't.'

There was a short silence while both considered. Then Bolly spoke.

'What the hell, we've come this far. I'm tired of feeling powerless. Shit or bust?'

'Okay, shit or bust.'

'What's the next step?'

'Well, for my plan to work we need the turbine to be static.'

Bolly laughed. 'That shouldn't be a problem. They spend three quarters of their life like that.'

'No, but we need to know in advance so I can get over there. Farmer's weather forecast sounds the best bet. The NFU have a local weather site on the Net. You just type in your post code. I'll do that. For obvious reasons we will need to do this under cover of darkness, right?'

'Makes sense.'

'Right well I'll go and splurge on the stuff we need. I won't ring you unless it costs more than a ton, alright?'

'Fine. And I'll pay you back when I see you. On the night.'

'You be able to get away alright?'

'Of course, Willy trusts me.'

'I wouldn't.'

'Freddy, don't go like that on me. If he doesn't know what I'm planning, he won't worry about it.'

'I know. I know. Okay. Will ring you asap when the weather forecast predicts a dead calm.'

'Right,' she said. The line crackled and then he was gone. No matter. This one's for you, Jumper. Applying physics to defeat these things really appealed. She couldn't wait to find out how Freddy thought he could do it.

The idea of being pro-active also appealed to her nature. Hitherto the developers had got their application through, put their feet up, relaxed and lined up their offshore bank paying-in slips. The opposition just curled up and died. Well, not any more. If it happened once, it could happen again. At least it would put the wind up them, she thought. Then she smiled at her own unintentional funny.

The people who had painted Green Shit on the turbines at Cloughgreen Moor had really inspired her. Of course, who had actually done it also fascinated her. Never in a million years could it be Willie or Carter Briggs or Dr Bentley. Or, frankly, any of the worthy middle-aged types from The Friends of the Living Moorland. Since Jumper's funeral she was pretty sure it had been the three lads from the rugby club.

They had to wait until July 15th for a more or less guaranteed period of calm. That's what the Pennine tops were like. Turbulent. Sometimes four seasons of weather in one day.

July 15th had been yet another rain-soaked one. But still. Not a whisper of breeze stirring the blades of grass. She checked the NFU weather site around 5pm, punching in her local post code. Like Freddy had said, it was a whiz of a site for short term localised weather predictions. It even predicted wind speeds. The site predicted no wind at all until the early hours. Perfect. She rang Freddy and told him the good news.

'I know,' he said. 'I was just about to ring you.'

Around eleven she told Willie she was feeling a bit stir crazy and felt like going for a drive in the car.

'Okay, I'll get my coat,' he said.

'No,' she said quickly, 'I just feel like being on my own for a bit. You don't mind, do you?'

He hesitated, then shrugged. 'No, just be careful, though. Keep the doors locked.'

'I will. Don't worry. You go to bed.'

She had taken the advice of Dr Mount and wore a black sweater and jeans. There was a black woollie top.

She put the Mini in gear and pointed its nose downhill into town. Then it was a a ten minute drive up the opposite side of the valley on to the tops of Cloughgreen Common.

The moon was brighter than she would have liked, but the world seemed to be holding its breath and that was good.

There was a black Transit van parked outside the gates of the wind farm when she got there. She drove off the road and parked next to it. Freddy Mount, looking like a commando with blackened face, bared his teeth in a grin and gave her a thumbs up as she got out.

'You alright?'

'Bit nervous,' she said.

'We'll just get in and out. But put some of this on your face first.' He passed her a tin. 'Black theatrical makeup.'

She did as he asked and he smoothed a few bits in. 'Great, the Cloughgreen Minstrels are good to go. You open the gates and I'll drive the Transit in.'

'Then I've got an industrial applicator, like a sort of giant foam gun, that they use for insulating lofts and cavity walls, stuff like that. The foam shoots out as liquid and then solidifies really quickly and acquires mass. I just need to shoot it onto the tip of one of the blades.'

'Simple as that?'

'Theoretically.'

'You're a genius.'

'Well, let's see first. The rotor blades are properly balanced. The idea is that a big solid blob on one of the blades once it's moving will create an imbalance. After that the movement of the blade will create enough stress and torque to tear itself off. That's the theory anyway'

'Like I said, you're a genius, Freddie.' She went to the big five-barred metal gate and dragged it open.

Dr Mount slid the van in and gestured to her to close the gate, as he drove up to the nearest turbine. He parked as near as he could and frowned.

'The tip is higher than I thought. Just hope the gun is powerful enough.'

'Need any help?'

'Yeah,' he said, looking thoughtful. 'I'm going to swing up onto the roof of the Transit. See if you can pass the foam gun up to me. It's quite heavy, but you should be able to do it.'

Bolly went to the open doors at the rear of the van as he contrived to lever himself up onto the roof. The gun was longer and heavier than she'd imagined. But she was able to lug it out and then push it up the side of the van and onto the roof.

'Christ, I feel like a spider on a milk bottle top up here,' he muttered. 'It's slippery.'

She watched as he shouldered the industrial gun and made a trial swing upwards towards the tip of the turbine blade.

'Okay, stand back.'

She retreated 20' from the van and watched in awe as he pulled the long, bayonet-like trigger. A thick gout of orangey-yellow foam shot upwards and past the end of the blade. He eased the trigger back, swearing. The thick orangey foam was congealing like egg yolk on the grass.

'Shit, this isn't as easy as it looks while you're balancing on a roof.. Still, let's have another go.'

This time he set his legs further apart and made a perfectly timed upward swing of the gun before turning it on. A large gout of the chemical lodged on the end of the blade and started to solidify almost instantaneously, leaving a ragged trail off the tip.

'Gotcha,' he exclaimed. 'That should do it.'

Then he stopped himself. 'On the other hand, now I'm up here.' He arced the gun up and fired again. The second burst of foam adhered easily to the first burst on the tip of the blade. 'Yesss...' Freddy said admiringly. 'Much more like it.'

He chucked the now much lighter gun onto the grass and crouched before jumping off the Transit roof.

'Okay,' he said, 'Job done. Let's get going.'

They were just closing the rear doors of the Transit when they heard it.

It was a high-pitched police siren. Then they saw it.

A white BMW saloon with flashing blue lights hammering down the winding moorland road.

'You go. Make a run for it towards Reddingley,' Bolly said. 'I'll drive towards them. They can't get both of us.'

'I don't think so, Bolly.' He grinned ruefully. 'I think this is what they call a fair cop. Must have closed circuit TV cameras on them.'

'Blast! I bet they did it after the Green Shit paint stunt. I was a fool not to think of it. But you run...'

'And leave you to face the music on your own. No. I'm not a scally. Some of us Scousers do have a sense of honour.'

'And it was just my luck to discover him,' she said.

Watching the police car race towards them she started to feel sick in her stomach at the thought they'd been caught red-handed. And a twinge shot up her baton-broken forearm. Then she remembered the cash she owed him. 'Here, take this,' she said, pressing a wad of cash into his hand.

The powerful white police car bored on through the moorland night. The sound of its siren echoing around, the cones of its headlights bouncing up and down on the undulating road.

It was still a good way off but there was no chance of outrunning it. The Mini Cooper might have done, but the Transit would have had no chance. They stood there, resigned, looking a bit like naughty children waiting to be punished, she thought.

He put his arm around her shoulder. 'Well, whatever happens, we've done it, Bolly. What we set out to do. Whatever happens to us, it's strike one for the good guys.'

Just then a wisp of hair blew in her face.

'Listen,' she said. 'The wind's getting up. It's like the gods are on our side.' The grass started rustling and then her hair started to stand on end. There was an ominous rustling and creaking and then clanking.

'Look,' she said, pointing at the turbines.

‘They’re starting to move. Let’s get back behind the gate.’ He jumped into the Transit and she ran and opened the gate.

He parked the Transit against her Mini and they closed the gate.

The turbines were picking up momentum as the wind rose. The whooshing slowly rose and the metallic clanking.

‘It’s the drive chains,’ Freddy Mount said. Then there was a sudden screeching noise as the nearest turbine, the foam-treated one, started vibrating violently on its pillar.

‘Christ, get down behind the Transit,’ Freddy yelled, pushing her down. They watched peeping from behind the front of the van, as the vibrations increased.

Suddenly she didn’t know what came over her. She got up and started a wild dance from foot to foot, chanting ‘Destroy the polluters, the ignorant ones, Destroy the polluters...’

‘Eh?’ Freddy said.

‘I feel like the Iron Woman. One of Ted Hughes’s heroines who fights river pollution. These dreadful things are visual pollution, as Willie would say.’

As Freddy looked at her in the starlight, she realized he fancied her. She looked quickly away. She didn’t need that sort of complication. She looked back at the turbine. Its foam-loaded tip was really oscillating now and whining.

Then there was a terrible shriek of over-stressed metal as the turbine blade wrenched itself off its axis and sailed over their heads. They ducked as it fell to the ground on the perimeter road. A plume of orange flame erupted from the amputation point as flaming oil spurted out and then black smoke swirled from the rotor head.

'YES!' Bolly punched the air. She felt elated beyond belief after months of having to sit and take it. 'Well done you, Freddy Mount. We've killed one of the monsters, shown they can be beaten.'

Freddy looked suprisingly calm, given his achievement, she thought.

'The trouble is, the UKWC have a lot of clout in the media. They have authority on their side. Your freedom fight is their atrocity.' He pushed his hands deeper in his pockets and looked bashful. 'Still,' he said, 'I love you for your spirit, for what you've done.'

Oh dear, she thought, dragging her eyes back to the wreckage.

The white police car screeched to a halt next to the Mini and two police officers spilled out. They ducked  as there was a colossal bang and an electric-blue flash illuminated the landscape.

Within seconds all the turbines ceased moving as some systems cut-out came into operation. They stood still, illuminated by the licking flames of their comrade's death throes.

'Jesus H...you've made a job of that,' the sergeant said. Bolly smiled defiantly and kissed Freddy chastely on the cheek. He deserved that. Freddy Mount just shrugged. The other policeman phoned for the fire brigade.

At three o'clock in the morning Willie was awoken by the house phone. His heart sank as the police acquainted him with the situation. Bolly, oh Bolly, what have you done?

Then the phone calls started. He rang his solicitor. He rang Bolly's father. He rang Gerry to give him a hand retrieving Bolly's Mini from the wind farm. The police rang Ursa. Ursa rang Dr Newall's mobile as the man on the spot.

'Can you go up and inspect it, Edwin? Give us a detailed report.'

'Hardly, I'm up in London on business.'

'Well in that case get yourself over here now. Can you do that?'

'Of course. Willingly,' Dr Newall said, resentfully. They may pay well, but he wasn't their creature to command.

An hour later he sat with Ilya Bakunin, Ursa's MD and Arkadiy Kovalenko, his right hand man and FD.

'The techies say the whole turbine may be a write off,' Bakunin said. 'The torque produced by the primitive device which tore off the blade may well have weakened all the other component parts in the turbine.'

'Couldn't have been that primitive to do such damage,' Dr Newall said.

'The device was fairly primitive. The thinking was first rate. One of the culprits is a physics don at Liverpool University.'

'Who are the others?'

'The other one is your old adversary, the beautiful Ms Dee,' Kovalenko said.

'Excellent,' Dr Newall said, beaming. 'Then at least some good can come out of this.'

'How so? We don't understand.'

'Well, don't you see. That abominable woman has really gone too far this time. This gives you the chance to get her out of your hair...'

'And your hair, Dr Newall,' Kovalenko said.

'...once and for all.'

'We're not here to be vindictive, Edwin. We're here to consider the wider picture before we instruct our legal people. Magnanimity might be a better way to proceed if we wish to have more turbines around Cloughgreen.'

'I agree,' Kovalenko said. 'Extract a grovelling apology for the damage done to us and to the electrical supplies of the people of Cloughgreen.'

'The juice just goes straight into the National Grid,' Newall said.

'They don't know that. What is it you call them, "the numpties of Cloughgreen?"' Kovalenko continued.

'I favour a generous view on our part, too,' Ilya Bakunin said. 'There are elements who resent us for not being Yorkshiremen, let alone being Russian. The last thing we want to do is turn Verity Dee and this physics teacher into local martyrs.'

'I think you're crazy,' Dr Newall said, fidgeting with his keys noisily. 'If I had my way I'd toss her into an oubliette and throw away the key.'

'An oubliette, Edwin?'

'It means a deep dungeon into which where people were thrown and forgotten about.'

'Thank you, Dr Newall. Even in Russia we have French teachers,' Bakunin said frostily. 'Both Arkadiy and myself know quite well what an oubliette is. We were just querying your strategy.'

'Edwin, I could even show you some modern-day oubliettes,' Kovalenko said, smiling. The smile never reached his eyes and Dr Newall felt all the old fear. With some men violence was always just below the surface.

'Well, I tell you one thing,' he said impulsively, wanting to lash out, 'If you let these two off lightly you'll have nutcases all over the country doing it. Especially now they know how to do it. And even if you want to take the risk it's not just about you. You owe a debt of solidarity to all your fellow renewables professionals to see this doesn't happen again anywhere else.'

The atmosphere in the board room chilled as the two wind farm executives considered the cost of renewed vandalism or activism countrywide.

'Will the insurers pay, Arkadiy?' the MD asked.

'I don't know yet. I have talked to them informally, but their senior claims people were not available, so their underwriters don't know. It depends what sort of line they take. I think this may be setting a precedent.'

'So we may have to take a three million pound hit on this? Still peanuts in the long term, of course. Even so, we can't afford a repetition.'

‘And other people within the renewables industry will say it’s down to us to take a stand,’ Kovalenko said. ‘But still, I can’t believe the beautiful Verity Dee would do this again.’

‘Sadly, I don’t think that’s the point anymore. I think Dr Newall is right. The last thing we need is copycat activists wrecking turbines just because they now know how to.’ Ilya Bakunin sighed. ‘I regret this as much as you do, Arkadiy. Such a beautiful creature should not be behind bars. And I don’t think she would do it again either. But this is too important to be thinking with our pants.’ Bakunin stared moodily out of the window and frowned. ‘Maybe not the oubliette treatment, but perhaps a demi-oubliette is needed.’ He turned to Dr Newall *‘pour encourager, les autres*, Edwin. French, too, you see.’

Dr Newall raised his palms to his face, feigning tiredness. Then he smiled deeply.

After Dr Newall left Ursa rang their solicitor. Their solicitor then rang the police. On the advice of their local adviser they said, they were taking a hard line, they were opposing bail. There was significant criminal damage, well over £100,000 worth. The turbine might even be a write-off. They were well within their rights.

Willie’s solicitor confirmed this. ‘With damage to property of this magnitude and interruption of services to the community they are well within their rights. It will probably be Crown Court. What she’s done is very serious.’

‘How serious?’

'If they want to play hardball, make an example of her, then £10,000 fine...'

'Bloody hell.'

'...and maybe 10 years in prison.'

'Good God. Prison. 10 years! Are you sure?'

'I'm afraid so, Willie. It will almost certainly be some sort of custodial sentence to reflect the enormous sum of damage. It's not like breaking a window, you know.'

'No, I can see that. These things can cost a few million each, I believe.'

'Exactly so.' He paused. 'There's also a good chance Ursa's lot will oppose bail.'

'Why?'

'Well, one the possibility she may do it again...'

'She wouldn't. I'll chain her to the bed if I have to...'

'...plus, as I said, the enormity of the damage she has already done.'

'Look, Willie,' his solicitor and long-time mate said quietly. 'This is way more serious than you realize. I can't genuinely handle it properly from 200 miles away here in London. And I've got things on. I'm going to hand it over to a very able, good mate of mine in Leeds.'

'Okay, what's his name, Bob?'

'He's called Jimmy Crossley. I'll explain everything and get him to call you.'

'Jimmy?' Willie said in astonishment. 'You really want me to entrust my wife's wellbeing to a solicitor called Jimmy?'

Bob chuckled. 'He's really sharp, Willie. What you must realize is that he's a specialist criminal lawyer unlike me. He finds "Jimmy" goes down better with his sort of punter.'

'I don't know. A solicitor called Jimmy? Maybe in Glasgow.'

'Willie, get serious. You have to realize Bolly's broken the law big time. She's committed a serious criminal act. She needs someone street-smart like Jimmy Crossley. Oh, and one last thing,' he paused for effect...

'Yeah?'

'Jimmy is a lot more expensive than I am.'

'But you're in London and...'

'...He's in Leeds, yeah. Should tell you something, right?'

'That bank robbers and white collar scammers have very deep pockets?'

'Funny, Willie. I'm glad you've kept your sense of humour. You're going to need it. Anyway I'll get Jimmy to ring you.'

'Okay, thanks,' Willie said. His mind was doing cartwheels. To his shame he found he was already counting the cost. Maybe a ten grand fine. Plus a more expensive brief than Bob. Plus court costs presumably. This was really starting to stack up. But what was the option? He had to try and extricate Bolly, whatever the cost.

Jimmy Crossley rang him twenty minutes later and they agreed to meet at his offices and go on to the main police station later.

His office was a smart one not far from the city's commercial centre.

Willie didn't know what he'd expected. Maybe a fag-ash version of Leo McKern as Rumpole of the Bailey. It certainly wasn't Jimmy Crossley. Jimmy Crossley was tall and elegant with aquiline features and long, slicked-back black hair. He wore a pale grey pinstripe three-piece, a generously cut grey silk tie with a pearl pin and expensive black loafers.

He had a confident, toothy smile and a firm dry handshake. He exuded success and yet still Willie felt he ought to be counting the fingers on the hand he had extended for the handshake.

Willie ran through the facts as he understood them and then they went down to the police station. As Jimmy had warned him, the police wouldn't let him see Bolly, so he was left to wait in the reception area.

Jimmy Crossley came back about an hour later looking serious.

'Ursa Power are jumping up and down playing hardball in the background. I can't figure it out. But it seems almost vindictive. Anyway, their solicitor is demanding she be remanded until trial in Crown Court.'

'When will that be?'

'Who knows? She's in the system now. It takes its own sweet time. She'll be up before a magistrate this morning and officially remanded to await trial in Crown Court.'

'I don't understand. Couldn't the magistrate deal with it, if she pleads guilty?'

'In some cases, yes. But only in cases where the damage is below £10,000. Above that figure it's taken very seriously and becomes a Crown Court matter. It appears the final cost of the damage may be many times £10,000. Then it appears Mrs Dee has a previous record for demonstrating and disturbing the peace. Ursa's solicitor is maintaining there is a real possibility she could go out and do it again.'

'But she wouldn't. She's made her protest now. She's been upset about a friend's death.'

Jimmy Crossley smiled a wintry smile. 'Having seen her, I'm inclined to agree with you. She's a very plucky woman, Mr Dee. But I think she knows she's overdone things. The trouble is the other side have very good cause on their side at this point when it comes to procedure. We'll have our chance later in Crown Court to plead mitigating circumstances. Did Bob tell you there is a possible maximum custodial sentence of 10 years for this offence?'

Willie felt the colour drain from his face and his legs go shaky. Neither of them would be able to cope with 10 years separation, let alone her having to deal with 10 years in prison.

Jimmy Crossley took his arm gently and eased him backwards into a chair.

'Sit down a moment. Take a deep breath. I have to warn you of this. It's part of my job. But that's very much a worst case scenario where Ursa and the judge seek to make a nationwide example of Verity. I'm pretty sure it won't come to that.'

'Ten years. You can get less than that for rape or murder.'

Jimmy Crossley smiled his thin wintry smile, the gleaming white teeth barely showing.

'You can do, yes. But English law takes a very strong view of crimes against property. You may remember deportation to Australia for stealing a sheep?'

'But that was the bad old days.'

Jimmy Crossley raised his eyebrows. 'In this country we still view crimes against property some would say overly seriously vis a vis crimes against the person.'

Willie put his head in his hands. Why on earth hadn't she talked to him about this? Well, he knew that, didn't he? Because he'd have stopped her. You'd have thought Dr Freddy Mount would have had more sense. There again, these damned turbines just seemed to inspire deep passions. Slowly through his turmoil he became aware that Jimmy Crossley was speaking.

'Buck up, Willie, we haven't started yet. We'll get our turn. The first thing is she has to plead guilty and show contrition.'

Willie groaned. 'Half of that will be no problem.'

'Willie, she doesn't have to mean it. Just play the game. That's what it's all about from now on. Playing the game. You leave it to me. We'll be okay.'

Will we? Willie thought miserably.

Ursa's PR woman, Victoria Flowers, rang Humphrey Drumm just after 9.30 am to tell him the glad tidings of turbine mayhem. It was not a good start to the day. His initial reaction was: "This time she's really gone too far". But he liked and respected the woman and wanted to protect her if he could. What the hell, she hadn't killed anyone. And the turbine was probably insured to the hilt anyway.

In the end he decided all he could do was keep her name out of the Recorder for now. But the story had to be told. He sent his snapper along for a picture of the ripped-off, bent turbine blade laying on the ground. Then he ran the piece under the headline Wind Turbine Vandalised. "Vandalised" didn't really do it justice, he thought. "Completely bloody wrecked" came closer the mark. According to Victoria Flowers the whole turbine might have to be replaced thanks to the stresses and strains imposed on the structure. Still, call it poetic licence. He rang a few chums on the nationals to pass on the item, but to his surprise no-one seemed to want to know. 'No mileage in dead ones, old sport,' was the closest he got to an explanation. 'We like moving ones waving gently and saving the planet.' But he tended to agree with Carter Briggs's conspiracy theory: that United Kingdom Wind Commission was running some sort of defensive PR screen. They wouldn't want people in other parts of the country being given ideas, would they?

# 27

Since Bolly had been arrested there had been no summer weather to speak of. Then no Indian summer in September either. Just as the previous year would remain memorable for its many-berried, long, hot summer, this one would be remembered for the unrelenting rain, Willie thought. On the few days it let up, you could watch reflections of the clouds gliding across the puddled grass of the saturated fields and lawns. Down in the town the rain was a matter of grumbling discontent. Up on the tops it made a big difference to peoples' everyday lives.

Leaving aside the unpleasantness of having rain driven into your eyes and ears the going underfoot became a nightmare. Going down steep hills was worst. Put your foot on saturated grass and you risked aquaplaning. Twist an ankle up here and God help you. You could die of exposure before the next walker came along. Normally Willie didn't want to be bothered by distractions but he took to taking his mobile with him. Just in case.

He increasingly had to change routes when he came across tame springs that had become whitewater torrents. The stepping stones in fords were under 6-12" of fast-flowing water. There was so much water the earth couldn't absorb it. It lay in massive pools in fields. Flowers were battered down, vegetables rotted in the ground and people lived under dark skies. In former times people would have believed the sun god was angry with them and started sacrifices to appease him.

October 1st, the day set for Bolly's trial, was no different. The sky was lard-coloured, the pavements sleek with rain. Willie's heart was heavy as he arrived at 1 Oxford Row, Leeds. As he watched midnight-blue police vans transporting criminals into Leeds Crown Court, he felt a sense of unreality. But also of dread. What was he doing here? What was his beautiful wife doing here? Wrecking a wind turbine, the idea was absurd. Except it wasn't. Hands up, she did it. All that was up for discussion was how painful would be her punishment.

He got a grip on himself, forced himself to enter the building and found Jimmy Crossley waiting in the agreed place. Apart from anything else he felt constrained. He thought he'd best try and look smart. So he was wearing the suit he'd bought for

Jumper's funeral. And the Lifeboats Supporters tie he always wore when anticipating a stormy meeting.

'Are you all right? You look a bit pale.'

'No, I'm not all right, Jimmy. The fact is I'm shitting bricks about how this is all going to turn out.'

Jimmy took him by the arm. 'Look, the milk has already been spilled, Willie. Let's see how much we can get back in the bottle, eh?'

Could you get 10 years for spilling milk? The metaphor was lost on him. Having apprised him several times of the possible outcomes, Jimmy pointed him in the direction of the public gallery and rushed off to see the barrister. His last words were 'We can still get a result.'

The atmosphere in the gallery had the same tension you felt in airports; nervous apprehension, a sort of collective trepidation. There were some pretty hard-looking types, all looking uneasy and edgy. Except for one toothless biddy in the corner who was feeding herself bananas from deep pockets and sucking them noisily down. A latter-day crone, who sucked happily as the tumbrils arrived and heads rolled. She was enjoying life.

While Willie was being horrified, Verity was ushered in by her police escort. He nearly jumped out of his seat. To judge from appearances she had handled her confinement well. But she looked nervous. He caught her eye as she looked around and waved a shy little wave. She smiled weakly back then turned to face the bench, suddenly solemn but serious.

As Willie had feared, Verity didn't do contrition very well. She stood proud as Boudicca before the Romans. Head held high, her long red hair like a battle ensign.

Where was Freddy Mount, he wondered. Then he remembered he had separate representation, some relative or other from Merseyside.

Eventually Jimmy Crossley appeared, chatting earnestly to their QC Duncan Forbes. Forbes was a slight, pasty-complexioned man who looked dwarfed by his wig. Next came Ursa's QC, Simon Willoughby. Willoughby was a tall, broad shouldered man with a handsome patrician face. He had the deep permatan that 6 weeks a year crewing a racing yacht to Bermuda or around the Greek islands gave you. He swaggered to his place looking confidently down his nose as though querying why he were being asked to perform on such a mean provincial stage. Willie's heart sank. Willoughby exuded success from his expensively cut, sun-bleached hair to his immaculately manicured fingernails.

The judge, His Honour Judge P.C.W Whittaker, was a tall, ascetic-looking man with jaundiced cheeks who appeared to have been sucking lemons. Willie had been warned that he had a reputation as a bit of a hanger and flogger. He spoke in a terse, flat Bradford accent.

His Honour testily got proceedings under way. The prisoner had pleaded guilty. Now what could be said for and against?

Simon Willoughby had steeled his features to reflect the gravity of Verity Dee's threat to Britain's entire future energy policy. Nonetheless he could not conceal his arrogance. He spoke in an affected Home Counties accent, posturing in a way that Willie knew was exactly what raised northern hackles. This gave Willie some hope. Willoughby's theatrical grandstanding might play well at the Bailey, but these were more down-to-earth locations. With folk who were determined to be unimpressed by grand manners.

It played pretty much as Jimmy Crossley and his old mate Bob had predicted. Simon Willoughby, for the prosecution, emphasized the seriousness of the prisoner's action; the enormous cost of the damage inflicted to the turbine; the loss of electricity to the community; the poor example it showed to the general public when renewables were the future we needed to embrace; the fact that Verity Dee had been known to the police before for actions in connection with wind farms; the strong possibility that if released without punishment she would reoffend; the need therefore to send out a strong exemplary message to other possible miscreants; the combination of these factors required the sternest punishment. Ten years.

Willie had been watching Judge Whittaker's reaction to Simon Willoughby's posturing. At times he looked as though there was a bad smell under his nose. It was pretty clear Willoughby wasn't Judge Whittaker's style.

When he first spoke Duncan Forbes's speaking style was a revelation. For a small, wiry man he possessed a powerful, carrying voice. He was reminiscent of Jose Carreras he thought, a smallish man with a powerful voice. Forbes's accent came from somewhere not far from Judge Whittaker's, with flat northern vowels.

He presented the counter case eloquently, Willie thought. A woman of good family who had no previous police record prior to her political action against wind farms; a woman who had previously confined her actions to strictly legal democratic protest; a woman who had been pushed too far by the death of a friend she believed attributable to the new wind farm; the assorted grievances such as dried up and redirected springs and blade rumble/flicker for which Ursa Power took no responsibility; the belief that a large fine would act as sufficient deterrent to others; Verity's statement that she would not reoffend and an acknowledgment she had gone too far. Above all, to jail a woman of such previous good character who had promised not to re-offend risked making a martyr for the anti-wind farm cause.

Judge Whittaker was brief in his summing up. Serious offence, damage to property. Interrupted power supplies were inexcusable inconvenience to community. Intolerable to take the law into her own hands. Need for exemplary sentence to send out strongest possible measure to others.

On the other hand, no purpose served by draconian sentence - here he stared at Simon Willoughby. Who seeks to break a butterfly upon a wheel? Therefore maximum fine of £10,000 plus 1 year's jail, less time served in remand.

Willie sucked his breath in. Bolly's shoulders drooped as she smiled wanly at him and was led away.

'We got a result,' Jimmy Crossley said later. 'Thanks to that southern arsehole, Willoughby. He got up Whittaker's nose more than his normal desire to make an example.'

'It's a year in jail, Jimmy.'

'Less what she's already done on remand. Less remission for good behaviour. She'll be out by the beginning of March.'

'Next year.'

'It'll fly over.'

'I don't think so, Jimmy. Not for me or Bolly.'

'Willie,' Jimmy Crossley took his arm in a get-serious gesture, 'Those wind farm bastards wanted 10 years. We beat the system. Those turbines cost three million a throw. You got a pop at one for ten grand.'

'Not me, Jimmy. I didn't get a pop at anything. I knew nothing about it.'

Jimmy put his arm around him. 'I know. It will be hard. But 10 years. That would have killed you both.'

Willie smiled bleakly. 'I may still kill her when she gets out.'

Jimmy Crossley made a wry smile. 'It was an expensive night out. I grant you that.'

'Yeah. If it would help, I'd volunteer to go back and help replant the bloody thing.'

'No you wouldn't,' Jimmy Crossley said.

'No. I wouldn't,' Willie admitted,

'Freddy Mount's brother-in-law did a good job as his brief. But then again Freddy had no legal history. I know he built the Gizmo but he wasn't cautioned for it. And he wasn't the instigator of the crime. And the judge took into consideration he would lose his career if he went inside.'

'What did he get?'

'£1,000 fine and 12 months suspended sentence.'

'Good. I'm glad he got off. If it wasn't for Bolly he'd never have been involved.'

'That's a pretty magnanimous thing to say. Seeing as how he enabled the fell deed.'

'What good would an extra 12 months of misery do? No, I'm glad he's got off. I think Bolly saw red and he got burned, too.'

'He's still lucky.'

'I don't know. He may still have his liberty. But for a moment of madness he's done something the stuffed-shirts at his Uni won't forgive or forget. They'll smile at him. But deep down the high-ups never forget.'

'True.' Jimmy Crossley sucked his teeth.

'What now?'

'I'll send you my bill.' The smile of a happy piranha.

They sent Bolly to a supposedly milder regime prison. But it was the far side of Leeds, in the middle of nowhere. Near farms, a small new airport and an illegal immigrants centre. Misery of a distant sort.

So he still had to contend with the Leeds traffic, plus the M62 was usually a crawl from Brighouse to Wakefield. It seemed a lot further away for visits, a lot more aggro.

And now she was a prisoner and not on remand the number of visits were strictly limited. The phone calls were erratic, depending on when she could get to the payphone and activate her account.

Reality bit suddenly. With Jumper gone, Willie had to put Bolly's horse Bushmills in stables. She'd had a horse since she was six. He'd never ridden one in his life.

More expense, he thought glumly. As he helped the stables lad load Bushmills into the van he suddenly thought "The winds of heaven blow from between a horse's ears". An echo of Bolly. But without her to ask he had no idea who had said it.

The next task was to take her Mini Cooper out and give it a run to keep the battery charged. It started first time. As the car warmed up, the residual smells of her perfume wafted around the car as though she were still there. It was too painful. He turned the engine off and got out. Charging the battery would have to wait till he was feeling better.

Now she was finally gone he sank into despair. He had been hoping against hope she would walk free. He would have paid double the fine for that.

Her imprisonment was like a sort of death. One minute she had been here, the next gone. He suddenly realized what a good marriage they had. How smug they must have seemed to singles like Gerry & Jumper. The perfect couple living in each other's pockets, finishing each others jokes and stories, content with each other's company. That comfortable feeling of living with someone who you know so well that nothing they do can badly surprise you. Ha! That was a good one, he thought.

How empty the house now is. What an old-fashioned husband he had been, doing only a few chores, cutting the grass, washing up, occasional breakfast. Now he felt as though half of him had been lopped off.

There was the terrible realization that without her he was nothing. Vagrant, his constancy gone, raggle-taggle gypsy, lost his bearings, no star to steer by, lost soul, wandering Jew. All of that. Plus the realization that until she came out he was living dead time. Marking time on the spot like a wind-up toy guardsman, going nowhere.

The first intimations of his dependency came after a month when he nearly set the house on fire. He loaded the washing machine, turned it on and went into the garden. Fortunately he smelt burning, ran back in, turned the smoking machine off and pulled the plug out. The washing machine guy asked why he hadn't cleaned the filter out.

Filter, he thought absently; they have filters?

He had lost his appetite for the first couple of weeks. When he found it he found he had no appetite for cooking. Bolly had always done all of that.

In his bachelor days as a successful photographer he had done what all his successful £2-3,000-a-day-plus-expenses mates did. Nights at flash restaurants or the occasional takeaway. It was a lifestyle.

One night a mate of his stopped dead in his tracks at a Chinese restaurant. Couldn't move. They had to call an ambulance. Turned out he had MSG poisoning from too much Chinese restaurant food.

Some issues sorted themselves out. Cloughgreen didn't have any great restaurants to lure him. And in the old days he hadn't dined alone; he'd taken models out to dinner. Neither of those were options now. Instead, Gerry Stansfield turned out to be an encyclopaedic source of great takeaway places.

One evening he bumped into Penny Wragg at the Red Fort Indian takeaway and she teased him, saying "We've got to stop meeting like this. Your place or mine?". He muttered something in embarrassment. Then he suddenly realized how friendly he'd become with her by chatting in numerous queues for Chinese, Indian, pizza, kebabs and South East Asian takeaways.

He liked her, found her long legs seductive in miniskirts and trademark purple tights. But Gerry was right. Even when she was being flirtatious there was a deep sadness in her eyes and her voice was too quiet, as if she was apologizing for herself.

Three weeks later he thought differently. He was at a low ebb and almost propositioned her. In the old days he wouldn't have thought twice. The plain and the sad were also worthy of sexual comfort. But he stopped himself in time and recognized it as a wake up call.

Another memorable night the Chinese waiter at the Lucky Dragon, the one who spoke poor English, took him aside and asked pityingly: "you got no cooker, mister?"

‘My kitchen is being refitted,’ he lied. ‘It’s taking a while.’ The Chinese guy knew he was lying.

Next day he went down into Cloughgreen and bought himself a microwave. Bolly, with her cordon bleu cooking, would kill him. They’d always sworn they’d never have one in the house. Still, there’d be time to get shut of it when he knew she was coming out. He was pleasantly surprised by how well Tesco catered for lone eaters like him. And how authentically flavoured a lot of the dishes now were instead of pandering to toned down English taste.

At lunch times he got into the habit of going down to one of Cloughgreen’s many chippies. They still used lard and the aroma was delicious. The smell on the wind of old-fashioned chips frying, wafting along the canal, was mouthwateringly reminiscent of the town.

Another revelation from his changed lunchtime circumstances: how the town’s army of small tradesmen lived. He suddenly realized that many of Cloughgreen’s tradesmen, builders, plumbers and sparks actually existed on lunchtime trips to the chippie. The queues went down the block. He wondered what our political masters would make of the health aspects of that. But then, fresh-sprung from a public school, uni and a job as a political researcher they had no idea of real life in the north and real, low wages.

A generous portion of fish and chips or chips and a saveloy was good value to a Cloughgreen tradesman who earned the same in a year as a good young PA earned in London. Our rulers had no idea. Let them eat cake.

Without Bolly to talk to he felt very lonely. He suddenly realized he'd lost touch with many of his mates who'd retired from London advertising and gone to live in the shires or abroad. Disappeared.

The days became much the same. He took Nelson for long walks. He did long drives to see people: Charley Fort in Brighton, his accountant in Mayfair, mates in Wimbledon, his dad in Purley. All down south.

Charley seemed little changed. In his non-PC way he grouched a bit that the gays seemed to be taking over Brighton. Willie wondered when Brighton hadn't been a gay mecca. Back in the days when everyone wore wigs perhaps, when the Prince Regent was still inventing it.

'Still not sold any anti-wind farm articles then?'

'Not a sausage, Golden Boy. The word is definitely out on that as a subject.' Willie had to laugh.

'What's up?'

'The Golden Boy days are long gone. I've been feeling more like a victim the past 2 years. It's not a nice feeling, but I had a good run, I guess. Before I fell to earth.

'What is depressing, quite apart from Bolly's situation, is that all the things you discovered on the Net about wind farms are all coming to pass in Cloughgreen. All the stuff you discovered in Frey & Hadden has come to pass. Not everything to everybody of course, but if you look around...'

Charley grinned a self-deprecatory silly grin. 'Well whatever they say about Charley Fort, he always gets there in the end. The bus may have gone the week before but he usually gets there.'

'What's been frustrating is that knowing all this was coming we still couldn't do a thing to stop it. Well, you've been spot on with this one, Charley, old mate. Funny thing is - although it's too late for us - there are signs the tide is turning. Hang on to those articles, don't bin them. You may sell some yet.'

Charley tapped his black laptop. 'All in here, sport. You know where to come if you need 'em.'

Apart from wind farms they didn't really have much to say to one another. Their previous link, articles in the Grocer, now being of limited interest to both. But first thing next morning, before all the anti-dog squad and the wowsers were out, they took Nelson down to a deserted beach. Showed him the sea. And laughed as he deliberately frightened himself with the waves. Doing a Canute, then running away and rushing back for more. Catch me if you can. Must be great being a Labrador.

When he visited Purley his aged dad was concerned for him. Once a GP, always a GP.

'You're going to have to look after yourself,' he said. 'You look like you're the one doing time.'

Willie looked at him. Was it that obvious?

'Your skin looks grey. You're putting on weight. You're flabby. Your eyes are red-rimmed. And you're drinking too much.'

'It does feel like I'm doing time,' he admitted. 'I never realized how much we are interdependent. Cut one of us and we both bleed.'

His father was staring at his chest. 'I bet you've been the same weight for about 20, 30 years haven't you?'

'Twelve stone 10,' he said automatically.

'Well, you're not that now. Look at your shirt buttons. And your gut.'

As though he were still 6 years old Willie did as his dad said and looked down. He was horrified. There were crescents of white flesh between the buttons on his denim shirt. And there was a shelf over the top of his trousers. Where had they come from?

His father looked at him sternly. 'This can't go on. Look at the shape you're in...'

His face must have dropped, he thought, because his Dad put a sinewy arm around his shoulder. 'Sorry, I didn't mean that literally. But seriously you haven't even mentioned your photography in months. It used to be your life. You've talked about nothing but Bolly. I think you may be depressed...'

'It would be hardly surprising, would it? I mean, losing your wife in these circumstances, depression would seem a reasonably sane response to me.'

'I agree. It is entirely understandable. And I'm not going to say you must pull yourself out of it, because it's not that simple. But I know someone who could treat you.'

'Happy pills?'

'If you like...'

'I think I'd prefer to pull myself out of it.' The old GP gave him a look.

'Drink is not the answer. You need to get back to work. Anyway, come and look at this,' his dad said, seizing his arm.

He took him out to the back garden and into the small Thirties asbestos garage, room for one Morris Minor. He'd rigged it for electricity and water and converted it into a darkroom cum gallery. The old mist-green Morris stood in the front drive behind the wrought iron gates.

His dad put the light on and closed the door. Then he took an old-fashioned cardboard portfolio with a maroon ribbon fastener from a plans chest.

'I've been working on a project called "Water",' he said proudly. 'Water in all its manifestations. Different types of water, different techniques.' Willie watched as his Dad took the large exhibition prints carefully out of the portfolio and passed them to him.

He shuffled through the prints slowly, giving each proper attention. All black and white. All needle sharp. All exquisitely printed on heavy matte paper. A showcase of the different techniques his dad had patiently acquired over the years.

There was a surreal multi-golfballed image that he knew was storm rain on a window shot close up with selective focus. There was a shot of a waterfall where the water looked like white treacle that he'd achieved using a tripod, tiny aperture and an overly slow shutter speed. There was another shot of spring rain falling past a gently blurring dark tulip, the rain captured as white elongated blips. Deliberate slow shutter speed, hand-held at about 1/25th of a second to allow movement of the tulip and the rain shafts. Dramatic.

There were about 20 in all. An impressive amateur assignment. Truly wonderful for a man of his father's age.

'Terrific effects, Dad,' he said. 'Still using the old Rollei?'

The old man beamed at the praise. Of course. She's got good optics that old girl. Had new springs and such put in, naturally, over the years. Must be 50 years old.'

Willie smiled back at the old man's pleasure. His Dad had always been interested in the "jewellery" aspect of new cameras. How they looked. What they could do technically. But he had never been covetous like a lot of guys. Just interested in the technical advances.

It was one of the things he loved about his old man. He was one of life's appreciaters. When he was 40 he'd finally aspired to a pro camera. A secondhand Rolleiflex. It worked well. It did him proud. He wanted nothing more. He would love it till he died. The way he had his wife.

Standing there in the old garage Willie remembered so well, a terrible truth revealed itself. He had neglected his father for months now, since Bolly had been jailed. Worse, maybe for years. He had been so wrapped up in himself and Bolly. That at least he could change.

Dealing with Bolly's parents was much worse. They were frailer in health and more easily shocked. They had been appalled at

Bolly's going to jail for "her political beliefs". Willie dared not say the actual charge was criminal damage. There was only so much he could tell them. They were too old and proud. He wondered if any of the Carberys had ever gone to jail. Probably yes. Probably back in the days when if it was serious they lopped your head off in the Tower. But Bolly was probably the first of the Carberys to be done for criminal damage. They'd fallen from aristos to the criminal classes.

He more or less counted the hours until his fortnightly prison meetings with Bolly. But they were unnaturally awkward, both of them trying to put a good face on things; both of them trying to remember things they wanted to say; both of them trying to avoid things they didn't want to say; both of them clock-watching the precious time. Probably both fretting over the changes in the other, he thought. On one of his visits he'd been getting over the fact she'd hacked down her beautiful long red hair. Then she calmly mentioned she'd kicked someone's shins in the day before.

'Why?' he asked, appalled.

'Oh, you know, things,' she said vaguely. 'It's like the schoolyard in here. If you don't fight back you get bullied. I think it was the Scouse playwright Bleasdale who said most people never get beyond the schoolyard in their perceptions and reactions to life. Well, it's like that in here. Plus most of them went to crap schools with crap schoolyards.'

She pointed at her hair. 'I've got it like this because if it comes to a scrap, long hair is too easy to grab hold of. Better like this, for now.'

Willie didn't know what to say. But he knew he could never tell her aged parents about the reason for their daughter's new hairstyle. Or why she was now kicking peoples' shins.

'Most of them in here are inadequates. They hate me on sight. Just the way I look and the way I talk turns loads of them into maenads, screaming furies. They'd kill me if they could because I seem like authority to them. The people who've been always telling them not to do stuff.' Then she smiled archly. 'But I still do a great Chinese burn if I have to. Something my convent school taught me.' She shrugged and reflected. 'I hit this fat baggage right in her flabby tits the other day. Hard. They soon get the message. Steer clear of the posh bird. She hurts you.'

Willie said nothing but was horrified. Chinese burns? Fat baggages? Where were the warders? What was happening to his wife? What worried him most of all was if she was telling him this, what wasn't she telling him?

Back in the Hamlet he told Gerry about this conversation. Gerry gave a short, hard laugh. 'Good for her. She's surviving. You should be proud of her. You don't want a twitching nervous wreck to emerge, do you?'

'But this might change her for life.'

'Probably,' Gerry said, 'but what's the alternative?'

'I'm serious. She's changing, Gerry. The experience is brutalizing her. I listen to her and I don't know her sometimes.'

'Like I said, she's surviving. Making a successful response to a challenge. Sometimes if you're going to survive bullying you have to pretend to be a better bully. It's the only thing bullies understand. The iron bar treatment. Uber-force.'

'I hope you're right. That's all it is. Pretending.'

'Anyway, we're all changing all the time. Even you. The whole wind farm nonsense and now Bolly - it's sapped your energy and the old Wille joie de vivre.'

'That's what my father says. He thinks I might be depressed.'

'Given what's happened you'd be a pretty insensitive guy if you weren't a bit depressed. And you are a sensitive guy, no matter what you say.'

One day he was checking out the wind farm situation on the Mac when he came across a newspaper interview given by a big northern landowner who also happened to be a peer of the realm.

As a man who employed many people and also had a duty of stewardship to the landscape, the patrician was saying he would never have wind farms on his vast estates because they were so divisive.

"Divisive."

That really gave Willie food for thought. This guy, probably Eton and Guards, had put his finger on one of the great wind farm truths.

They were ultimately divisive. Ironically, that was something we could all agree on.

He got himself a Pentel and a pad. Then he jotted down the divisive elements he could think of.

They divided city and country; the emotional and the rational; the philistines and the visual aesthetes; the sacrificers and the sacrificed; those who had house values to worry about and those who didn't; those who felt a religious devotion to the planet and those who were objective; those who understood the health concerns and those who were ignorant of them; those who would do anything to ameliorate climate change and those who wanted to do the most appropriate thing; those who cared about birds and bogs and nature and those who didn't; those who found the countryside boring and those who took passionate pleasure from it; those who saw wind farms as an expensive short term fix and those who believed they were a technical miracle; those who saw them as obsolescent technology and those innocents who saw them as a sort of natural magic...

Divisive was the word, alright, he thought. The problem was, because of all the squillions of quid involved and the political bias, only one side of the story was being told. The public were being given the fairy tale version of wind farms. This innocent, magical device which captured free electricity out of windy thin air with no nasty downsides. A picture book Hansel & Gretel, not a folk memory of starvation and child neglect in the German forests.

Some days later he went to the NAWAG site (The National Alliance of Wind Farm Action Groups). Someone had posted some press releases concerning Denmark, home of the wind farm. The facts surprised him.

"Denmark, the world's most wind-intensive nation, with more than 6,000 turbines generating 19% of its electricity, has yet to close a single fossil-fuel plant. It requires 50% more coal-generated electricity to cover wind power's unpredictability, and pollution and carbon dioxide emissions have risen (by 36% in 2006 alone)."

The German experience is no different. Der Spiegel reports that "Germany's CO2 emissions haven't been reduced by even a single gram," and additional coal- and gas-fired plants have been constructed to ensure reliable delivery.

Indeed, recent academic research shows that wind power may actually increase greenhouse gas emissions in some cases, depending on the carbon-intensity of back-up generation required because of its intermittent character. On the negative side of the environmental ledger are adverse impacts of industrial wind turbines on birdlife and other forms of wildlife, farm animals and wetlands. Industrial wind power is not a viable economic alternative to other energy conservation options. Again, the Danish experience is instructive. Its electricity generation costs are the highest in Europe.

He printed off a hard copy and put it in the envelope for his next letter to Bolly. That should cheer her up. Then again, being proved right was no consolation if you'd lost, was it? He'd send it anyway.

The four months from mid-July when Bolly was remanded to November passed in an alcoholic blur as he tried to wish his life away until April when she was released.

No, to be exact it was booze, wind and rain. Then more booze, wind and rain. A world of booze, wind and rain. On November 1st, purely on a whim, Willie put Nelson in the back of the Range Rover and drove over to the riding school he and Bolly had visited the previous year. They'd warned the owner about the possibility of having a wind farm as their neighbour and advised selling up. Got a flea in their ear as thanks. Wonder how he felt now?

He parked in the car park of the derelict pub and let Nelson out. Above them the massive wind turbines flailed the air. No way he was going to the summit of the Common to admire them. He took Nelson's lead off and they followed the twisty, packhorse trail over smooth, rain-hollowed black slabs downwards towards the stud. Nelson stopped from time to time 'pointing' at rabbits in the heather or kestrels hovering. The brisk wind had got up his tail and was exciting him.

Nelson bounded through the long grass, splashing and drinking in deep puddles, glorying in the wetness on his feet and the wind scouring his fur. Soon enough Willie hung a right on to another packhorse trail and started the descent that would bring him down past the stables.

From a distance the place seemed deserted. There were no horses in the fields or paddocks. And no sounds from the stables. The only movement was from the angry thrashing of the skinny trees against the buildings. At first he thought the stud was boarded up and abandoned.

But when he got closer he saw a big black Jeep 4WD up near the house. The owner came out as Willie was passing the five bar gate at the lane up to the house.

'Hey, you, mate,' he yelled, 'Hang on a minute.'

Willie hesitated, mindful of his reception last time. Then he stopped and called Nelson back. The dog sat down next to his legs and watched as the man approached.

'Morning,' Willie said.

'Morning,' the man said, touching his brown flat cap with one finger in an old-fashioned gesture. No belligerence this time. The guy looked chastened.

'Seems a bit quiet,' Willie ventured.

'Closed a few months after those buggers went up,' he jerked his thumb over Willie's shoulder in the direction of the wind farm. 'None of the mummies wanted to risk their little darlings on frightened ponies.' He sighed deeply. 'Can't say I blame them, really. Them bastards whirling and rumbling put the fear of God in all the animals, horses and ponies. They were never the same from the day the turbines started. Even when they were quiet and still, the horses were nervy, looking over their shoulders, like.'

From six feet away Willie smelled the sour smell of week-old booze and unwashed clothes. Misery made manifest as it leaked from the man's pores.

'Closed,' Willie repeated quietly. 'I'm sorry.'

'You warned me. You tried to tell me, but I wouldn't listen. I remember being rude to you. I thought they were wonderful green inventions. Pride before a fall. You just don't realize 'till you're close to them. Nobody tells you. What it's like being close to them, I mean.'

Willie smiled a tight little smile. Nobody tells you, no. UKWC don't want you to know. You have to find out the hard way.

The man shuffled forward awkwardly up to the five-bar gate and thrust a calloused red hand over the top.

'I owe you an apology,' he said. Willie leaned forward and shook his hand, so close now he could identify the actual booze. Gin. Ten-thirty in the morning. But then who was he to judge? He'd sunk a few these last few months.

'Where are the horses?'

'Oh, they're all gone. No problem selling the horses. Wife and kids gone, too. The wife loves horses. Grew up with 'em, see. Living with a bloke with a proper stud now. Might have left me anyway, of course, but this didn't help. Problems there before, but...

'Selling this place, a stables next to stuff that drives horses crackers...now there's a puzzler for you. No takers. They drive up, take one look at that lot up there whirling and banging and they're off. Don't even come in to talk. Reckon I'm hanging in for the bailiffs now. No income for the mortgage,' the man said, grinning stupidly. Alcoholic bravado.

Suddenly a stable door swung open and banged back, sharp as a pistol shot. Both men jumped.

The stud man laughed out loud. 'No point closing the stable door now the business has bolted... and the missus, too, ha,ha,ha.' Then he turned on his heel and strode back inside to his empty life and his gin bottle.

Willie thought about going after him. To do what? To say what? That other people had lost their livelihoods in similar circumstances. Caravan site owners and such. What consolation was that? It was all over. His business was just another living thing the turbines had killed. They were bad neighbours. Period.

He shook his head and exhaled slowly, trying to repel the misery. 'Come on, Nelson,' he said, pointing the way to the pub car park. Getting back up the hill was a bit of a slog. One small mercy. When the bloke had said his missus had done a runner, thank God he hadn't asked after his own wife.

On 12th November he had a phone call at three in the morning.

'Willie, it's Jenny Swinburne, Dave's wife. I haven't seen him now for 48 hours and some of his clothes are gone. I wondered if he'd told you where he's gone. Or what arrangements you'd made for the gallery.'

'I haven't spoken to him for a couple of months. We've had some problems up here with wind farms...'

Jenny didn't hold back.

'Bolly going to jail, you mean? Yes, Dave told me. I was sorry to hear that. She seems a nice lady, your wife...'

'So, no, I don't know anything about him disappearing. He hasn't told me anything. I know he hadn't been enjoying the gallery for a while.' He paused, then decided to tell her. 'It hasn't been doing very well financially for a long while, Jenny.. Just breaking even really, paying Dave's wages and the rent.'

'Yes. But what else would he do?'

Jenny's voice was sharp. What else indeed? Dave was a really nice guy. But a lousy photographer. And now a lousy salesman.

He'd only kept the gallery open as a sort of hobby and because he knew Dave needed a job. And of course he had the flat above as a bolt hole if he ever needed it.

'I don't know what to say. Have you called the police?'

'Yes. They say it's early days. People often go missing for days and turn up again. But not Dave. You know Dave. Whatever else, he loves me and the kids. He's not a drunk or a womaniser. I don't know who else to talk to. After all these years you know him better than anyone. I thought maybe if we chatted we may come up with where he's gone.'

'Would you like me to come down?'

'Oh, please, Willie. That would be great.'

'Okay if I bring the dog?'

'Of course, the kids will love that.'

He got up at six, threw a few clothes in a bag, had a tea and toast breakfast and walked Nelson.

Then he put Nelson in the boot with some food and water and his bowls and lead. He instantly went to sleep on his old plaid blanket. Him and that blanket, friends reunited.

As he turned the ignition the clock on the dash read 8 on the dot. What awaited him in London and what he could achieve the Lord alone knew. But at least it would take him out of his own misery. Why was it other peoples' problems were always easier to solve than your own?

He put the car in gear and set off for the M1. He'd fill the tank on the way through Cloughgreen.

# 28

November 13th

Wipers clunking, Willie Dee negotiated the last bend into town and night turned into nightmare. Clouds of impenetrable brown murk swirled up in front of him, masking the street lights. At gutter level the Range Rover's full beam showed torrents of whitey-foam/brown-malt-vinegary water surging towards him.

100 yards away a police officer emerged from the gritty brown clouds. The copper waved him down, indicating the side of

the road. For months and months, no, maybe getting on for two years, they had warned them and warned them about this.

But the developers and their backers hadn't listened. Willie and his friends had been brushed aside in the stampede for Big Wind. The dash for cash was on.

They had fought Big Money, Big Government, and the biggest PR campaign for decades. But the unholy trinity had steamrollered them. And the all-important hydrology survey had been overlooked.

Now what they feared had happened. And it was worse than anything he could have imagined. The powerful halogen lights above the loading bay of the Storm-n-Shine factory burned through the swirling grit like gleaming stars in a faraway galaxy. But nothing else was visible. It was like something from Dante's seventh circle of hell. Except for the noise of the sirens.

Willie drove into the side of the road and cut the engine, watching as the young policeman trudged up to him through the dense brown fog and muddy water. His face was streaked with filth and there appeared to be smudges around his eyes from tear stains. He held a grubby white handkerchief over his nose and mouth. He looked more like a stressed-out squaddie emerging from combat than a copper, Willie thought.

He lowered his window and an alien atmosphere surged in. Huge, clogging particles of grit, moisture, and a funny smell like malt whisky. Peat, that was it. The young copper leaned in close, showing the red-raw whites of his eyes. Close up, China blue eyes, pocked red acne scars, he looked about 20.

'You'll have to turn round and go back, sir. The road is closed for emergency rescue work.' The young man blinked hard, bit his lip. 'Could be days...weeks even...it's a disaster...'

'What happened?' Willie heard himself say, knowing full well.

'Hard to say yet, sir...'

'Christ, what a mess,' Willie said. He could have told the copper exactly what had happened. They'd warned of it often enough. Peatslide.

'Just get out of the way, sir, please. Quick as you can,' the police officer said, 'Let the emergency vehicles through. Ambos, fire guys...' his voice trailed off, not wanting to mention the unmarked undertakers' vans he'd also been briefed to wave in.

Willie looked at the young policeman and felt the instinctive pity of an older man for a younger one pushed way beyond his comfort zone to deal with horrors beyond his years. Struggling, but coping.

'Will do, officer,' he said and nodded. The boy copper touched two fingers to the brim of his flat cap in salute and spun on his heel.

Willie turned the key in the ignition, did a u-turn and headed the 4WD back the way he'd come towards the alternative route near Woolton. As he changed gear something rattled, it had been doing it spasmodically for about a month. Something else to sort out.

Suddenly his face was flooded with light. A fleet of chequer-banded cream coloured ambulances, sirens screaming, hammered past him heading for the old mill.

He felt stiff from his 200-mile drive. He resented being forced into this unlit, hairpin-bending, 300' climb up to the moors in the dark. Then something clicked. His tiredness was numbing his humanity he realized and suddenly felt guilty. What was he thinking about with those poor bastards down there trapped in the Storm-n-Shine factory?

What he and Verity and Carter and Phyllis had foreseen was unfolding like some apocalyptic Greek tragedy. Poor old Jumper Lonk was dead, Verity was banged up and townspeople had been left without their spring water or in respite care. Now this.

Down there in the old mill innocent people lay dead or dying. Waiting to be dug out of the hillside that had slid out of the dark and engulfed them.

As a professional photographer, visualization was a big part of his job. Only amateurs snapped what they saw. Pros imagined what could be achieved and constructed their pictures to suit.

In his mind's eye he saw thousands of tons of wet peat and rotted pit props travelling around 100 mph downhill. He saw the black mass smashing through the back wall and doors and windows of the mill, roaring through the work spaces choking men where they stood. Screams for a moment, then silence. Please God they were all killed quickly, not left to choke or suffocate.

The horror of it made him gag. He stopped the car, got out into the thin drizzle and vomited. He wiped his mouth with the back of his hand and rested his arms on the roof of the Range Rover, facing away from the mill.

He filled his lungs with the chill night air and took deep breaths. The east wind ruffled his blond hair. This is what the high Pennines is all about, he thought. Rain, wind, cold. Millstone grit and heather. Dirty sheep. Space. A beautiful wilderness place still. Except for the bloody wind farms.

On clear nights you looked up and the sky was like navy velvet with twinkling gems some drunken Greek god had spilled. Not tonight though. He felt he could almost reach up and touch the low cloud.

With an effort of will he forced himself to turn around. He didn't like looking at ugly things, but he'd been forced to do that this last 2 years. He felt a savage joy as he looked back on the crimson and yellow flames dancing around the downed turbine on the far side of the valley. It seemed as big as a bloody thumbnail in the black void. Then the vengeful feelings drained. And he felt heartsick as he thought of the men trapped inside the mill. From what you could see it looked like half the hill had slipped away. He held out little hope, except for a quick death.

Slowly he hoisted himself back behind the wheel and resumed the blacked-out upward climb. Tiredness strained his eyes, making them water.

After negotiating the 9th hairpin bend on the upward single track road he emerged on to "the tops", high above the valleys.

The road up had narrow passing places but no lighting and he blessed his luck he hadn't encountered a drunk going the other way. There was a long drop over the edge if you miscalculated.

Now he was on the tops the road widened into a long level road through small, sleeping hamlets. For hundreds of years they'd called it The Long Causeway. It was the old straight track the Bronze Age people had walked, high above the wolves, bears and bandits in the woody valleys.

Even without streetlights it was a much easier drive. But he knew he was too tired to be driving really, even without the emotional upset.

Since he'd turned the car in front of the mill he'd come around almost 270 degrees. The burning oil from the flaming turbine was clearly visible now he was up high.

After about 5 minutes he turned left onto the rough track that led to his old laithe house. There were no lights on in the neighbours' cottages or Jumper's old farmhouse as he drove down the lane. At the end Greenwood Royd lay outlined blacker than the darkness like some ancient, supine beast. It exuded the security of having outlasted many crises these past 400 years.

He eased the 4WD into the courtyard between Greenwood Royd and the outbuildings and turned off the engine. Then forced a thin smile as the stillness woke Nelson in the boot. The black lab shook himself and did his customary four-foot fandango, stamping his paws as he revolved and stretched, impatient to be out now they were home.

Willie opened the front door and the dog shot along the hall and into the kitchen. He could hear him slurping from his water bowl. Stale water or fresh seemed to make no difference.

He turned on the lights and headed for the stairs. Then the lights failed. It had happened before when there had been problems with the wind turbines. No electricity, so no 24-hour news on the radio or telly.

No matter, he'd find out soon enough the full horror story, he thought. The latest sacrifice they'd all been forced to make for Big Wind.

He went to bed but he couldn't sleep. Bolly was still in that awful gaol. Doubtless also unable to sleep listening, to the yelling and sobbing of the unhappy women around her. He found his mobile and rang Carter Briggs.

Carter picked up and sounded bleary. Well, two in the morning he was entitled to, wasn't he?

'Sorry to disturb you. Have you heard about what's happened at Storm-n-Shine?'

'No.'

Willie told him. To his amaze, there wasn't the surprise he'd expected.

'It's happened before, you know.'

'You're joking. No, sorry, of course you're not. Stupid thing to say, I'm tired.'

'I thought we'd told you. Phyllis discovered it on the Net. It happened in Ireland at a place called Derrybrien in County

Galway. There was a peatslide, just like this. They were lucky, though, there were no people around.'

'So what happened?'

'The EU said it was poor environmental impact assessment before they started construction. Anyway the landslide dislodged 450,000 cubic metres of peat and polluted a river. They got off lucky. Only 50,000 fish copped it.'

'So what happened then?'

'Well, the EU fined the Irish government...'

'But what about the site?'

'Well, they secured the site, sorted it out and quietly got it up and running again. That's what they'll probably do here.'

'This is bad, Carter. There may be 50 people dead. However many there are on the night shift, anyhow.'

Carter noisily sucked his teeth. 'Well, it's a major disaster of course. But the developers don't see things the way you and I do. They'll probably think it's regrettable that people have been killed, give them that. But they'll also think it's regrettable that the wind farm hasn't even started to clear its start-up costs yet. Neither they nor their merchant bankers are going to pull out of their investment that easy, believe me.'

'Bloody hell, Carter, you shock me.'

'I didn't say I thought like that. I'm just giving you the hard-nosed businessman's view. I mean, they'll probably send a few wreaths, but they won't admit liability or pay compensation. They haven't done for anything else, so far. Not even for the blocked and diverted springs. You mark my words.'

‘Goodnight, Carter,’ he said and put the phone down. He couldn’t take anymore for one day.

As he lay in bed his thoughts turned to Bolly. She tried not to moan but her arm was still giving her trouble. Consensus was that it had been a bad break that had never knitted well and that she would have twinges all her life. As she got older she might develop arthritis in it.

More worrying was the fact she wasn’t coping too well with prison life. He guessed a lot of ordinary people who ended up in prison for traffic offences or white collar crime didn’t. To them it was an alien environment. Whereas for some people prison was like everyday life but with free regular food, heating and amenities. They’re dealing with the same people they deal with in their pub or local shop. Tough people from tough walks of life. Bolly was tough, but not street tough. A lot of the women inside hated her perceived posh accent, her education, her attractive looks. Lady La-di-dah, the posh cunt, Authority.

Bolly hated the smells, the noise, the violence in the air. She was putting a brave face on it. She knew she only had herself to blame. But she’d once let slip that every day seemed like a week to her. Everyone in there had lost their liberty, he knew. But for some people the prison environment was a bigger punishment than for others. Why, oh, why, Bolly didn’t you tell me about killing the turbine, first? Because I’d have stopped you, that’s why.

We fought and lost, Bolly. Only you still don’t get it.

Then there was the mess with his so-called assistant, Dave Swinburne, down in Covent Garden. What with Bolly and the wind farms he'd taken his eye off the ball with his gallery.

The 3am phone call from Dave's wife saying he hadn't come home from work did he know where he was, had been a bolt from the blue. It seemed Dave had done that Reggie Perrin thing. Just seemingly walked out on his life. Done a runner. Didn't want to be found. Unless he'd fallen foul of some bad lads. But what would Dave be doing with bad lads? He was straight as a die. But then how well do you ever know anybody? Look what Bolly had gone and done.

Seeing Dave's wife had been horrendous. He liked Jenny. Knew she'd done the same job in Dave's personal life as he had done in Dave's professional life. Basically taken responsibility for him and his shortcomings. Kept him afloat. He'd had to leave her some cash for her and the kids till Dave surfaced. Or didn't. It had been awful. Her blubbering, more or less saying he should have noticed Dave was unhappy, not doing the job properly, basically cracking up. And she was right probably. Another session of feeling powerless with circumstances. He was getting used to it. And of course there were no developments with Dave. The police had no clues. As they quite reasonably said, there were nearly seventy million of us in the UK, hundreds of people did this every week.

When Nelson lined up alongside the bed at 6am he hadn't slept a wink. He patted the bed and the dog jumped up and shared his misery for a couple of hours. It still wasn't light when he fell out of bed at 8.30. But he could hear his mobile playing the ride of the Valkyries, which no longer seemed amusing. It was Humphrey Drumm in a tearing panic, speaking forty to the dozen.

Deadline was 12 noon. Tell him what he knew. Been in touch with Carter. Etc

So he told him what he knew.

Even as he spoke, Humphrey said, reporters would be hastening towards Cloughgreen by car, rail and helicopter. Such was the magnitude of the disaster, the worst since Aberfan. He would be trounced on his own territory because The Recorder was a weekly and didn't come out until 48 hours later. But he would have the inside track on a later, considered view, he promised.

When Willie turned on the TV there were already "reports coming in" of a disaster at a Cloughgreen factory involving a wind farm.

The next week became a whirl of strangers flooding the town and poking cameras and microphones in people's faces. Feelings ran high. Tempers became frayed. Insensitive media sharks ran into meaty Yorkshire fists.

Finally he saw Humphrey Drumm's first efforts. He'd only had time to change the front page. And he seemed to have drawn heavily on what Carter Briggs had told him and an interview with the MD of Storm-n-Shine.

50 DEAD, BUT URSA WAS WARNED

THIS WOULD HAPPEN

When Humphrey had written it, it seemed as though the entire night shift had been engulfed. It later transpired that the security guy had illegally popped outside on to the loading bays for a crafty smoke. So Humphrey had got the body count wrong. Only 49 dead, not 50. Only 49.

The security guy had since fallen apart with survivor's guilt. He shouldn't have been having a fag out front. He should have been out back. He should have seen the peatslide coming. He should have raised the alarm. He should have got them out. He could have saved them. He should be dead, too. All of it totally ridiculous, Willie thought. Nobody could have seen the peatslide coming out of the darkness.

By way of survivor guilt, to compensate, he'd had a heart attack. Whatever happened, it didn't seem as though he would ever work again. He was a broken man.

# 29

November 21st

The day of the Storm-n-Shine funerals arrived with a lemony yellow light. For November it was not a bad day, except for a sneaky northeaster which crept between your collar and your skin. Always the wind. Alas, always the wind. The main funeral service at St Nicholas's was broadcast live on local radio, with highlights on the national lunchtime TV news.

It was standing room only in all the churches. Willie and Gerry decided to leave the live service at St Nick's to those who had lost friends and relatives. Gerry had driven up to Greenwood Royd to watch it from there.

The whole town closed for the morning. Partly as a mark of respect and partly because the small town centre couldn't cope with the crush of traffic. Burly West Yorkshire coppers, unsmiling, strode around in their helmets and motorcycle leathers, shepherding mourners and the international media.

The two friends sat silent through the radio broadcast of the service then Willie got to his feet.

'You ready for a drink, too?'

'Too right.'

Gerry looked terrible, he thought. His chopped-off brown spade of a beard and his shoulder-length tonsure looked greasy. And his eyes were red raw from lack of sleep.

He brought back a pint bottle of beer and and a whisky chaser.

'Pie and a bit of salad be alright?'

Gerry nodded and he went back into the kitchen. He took the large pork pie he'd bought and sliced it into four portions with the breadknife. Then he put two quarters on each plate, ripped up a lettuce and tossed a couple of tomatoes on. Finally he placed condiments, English mustard and cutlery on the tray. Plus his own bottle of beer and a chaser.

Gerry, looking grim, had already finished his liquid refreshment. 'I'll get you some top-ups,' Willie said.

But Gerry motioned him down.

'I know where they are, I'll get them.'

They sat with the sound off the TV until the news item came up. Then Willie dabbed the remote to get the sound up.

They watched as the camera slowly panned down from the St George's flag at half-mast, whipping around the flagstaff, to black-clad mourners, their skirts and trousers riffling in the wind, their hands clutching hats, as they entered the church.

A large crowd of townspeople had gathered outside to hear the service relayed through speakers. A woman newscaster conveyed the usual words of respect and regret from outside the church. Then she mentioned the terrible tragedy at Aberfan decades earlier.

'You can't compare that to this,' Willie said. 'That was even more horrific if it's possible. If I remember correctly there were a lot more people  and most of them were young schoolkids.'

Gerry nodded. 'Yeah, all those innocent kids had no life at all. Some of these guys were nearing retirement.'

'Yeah, but there was an apprentice and a lot of young guys.'

'Guys of all ages,' Gerry agreed.

Two minutes later the newscaster finished her piece to camera and they cut to pictures of the land above the peatslide. You could see cleared away wreckage from the burned-out turbine and gaping black holes in the brown hillside.

'Looks just like a giant chunk of Aero,' Gerry said.

'Yeah, you can clearly see they're cross sections of old mine workings. The ones Carter and Phyllis raised concerns about in the hydrology report.'

'The whole hillside looks rotten,' Gerry added.

The broadcaster mentioned that the hill was being stabilized by civil engineers. Then it was on to the latest explosions in Afghanistan. Willie turned the TV off and frowned.

'It sounded trite. Somehow the media seem to trivialize everything.'

Gerry shook his head. 'What can you say? 49 innocent people died who should still be alive...'

'That's what should have been said.'

'...If only this whole wind farm hadn't been forced through.'

'The rape of the countryside, the intrusion on innocent peoples' lives, all for a pitifully small amount of electricity, it doesn't make any sense. It just doesn't add up.'

'Those are the things that should have been said. But nobody will. Not with Ursa Power's lawyers on stand by.'

Gerry tugged his beard thoughtfully, then continued. 'The pigheadedness won't change. What's happened here in Cloughgreen is an extreme example of what can happen. But the reality is it did happen. It happened in Derrybrien, too. And it could happen again tomorrow or next week. There is still the same bloodyminded mentality to force these things through no matter what.'

They chewed in silence for a while.

'Old Humphrey Drumm got it right,' Willie said eventually. 'Those people who died were martyrs to a false technology in land-based wind farms. And there are a lot more people whose lives have been ruined in different ways who are martyrs. Both in this town and all over the country where these bullyboy tactics have been used.'

'Well, you know how close-knit a local community this is. There's that old saying, "scratch one Cloughgreener and seven bleed". Well, there's a lot of bleeding being done in different ways right now.'

'Dead right. Storm-n-Shine was the town's biggest employer. It's not just the night shift that's been wiped out. The much bigger day shift have got no work to go to,' Willie said.

'Me neither,' said Gerry.

'How do you mean?'

'Well, it's not just Storm-n-Shine who will suffer. It's all their local suppliers, too. And I'm one of them. One of their biggest. I'm gonna go bust, Willie.'

Willie looked at his sleep-deprived features. Now it all made sense. 'Oh, Gerry...' he groaned.

Gerry leaned forward, his lips so tight they were razor thin. His normal stoic stance and merry cynicism were washed clear by the pain in his eyes.

'I'll get us some more drinks,' Willie said and returned with the scotch bottle.

He gave them both a generous measure. 'Surely you've got more clients? I've nagged you about this for ages. Not to leave yourself exposed, dependent just on them.'

'Oh yeah,' Gerry smiled sadly. 'I've got another fifty clients. No trouble there. The problem is they're all tiddlers who pay peanuts and ask the price of everything before you even turn the Mac on. There's slim pickings from them, Willie. It would be nip and tuck whether I could even eat if I depended on them.'

'You're exaggerating surely. You're upset because you knew some of the guys who died.'

Gerry raised his head and looked Willie straight in the eye.

'That's true enough. I knew a lot of the poor buggers who died. But no. I ignored your advice. And now I'm bust. It's the oldest story in the book for a small ad agency. You have one massive client. Instead of just doing the design and artwork you act as the print buyer, too, so you can make a bundle on that. Only problem is you're bearing the financial risk. If anything happens to the client you get left holding a massive print bill. It's happened since Noah was a lad.

'I'm personally finished. 80% of my business was with Storm-n-Shine. I spoke to Ronnie Green, their sales director yesterday. He's a good bloke. We're drinking pals. They've got insurance and stuff. But obviously they can't produce any goods till they get new premises. So they need sales material like a hole in the head.

'The whole company is walking wounded. Willie. An old-fashioned family firm who looked after everyone from school-leaving to retirement if they could. They don't know what's hit them. Let's face it, this isn't an everyday sort of occurrence even if you've been in business a hundred years like they have.'

'Can't they bale you out?'

'I think they would if they could. They're decent people. But I'm not staff. You know it doesn't work like that. Besides, like I say, the management is still in shock. They've now got their own cash flow problems.'

Gerry stopped talking. His eyes had a faraway look as though he were visualising the traumatised directors of Storm-n-Shine. Then he went for another swig of scotch and saw his glass was empty. Willie quickly filled it.

'The directors think the mill is probably still structurally sound. In 1860 they were built to last. The trouble is no-one is sure they want to go back to work in a slaughterhouse. With the ghosts of all their mates around them. And I can't say I blame them. So if they do re-start, it may well be elsewhere.'

'So what happens now?'

'Well, they owe me a whacking great print bill for their next Spring catalogue. If they can't pay that soon I'll go under. And so may the printer, too. Which will pain me mightily. I had to let Penny Wragg go yesterday, which was awful. She cried. But there's no work even for me at the moment, let alone her.'

Gerry looked bleakly at his friend.

'She'd seen it coming. Had even given up the pretence of going to the loo for a crafty vodka. Yanked her flask out of her bag and had a swig when she felt like, sitting at her desk. Thinking of going to stay with her big-brained, busty sister and her banker husband in Dulwich. The banker apparently compares his bonuses with the GNP of the Isle of Man to see how well he's doing. She loathes them. But it may be her last line of retreat.'

Willie sighed. 'Poor old Penny Wragg. But surely Newall will look after her, won't he?'

'Do you think so?' Gerry said. 'I'd hate to have to depend on Newall.'

Willie said nothing and Gerry resumed his tale of woe.

'It's all about Storm-n-Shine's cash flow and how long the insurers take to pay up. If they pay up that is, and don't declare it's an Act of God.'

'Surely a landslide isn't an Act of God, is it? Not if someone has recently weakened the hillside.'

'Depends on the company and the policy and the small print, I guess.'

'Even so, Ursa must surely be responsible. The hillside was sound until they put the turbines in. They could be sued surely?'

'You and I believe that. But can you see them admitting it?'

'No.'

'Too right. They've never admitted anything so far. How long do you think it would take to go to court and slug it out?'

'A lot longer than it will take for you to go bust.'

'Exactly.'

'Something will turn up,' Willie heard himself say. Idiot.

'The problem is, we've all got to be different now. You, me, Bolly, the whole town. The wind farm has changed all of us. One way or another.'

They drank their way through the afternoon, batting the problem back and forth. Venting their spleen at Ursa. Gerry needed to get drunk and Willie knew it. He throttled back on his own drinking and made sure Gerry had plenty of nibbles to go with the booze. Drinking Greek or Spanish style. Finally he made him drink a pint of Alka Seltzer. Then he helped him up to bed. He was asleep as soon as he lay down. Willie threw a duvet over him and closed the door. Oblivion wasn't the answer, but sometimes it was a relief.

He lay awake a long time. In retrospect, what Gerry had said was true. The wind farm had changed the lives of most people in the town. For most the changes had been catastrophic. Nobody had materially benefitted except the owners of Cloughgreen Common who rented the land out to Ursa Power.

That day at Leeds Crown Court when Bolly went down he had passed over a line into the shadow lands. Hitherto he had been The Golden Boy. Spring had followed winter. And summer had followed spring with a magical mystery to delight him. Only the greying of Nelson's muzzle had marked the passing of time as he basked in certainty and the love of a beautiful woman.

Now for the first time in his life he dwelt in those shadow lands, where there were no certainties. He was fearful for his wife, his marriage, his friend, his future if he was unable to sell his house, and even the economic future of the town.

Furthermore Bolly's long months in prison had brought a terrible awareness of how isolated he and Bolly had become. He could at least change that. Make a positive out of it. And he knew just how to make a start.

Next morning he let Gerry sleep in as long as he needed. Then he loaned him a pair of wellies and cover-ups and they took Nelson for a pre-breakfast walk.

Gerry seemed better to have let it all hang out. And the long sleep had made his eyes less red and puffy.

'Are things really as bad as you made out last night?'

'Willy, I'm down and out on my arse. Finished. Skint. Kaput.' Gerry made a stupid, brave grin. 'You tried to help me years ago. I didn't listen.'

'While you were asleep last night I did a lot of thinking. You need company right now. You could stay here until you sort yourself out. There's bags of room. You need to work and maybe I do, too. Maybe I've got too cosy. If this place isn't beautiful to live in anymore, it would still be a good place to work. We could maybe set up a small design group together. Specialize in brochures, pack design, stuff like that, where you just need a good designer/art director and a handy photographer, just the two of us. Low overheads. No overheads almost apart from materials if we work from here. What do you say?'

'I don't know. It's asking a lot of you. And you'd have to ask Bolly about me living here. Plus the good old two-or-three-grand-a-day-plus-expenses days of photography you knew are long gone...The business has changed mightily. Everything is wanted for tuppence these days.'

'Oh I know that. And I'm not a superstar anymore. Most of the kids would see me as an old fart. But you'd think about it?'

'Of course I would.'

'Great!' Willie jumped up and punched Gerry lightly on the shoulder.

'We could even use the bastards over there on the hill for our name. Turbo Design, what do you think?'

'I could do better. Just wait here while I get a pad and Pentel from the car.'

They went and sat in the Music Room and Willie crossed behind the white piano and put some early Stones music on the CD player. Good, clanking defiant blues. Gerry sat down with the pad and ticked in three words in a cursive script. He turned the pad to show Willie.

Willie looked at it and roared with laughter. 'Windy Beggars Design! I like it.'

Gerry took the pad back and wristed in a quick cartoon which he turned and showed to Willie. 'Here's our logo.'

The cartoon showed two figures. One a bean string with curly blonde hair, the other chunky with a tonsure and beard. They were sitting cross-legged in front of a begging bowl in the shadow of a turbine. Again, Willie hooted. Gerry grinned.

'Well, maybe it's an idea. Or maybe it's too close to home. Let me think about it.'

'Okay. Can I borrow a sheet of paper and your pentel?'

'Borrow away.' Gerry passed them over.

Willie scribbled furiously.

'Can I see?'

Gerry read "Bolly's Welcome Home party". Then 14 names.

'That's the start. I reckon there's another 186 names or thereabouts to add. I want to have everyone Bolly and I have ever liked here under one big marquee for a gi-normous party to celebrate Bolly's release. Re-forge all the old links. Get back into mainstream life.'

'Better and better. I like this new positivism.'

'Maybe even invite Newall.'

Gerry looked quizzical.

'On condition he comes as Guy Fawkes.'

'It's amazing what a good piss-up can do, isn't it?' Gerry said, laughing.

'I'm even going to consult the dread Grainne for more names for the party.'

'Who be "dread Grainne"?'

'You don't really want to know. Bolly's best mate from convent school. Sucks men in and blows them out as bubbles. Dad's an Irish brewer. Grainne can drink for Ireland, shop for Europe and fuck for the planet. Three previous husbands and just warming up. More credit cards than there are guns in Colombia.'

‘Sounds fun.’

‘At a distance.’

At the mention of Grainne, fallen angels flew over the proceedings and silence fell. Then the sun came out and the blade flicker started passing over the wall of the Music Room. Willie sighed.

‘You know the one thing I keep coming back to, the one thing I can never get my head around?’ Willie said. ‘How can people supposedly committed to the good of the planet and the environment reconcile that with ripping up precious bog and destroying all the wonderful plants and animals and insects that live there?’

Gerry made a face and raised his hand like a spoof Red Indian chief. ‘Hah! Green spirit breathe life into wind totem,’ he said in bogus Hollywood voice. ‘People look up, see wind totem on skyline. And it is good. Remind people of planet and greenness. No matter totem empty gesture. Wind totem him big medicine, big icon, must go on.’ Then he burst out laughing.

Willie made a pretend gun with his fingers and shot him over the case of Bollinger on top of the piano.

‘Pow! Chief Cynic, him speak with forked tongue.’

Gerry laughed too. ‘Well, at least we’re laughing again this morning,’ Willie said.

# 30

Ernest Maitland, chief planner for Woolton MBC, lived in a Victorian gentleman's residence called The Poplars. It was set high above the town. But safely below the tree line and the ravages of the scouring winds.

The former owner who put in the encircling poplars had named the house in their honour. 60 years later the trees were massive-trunked and ever-dappling in sunlight. They surrounded the modest detached house which sat amid lawns in the centre.

When the wind rose they sighed gently around the house like protective nymphs.

Ernest had bought The Poplars in the Seventies for the price of a secondhand 3-litre Capri. The house was a dilapidated wreck. But he had seen its inner beauty. It had been his delight to reroof it, rewire it, replumb it and restore the interior with genuine Victorian fittings. He relished DIY, was an accomplished carpenter. He found satisfaction in the fact that a precisely cut mortise and tenon joint was as dependable as a planning reg. It was people who were unreliable.

Living behind the screen of gently swaying, leaf-dancing poplars he and his elderly mother, Lilian, had felt safe as any Englishman in his castle. There were certainties to be had there. For example, at precisely 7.45 am every day he sliced a pink grapefruit and put brown sugar on hers, left his own as it came. Every day of his grown-up life this cosy ritual had been fulfilled, like some talisman. Even when they were travelling they had obtained grapefruit for breakfast. He had hoped to retire to The Poplars. It felt sad to be leaving early.

He looked fondly at his mother sitting in the front seat of his old Rover, safely ensconced amid the leather and walnut. Dark green, reliable, built like a tank, he loved that car - even if it did drink like a dipso camel. Not very Green; but never mind, there were more important things to worry about.

Now he pulled the front door towards him. He took pleasure in how the beautifully hung oak slab eased shut and turned the key in the lock. Then he took a stamped, buff envelope out of his inside pocket, addressed to his solicitor, slipped the key inside and sealed it.

'Be two minutes, Mum,' he said, after pulling her car door open to talk to her. She smiled gently. Okay. He clunked another well-made door shut. Doors closing one after another.

He took his time walking to the George VI red post box. No rush to do anything any more. He popped the letter in. Then he put his hand in and checked that it hadn't snagged on the inner mechanism, careful as ever.

He took one last look around before getting in the car. A sudden gust of wind blew the poplars over at 30 degrees he guessed, meshing and unmeshing their denuded branches with a hiss like flails beating the guilty. Not like the spring and summer dappling, but still beautiful, he thought, photographing the thrashing brown tops with his eyes. A postcard to file in the memory.

Then he turned the door handle and got in the car. He looked to check that Lilian had got her seat belt sorted properly then started the engine and moved smoothly away. He smiled to himself. Although his mother still did the shopping and light housework, it had been a good while since they had reversed roles as parent and child.

She still had her faculties, but it was a much diminished world she now inhabited. Her enthusiasm for the arts and music alone was undimmed. For the past 20 years they had taken 3 weeks in June - before it got too hot - to see the artistic things the world had to offer. One year Florence and the Amalfi coast.

Another year Paris and the Louvre. Another time the Nile and the pyramids. Petra, rose-red city, old as time. They'd seen them all, been good travelling companions.

He drove slowly, thoughtfully, the way he did most things in life, as he navigated the car out of Yorkshire towards a prettier, softer landscape in Lancashire.

Many people think of Lancashire as scruffy little mill towns with rows of redbrick Coronation Street back-to-backs and venerable football clubs. Well, there was that, he acknowledged. But there was another part of the county where the Queen still held substantial country estates in the Duchy of Lancaster. This ancient wilderness once held wild boar, deer, wolves and wildcats. Now it was a little known area of exquisite beauty with relatively few tourists. That was where he was heading. Somewhere they could be alone.

'Where are we going, dear?'

'The Trough of Bowland, Mum.'

'I like it there,' she said, eyes twinkling.

'Yes, you do, Mum,' he said, patting her hand in her lap. 'We're going to your favourite pub for lunch. Then later we'll go for a little walk in the woods.'

Weekends you got troops of bikers roaring and weaving along this winding, undulating road. Today the traffic was light. He was able to let his mind wander. His father, an accountant, had married late and died when Ernest was eight. It was funny, what he most remembered about Dad was how his eyes seemed always red-rimmed and sore. Probably from checking thousands of columns of figures. After his father died his much younger mother had been the best parent a lad could have.

He remembered her buying the jam that enabled him to have enamelled golliwog badges for his blazer lapel. And the cereal packets that held small plastic puzzles which you made into cars or ships. And mini submarines you put baking powder in to make them surface from the bottom of the bath. And his boys' newspaper that had free magnets and brown paper clappers.

Then nearly fifty years of making him a new cardigan every Christmas. He knew they sneered at his cardigans in the office. But what was that against giving pleasure to an old lady in return for a lifetime of motherly love? As he grew older he felt some younger people had no normal human feelings, only sexual ones. He knew his values were out of kilter with the times. He felt there was little honour left in life. Well, he knew what he believed.

'Do you think I will be able to have scampi, Ernest? With mayonnaise.'

'I don't see why not,' he said, patting her hand once more.

'You've been a good and loving son to me,' she said. He looked closely at her when she said that, but he detected no special significance.

'They'll probably have your favourite lemon sorbet, too,' he said. And after a couple of gin and tonics you'll probably fall blissfully asleep, he thought.

Then he went back to watching the gentle green valleys and clear, tinkling streams. The grass looked as if it came out of a Hollywood movie about Ireland - unbelievably emerald. The fat sheep looked like blow-up cartoon sheep. It was so, so different from the dirty Yorkshire sheep and scrubby Pennine grass on the moors above The Poplars. It wouldn't be a bad place to rest your head.

He was still baffled. He had no idea how this situation had come about. Just one mistake. If it was his mistake. He wasn't sure how it could have been, but it must have been. One giant black mark against what he felt was a lifetime of public service.

He was proud to have been the sort of planner who used all his expertise to facilitate change for the public good. He had very much wanted to be a facilitater. He saw it as his job to exercise his skills as part of a team to enable better places for people to enjoy better lives. Unlike that egomaniac Newall who wanted to impose his lunatic political views on the public.

Newall was a throwback to the Fifties and Sixties and the arrogant planner advocates who believed they knew best and must impose their views on an ignorant public. Planner as Hero, they called it. It was they who had enabled tower block battery farms of people and dark mugger-friendly underpasses. It was they who had razed to the ground historic buildings, turning ancient city centres into motorway race tracks.

Now Newall's crowd wanted to do the opposite. They wanted to drive cars out altogether, failing to understand they'd drive the trade out, too, and kill the very town centres they sought to revive. Under the guise of urban renewal and the patronage of secretive, unaccountable quangos the know-it-all planners were coming back. He sighed at the fashionable lunacy of it all, exasperated.

At least he understood where Dr know-it-all Newall was coming from. But he had been shocked by Dave Summit's views. And the implicit suggestion he should take full responsibility for the faulty hydrology report and fall on his sword. He sighed again. What could you do? He had never understood people.

But if the MD of Woolton MBC had pointed the finger at him then it must be his responsibility, surely? Unknowingly somehow he'd failed in his duties and brought about this terrible catastrophe. By neglect, maybe, he'd unconsciously killed the town, while Newall would have killed it by determined, ignorant dogma. Such were the ironies of life.

'Are we nearly there, Ernest?'

'Yes, mother,' he said. 'Our journey's almost over.'

# 31

November 28th

Humphrey Drumm, urbane editor of the Cloughgreen Recorder, felt downright agitated. He hadn't slept well. He kept turning over the enormity of what had happened in his small town. For some time he had thought of of it as "his" small town.

Now he looked hard in his shaving mirror. He saw a 5'8" guy in his late fifties with bleary eyes, wings of silvery hair, rimless specs, pink cheeks and extrovert mutton chop whiskers. With his ample paunch he looked not unlike John Bull or Mr Pickwick, he thought.

But appearances can be deceptive and he knew that deep inside he wasn't a genial figure of fun. He had steel in him. And one of the things he liked about himself was he was one of life's white knights. They must surely come in all shapes and sizes, he chuckled to himself.

Then he frowned and became serious. Fuck you, Newall, you arrogant little green fascist. I may have had to publish your letters, but I've never had to like you. You and your sort have a lot to answer for. It may be that I am going to write the longest suicide note in history, but I'm still going to do it. I'll put a stop to you and your greedy pals if I can.

In truth after the tragic events were confirmed it hadn't taken him long to realize he must rush out a memorial edition.

What had taken him longer was to wrestle with whether he could maintain any semblance of impartiality on wind farms. Whether he could come right out and say what he was in a unique position to say - even if it meant losing his job.

He had come to very much like his job and living in Cloughgreen. And to understand how a small town newspaper acted as the heart of a whole community. Although it was easy to scoff from metropolitan heights, he now realized you had a far greater chance of making a difference to a community than any national journo could.

But now a national issue had visited his small town. And he had a real opportunity to serve both his town and the nation. The real clincher, because he was a white knight, had been this realization that he was in a unique position. He was johnny-on-the-spot with in-depth local knowledge. But he also had the major league experience to tell it the way it was and to make it count. He had a strange feeling of destiny as though all his time acquiring journalistic skills had been in preparation for this moment. The adrenaline zinged through his blood.

As he left the bathroom, mere physical entities like stairs and doors were negotiated on auto. He was deep in his head, drafting the special memorial issue he hoped would expose this wind farm business for the dangerous nonsense he now knew it to be.

The Cloughgreen Recorder was still old-fashioned broadsheet size, so a 4-page special gave him plenty of space to tell his story and to use emotive pictures.

The tradition with such editions was to have all the pages black-edged and he would definitely want that.

On page 1 the header read "Clough' in Mourning" and showed pictures of the long funeral cortege winding its way up to the parish church in the town centre. The copy was both descriptive of the day and factual in times and numbers. It also told when different faith ceremonies had been held.

On pages 2 and 3 Humphrey ran a giant headline across the gutter which read simply "THE WIND FARM MARTYRS". Below that he ran the pictures of the 49 dead with their names and age and marital status.

Below that was a subhead above the editorial copy which read "A FAILURE OF TECHNOLOGY, PLANNING & DEMOCRACY".

There was another panel let into the bottom right hand corner. The headline ran "THEY TOO ARE MARTYRS". Underneath were pictures of Frank Bottomley, the traumatized security guy from the mill; Sam "Jumper" Lonk; Verity Dee; Joe Stansfield, the farmer whose water had dried up; 10 more people whose spring water had vanished; plus pics of two families who had had to move out of their homes because of noise and/or blade flicker.

Humphrey scratched this outline on his pad and alerted the printers and his support staff. Then he picked up his mobile and rang Willie Dee.

'Willie, has Verity got any material I could run on the back page of a memorial edition of the paper spelling out the pros and cons of wind farms?'

'I don't think so, Humphrey. You know she's still banged up? It's tricky sorting things like this out quickly. And you've obviously got a deadline, right?'

'Too right. Not to worry. I'll work something up.' He put the phone down and then picked it up again when it suddenly rang. It was Willie again.

'I just had a thought. We know this guy called Charley Fort who's a journo. He helped us discover things a couple of years ago. He's been trying to flog anti-wind farm pieces without success ever since. He's probably your man. He's got a stack of stuff already written.'

'Good thinking. Give me his number.'

Humphrey Drumm rang Charley Fort immediately. Charley had a piece entitled "What wind farms do and can't do" emailed to him within an hour. He re-titled it "A TRAGEDY WAITING TO HAPPEN" and subbed in an intro about a previous peatslide at Derrybrien in Ireland. Then he just slanted Charley Fort's piece around the rush to get these things in and how health and safety were being overlooked for the sake of very little electricity.

Then, with everybody else rushing around getting photographs of the victims, producing layouts etc, he sat down and wrote his editorial piece.

THE WIND FARM MARTYRS

A FAILURE OF TECHNOLOGY, PLANNING & DEMOCRACY

Our town lies in mourning with 49 people dead and one man terribly traumatized. The town's largest employer, Storm-n-Shine has effectively been put out of business. Its return is currently in doubt.

This is a disaster that should never have happened. That it did so is down to an unholy combination of big business in a dash for mega cash over the next 25 years, irresponsible Green zealots who want their own ideology at any cost and an over-mighty government.

For a long time now we have had a debate within the pages of the Cloughgreen Recorder about wind farms and their suitability. It seems to me the cost of saving the planet is too great if it means sacrificing our own people.

In the early days when the wind farm on Cloughgreen Common was first mooted, Dr Newall and his supporters called for us to make sacrifices. Now nearly 50 of Cloughgreen's citizens have made the ultimate sacrifice. I hope he and his friends take note of this. Without the wind farm, they would all still be alive today.

This town never wanted the wind farm. The Friends of The Living Moorland raised serious hydrology issues. Our Town Council listened to the people and weighed the arguments and voted against the application of Ursa Power to have this wind farm.

This government knows very well how many people disagree with wind farms and the despoliation of the environment. It is why they have used their powers to constantly amend the planning processes and make it easier to get applications pushed through. To further ensure this they have employed a combination of draconian powers and penalties to influence metropolitan councils to grant planning applications.

The perception is that where there are borderline decisions or grey areas then government inclination is to push on regardless.

The Friends of the Living Moorland have long questioned the hydrology issue in this case. It is notoriously difficult to stop wind farms on the grounds of impaired scenic appeal, as it is pointed out that it is all a matter of personal taste. But the Friends of the Living Moorland also pointed out that health issues involving sound emissions and blade flicker are also often over-ruled for lack of measurable scientific proof until it is obvious and too late. When it is then ignored by the developers, who wring their hands, cry crocodile tears and do nothing.

This digging in of feet and refusal to accept objections when commonsense dictates their may be real problems must be reversed. So that we may have a situation where if there are potential problems wind farms are not allowed to proceed. In reality, given that the technology is inherently flawed by both the inefficiency of the turbines and the intermittent and unpredictable nature of wind perhaps it would be better to cease pushing for wind farms at all. Producing even small amounts of electricity requires we sacrifice huge tracts of our beautiful wild places which are non-renewable. God has ceased to create them.

With their small footprint, micro turbines work well to make individuals self sufficient in energy and offshore wind farms can be sited well away from people and wild life.

But onshore wind farms are bad neighbours to all living things and therefore impractical on a small, overpopulated island like Britain. People and industrial wind turbines are simply incompatible.

Nobody wants to live near them. For very good reason.

Everywhere a planning application goes in, a resistance group is formed. The government knows this full well. It is high time they abandoned gesture politics for the Green faction and started listening to the real people of this country. Nobody wants to live near these things. And if you won't live near them yourself you should not require other people to, either. The sacrifice must be made by all or none.

In particular, the especial lessons of Cloughgreen Common must be learned so that it cannot happen again. Heads must roll. And an inquiry into the all-important hydrology issue conducted.

At least 49 innocent people have died. Others have been either traumatised or criminalised by this wind farm. Somebody must be held accountable for this terrible tragedy. The whole nation awaits.

But above all, could we please stop the wind farm propaganda and start implementing the better solutions that are out there? At least then some good may have come from this tragedy."

The magnitude of the tragedy initiated a sea change in the national press's attitude to wind farms and turbines. It was big news all over the world. So it skipped over the obstacles UKWC had put in place. But a lot of people had to die, to get the other side of the wind farm argument heard, Humphrey thought.

He syndicated his memorial edition and made a substantial amount of cash for the Cloughgreen Emergency Fund.

Willie and Gerry were sitting in their usual places in the Hamlet. Both Wes and Hilda had been a bit odd since Bolly had been jailed. Wes had cut down the banter in place of a sympathetic smile and Hilda acted as though Bolly had actually died.

Willie had brought Humphrey Drumm's memorial edition in for Gerry to read.

'Good for Humphrey. Good strong stuff,' he declared, after casting his eyes over it. 'Tell you one thing, though, the chickens will be coming home to roost all over Woolton. Protect the guilty, search out the innocent and make them pay...'

'Good to hear you're back to your cynical old self.'

'Not that old. But seriously someone is going to be made to pay. It won't be Ursa Power. And I bet it won't be Dave Summit, the CEO of Woolton MBC.' He took a pull of his pint and wiped the foam off his lips. 'You mark my words, it won't be anyone like Newall who ends up being the fall guy.'

Dr Newall was startled by his mobile at the ungodly hour of 6.45 am. He was already awake, having been woken up by Penny Wragg laying on her back with her mouth open, mascara run and snoring.

He had been furious. He'd been on about her snoring for months now. It was so unladylike. Had she any idea what she looked like, he'd said. She'd made some sort of non-commital answer and gone on snoring.

This morning had been the last straw. Her snoring had woken him out of a deep sleep. Incandescent, he'd walked quietly into his office and taken out the old Polaroid Land Camera he'd used for site inspections pre-digital. Then he'd taken a close up of her with her mouth wide open, wrecked makeup and all and left the print on the pillow beside her. See how she liked looking at that first thing in the morning.

Angie Snow sounded faint down the phone as though she were whispering. 'I thought I'd better warn you,' she was saying. 'There's a witch hunt going on over here at Woolton MBC. Dave Summit had old Maitland in for a meeting late Thursday afternoon and he resigned yesterday.'

'Why, Angie? The old fool only had a few years to pension time, didn't he?'

'A year actually.'

'Admit nothing, apologize for nothing. The old fool.'

'Anyway, the ripples are spreading wider. Our favourite hydrologist, Paul Vennis, has been summoned for Monday. If I were you I'd make myself scarce and unobtainable pronto. You're not linked in any way. But just to be on the safe side.'

'Thanks for the tip off, Angie. I think I'll leave the country for a week or so.'

'Republic of Chad or Van Diemen's Land sound good to me.'

There was a pause then Angie Snow started speaking again. 'It was a terrible tragedy, the peatslide. But no-one could have known. There were simply no records of the mining. The galleries could have been anywhere. It was just rotten luck.'

'No,' Newall agreed. 'There was no evidence of where the galleries were.'

'Not even Vennis could have known.'

'No. There were just no written records. Anyway, how are you?'

‘Oh, I’m okay. I’m acting Chief Planner. Summit muttered something about needing younger blood around and appointed me acting Chief. The subtext is he’s such an mcp he thinks that as a girlie I’ll be no threat.’

‘Don’t disillusion him.’

‘I won’t. Anyway just go. Speak to you when you get back. Maybe I’ll be getting you a few more jobs out of Woolton in the future.’

‘Cheers, Angie,’ he said. Then he packed a bag, grabbed his passport and fled, leaving Penny to her portrait on the pillow.

Before he got to the airport he phoned Ursa to tell them of developments at Woolton MBC and the possible problems with the hydrologist, Paul Vennis.

‘Thank you for telling us. We’ll deal with it,’ Arkadiy Kovalenko said.

Dr Newall took the first available flight out of Manchester to the Canaries. Sunshine and sangria and fresh bananas and warm water to swim in. The perfect antidote to a political stink and never-ending rain.

The Monday morning papers were full of stories about the death of Ernest Maitland, the former Chief Planning Officer for Woolton MBC who had been found dead at a beauty spot in the Trough of Bowland. Foul play was not suspected. But the first indications were that he may have taken an overdose of prescription drugs he had been taking for a stress-related heart condition. His mother had also died in the car.

The winter wind and rain howled around the corners of the glass and concrete tower that housed Woolton MBC. It was a disconcerting acoustic that served to emphasize the grim weather and inadequate heating in this executive corner office.

Dave Summit, CEO of Woolton MBC, was not a happy bunny. He clutched a large mug of sweet black coffee for warmth. He was wearing a thick white cricket sweater he had been forced to wear for warmth. He thought he looked cool. No tie.

He was having a particularly stressful Monday morning. First, Paul Vennis, the hydrologist hadn't turned up for his 9am meeting. Then he hadn't returned any of his calls.

At 10am he'd fielded a phone call from someone high up in the Planning Commission claiming to speak on behalf of the government and telling him in no uncertain terms not to tell the press anything.

The press were besieging him about Ernest Maitland, the old fool. And doubtless they would be querying Paul Vennis's report once they'd got their act together. He had been hoping to tell Vennis to be tight-lipped. But the fallback position was that if other heads had to roll then Vennis was expendable. Maitland had already made himself the Council sacrifice. That ought to be quite enough blood-letting. Still, he couldn't understand why Vennis wasn't answering his calls. Surely he realized he needed powerful friends at a time like this.

While Dave Summit was freezing in his office Paul Vennis was cosy in furs and marvelling at the frosty beauty of the old Winter Palace in St Petersburg, now the Hermitage art gallery. Since Arkadiy Kovalenko had sent a limo to fetch him last Friday night his world had improved immeasurably.

To his surprise, Kovalenko spoke perfect English and had proved to be a very impressive friend. Although Ursa had supplied the wonderful Jag he'd been forced to leave behind he had never met Ursa's FD before.

The man exuded the warm charisma that comes from physical fitness and the confidence that comes from power and wealth. They had flown by private jet early on Saturday morning. Private jet! His humdrum life had become exotic and luxurious.

Kovalenko had explained the political ramifications of the witch-hunt going on after the Woolton peatslide. And the fact that he would be a likely scapegoat with no possible future. Beyond maybe prison.

That sort of outcome would suit neither him nor Ursa Power. Better, he said, to come to the burgeoning new Russia and disappear. We know many people who can make you disappear, he said. We have people who can discreetly sort out all your affairs in Britain for you. It was sad about the beautiful Jag, but there would be other fast cars. And wine, women and song within the Russian end of the Ursa organisation. They would be very grateful. No-one would spill the beans. He would have a new life and a new career. Everyone would live happily ever after.

Paul Vennis was a single man in his early forties. Russian wine, women and song and a new career sounded fine by him. Particularly when compared with the alternative. He gladly volunteered to be “disappeared”. And was never seen in England again.

Back in London Ilya Bakunin had received discreet communications from the government that the Cloughgreen Common wind farm should be expeditiously repaired and brought back into production. He assured them this would be the case. Move on.

## 32

Dr Newall was not amused. 'Have you seen this latest copy of the Recorder?' he yelled at Penny. 'That has-been Drumm has taken leave of what few wits he had. He must be senile. I'm going to have words with the powers that be on the Recorder's editorial board in Woolton.'

'What's he done now?' Penny asked. She had been very hurt by Edwin's Polaroid snap and had thought seriously about their future. And then he'd run off to Spain without telling her. But then that was just him, wasn't it? He didn't really mean it. He just didn't realise how hurtful some things could be. Being a genius, he was just on a different plane sometimes from everyone else. You had to make allowances.

After ten days apart, here they were back together as though nothing had happened. Whatever other people may think, Edwin had needs. And so did she. She wouldn't be able to keep her flat on much longer. And she was quite keen to move in with Edwin.

She had been terribly upset by the peatslide and had cried herself to sleep. She knew Edwin saw it as "an unfortunate accident", so she didn't talk to him about it. But she still felt raw about it.

They were supposed to be having an Indian takeaway and an evening of booze and bliss. She certainly didn't want to listen to Ed rant on about damned wind farms all night.

Quite apart from anything else, although she couldn't say too much, obviously, she had come to have her own reservations about wind farms since the Storm-n-Shine tragedy. How could you not? The picture of the wind turbine blazing into the night like a distress beacon and illuminating the inundated mill would live with her all her life.

'That old fool Drumm's written this so-called editorial blaming wind farms for just about everything other than original sin. Lies, all damned lies.'

'Not myths, don't you mean?' Penny asked mischievously. She'd only had one glass (apart from a few from her handbag of course). She didn't know what came over her.

'Don't get funny with me, my girl. Gaia, what have we lost?' Dr Newall held his hands to heaven. 'A few birds, a few bats, a bit of clapped-out bog - an old lech on an old horse - if you believe it. And now a few lower grade routine functionaries, mere manufacturing peasants really. 49 peasants. What's that against saving the planet? Against the reputation of wind farms? Collateral damage, as the Americans would say. Get over it. The Planning Regs are too soft here. We should be more like China or Russia. Once you know what's right you just get on with it, do what's right. Really, in the big equation, the peasants don't matter. They're breeding all the time. Plenty more where they came from.'

As Dr Newall paused for breath, Penny noticed he was going purple in the face. It crossed her mind to ask who decided who the peasants were. Was she a peasant, for example? But she knew she daren't risk it. Christ, she hoped he wasn't working himself up into some sort of seizure or heart attack. She wasn't married or even on the deeds of this beautiful house yet.

'Have another drink,' she said, helpfully pouring from the bottle of Aussie Cab Sauv and passing a glass to him.

He took it without thanking her, she noted, and swigged deeply.

'I have had a dream,' he announced portentously and paused looking at her for effect. Why was he looking at her like that?

'I have had a dream,' he repeated.

Christ, what did he want her to say, why all this pause for effect? 'What was it?' she eventually asked.

'That we have green, self-sustaining communities. The prototype will be known as Purity Valley and will be manned by purists, volunteers under strict covenant. No smoking, no drinking, no casual or illicit use of energy for recreation or personal indulgence, no personal radios or TVs or stereos or computers or washing machines, vacuum cleaners, garden appliances etc, no cars; the community entirely self sustaining through rotas and our own communal electrical devices and utilities, communal trades and tools, transport, flocks and herds and crafts...it will have sensible communal buying, wind farms, solar heating, water turbines, underground heating, strict supervision...'

Penny tuned out, considering whether it was time to have a change from Tandoori Chicken Masala which she absolutely loved, or whether she should indulge in a Madras which she hadn't had for ages.

'As a radical planner, I must constantly be reviewing land use. Take the Storm-n-Shine Mill. Despite the loss of life, that's not really a tragedy. Well, it is of course in a way, but it's also a heaven-sent opportunity to use that site in a more beneficial way...'

On the other hand, Penny thought, Gerry Stansfield had mentioned a new place that had just opened near Reddingley that did South Indian cuisine. Quite hot and coconutty, with distinctive light, lacy pancakes with spicy mashed potato filling. You ate them with raw green chillies which was a bit daring. And wet, spicy vegetables.

'It's important they get those turbines on Cloughgreen Moor up and running again, if possible. Their prominence over Cloughgreen is symbolic. It's not just the energy they produce. It's the totemic effect, singing out over the whole region our green credentials and future. The fact that the windfarm is in their faces is actually really important. They're little people, who only care about themselves, their property, the view from their bedroom window, their house prices, the fact they want to ride bikes or horses and walk dogs, they need to be constantly reminded...'

'What do you think about hot potatoes?

Dr Newall didn't miss a beat. 'If Ursa can just ride out the storm we can have smaller wind farms in the spaces between the large wind farms, fill in the gaps, designate the whole Ted Hughes landscape a National Wind Farm Area.

'Then we can get the whole area re-zoned for light industrial use the way it used to be. Get some production units on the tops, clear off the mangy sheep and whingeing farmers...become a green beacon for the nation...for the world even...' Doctor Newall smiled fondly. 'It's a brave new sustainable world, we're entering into, Penny.'

'I expect you're right,' Penny said, dribbling a little. South Indian, it was.

December 10th

Dr Newall let the Storm-n-Shine saga work itself out. A fortnight after the funerals he rang the Ursa guys to set up an urgent meeting. It was time to move the whole Purity Valley agenda to the next stage, to lay in planning apps for the final smaller wind farms which would make planning re-zoning possible.

He broke the habits of a lifetime by inviting Bakunin and Kovalenko round to his office on the third floor of his house in Radical Road. He regarded his office as his holy of holies.

After the pleasantries he sat them down with coffee.

'I think, he said the time is now right to put in apps for the smaller, fill-in wind farm sites we discussed. Utilizing the gaps between the so-called "pretty moors" at Thor Fell etc.'

'Are you mad?' Bakunin said. 'They've hardly buried their dead.'

'So what? Life goes on.'

The colour rose in Bakunin's cheeks and he clenched his fists by his side.

'I really do not understand you, Dr Newall. Are you not human? What have the people in this town done to you? We find the timing of these suggestions offensive. Perhaps it might be better if another company developed these smaller moors you talk of. We will pay you any monies outstanding. Then we are finished.'

From where he was sitting Dr Newall could see the Russian's hands were shaking and his face had gone white with anger.

'But why? I don't understand.'

'No, clearly, you don't,' Ilya Bakunin, said, rising from the settee and heading off towards the stairs. 'Goodbye, Dr Newall.'

Newall sat looking at Arkadiy Kovalenko. They sat in silece until the sound of Bakunin's footsteps ceased.

Then Kovalenko, the ex-special forces man, rose, too. He walked over to Dr Newall, who felt a frisson of fear. Kovalenko's hand moved so swiftly he had Newall's cheek between thumb and forefinger before he saw it coming.

Before he could protest, Kovalenko released it and dealt it a good, hard slap. Not enough to knock him over. Just hard enough to leave four red finger marks on his cheek.

But it was a slap. Not a punch. A girlie hit. The way men used to deliberately incite enemies to a duel. Dr Newall knew all this well enough from being Colonel "Nasty" Newall's son. No way was he stepping up to the challenge. He felt very small and looked at his feet. Took it.

Kovalenko smiled and shook his head. 'Goodbye, little Eddie,' he said. 'I have known some bad people in my life. But at least they had guts. You are one little piece of shit.' Then he followed his boss down the stairs and out of the house.

Dr Newall rubbed his cheek and swore under his breath. Little fucking Eddie, indeed. He opened the top drawer of his desk and took out his address book, ripping it open. How could you work with bastards like that? There were plenty of other wind farm developers out there. People who appreciated planning expertise and understood commitment when they saw it.

One accident didn't mean a thing. Accidents happened when you were pushing the frontiers. Like the American generals said, it was just "Collateral damage". Regrettable. You had to push on.

# 33

December 15th

The fifteenth day of December had started with storm rain and Willie had dug out his knee-length 'Hoggs of Fife' pro ghillie's waterproof jacket. It was knee-length with copious pockets, zips and studs and a hood with tie-through toggles to keep it on through gales. He teamed this with waterproof lightweight plastic trousers. But the weather was still vile. The Hoggs of Fife gear was wonderful rainwear. Their catalogue cover boasted "HIGH PERFORMANCE CLOTHING AND FOOTWEAR". But nothing would have kept him dry today. The gale drove rain under the hood and tried to force itself up the elasticated sleeves. Turbo-driven, the rain felt cold as a whetted knife along his cheekbones.

After half an hour he decided it was pure masochism to continue. He turned around and Nelson looked up at him questioningly. Surely not turning around so soon? He immediately felt guilty, but what the hell? This morning Churchill's mythical Black Dog was sat firmly on his back. He justified himself by observing Nelson was soaked and bedraggled already.

On the way back he passed Joe Stansfield standing out in Jumper's fields in the purple overalls and grey flat cap he seemed to live in. Because of the depressed economy it was taking a while to sell Jumper's farm. And nobody wanted to buy the sheep.

Joe was still looking after Jumper's sheep in exchange for daily water for his herd and a small fee from Colin Combe, the solicitor. The "small fee" might just about cover his diesel money driving over here, Willie thought. He waved to him and Joe waved back.

'Alright, Willie,' he yelled over the roar of the wind. Willie nodded, taking in Joe's battered ex-Army Defender with its bald tyres and the dented, rusty grey bowser by the farmhouse. He guessed the bowser leaked not much less than it carried. Rural poverty, but make do and mend, carry on. Hope something will turn up. In the meantime, there's always orange baler twine to hold everything together. Whole lives, maybe.

'Any progress with your borehole?' he bellowed above the wind.

Joe walked about 20 yards closer and cupped his hands to shout back, rain running down his face. Close enough for Willie to see the big grey bags under his eyes.

'Got a co-operative up. Twenty of us in the same boat hoping to do a bulk deal with this guy who has a big ex-US Army driller. Money up front is the problem. Tryin' to get some sort of grant to help fund it.'

'Great,' Willie said, feeling stupid. 'When will it all be sorted out then?'

Ted shrugged. Waved his arms hopelessly. 'Next Preston Guild, mebbe.' Then he smiled a thin smile. 'Gotta stay positive, ain't you?'

Willie waved and moved on. 'Next Preston Guild'. Once every twenty years in other words. Some time. Maybe. Never. Yeah, stay positive, Joe.

He wandered through the back door into Greenwood Royd and Nelson followed him. He took off his soaking waterproofs and boots and put his loafers on. The dog stood patiently watching him, small pools forming around his paws on the stone slabs. He took the dog's towel from the back of the kitchen door where it hung with spare leads and collars. Then he carefully towelled the dog down paying close attention to his paws and back legs. Didn't want him getting arthritis there if he could help it. Curse of the Labrador, arthritis.

When he'd finished, he left the kitchen and walked into the lounge, collecting yesterday's Sunday Telegraph. Then he went through to the Music Room and looked idly at the white grand piano. Another failure. Like the last two years had been. Better to have fought and lost than never have fought at all? No, it didn't feel like that. If they hadn't fought the wind farm then Bolly would still be here, thinking of silly Christmas presents and suprises and whether it would be turkey or goose.

His eyes rested on the case of Bollinger on top. Christmas in prison for Bolly. No Bolly here to appreciate the Bollinger. God, what will that be like for her? Stuck in there. With all the wailing and human misery. Women away from their men and their children and thinking of paper hats and turkey and toys and booze. And all the rest of it they'd be missing. Probably better in memory than the reality had ever been for loads of them. But no weaker for that. God help you, Bolly. He went to the disguised drinks cabinet and took out a bottle of Bells and some ice cubes.

He slouched down into a leather armchair and sipped his scotch. Then he picked up the Sunday Telegraph. The front page talked about email smears and Gordon Brown paying the price. He flicked through to Christopher Booker's column, the one journo who had steadfastly told the whole truth about wind farms from the start.

This week his column reported an outrageous comment from Ed Miliband, the Energy & Climate Change Secretary, he'd already heard on the radio. Ed Miliband had said that "opposing wind farms should be as socially unacceptable as not wearing a seatbelt."

At first Willie was so incensed he thought he must have misheard the quote. And he'd ended up rooting out an old packet of mint tea to try and calm down.

Now here it was in black and white. It had become a matter of public record. And Willie was incensed all over again. He paced the floor. How dare he say that? It was inflammatory and it was blatantly wrong. Mr Miliband was a young man, passionate and sincere, no doubt. But he was also a Cabinet minister. He really ought to know better.

What happened to Voltaire? "I disapprove of what you say, but I will defend to the death your right to say it..." If nothing else that was what democracy should be about.

In any case, you may as well say that recklessly destroying the remaining high wilderness places with their rare bogs, birds and mammals was "as socially unacceptable as not wearing a seatbelt". Or that future Britons may well view the government minister responsible as an eco-criminal for his part in the once and for all despoliation of wilderness countryside. What made his opinion gospel truth?

If you weren't allowed to peacefully protest any more, where did it all end? Book burning next? Then burning people?

He picked the paper up and read on. It seemed that some lesser lights in leftwing politics had picked up on Ed Miliband's statement and decided it was the way to go. Naturally, if this was how the guys at the top behaved...

A woman politician was stating that flying to Spain on holiday was "morally comparable to knifing someone in the street". Eh? Sounded like she needed a knife in the hyperbole.

Another politician was saying that failing to ensure one's home was "energy efficient" was a "a moral crime" as "anti-social as drink driving".

Ye gods and small fishes, what planet do these people inhabit, he wondered. How have we come to this stage when name calling and completely disproportionate statements like this constituted mainline politics? It reeked of ugly fanaticism. We don't like your point of view, particularly as it may cost us votes, so we vilify you. Tell the unpleasant truth about wind farms and they say things which impeach your personal honour and attempt to criminalize you. And these are senior political figures, supposedly attempting to influence us. What hope for the yobs on the sink estates? He felt heartsick at the whole issue of the bully boy politics Britain now seemed to have.

You saw the creeping industrialization of rural Britain by stealth and you were supposed to shut up, play nice and let them get on with it. Otherwise you were a social deviant, a person who consumed alcohol before getting into your car and driving off without wearing a seatbelt, having previously knifed someone in the street. Where have these people come from? he wondered. Who educated them? Even worse, why do they think saying these appalling things is the way to win people over? Was it gutter politics, as Gerry would say?

The only good thing about it was Bolly hadn't been here to read this inflammatory rubbish. But having her incarcerated at Her Majesty's pleasure was cold comfort. And he worried that her arm still wasn't right, would never be right.

'What are we going to do, Nelson?' he said. 'We're buggered, old mate. Bolly and I have thrown our hearts behind this, been conscientious in finding out all the facts about it, we've been energetic, spent our own money funding the fight, risked being pariahs with the PC wankers and still we're stuffed. I may as well have been Don Quixote and you Rocinante for all the good we've achieved.' The dog looked at him, head switching from side to side, his one eye wide, trying hard to understand.

'Worst of all, the wind farm bastards and the politicians we've now got have managed to criminalize Verity, a person with a previous unblemished record, for basically not wanting to be lied to and fighting for what she believed in.'

But sooner or later she will be out. Maybe in only three months now. And then he would have to confront her with the news that they really and truly may not be able to sell up and move away. That they hadn't had a single enquiry for Greenwood Royd. It was a very large house with outbuildings and acreage. A great deal of his capital was tied up in it. Having to carry on living the rest of his life with these things defacing the landscape, a man who loved beauty, would break his heart. But the ugliness and the inability to change things would break Bolly's spirit.

He'd spoken on his mobile to Davie McPhee his accountant about what to do with the gallery business in Covent Garden. Sell up and have an email gallery was the answer. Davie knew someone who could organize it. Later Davie had asked about the wind farm. So he told him the full horror of them whirling in their faces, looking down at them. Rumbling whenever the atmospheric pressure was right, flickering whenever there was sunlight.

'Never mind,' Davie'd said. 'In six months you'll not even notice they're there.' But Davie was the sort of guy who strained his eyes finding a matching pair in his sock drawer. On the other hand he, Willie, could go into his butchers, buy a pound of cubed stewing steak and tell you which of the three butchers had prepared it. One cut large cubes, one cut minuscule cubes and one cut cubes which hung together with threads because he never sharpened his knives properly. His eyes were the tools of his trade; he had enhanced visual sensitivity. The turbines were like a thumb in his eye.

You can only despair, he thought. Are we the last generation who see beauty in the countryside and take joy in the flora and fauna? Have we now got a population that is so urbanized they are only interested in technology and living their lives through electronic sights and sounds? Who find the countryside boring and don't care if you turn it all into a junkyard. Maybe Joni Mitchell was right all those years ago. And soon we'll be taking kids to see a tree in a tree museum.

When did the Nature table disappear from the corner of the classroom in primary school, he wondered. Remembering his own childhood with kids bringing in "special" leaves of different colours and shapes. And stray feathers and cracked birds eggs. Dead hedgehogs in shoeboxes. Acorns and conkers from Boxhill. Seaweed and shells from Brighton. Even sticklebacks, "taddies" and newts from ponds in jam jars and little tanks for the day. Teacher drawing robins and lapwings on the blackboard. Maybe when the Nature table went, the natural wonder went. Now the little buggers would want everything with an AA battery rammed up its arse so they could make it work. He sighed. Getting old, Willie.

The Scotch had gone down appreciably, but he had the feeling that today he could drink the bottle dry and see no light at the end of the tunnel. His glass was empty, but he left the bottle of Bells where it was. Enough.

He looked at the date on his watch. Reminded himself it was still December 15th. Christmas soon. Never mind Bolly in prison, it would be a poor Christmas in Cloughgreen. The town still mourning. Too many eyes red with grieving for the dead. Breadwinners now in the grave. Literally no longer able to bring home the bacon, let alone the turkey or the toys. Besides, who felt remotely like celebrating?

His mind swung back again to Bolly. First Christmas away from him since their marriage. First in jail, for Christ's sake. How would she cope? How would he cope? Where would he go? See it out with Gerry here? Go and see his father? Or take his old man to Ireland again and sit with Bolly's parents staring silently at the empty place setting? Would Gerry take him up on his offer of free board and setting up another design group? He'd not said anything about it since they'd mooted it. There were a lot of unanswered questions. He changed his mind, opened the bottle of Bells again and took a small measure, sipping it slowly.

He looked down at the dog once more. 'What are we going to do, Nelson?' The dog looked at him mournfully, sensitive to his mood. Then he sidled off. A minute later he was back. He dropped his worn yellow tennis ball at Willie's feet.

'Indoor cricket? Okay, old mate.' He dragged himself out of his armchair and walked back into the kitchen. The rain had stopped while he'd been reading his paper and the sun had come out.

'In you go,' he told the dog. He pointed to Nelson's position on the top step in the raised-up doorway at the end of the kitchen and the dog assumed his stance at the wicket, wagging in anticipation of the first ball.

'Ready, Nelson?' he asked as he wound his arm back for a slow lob. Nice easy one, let the dog get his remaining eye in.

Just as Willie let the ball go, the sunlight brought the blade flicker into the house, across the kitchen and onto the far wall where Nelson stood. The dog blinked and missed. Then he blinked again and inclined his head to Willie in puzzlement.

What happened?

Willie knew exactly what happened. He walked across the kitchen, reached down and patted the bewildered dog's head.

'I'm sorry, Nelson. Wind farm stopped play.'

He looked back out of the window at the blade flicker and continued talking. He knew he was talking to himself now and to Verity and all the people out there who'd been shouted down by Big Wind hype.

'If you're alive in any way, be you man, mammal, bird, bug or bog,' he said, 'wind farms make lousy neighbours. Isn't that the plain truth of it, Nelson?'

Nelson brought him the tennis ball back.

# 34

December 20th

Humphrey Drumm had his feet on the desk and was contemplating Christmas. It would be miserable here in Cloughgreen. So he had decided to spend it with his poultry-farming brother in Norfolk. Two old bachelors together, quaffing ale and watching the Christmas jollies on the telly. How had it come to this? Oh well, he'd had his moments. He looked at his watch: 2.30 pm. Bit early for the staff to be back. The Cloughgreen Recorder only had half a dozen staff at the office here in Cloughgreen. Not enough for a proper party. So he'd loaned his number two his Amex card and sent them off to the Happy Dragon. He stifled a yawn. He didn't expect them back till around 4. The place was like a morgue.

Suddenly he heard a fierce rapping at the downstairs reception door. Sounded like the police or the bailiffs. He put his jacket on and went downstairs to investigate.

He worked the locks and discovered a young guy who looked to be about 25 with a laptop slung over his shoulder. Medium height, short blonde hair with left parting, blue eyes and high dabs of ruddy colour on both cheekbones.

'You Humphrey Drumm?'

'I am. Who are you?'

'Jones. Bill Jones from Head Office in Woolton. I'd better come in.'

Humphrey beckoned him inside and locked the door behind them.

He gestured at the empty reception area and the deserted office behind it. 'All off having their Christmas lunch.'

'Maybe just as well,' Jones said.

'Follow me,' Humphrey said and set off up the steep narrow staircase to his office.

'So what does Head Office want?'

'They want to see you.'

'Not paid their phone bill? Couldn't have just rung me?'

Jones ignored him. 'I have to ask for your keys. I'm taking over. For now at least.'

'Eh?'

'They say you exceeded your authority with the memorial edition. In particular that *J'accuse* piece. Said it upset too many people in high places.'

'So they're firing me?'

Bill Jones suddenly looked like a naughty pupil on the carpet in the Head's study. He refused to meet Humphrey's eye, looked steadfastly through the window. 'I think so, yeah.'

'Hardly worth the bother of going to Woolton then, if it's all cut and dried.'

'I'm sorry. But there it is. I'm supposed to be your replacement. Big chance for me. Awkward though, I've always been a big fan of yours. I thought the memorial edition was first rate.'

'Thank you, Bill,' Humphrey said, recovering. He reached into his right hand trouser pocket and fished the office key ring out, tossed the keys to the young man. 'You'll soon discover what fits what. Not many keys in this place. The girls will sort you out. They're a good lot.'

'This is really embarrassing. I have to supervise you while you sort your stuff out and escort you off the premises.' He reached into his laptop case and extracted two large black bin liners, placed them on the desk.

'You mean right now?'

'Well, yeah. That's what they said. Immediate dismissal.'

'Right.' Humphrey took a bin liner and emptied his drawers into it. Only took one black plastic bag. He left the other on the desk. 'Keep this, you may need it.'

The young journo flinched. Then looked hesitant.

'Spit it out. What else?'

'They want a personal cheque for the memorial edition proceeds you donated to the mudslide benevolent fund. They say you had no right to donate it. It was their money.'

Humphrey smiled and shook his head. 'Well, you have to admire their cheek. As well as the humanitarian gesture I thought they'd appreciate the PR value. Well, they can whistle for that... or go to the benevolent fund itself and claw it back. That should just about put the paper out of business before you've even started.'

Bill Jones looked miserable. The high patches of colour on his cheeks had caught fire. 'I tried to tell them that.'

'Well stick to your guns. Don't you do it. Let them do their own dirty work.'

'What will you do now?'

'Return to a life of crime.'

Bill Jones looked alarmed.

'I used to be a crime reporter. But don't worry. The novel every journo is supposed to have in a drawer somewhere? I've got one. Called Deep & Dazzling Darkness, it's a crime novel. I'll get off to a little villa I have down by the Guadiana River just over the border from the Algarve. A bolt-hole paid for by the glory days in London. Warmer there, quiet, good place to write.'

'Well, good luck then. I'm sorry about this.'

'Don't be. I've had good times here. But the wind farm troubles have spoiled it for me. Now the peat slide. Besides it's you who has been landed with someone else's dirty work. It's not your fault.'

Humphrey hoisted his bin liner and walked around the other side of the desk. 'You'd better come around here now. The business side of the desk. Make it official.'

The young journalist walked around the desk and stood there a moment before smiling shyly. Pride fighting with a sense of decorum for the old guy being booted out. Editor already.

'One last thing, Bill Jones. Did you like it at Woolton?'

'Loved it.'

'Well then you'll love it even more here. This is a great place. And don't take things personally. If it hadn't been you, they'd have sent someone else. Think of it as the end of an era. All eras come to an end. You'll discover that as you get older.'

Humphrey stretched out his hand and Bill took it. A dry, confident clasp.

'Thank you for being so civilized.'

'It may well be for the best. Good luck with the new Jones era.' Humphrey picked up his bin liner and headed for the door. It wasn't the first time, but it would be the last. The era of Drumm as journo had also ended.

As he was passing through the door, Bill Jones spoke over his shoulder. 'Happy Christmas, Mr Drumm.'

Indeed, Humphrey thought wryly. Oh, yes, Happy Christmas indeed. Being fired days before Christmas always made it special. You had the comfort of knowing that those doing the firing had done the dirty deed now so they could relax and enjoy their Christmas. Good will to all men.

He let himself out the front door and unconsciously speeded up, not wanting the mawkishness of explaining to the girls and them getting emotional. He suddenly remembered his Amex card. No problem, he'd get his number two to mail it to him. Head down, he headed up London Road to the travel agents to book a flight to southern Portugal. He'd cancel his brother, invite him to join him maybe. The Algarve would be a lot warmer than Norfolk this Christmas.

After all that had happened Cloughgreen wasn't such a bad place to be leaving this Christmas. Death overlay everything, like ashes on holly.

Willie was awakened by Nelson licking his face. It was pitch black. He turned the bedside light on and looked at his wristwatch. December 23rd 5.10 am. He was about to tell Nelson to go back to sleep when he became aware of the house phone ringing downstairs.

He fell out of bed, still half asleep, and made himself tread the steep stairs slowly. Forebodings swarmed in as he descended. Who normally rings at 5 in the morning? It's not to tell you you've won the lottery or your new car is ready to collect. Death or mishap. Next of kin. Those are the sort of calls that are made at this time of day. Had his dad been taken ill? Had someone attacked Bolly and wounded her badly?

Having been woken up, he was aware he wasn't functioning properly. But he made his way to the lounge and picked up the phone.

'I'm sorry. Just so sorry...' a trembly voice said, before bursting into deep, racking sobs and putting the phone down.

'What the hell?' Willie said. Or who the hell? He replaced the receiver and picked it up once more. He tapped in 1471. The number was not familiar. Just someone in London. But he wrote it down on the pad. His finger poised over the callback button. But then he thought, no, he wasn't at his best. He would call back after breakfast.

He had just about got back to sleep when the phone woke him again. From the chink in the curtains he could see it was still pitch black outside. He switched the bedside lamp on and looked at his watch. 7.15 am. It was rare for anyone to use the landline these days. Usually someone cold-calling or a sales pitch from a Bombay call centre. Now twice in two hours.

He retraced his steps, thinking vaguely that at least now the central heating had been on an hour.

He picked up the phone and this time it was a different voice.

'Hello, Willie, it's Jennie Swinburne. Sorry to disturb you again, but Dave has just told me what he did earlier on...'

'He's back then?'

'Yes, a few days ago. I wanted just to let him get a bit better before I rang to let you know. Foolishly I was telling him last night he ought to ring you himself. And he's gone and done it. His sleeping is all over the place at the moment, he didn't realise what time it was...'

'So that was Dave? He sounded in a terrible state.'

'He is. But he's going to be okay in a few weeks, they say. He's on sleeping pills to repair a "sleep debt" the doctors say he has. So he sleeps sometimes for 12-15 hours then wakes up and doesn't know where he is. And he's on anti-depressants.'

'Jesus, what happened?' Shock had got the adrenaline running and Willie felt pin-sharp now.

'Some sort of midlife crisis apparently. He doesn't remember anything except worrying he was letting you down with the gallery. He was gone almost a month before they found him. He was on a platform at Inverness Station with two carrier bags full of spare clothes and food like a bag lady. But he was wandering around frightening people, begging, he had no money. Someone called the police. He has no idea how he got there or what he's been doing...'

'Jesus, Jennie, poor you. But Inverness. Bit off the beaten track, isn't it? Why there?'

'He's no idea. The local police rang me. They were very nice about it. Took him in, helped clean him up, fed him and asked me to come and collect him. He still had his wallet on him with some personal details. I took the Caledonian Sleeper to collect him.'

Willie winced. Thinking I bet that cost a lot more than they could afford. Been cheaper to fly probably. But then at a time like that you don't think straight.

‘The clothes he was in just stank. We came back on the Highland Chieftain. It was awful, people shunned us all the way. I had to burn the clothes eventually. But anyway, I wanted to let you know he’s safe. The doctors say he should be fine in a month. Plenty of rest...’ There was a pause.

‘You still there, Jennie?’

‘Yeah. It was just I had a proposition. Say no if it’s rubbish...’

‘Okay, what? He doesn’t sound fit to come back to work...’

‘No, he isn’t. But he’s okay for child-minding. I thought if you wanted to re-open the gallery I could run it for you. It’s not making any money closed.’

Willie thought for a moment. Why not? She was right, the gallery wasn’t making money. And it was a long lease. She could be no worse than Dave.

‘Okay. How about a month’s trial? Start Jan 2 after Christmas?’

‘Great. Thanks Willie. You won’t regret it. I used to run a perfume counter at Selfridges.’

Willie blinked. He wasn’t sure how selling fragrances compared to selling photographic prints. But thinking about it she was no mouse, like Dave, she was good with people. It could work.

‘Well, great. We’ll give it a go.’

‘Thanks, Willie. We really need...’

‘Don’t say it,’ he interrupted, ‘I know. Tell Dave not to worry about anything. All is forgiven. Just take his time and get better.

I'll be down to see you both when I can. At least he's home for Christmas. Try and have a good one.'

'Will do, Willie, and once more thanks.'

She put the phone down. What a thing to happen. Suddenly he felt in need of one of old Jumper's early morning heart-starters. It felt more like midday than seven-thirty. Instead he settled for a cup of Colombian freeze-dried.

He had mixed feelings. On the one hand he was relieved Dave had turned up more or less okay. But on the other hand he was amazed dull old Dave had had the imagination to have a mid-life crisis. Just goes to show. But what mental process propels you from Wandsworth in south London to Inverness in the middle of the Scottish Highlands he wondered. Maybe if you just panic and run it's hard to know where you're running to?

Anyway, be good to get the Gallery up and going again. Try and earn a few bob to pay for Bolly's little brainstorm. Thinking about it, Jenny's people skills might be just what was needed. He had the beginnings of an idea for an exhibition called 'Saved Landscapes'. The large prints would show virgin landscapes as they had been with maybe a cameo in the corner showing the despoiled wind farm landscape they had become. If he couldn't literally save the landscape, maybe he could at least save the remembrance of it.

Carter rang him on New Year's Day to extend the greetings of the season as he put it. He sounded down.

'You know, Willie, we played it all wrong.'

'How do you mean?'

'The anti-nukes showed how it should be done. Governments have always been far more frightened by the anti-nuclear lobby than of us. The anti-nukes got organized better, got themselves into crowds, got militant, shouted, demonstrated and generally made a nuisance of themselves. Got arrested. Above all else they got themselves on the telly. That is what matters these days. Get yourself seen. Nobody reads manifestos any more. Few people read the serious newspapers. The telly is what matters. Big images, being seen, that's what it's all about. No heavy brain work. Pictures.

'That's why all the expensive PR the UKWC pumped out worked. Big soft images of softly waving white blades on blue skies. Peaceful. Non-threatening. Repeat and repeat. No hard thinking. Soon everyone thinks wind farms are good. Without knowing anything about them.

'By comparison, we were a kind of civilized, middle-aged, middle-class, invisible underground movement. Disorganised. Completely cut off from each other. Letting government fight on its own ground, writing letters to the council, being reasonable, law-abiding, talking to each other not to the public, easily picked off, irrelevant...'

'I think we tried harder than that. Bolly's letters made a big difference. We won the battle here.'

'Oh, sure. Locally, via the Recorder, we won the battle. But I'm saying all over the country, as a national force, we've missed the boat.'

'I'm not sure I follow.'

'We should have organized mass rallies and demos, too. Shown people pictures of what an eagle looks like with its head chopped off by a turbine. Showed pictures of turbines on fire or with fractured blades spinning off. Showed what ripped-up, cast-aside rare bog looks like. Anything to inject a bit of reality into the debate. But let people see it. Done what the Moorsyde Wind Action Group have done on their website. But have it on telly, not tucked away on the Net.'

'Aren't you forgetting something?'

'What?'

'The power of UKWC's PR machine to block any anti-wind farm messages reaching the media. When Bolly wrecked the turbine at Cloughgreen Common it was kept out of the broadcast media. Just a short mention of "an incident involving a turbine in West Yorkshire". And a few column inches in the papers, no pictures. Even then they made Bolly sound like some poor soul who'd gone over the wall from a mental institution.'

'Okay, so we make it into a film and organize free viewings. There's other hands on stuff. We could organize trips to those places where people are really suffering from being too close or been driven out of their homes. Let people go and see and hear what it's really like. Get a bit of word of mouth out there...'

'You don't think it's too late, Carter?'

'In some ways, yes. Cloughgreen Common is gone and Reddingley Moor. But who knows what else Newall has got up his sleeve. And you and I have never been just Nimbys; we don't think anyone should have 'em in their back yards. There's still a lot to fight for.'

'I suppose,' Willie said. Fighting the power of Big Money, Big Government and a big green lobby was exhausting.

'The joke is we've been too democratic. Then in an Alice-in-Wonderland way Ed Miliband says it's undemocratic to make democratic objection. Now if we'd had a few thousand like Bolly it might have been different...'

Willie winced. 'I'm not sure that's the answer either,' he said quickly. 'Anyway, talking of Bolly, it's not that long till she gets out.'

'We'll have a big party for her.'

'My thinking exactly,' Willie said. 'That is, if she wants one...'

'How do you mean?'

'She's changed, Carter. I'm not sure quite who I'll be getting back.'

'It'll all be fine, Willie, you'll see.'

But will it? Willie wondered.

January 10th

'I've gone,' a familiar voice said down Willie's mobile.

'I sort of guessed.'

'You were good to me, Willie. But I hate goodbyes. And it would never have worked out. You and Bolly are an item. I'd just have got in the way. Too old to be a bloody gooseberry.'

'So where are you, Gerry?'

'Staying with Keene, erstwhile star copywriter down in London.'

'How's it going?'

'Bloody awful. I was telling you the ad world had changed. I hadn't realized just how much. Old Keene's just hanging in really. They don't seem to need words or ideas any more. Just loads of pictures and effects. The art director is king.'

'Well that's good isn't it? From your point of view as an art director.'

'Not especially. It's all the kiddywinks art directors who are shouting the odds. It's all digital and electronic. I feel like a caveman daubing the walls. Be lucky to survive as a Mac operator.'

'I'm sure you'll find your feet.'

'Yeah.'

'Give it time.'

'Another thing. Nobody wants to pay anything for anything. So there are loads of sweatshops. And it's hard to get out for a good drink. It's all drugs in the bogs behind closed doors, apparently...'

'Anything else?'

'Yeah. They don't fry the chips in lard. I miss that wonderful aroma floating around Cloughgreen.'

' So it's not Yorkshire then. You'll live. Probably longer.'

'Yeah. Anyway, just tell me when Bolly gets out and she has her party. I'll be back like a shot.'

'Trailing clouds of glory...'

'Yeah,' Gerry said. He didn't sound convinced. 'Take care Willie.'

Gerry, Gerry, Willie thought, you can be one miserable sod sometimes.

January 20th

The estate agent rang to tell him there was a guy who might be interested in buying Greenwood Royd, was it okay to come up?

'Why not? Send him up, I'll be waiting.'

'Don't get your hopes up, Mr Dee, not until you've spoken to him.'

'Okay.'

Half an hour later a black Jag XFR pulled up outside. Willie looked at the low sleek lines and was well impressed. The man who got out was of medium height, wiry, with crinkly black hair. He wore a dark suit and expensive black brogues, pricey camel coat on top.

Willie went out to meet him and introduced himself.

'Nice house, great location. Apart from that,' the guy said, indicating the turbines on Cloughgreen Common, opposite. Straight to the point, Willie thought.

'Well some people really like them,' he said. 'Come on in and I'll give you the grand tour.' The man's manner was confident, pleasant enough. He stopped to pat Nelson.

‘Well,’ he said, ‘It’s a nice house in good nick. “Well appointed” I guess is estate agent speak. No problems there.’

‘So what do you think?’

‘I hear it’s been on the market a while. Not enough people liking the new view. The estate agent said you might be open to offers.’

‘Everyone is open to offers these days.’

‘Quite so.’

‘So what’s your offer?’

The guy smiled and named a figure. Willie took it in the solar plexus. He almost grunted. About sixty per cent of the asking price.

‘That’s way below the asking price.’

‘Yeah. But you’re having difficulties. Your asking price was probably fixed before they put the turbines in, right?’

Despite himself, Willie nodded.

‘Well, I’m offering you a way out.’ He smiled again. ‘I’m not going to twist your arm, okay? But business is business and if I’m going to sell it on I need to leave a margin.’

‘You’re not thinking of living here yourself then?’

The man looked at him as if he were mad.

‘No,’ he said, finally. He reached inside his suit and passed over a heavy, beautifully embossed card: William Benson, Property Management. ‘No rush. Think about it. I’ll leave the offer on the table.’ He reached down and patted Nelson. ‘Nice dog.’

Willie watched as the guy let himself out. Calm and smiling slightly, he opened the door to the Jag, started it up, put full lock on and negotiated the courtyard before returning up the narrow lane.

'Shit, Nelson, I don't think we'll be telling Bolly about this,' Willie said.

He went and poured himself a small Bells. *Offering you a way out. Not going to twist your arm, okay?* Thank Christ, we're not desperate to pay a mortgage.

Then the penny dropped. That's what the guy is doing. Touring the estate agents during difficult times, asking about stuff that had been on the market a while where people might be forced to sell at any price. No hard sell or arm-twisting, Mr William Benson was sniffing around for the scent of blood and desperation. Then if there was blood in the water he'd make a killing. William Benson was a property shark.

And he's the only inquiry we've had, God help us.

# 35

February 15th

In the end Bolly served only seven months. Because of overcrowding and whatever else, they decided to let her out before the end of her sentence. When Jimmy Crossley rang to tell him he sounded as though they'd won the lottery rather than achieved the early release of a felon.

'Result, Willie, you should be dancing in the streets.'

'Somehow,' Willie said, 'It doesn't feel like that. But thanks for calling. And thanks for everything. But you'll forgive me saying I hope I never need you again.'

Jimmy Crossley just laughed and Willie imagined him kissing his wallet.

'Curmudgeon,' Crossley chuckled. 'You mind you take care of her now you've got her back.'

Willie picked her up from the gaol first thing. She looked small and diminished in size as she trudged over to the Range Rover. Red hair short, dull and neglected. Even the blizzard of cheery freckles looked knocked back and faint. He got out and they embraced. She clung to him like a frightened animal and didn't want to let go. Then she made a funny mewing sound under her breath.

'It's okay, you're out now. The nightmare is over.'

'Thank God, you're here,' she said.

'Why wouldn't I be?' he said. She said nothing, looked over his shoulder. The question hung unanswered in the chill morning air, smell of manure from the farms around the prison. It was in a to hell and back sort of place in the middle of nowhere.

'Let's get away from here,' she said. They got into the car and left. From time to time he leaned over his left hand and squeezed hers, but it was cold and unresponsive. She didn't seem to want to talk and he was frightened to say the wrong thing.

First thing back home she'd demanded to go and have a shower "to wash the prison stink off".

He hadn't imagined this but they were nervous as teenagers, chattering away all day and hugging each other. But not risking much of any importance. To Willie they felt like some strange other couple.

Distances had appeared. Perhaps it was inevitable. Be patient.

Nobody felt like cooking so they called up an Indian takeaway, got drunk and went to bed. They clutched each other tight and fell asleep. Emotionally exhausted, they slept like shipwrecked mariners on a warm and sandy shore.

Next night was different. They lay like spoons facing east. His left hand came over her left shoulder and kneaded her right breast. His right hand cupped her sex from behind, squeezing gently and massaging it.

They did not speak and the world's sights and sounds shrank to three very sensitive pieces of flesh. He felt her nipple enlarge and her sex become wet and palpy as it drew itself open. All the time he counted slowly in his head, trying to ignore his own sensations. Somewhere around two hundred she moaned and said 'Come inside'.

He only managed six thrusts before he felt her collapse around him, silky wet like a collapsing Big Tent after rain. As she clenched and unclenched tightly around him he could hold back no longer.

'Wheeew...' she said, bursting out laughing, 'We needed that.' He laughed too, the way they always had. Opening his eyes and looking down at all those sleepy tawny freckles on the pillow he had felt things were going to be alright. He was relieved to discover things felt good as they always had.

But of course other things weren't the same, were they? Not really. Because as Gerry had predicted he'd got back a different woman from the one who had gone to prison. A survivor, but a changed woman. A woman who talked a lot about her cell mate, Elinor.

Bolly's return had not been as anticipated. Yes, the second night had been wild and passionate and a desperate relief for both of them. But the next day he had been forced back on his heels and forced to listen to 3 hours of political rant. She had been banged up for months with an impassioned civil rights supporter called Elinor. Elinor, a redoubtable woman in her sixties, loathed the current government with a passion. Why were we not all on the streets, ripping up cobblestones and rioting, demanding the return of our civil rights? After months of indoctrination the iron had entered Bolly's soul. She had become a political activist.

Within a week Willie could have written a book entitled The Words & Wisdom of Elinor Boyd. As well as all the stuff they'd discussed in clink he was dismayed to find they spoke regularly on their mobiles.

The only good thing about Elinor Boyd, he thought ruefully, was she lived in deepest mid Wales. In a place seemingly surrounded by meandering lanes with wooden signposts indicating the same 6 hamlets. Thankfully it was a heck of a journey and devilishly hard to find. What if she had lived up the road in Woolton? he thought grimly.

As a new-made political activist, Bolly loathed this authoritarian, big state, Labour government that had taken all the power to itself; which did its best to erode the rights of the individual and locally elected bodies whenever it could.

With all the infomercials it was running on TV and radio it was in your face from breakfast 'till cocoa time. Government department after department dictated how you should behave. Big Brother was now in your car, your living room and your bedroom. And despite all evidence to the contrary, like Stalin's regime in Solzhenitsyn's eponymous book, they declared We Never Make Mistakes. And that was really scary. And so on. And so on.

The terrible thing was he agreed. He hated the nanny regime as much as she did. The nanny they were modelled on certainly wasn't Mary Poppins: no spoonfuls of sugar helped this medicine go down. Just double doses. And a lot of stick.

What he came to dread was that every new Labour nonsense brought the full catalogue rant out. Repeating the whole awful anti-democratic inventory seemed to reinvigorate Bolly. But it wearied him. According to Elinor there were now 3,700 more criminal offences than when the government came to power. Did he know that? Yes, he did, he did, he did. The terrible thing was he had started to tip toe around her, hide stuff that might upset her. Anything to avoid the long political rants.

He longed for the old idyllic days of enjoying each other and their surroundings. Watching the constantly changing weather and seasons work their light play over the giant skies and moors. Walking, tending their garden, lunching in country pubs, delighting in Nature. And him taking landscape photographs for the first time. Savouring her wonderful meals and company. Just enjoying each other, being content and minding their own business. But those days were gone forever.

He had come to realize he was now, perforce, a vigilant, auxiliary activist. More exactly, he had elected to become Bolly's minder. No way was he going to let her sneak off again and break the law. The state would throw the key away next time.

The extra political baggage she had brought home was a real pain. But if it was the cost of having Bolly warm in his bed every night, he was willing to pay it. Everything in this life had a cost. Like the cost of wind farms was the loss of all our wilderness places. You had to work out whether it was worth it.

March 1st

Spring was on the rise. Up in the bedroom Bolly yelled 'White rabbits, pinch and a punch,' and administered both.

But never mind what the calendar said. Up on the moors he had seen and heard his first curlews of the year with their wonderful long wings and beaks and plaintive cries. Sometimes, gliding high over the moors, their mournful cries sounded like sailors on some windswept wreck.

Two days later the lapwings arrived. His heart soared as he watched the stubby-winged birds stunting around the sky. Soaring, doing barrel rolls and then dropping like a stone.

Three days later he was mooching around the kitchen when Bolly's mobile started ringing where she had left it on the table. She was down the garden, so Willy answered it.

'They've started putting the next phase in hand,' the voice said. 'I must speak to Bolly urgently.'

Who has? Willie wondered. Instead he heard himself say 'I'll get her. She's putting peelings in the compost bin.'

'Go on then,' the shrill voice demanded.

'Who shall I say it is?'

'Elinor.'

'Right.' His heart sank. But he forced himself to walk down the garden to where Bolly was forking over half-rotted kitchen waste in the big black bin.

'Elinor,' he said, handing her the mobile and making a face. She brushed her hands on her gardening sweater and took the phone.

When she came back her cheeks were flushed and her eyes were glistening. 'Elinor needs to see me right now. Urgent update.'

'Right now?'

'Yeah.'

'What about me?'

'You can come if you like. Might be useful.'

Too right, he thought, I'm not letting you go off on your own any more. 'You're not driving all the way into the Celtic fastnesses are you?'

'Meeting in a supermarket car park just outside Chester.'

'Very hush-hush.'

She play-punched him on the arm. 'No, idiot. Just about halfway for both of us.'

'Bring Nelson?'

'Bad idea. She'll have Cain and Abel with her.'

'Who?'

'You'll see. Her bodyguards. Lots of people would like to hurt her.'

'Why not Chester itself and we could go for a nice meal later?'

'You ever driven in Chester?'

'No.'

She just smiled at him, pityingly. Okay.

The sat-nav guesstimated an hour and twenty-eight. But Bolly drove the Mini Cooper as though its tyres were on fire. Willie found himself depressing an invisible brake pedal in front of him. Despite weekend shopping traffic they did it in an hour and ten. They pulled into a car park crowded with Saturday shoppers, all of them obsessed with Sunday roasts and stocking up with weekend booze, no-one looking before pulling out or nipping in. Bolly muttered a bit under her breath and did a slow-mo circuit of the huge car park. She'd started swearing since she'd been in jail.

'There she is,' she said, indicating a rusting orange and cream Combi camper van. Willie followed her scarlet-painted fingernail. Two large black and tan Alsatian heads glared out through the side windows.

'Cain and Abel, her guardians,' Bolly said, smiling.

A wiry older woman of middle height in jeans and red anorak had stepped out of the Combi. As the Mini pulled up alongside Willie had the feeling he was looking at some former-day priestess. Many serpents of greasy grey and black hair were complemented by fiercely intense blue eyes. No makeup. So this was Elinor Boyd, political activist. She looked intimidating, Willie thought.

She grabbed Bolly and wrapped her in a bony bear hug. 'Good to see you, cell-mate,' she said. Then she released her and strode up to Willie, grabbing his hand in an iron grip.

'Willie. We meet at last. Good to see you.'

'Heard a lot about you,' Willie said with understatement. He resisted sucking his mauled hand.

'Come inside, I've got tea in a Thermos. The lads won't touch you.' She indicated they should sit around a small pull-out table and served up sweet tea in mugs. Too bad if you didn't take sugar.

He was aware Cain and Abel were giving him hard, calculating stares. He knew confident dogs don't always bark before they bite you.

Elinor suddenly brandished a brown envelope at Bolly, which she appeared to have magicked out of an anorak pocket. Her movements were quick and nervy, Willie thought, disturbing. Disturbed even?

'They've started. Have you had one of these?' She indicated a maroon and black sheet of A4 headed The identity card is here. ID at your fingertips. 'It's an invitation to pay £30, recurring, and get your state ID document. Your chance to give them your fingerprints, personal details and lord knows what else. Later they'll probably want full biometrics.'

'More Transformational Government,' Bolly said.

'Exactly. They couldn't force us all into paying thirty quid each to restrict our own privacy and liberty. Too much uproar from civil lib groups. Quite right, too. So they're sneaking it in through the back door. Rolling it out on the quiet through direct mail. Conning the gullible it's for their own benefit.' She brandished the sheet again and read from it. 'Use it like your passport. You can use it to help prove your identity. Protect yourself against fraud...all supposedly for your good. And you get to pay another £30 every 10 years... '

Willie looked puzzled. He raised his hands. 'Transformational Government? Translation please.'

Bolly leaned in to him. 'Transformational Government is what our Big State government calls centralizing all the databases so the state can know everything about you at the press of a button.'

Elinor drummed both forefingers on the table and said 'They spin it so that it's all supposed to be for our protection or for ease of access to save us in medical emergency or general efficiency to let them help us quicker. The reality is that it's for state power. For control, to put it bluntly. They want every scrap of information about us, each bit helping to nail us down better. Control, control, control.'

'Just think about it, Willie. All your private medical and dental info. Your tax records. Where you travel. When you travel. Gathered via passport or surveillance on streets and rail stations. Your sexual preferences. Your academic achievements. What you buy, where, from which credit card companies. Your credit ratings. Everything from cradle to grave. We've already got more surveillance cameras than anywhere else in the world. On motorways. At stations. Airports. Garages. Hotels. Hospitals. Public buildings. In lifts, you name it... They even have spy mikes...'

'What?' Willie said. 'Spy mikes?'

'Yeah. On some of the spy camera pylons they also have spy microphones which can pick up the sound of arguing or of gun shots. Gun shots, obviously, you don't mind. But the idea they can listen in to raised voices about anything, well...' She let her shocking revelation hang in the air, then she was back to the main drift of her argument.

'Once they get your fingerprints and other biometric details such as your personal eye configuration, they've effectively got you tagged for life. They may as well give you your own personal bar code.'

Elinor paused. 'If this stuff continues that's probably where it will all end. Everyone will have an electronic chip slipped under the skin at birth, like they do with pedigree dogs. "A moment of discomfort, but think of the benefits - your blood group, medical history all available in a quick scan if you have an accident." That's how they'll sell it. The way they pretend now that all the surveillance and pooling of information is to help against terrorist threats. Believe that and you'll believe anything. Surveillance. Restriction. Compulsion. More Big State

Government and you'll have a police state. Dunno why they don't just bar code all our foreheads now and have done with it.'

Willie felt a chill go through him. All this regulation and restriction of people was total anathema to him. Elinor looked wild, but what she said made a lot of sense.

'Any more tea, you two?'

'Please,' they said in tandem.

'We haven't had our mailing yet...'

'You will. They'll be rolling it out slowly region by region to try and achieve stealth. Conning people that they're doing it to help them.'

'It's depressing, isn't it?' Willie said.

Elinor sighed. 'You don't know the half of it. The whole political class seems to have lost touch with ordinary people. They think they are above the people they govern, a special class. Some of them need to travel in special train compartments innoculated against the hoi polloi. Others seem to think they can live their lives on special expenses, be it for moats, porn DVDs, bath plugs whatever. Then they have special pensions which are now outmoded from when they were introduced...'

She paused. 'A lot of these things were a good idea originally when many socialist MPs had no private means or incomes. And when people in ordinary walks of life had jobs for life and the pensions that went with them. For the rank and file in the private sector, all that went about 30 years ago, the jobs for life and the featherbedded pensions. It's renewable contracts and save for your own pension. The public sector, including MPs, still live in a cushioned, parallel universe.'

'It seems to me loads of them have no idea how ordinary people live,' Bolly said. 'They've totally lost touch. Good guys like Frank Field and Dennis Skinner who understand real life are thin on the ground. Too many of them on all sides now come from well-off families, good schools, good unis, a spell as a researcher or personal assistant and then fast-tracked into a safe seat. They never get their hands dirty with the facts of real life... They've literally no idea.'

'So what's the answer?' Willie asked.

'Take away MP's special privileges. Pay them more for the responsibility they have. But put their remuneration levels back into the real world, where tax bands hurt them, too, same as everyone else. And the same pension provisions obtain. So, let's pay MPs £110,000 a year and let's pay ministers £150,000. Let them be more like the rest of us, share our pain and frustrations and taxation. Give them only strictly monitored travel expenses, second class, so they travel with the rest of us. Get to hear what we groundlings actually have to say.'

'It would be a start,' Willie said.

'I don't know how you inject management know-how and real-life experience into them,' Elinor moaned. 'The other day a social worker was telling me about a case where a young lad, who lived with his two feral older brothers, had never seen a news programme on TV in his life. He thought it only worked as a monitor to see porn movies and video games.'

Willie was shocked.

'My Dad was a GP. He used to tell us how many of the people who came to see him were malnourished. How many families spent up to the last penny until their next dole or week's pay came through. Went to school or work with a packet of crisps and holes in their shoes.'

'There's still a lot of that about,' Elinor said. 'Despite all the satellite dishes.' She suddenly looked exasperated.

'Then there's all the wrong sort of social engineering and form-filling. Both those things kill small and medium businesses. Did mine anyway...'

'I didn't know...'

'Elinor had a small company in Cumbria that made up-market fishing tackle.'

Elinor smiled wearily. 'Long-established company. My husband bought it. Good product. Customers kept coming back. Set in a small Cumbrian town. Provided scarce employment for about 30 people. Then we had the sort of legislation and employees rights introduced that companies like Tesco or Unilever can cope with; but they kill small businesses. Big Government, run by people who've never run a market stall, suddenly in charge of multi-million pound budgets. They just don't get it. They think all the self-employed and small company directors are creaming it and running yachts in the Bahamas. If only. My husband never lived to see all this nonsense, thank heavens. Dead before red tape strangled the business.' In the silence Cain or Abel made a truffling noise.

'You want some water, lads?' she said, padding over to the Alsatians with a large water bowl. She suddenly looked stooped and older. She came back and sat down.

'The nanny state, eh,' Willie said. 'God help you if nanny is blind, deaf and bloody-minded?'

'I hate it that we're all so passive,' Elinor said. 'Ever heard of Ochi Day?'

The Dees looked blank.

'They celebrate it every year in Greece. It is a remembrance of a day in 1942 when Mussolini demanded General Metaxas, the Greek president, surrender Greece. General Metaxas simply replied "Ochi".

'No. That's what I'd like to see us all do as a response to this last sleazy, oppressive lot. Everyone goes to the polling station and marks their ballot paper NO.'

'And what would that achieve?' Willie asked mildly.

'Give 'em a jolt. Give 'em something to think about. How they're killing democracy when they obfuscate everything and ignore us. If nobody votes, that makes them obsolete. Back to the military, which surely nobody in this country wants.'

Bolly could see everyone looked depressed and changed the subject back to the classic fishing tackle Elinor's company had made. She was admiring a couple of colourful fly-fishing lures Elinor had hooked through the Combi's sun visor. Then a couple of small kids started pogoing up and down outside the Combi to see inside, shaking the side panels. That woke Cain and Abel who started offering deep violence and jumping up. The kids ran for their lives.

Elinor quieted the dogs. But the mood was broken. Willie and Bolly made their goodbyes and left. The driving in the supermarket car park was still obsessively blinkered as customers floored the pedal to back out or raced into spaces ahead.

'Saturday drivers,' Willie said.

A massive, drug-dealer-black 4-WD with can't-see-me tinted windows carved her up. 'Bloody Sunday drivers you mean,' Bolly said, leaning on the horn. 'And you, mate,' she yelled out the open window.

A human pit bull with multiple face piercings, shades and stubble powered his window down and gave her the finger. Slowly and deliberately. 'Wot yer gonna do about it, bitch?'

'Down, girl,' Willie whispered, as Bolly bethought herself and waved the yob through.

'They're still bloody Sunday drivers,' Bolly said. 'Even with guns'.

Nursing his bruised hand, Willie felt a little confused. Personally he'd found Elinor as disturbing as he'd expected. But she spoke a lot of sense. On the other hand, being locked in a cell 24/7 with her wild-eyed, scraggy-haired intensity would have driven him nuts.

Bolly eased the Mini out on to the main drag and put her foot down. The car snarled happily at being let off the leash and she double declutched and went through the gears.

'Good old Elinor,' Bolly said. 'She was the one thing that kept me sane in clink.'

Maybe, Willie thought, but a little goes a long way. Whatever else happened in the future he was going to keep Bolly well away from Elinor. They were like fire and petrol. Not good in close proximity.

# 36

Spring came on like an avalanche. Suddenly there were fifty shades and shapes of virgin green leaf. From pale grey-green to dark pine green. Vibrant red-flowering currant, tiny blue forget-me-nots, red Wandas, purple wind flowers, scarlet and gold tulips and purple aubretia, a riot of fresh colours all at once. Pairs of birds shot across the garden in lustful hot pursuit. Bees appeared. And sun.

The sixth of April dawned with an outpouring of molten gold sunlight. In the garden battalions of daffs turned their faces to heaven. It was beautiful but Willie quickly dragged the curtain over the dining room window. It might just conceal the blade flicker before Bolly came down to breakfast. To have his Sunday start with a flickering golden intrusion and the resulting rant was not what he wanted. Even so, having half her dining room closed off from the sunlight would annoy her.

As he made the coffee he watched a cloud of crows flapping around the bottom hedge. Something invisible lay dead or dying. He banged the window and watched the crows soar up and away.

He thought of hiding the Sunday papers in the hope of peace. But he knew it wouldn't work, she'd heard the lad delivering them.

He would have stopped all the newspapers if he could. But Bolly wouldn't let him. As it was, he folded the Sunday Telegraph and The Sunday Times next to her place and hoped the government hadn't done anything else overriding.

She was upset enough that British soldiers were dying at the rate of one a day in Afghanistan. He just wanted a quiet Sunday morning.

Later they were planning a walk around Skipton. They were walking further and further afield to escape the turbines. But it was becoming more difficult.

Just then his mobile went off. To avoid upset he was becoming a secret squirrel like Newall, he thought. He read the caller ID and stepped outside into the garden.

‘Sorry to disturb you, it’s Carter, here.’

‘No problem.’

‘You know Phyllis and loads of other members of The Living Moorland have been writing to the Tories about their wind farm policy?’

‘Yeah,’ Willie said, wondering why this should disturb his Sunday morning.

‘Well, there have been precious few replies. Which is fishy in itself. Earlier in the year the Tories published this paper saying they will seek to incentivize councils to “host” wind farms if you’ll pardon the expression.’

‘Hadn’t heard that.’

‘Yeah. So whether Labour or Tories get in at the next election we still get stuck with the ghastly things.’

‘Some choice then.’

‘Yeah.’ There was a pause on the other end of the phone. ‘It’s been puzzling me this. The Tories aren’t stupid. They know all middle England hates these turbines. No-one wants to live near them. So why persist? I’ve been worrying at it like a dog with a bone. Then last night I had this dream...I could be wrong.’

‘But?’

‘I think I’ve sussed out a dirty little secret that Labour and the Tories have shared this last 30 years. They’ve both worried about how long the coal would last, then how long the oil and gas. But both of them have fought shy of putting in hand the obvious long-term solution.’

‘Which is?’

'Nuclear. They've both been terrified of raising the nuclear bogey. So they've effectively conspired together. Each hoping the other would have to face down the anti-nuclear lobby and commission nuclear power stations when they were in power. A sort of nuclear "pass the parcel" with both parties hoping the other would be in power when nuclear was unavoidable.'

'I remember you saying something similar before.'

'Yeah, but now I know the kicker. Suppose we've now passed the point of no return? That we don't have time to get the nuclear power stations up and running, comply with Kyoto and the EU and keep the lights on?'

'Shit. You mean without even pitiful amounts of wind power we could have power cuts?'

'Exactly. Christopher Booker, the journo, has been warning about it for years. What we're going to need and what is going to be available; the figures don't tally.'

'So the only short term solution to raise extra energy will be to pile in the turbines?'

'Yeah. Let's say the Tories have seen the figures and are panicking, too. That's why they'll try and bribe people to accept more turbines. They'll be desperate for every last scrap of energy, even if it does mean building new coal-powered stations to support them. Anything to keep the lights on.'

'God help us,' Willie said. 'Having to depend on the undependable.'

'Exactly. It won't save any carbon because you'll have to have standby conventional power running all over the place, supporting them, actually wasting energy. But...'

'I see where you're going. So far as the politicians are concerned this whole Green issue has been an elaborate front to mask their own shilly-shallying and get the turbines in before the lights start going out...It's not necessarily because they're green but because there's no short term alternative. Dirty little secret is right.'

'How does that sound to you?'

'Plausible. And like you and me should be investing in candle manufacturers and generator companies.'

A dry laugh came back down the phone. 'Glad you've still got your sense of humour, we're going to need it. If my theory is right we're well and truly fucked...'

Willie caught the expletive. He couldn't remember Carter swearing before.

Now he felt his blood pressure rising. 'So what it comes down to is the cost of saving politicians' red faces is to blight the whole of the British countryside. All done hypocritically under the guise of greenness, but really because of decades of energy mismanagement and fear of the anti-nuclear lobby.

'Although they're selling wind farms in as renewables and green etc, the reality is they're the fastest stop-gap energy source they can whack in 'till the new nuclear plants or tidal come on-stream.'

'That's about the size of it, if I'm right,' Carter said, sighing.

'You sound tired.'

'Didn't sleep too well after the dream woke me up. I have these long dreams like movies, very real. This one woke me sweating...'

'I'm not surprised. What does Phyllis think?'

'She thinks I'm right.'

'So do I. It would totally explain the Tory stance. Otherwise they could be landed with the lights going out if they get elected.'

'What are you gonna do?'

'Lay in stores of candles,' Willie laughed bitterly. 'What can we do? Say it's a choice between blackouts, no TVs, no computers, no kettles or lights or heating. Or cramming the countryside with turbines. It's a no-brainer. Especially for city dwellers. Shame about us in the country who don't want them. Don't be selfish. Sacrifice and shut up.'

'No surrender,' Carter said. 'Hope against hope is the motto. And lay in the candles like you say.'

'I think we're fucked, Carter. But you know what...'

'What other little thing?'

'Whichever lot get in at the next election if this energy crisis turns out to be the way you see it, ie of their own making, we should never let the politicians forget it. We should rail and rail against them for all their political cowardice. Not just for being so self-seeking, but for taking all our wild places from us. To pretend to be doing it for moral environmental reasons rather than covering their own cock-ups just adds insult to injury.'

'They'll never admit to it. Skins like rhinos.'

‘Take care, Carter,’ Willie said. ‘Large malt should improve matters.’ Then he forced a rictus, relaxed it into a sunny Sunday-morning smile and went back inside.

He turned to Classic FM on the radio as Bolly appeared and sat down at the breakfast table. A government commercial was warning of the dangers of unmanned level crossings.

‘Not saying anything about the dangers of crossing Afghanistan with insufficient helicopters or inadequately armoured vehicles, mind you,’ Bolly said. ‘British soldiers dying at the rate of one a day and they’re spending a fortune on level crossings advertising. Talk about fiddling while Rome burns.’

‘Yeah, they sure know about priorities, this government,’ Willie agreed. ‘They seem to understand advertising as little as everything else. Do you remember them running ads to saturation point for adult literacy and numeracy on this station?’

‘Yeah, while the station’s own “trails” feature people wanting a little Mozart as they work on their dissertations...How much literacy and numeracy do they need? It’s a bad joke. But it’s our money.’

‘Did you hear that government commercial telling you to make sure you put your socks on with the lumpy shape at the back, Bolly?’

‘Must have been while I was in clink.’

‘Joke,’ Willie said.

‘Not much of one. They’ve spent squillions telling us to do everything else.’

‘Marmalade or Marmite?’

'Marmite,' she said as he laid the toast down on the table. 'Unless that's now banned.'

'Coffee's just coming.'

Bolly picked up the Sunday Telegraph and turned first, as was her wont, to the Christopher Booker column to discover the latest wind farm madness.

Willie put the coffee down and watched as she read.

She had returned from prison with a half-inch long white scar in the fleshy skin above her right eyebrow. The result of another inmate skimming a metal pan lid at her. She was embarrassed about it and normally covered it with cosmetics. Now Willie watched as the white scar tissue flushed red with anger.

'You'll never believe what the shits have done now.'

'What's left to do, short of rounding up everyone who disagrees with them and shooting them?'

'They're going to institute a new planning body called the Infrastructure Planning Commission. This is what Christopher Booker says: "the purpose of this organization is to force through thousands of these absurd objects (industrial wind turbines) over the wishes of local people and councils, who will be deprived of any democratic say in the matter".'

'Bloody hell,' Willie said. The scar tissue above Bolly's eyebrow was throbbing with engorged blood.

'Our faraway metropolitan masters have once more shat upon the shires,' Bolly said.

‘Tony Blair once joked about the “great, clunking fist” of Gordon Brown,’ Willie said. ‘Well he wasn’t joking. The great, clunking fist has come down to quell any democratic opposition to wind farms.’

‘Britain has entered a new phase of bully-boy politics. In other countries, like Elinor says, we would all be taking to the streets,’ Bolly said. ‘You don’t like people disgreeing with you so you move the goalposts.’

‘The thing is, John Prescott has already moved the planning goalposts with PPS22...Right from the beginning the whole point was to make it too difficult and technical for ordinary people to object. Except middle England has got a lot of clever people who swatted up on the planning regs and fought the government on its own terms. This is really a government defeat. They haven’t been able to win on their own terms. So now you’re not allowed to protest at all.’

‘They may change the planning regs but they can’t change how people feel. It will just make people more bitter. Because no-one wants to live near them.’

‘All this means,’ Bolly said, ‘is they’re determined to use the overwhelming power of the state to impose this crappy, land-hungry technology on us all’.

There was a silence over the breakfast table and Nelson, gauging the atmosphere, whimpered. Back when he was a puppy his previous owners had sometimes beaten him. Now when times were tense he assumed it must be his fault and got nervous. Willie smiled a tight little smile and and leaned down to pat him.

'You're okay, Nelson. It's not your fault.'

'What it means is we are all effectively denied the democratic right to prevent our countryside being swamped by these things.'

'Who will they silence next?' Willie asked.

Bolly didn't hear him. She had left the table, pulled back the curtain and was staring out of the window at all the flickering on Cloughgreen Common. They will be there for 25 years, she thought. And now there will many more thousands across Britain, whether the locals want them or not.

These things would be the visible legacy of a government which systematically took power away from the small people and their elected local bodies and eroded civil liberties at every turn, creating a sort of democratic Dark Ages. Let people remember it was a Labour government.

Sighing, she went back to the table. Willie carefully folded the newspaper back into place. He had come upon another piece about redefining brownfield sites to push planning apps through. He couldn't bring himself to mention it.

'No,' he said, smiling at her, feeling like Judas.

'No what?'

'No, we don't have to go to Skipton today.'

'Don't you mind?'

'No, you've got more letters to write, haven't you?'

She smiled. 'You're a good man, Willie.'

'Dunno about that,' he muttered guiltily. 'But I will take Nelson out over the moors.' He got up from the table and went out to the kitchen to get Nelson's lead. As he took it off the back of the door a thought occurred to him.

Bolly had already got out the A4 pad and Pentel. She sat poised in thought at the breakfast table.

'Just still be here when I get back,' he said. 'No more unilateral gestures. Promise.'

She laughed and blew him a kiss. 'Relax, I've learned my lesson. It seems to me I'm not the only one who has changed. When did you get to be so distrustful?'

He shrugged, attempted a lame smile. She pointed a finger at the door. 'Go.'

He left Greenwood Royd by the back door and headed for the moor and The Hallow Stones, deliberately averting his eyes from the turbines on Cloughgreen Common.

Nelson suddenly sat down and pointed. Willie followed his gaze. High above the moors two enormous ravens, mega-crows, played love tick. They flew close up, mimicking each others flight, suddenly darting left or right, rolling over, diving, soaring up over miles of countryside, their thick, raggedy black wing feathers extended. Completely in their element.

The sunlight was warm on his face, the grass underfoot sparkled from the heavy dew. Pure white lambs come fresh into the world suckled their mothers. To make it idyllic the breeze died completely. It was tempting to believe God was in his heaven and all was right with the world.

But the serpent had entered his paradise and it was spoiled. Now the wind had dropped, he knew if he turned and looked the turbines would be hanging limp as wet washing. Somewhere, invisibly, a coal-fired power station would be kicking in to take up the slack.

The latest moves to force the turbines in disturbed him. The new planning body was a crude instrument to crush all dissent. But this other thing, the proposal to brand any place with pylons on it a brownfield site, showed the lengths this government would go to.

If it weren't so dreadful it would be hilarious. Nicolas Sarkozy, the French president, having seen the visual ravages caused by wind farms on his travels over Europe, had declared that only brownfield sites could be used for wind farms. He didn't want to ruin the countryside of la belle France. The British response was simple. By declaring anywhere with a pylon in sight a brownfield site, they made most of rural Britain a brownfield site. If it's got a pylon on it, it's obviously a brownfield site. So you can't complain about that, can you?

The dewy conditions had preserved the overnight smells, making the scents of small nocturnal creatures hyper-fresh. Nelson rushed urgently from sniff to sniff, tail never-endingly wagging. Sitting down and waiting when he got too far ahead and demanding a gravybone for his consideration.

The heavy dew made the surfaces greasy. Willie had to watch his footing and take care not to reach out for the red-rusty fence wire to save himself. A palmful of rust and blood would ruin anyone's Sunday.

The sky was a cloudless deep blue. The sun was warm on his face. The moorlands rang to the singing of the sky larks and the mournful cries of the curlews. And he had a happy dog to share it with. A couple of years back, he thought, his soul would have been singing fit to burst.

Now he wondered glumly where Bolly's activism would end. The obvious thing would be to sell the house and move, emigrate even. Get her away from wind farms and this Big State government that so antagonised her. But if they couldn't sell the house, they were stymied. Catch 22.

As he crested the next ridge he had a clear view into Lancashire. The new wind farm beyond Reddingley hove limply into view. It had been erected by another carpetbagger developer with no prior power experience and had been flawed from Day One. Although the turbines were huge, they hardly ever seemed to work. He suspected they'd greedily gone for the biggest yield and picked an inappropriate size of turbine for the location. Thus they rarely moved.

If he walked another 15 minutes there would be another limp-standing turbine site on his left, just over the Yorkshire border. Also waiting for a coal-fired station to kick in, presumably.

This was the brave new world planned for the rest of the country. Wall to wall turbines. Carbon-powered plants waiting to kick in when the turbines failed.

Did the government not realize the consequences of this planned coercion? In a democracy legal protest - and the possibility of winning your case - enabled discontent to be vented. Civilized people felt compelled to work within the law. But if the law was rigged so that it denied the possibility of fighting your corner through proper democratic process then people felt differently. If the law didn't look after you, you reverted to looking after yourself. This was when certain elements reached for the AK47s. Thinking of which, he thought wryly, he'd better be getting home.

You couldn't govern people by beating them over the heads all the time. People soon tire of having bloody, bandaged heads. In the same way that 24/7 megaphone politics make you turn a deaf ear. At some stage the carrot and the quiet word had to be an alternative.

The thought of turning the bend and viewing the next wind farm dispirited him.

'This way, Nelson,' he said and veered off down the stony track that led towards Halfpenny Meadow, turning his back on the prospect of the next Yorkshire wind farm. The rocks on the downhill track were treacherous with dew and he clutched the broken-down dry stone wall for support. After half a mile of downhill scrambling he gingerly jumped the shallow stream and opened the small gate to Halfpenny Meadow. Halfpenny Meadow's emerald pasture looked like sheep heaven.

They crossed the meadow and climbed back up to the moor. Immediately the wind farms at Cloughgreen Common and The Delf loomed large.

'This is their vision for the rest of Britain, Nelson. The Green lobby may say it's 5 minutes to midnight for the planet. But it's 10 seconds to midnight for our wilderness places.'

Nelson wagged happily. He loved this place with its wind, moorland pools and long, tickly grass.

Back home Bolly had a strange look on her face. 'This new Infrastructure Planning Department, I've rumbled it. You know what it's all about, don't you?'

'I've a pretty good idea. They'll use it to rubber stamp all wind farm planning applications. I should think all the Scottish islands will be fair game and large tracts of Wales, as well as places like us...'

'It's cleverer than that. They'll use it to steamroller all opposition to the new nuclear plants, we desperately need pronto. They're terrified of the anti-nuclear lobby. What this will allow them to do is supposedly sit even-handed saying the energy security of the state means we need all these things. Anti-wind farm supporters are being forced to make sacrifices. So you anti-nuclear protesters are going to have to make sacrifices, too. End of.'

Willie looked at her. The scar above her eye was pulsing red. He knew she was right.

'Various UK governments have shied away from commissioning nuclear power plants. Now we're at the last possible moment to commit before the country is plunged into darkness. They can't afford to allow lengthy on-going anti-nuclear planning protests. So we have a draconian one size fits all planning policy.'

Willie nodded and went out into the garden. He couldn't bear to tell her the reality might be far worse than that.

'It's started already,' Carter said. His mobile sounded as though he was in Turkestan.

'What has?'

'The new rubber stamp policy for all wind farm disputes.'

'How do you mean?'

'Well, I've heard from 5 disputed wind farm apps that were referred to the Secretary of State. They've all been waved through. They haven't waited for the new Infrastructure Planning Department to be set up. The draconian new policies have started. The inspectors at the Planning Inspectorate seem to be viewing every planning app in the light of national energy security.'

'How can you be sure?'

'Well, I can't be sure. But in each case the strategy seems the same. The planning inspector and the Secretary of State mildly concede various issues, acknowledge the fact that the new wind farms will adversely affect some things. But that the benefits outweigh the adverse effects. And wind farms are necessary to make a limited but valuable contribution to the security of the national energy supply.'

'You mean they admit there may be problems?'

‘In a restrained way. But no problem will be allowed to stand in the way of national energy security. That is the catch all.’

‘What can you say?’

‘You can say farewell to all our remaining wild places, that’s what...’

When he put the phone down Willie felt like crying. The barbarians had won. For the sake of symbolism and short-term relief they were going to impose these hopelessly inefficient machines on the whole of the British countryside. They would kill living things which were completely non-renewable. The joke was it was all unnecessary: there were far more reliable sustainable energy sources. Just not as cheap or immediate.

He didn’t know what he would tell Bolly about the dirty little secret both main parties seemed to have connived at.

That for personal popularity both main political parties were happy to sacrifice Britain’s whole rural heritage.

If this turned out to be the case, then both main parties should be vilified. He thought of Elinor and her NO vote to the lot of them.

Later in bed Willie was overtaken by a fit of giggles. Bolly looked up from her book.

‘What’s up with you?’

‘I was thinking about something Carter said. He was saying how desperate we may be for energy from the wind farms just to keep the lights on. And I had this funny vision.

‘Just imagine future Cabinet meetings. Picture it, there is a tentative knock on the door. A timid figure is given admittance. He passes a note to the PM, who waves him away and addresses the Cabinet.

‘“Bad news, ladies and gentlemen,” he says. “The Met Office predicts becalmed conditions all over Britain today. More work for Aiolos, I’m afraid. I ask you to join me in prayer.” They all bow their heads and close their eyes. The PM intones, “Mighty Aiolos, Greek god, keeper of the four winds, powerful since ancient times, we humbly beseech you to release your mighty winds on our becalmed island. Come to our aid and dig us out of the deep and smelly stuff. Send the right winds swiftly, always acknowledging, through your all-knowing omniscience, the start-up wind speeds of our feeble turbines and also their close-down speeds. Let the crosses of Aiolos move and let there be light across our land. Amen”. And then they sit around and hope. Not an African rain dance exactly, more a British wind chant.’

They laughed until the tears ran down their cheeks and their ribs hurt, thinking of the Cabinet at prayer.

Eventually Bolly had to go to the loo.

When she came back to bed she turned to Willie and said ‘It isn’t really funny, is it? I mean, if it’s come down to depending on the wind, God help us all.’

# Epilogue

One Monday morning they sat down to breakfast and Willie said 'This is the first day of the rest of our lives, what are we going to do with it?'

'Funny you should say that,' she said, 'but I've had an idea. It will cost us money at first, but it will get us back into harness. And we'll be doing something useful instead of sitting here moaning.'

Willie gave her a funny look. 'Okay...say on.'

'Well, I've been looking through my notes on what industrial wind turbines are doing to birds and bats around the world. The notes would make a consciousness-raising book. And you could illustrate it, actually show the nature of the problem. Call it Blood on the Wind.'

Willie just whistled and then broke out in a big slice-of-melon grin. He thought of what Carter had once said about showing people what an eagle looked like with its head chopped off. 'I like it,' he said. 'So you mean like go around all these places in Wales and Scotland where the wild life is being mangled...'

'And California and Canada and Tasmania and Spain...the Straits of Gibraltar, the Straits of Messina, it's a worldwide problem. I've just read the Swedes are organizing anti-wind farm concerts in beautiful places to highlight the plight of wild life. Plus it gives us a wider market.'

'Woweee, no half measures with you, Bolly. Go, girl. Okay, that's the brief. Can do.'

The more he thought about it, the better it seemed. It could only be good to give Verity a break away from their unsaleable house and the strobing blades.

By the end of the week they had their itinerary and were on a plane to LA. Willie had left his digital hardware at home, brought his film cameras and fine grain film. They started at the oldest, biggest wind farm in the world at San Joaquin Valley, at a place called the Altamont Pass.

It had been built in 1981 after the global oil crisis of the Seventies, with over 5,400 wind turbines. And right from the start it had a bad reputation with wildlife enthusiasts. Depending who you listened to, it had either killed 17,000 raptors over 25 years or was killing birds in general at the rate of

10-15,000 a year. Now it was the subject of much legal activity between environmentalists and the power companies. To be fair, the power companies had tried different things over the years to alleviate the problem; but the development had been built at a different time with less awareness of avian conservation needs when it came to siting.

They had more or less known what to expect. As Bolly had warned, it was a huge site fenced in with warning signs and locked gates advising no unauthorised entry. Nonetheless, the scale was gobsmacking. They got out of their hire car and just leaned their bums on it and looked.

'Wow...' Willie said, stunned by the ranks of turbines running away and away from them.

'It's just massive,' Bolly said.

'Worse than that, this could be the shape of the future,' Willie said.

'If this new Labour planning super-quango goes through - where you have no rights to object - this could be the face of huge parts of the UK. Just massive industrial wind farms in all the open spaces.'

'Christ, don't say that,' Bolly said.

'But it's true. If you can't object, they'll just pile 'em in.'

Bolly squeezed his hand. 'Have courage. It's not all over yet. Who knows, they might not even get in at the next election?'

'I wish I had your faith.'

She suddenly started singing. 'Oh, I am the eagle, I live in high country, in rocky cathedrals that reach to the sky...'

He listened till she finished, happily distracted.

'What was that?'

'John Denver. "The Eagle and the Hawk".'

'Great lyrics.'

'Yeah,' she said.

Then they poked around outside the wire fencing and Willie shot a fair number of shots to illustrate Bolly's text.

In the days that followed they visited wind farms on the Appalachian ridges. And the north shore of lake Erie. And Ontario's Wolf Island where a wind farm had allegedly been responsible for 2,000 bird and bat deaths. The fatalities were said to cover 33 different bird species and 5 bat species.

It allowed Bolly to remind readers of the full horror of bat deaths. That mostly the turbine blades themselves didn't kill the bats. The blades chewed up the air creating changes in pressure in some zones. Canadian scientists had discovered that 90% of the dead bats had no mark on them. But their internal injuries were consistent with their lungs expanding suddenly in a low pressure zone, capillaries in the surrounding tissue bursting and causing their lungs to become flooded with blood. The condition was known as barotrauma and was similar to the condition suffered by scuba divers. What a way to go, Willie thought. The thought of it made him feel ill.

According to Bolly, on one site alone up to 3,000 bats had been killed in a 6-week period as bats migrated along ridges searching for insects, but finding turbines. The scientists were experimenting with radar to warn them off.

They took in a wind farm in NW Tasmania where 18 endangered wedge tail eagles had been killed. Plus the Starfish Hill site in Australia and the controversial Bald Hills site where there was strife about the rare orange-bellied parrot.

Then back to Europe and Spain. The southernmost tip of Spain where it leans out to kiss Morocco has a large wind farm which they sometimes have to turn off for months at a time to protect migrating Griffon vultures. As Willie read Bolly's text it hit him right between the eyes that rare raptors, big predatory birds, were so often the victims. Clearing the sites for wind farms killed off the ground nesting birds, but the turbines got the raptors. Apart from the wind farms being sited on traditional migration routes or on high-ridged hunting zones nobody really knew why. Research was suggesting that maybe in their hunt for small mammals raptors "saw" life differently from other birds and were therefore more vulnerable to the blades.

Whatever the reason, Spanish conservationists had calculated that some rare raptors could be rendered extinct.

Same problem at Smola Island in Norway where white tailed eagles had fallen foul of a wind farm.

And similar tales in Scotland, Wales and Yorkshire.

To begin with the work he'd once been so proud of had seemed shallow by comparison with this important new work. Stuff like a giant prawn, the glossy image three times normal size drenched in mouthwatering Chinese sauce dribbling down it, a hint of steam coming off it. Or an expensive new car so buffed and burnished and brilliantly lit it looked like automotive sculpture, car porn. He had been proud of the craftsmanship and they had won awards, established his credentials as just Dee - one word fame. But the fate of wild life confronted by all these murderous blades had seemed of real value, something that mattered. Eventually though, the job had soured and Willie had sickened of it all. Photographing killing grounds and dead and dying creatures made him feel more like a war correspondent than a wildlife and landscape photographer.

Blood on the Wind achieved remarkable sales for Bolly and Willie.

After all the wind farm PR about what such fluffy wonderful things "windmills" were people couldn't believe the reality. They bought the book to gorge on the unexpected avian/bat horror. Same old, same old, Willie thought cynically. We live in a visual age. If you want to convince people you must show them. Stick it to 'em where they can't ignore it.

Most importantly the book got Willie out of retirement. He now devotes himself full time to photographing all the wild places in the UK where wind farms are being pushed through. He aims to spend a week at each site before the bulldozers move in. Then go back once the site is completed. But there are so many different sites being forced through it isn't always possible.

He has restyled his gallery in London to show current work and has a running exhibition on the doomed landscapes. He juxtaposes shots of landscapes before and after the turbines. At the same time he is putting together a coffee table book which is as beautiful as he can make it of the "before" shots; he calls it Lament for the Wild Places.

'It is important,' he says, 'given the scale of the government's plans to build these things that there is a record of how the British countryside looked prior to the great desecration. So that future generations can look at the countryside in its proper scale before the so-called sustainable wind farm landscape.

'I refuse to entertain any such thing as a "wind farm landscape," he says, 'where we use the power of words to dissimulate or camouflage the truth. Why not call it a junk yard landscape?

'At any rate I hope future generations will look at my pictures and get an idea of what a wild countryside looked like when the only movement in it was made by clouds or rivers or birds. To that end I look to try and include birds or wildlife whenever I can. A kestrel hovering, a sky lark ascending...whatever is live and wild and still flourishing.

'Without these pictures an unblemished countryside will soon be a folk memory. The first generation of wind turbines were about 200' high. The ones now replacing them are over 400' high; and there is every possibility the third wave will be 600' or even 800' high.

'By stealth and the might of the state the whole face of Britain's countryside will have been drastically changed in less than a generation. The visual impact will be horrific. The cost to the nation's landscape immeasurable. And this fact, because it does not include money, is never taken into the equation when the true price of industrial turbines is considered.

'At the same time, because Britain is such a small, crowded island already, there will be real problems in absorbing the thousands of more wind turbines proposed. To cram them in, they will inevitably be pushed ever closer to peoples' houses and eventually the health problems, so far denied, will become a scandal. The people who are being forced to live close to these things seem very low on the list of priorities.'

Bolly accompanies Willie and Nelson on these photo shoots. Most days she acts as his assistant, helping set up the shoot, passing him filters and lenses and such. But sometimes she gives talks.

This is an extract from a recent speech: 'Reading the Secretary of State's comments when upholding recent planning applications you will notice a subtle change. He now accepts that these huge turbines will inevitably destroy the elements of wildness in these places. It is a price he is happy to pay. He allows that some, nervous, horses will be frightened of them. Get a more robust one, he implies. He acknowledges that many walkers and riders will be driven away - they may go elsewhere - although God knows where there will be left to go. But all this must be ignored in the greater interests of the state. Later generations will ask what all this involuntary sacrifice was for. Why did we allow our last wilderness country to be raped when we have almost 8,000 miles of coastline with totally reliable, totally predictable tidal energy? Plus there's also wave energy.

'The answer to later generations denied their scenic birthright must be that a great many people did fight on their behalf. In some cases making themselves ill with all the hard planning work they put in to fight democratically. They fought so hard that an over-mighty government was forced to keep changing the legislation and making objection ever more onerous. When even that didn't work, the state made dissent impossible. Aesthetic barbarism triumphed in the cause of short term political aims and political symbolism. But please tell later generations that we did fight. We saw these overshadowing rings of steel coming to our small towns and recreational places and we fought till we were denied the right to fight.

'All we can offer the British people now is Willie Dee's photo book: "Lament for The Wild Places". Paper and ink in place of sky larks and solitude. In the end it was all they left us.'

# AUTHOR NOTES

This is a work of fiction. So I'm not describing events, places and people exactly as they are or were in real life. In fact, for the sake of dramatic licence and hoping to make it a better read I have taken many liberties with the dates things happened.

The only real people in the book are nationally known politicians, writers and Mrs Jane Davis who was forced out of her home and is, as I write, involved in a High Court case seeking recompense. Where I quote real people I have been at pains to quote them as accurately as I could. The web sites I mention are real. And the numbers as accurate as I could manage.

People wanting accurate figures should seek out '*The Wind Farm Scam*' by Dr John Etherington. And the wind farm performance website: www.renewable-energy-foundation.org.uk

Certain events, such as the peatslide at Derrybrien, where thousands of fish were killed, and the embarrassing failure by Radio South to power their outside broadcast by wind actually happened. Similarly the fires at Raasay and Sheffield University. You can find details on the Net.

However, the vast majority of people and events are fictitious; they are composites. When you are writing fiction about a wind farm struggle there have to be developers, activists, councillors, farmers and planners. But nobody should think my characters have been based on themselves. All the characters are fictional beings made up of several people.

However, there have been several hundred wind farm struggles in this overcrowded little island of ours. So it is quite possible that some of them could have been like the one at Cloughgreen. The intention has been to point up these possibilities and to contrast the harsh realities of wind farms with the fluffy PR image Big Wind projects.

Keith Milligan
April 9th 2010

# ACKNOWLEDGEMENTS

The difficulties encountered in bringing this book to publication made it impossible to seek all the permissions for reproduction. However, I happily recognize my debt to all of the following people and would point readers towards their works. Most of which are easily available via Amazon.com

Ted Hughes, the former poet laureate was prolific and almost all, if not all, of his wonderful work is still in print. Two good introductions would be: *Ted Hughes poetry – Elmet.* Poems by Ted Hughes with photographs of the West Yorkshire area he wrote about by the celebrated photographer Fay Godwin (Faber

& Faber). And *Ted Hughes - Poems selected by Simon Armitage* (Faber & Faber).

The whole factual background, how wind turbines work, their performance, the subsidies, the ecological consequences etc are clearly spelled out in *The Wind Farm Scam* by Dr John Etherington (Stacey International).

For how individual wind farms actually perform, as opposed to claimed figures, check out www.renewable-energy-foundation.org.uk

Details of health concerns can be found in a study by Dr Nina Pierpont called *Wind Turbine Syndrome* (K-Selected Books, Santa Fe).

Almost singlehandedly Christopher Booker, the famous writer and journalist, has battled the follies of the wind farm lobby in his Sunday Telegraph column. You may find his book *The Real Global Warning Disaster* interesting. Examples of his journalism are widely available on the Net.

One of the most influential voices about climate change has been the former NASA scientist, James Lovelock, originator of the Gaia Theory. For details of the Gaia Theory and James Lovelock's current thinking I recommend *The Vanishing Face of Gaia* (Penguin Books).

People interested in how big states are eroding civil liberties may find the fiction trilogy of John Twelve Hawks interesting. John Twelve Hawks - *The Fourth Realm Trilogy* (Bantam Press).

This novel mentions the lyrics from the Beautiful South hit, Perfect 10. You can hear this on *The Beautiful South: Solid Bronze - Great Hits* (Go! Discs Ltd/Mercury Records Ltd).

John Denver's song The Eagle & The Hawk is available on a CD entitled *A Song's Best Friend, The very best of John Denver* (2004 BMG UK & Ireland).

There are two outstanding versions of Bolly Dolly's "anthem" available. One is by Dr Hook - *The Ballad of Lucy Jordan* (Hits & History, EMI). The other is by Marianne Faithful.

INTERESTING WEBSITES:

www.moorsydeactiongroup.org.uk

www.moroccanbirds.com - link to Bird Slicers video

www.windturbinenoisehealthhumanrights.com

www.renewable-energy-foundation.org.uk

www.nawag.co.uk

www.yes2wind.com

www.Renewables.UK